For Her Sins

Shadowdance

Saga

Song Two

By

Mark Wooden

To Aunt Marion! Thanks for all the love and support!

Mark Wooden

ISBN: 978-0-9913074-5-6

Master Edition

Published by Writer Geek Press at CreateSpace.com

For information, contact us at

www.shadowdancesaga.com

or

wgp@shadowdancesaga.com

"SHADOWDANCE" SAGA CHRONOLOGY

"A Reason to Live: A Shadowdance Variation"

"By Virtue Fall: Shadowdance Saga Song One"

"For Her Sins: Shadowdance Saga Song Two"

What people say about
"By Virtue Fall: A Song of the Shadowdance"

"This author has a wonderful imagination, and I like the way he mixed historical fiction into his modern day setting making his writing style unique for this genre."

— *The Book Diaries*

"Love the story. You're on my list of great reads waiting for the next in the series. Who needs romance?? I'd rather read a great story. ["By Virtue Fall"] reads like an action movie."

— *Kris Blankenship, editor at the University of Tampa Minaret newspaper*

"Reminded me of an RPG game – an unbelievable infrastructure rooted in historical fact with action from all angles, and every character with their own ulterior motives that could take the story in so many directions."

— *Audrey DeLong, producer at Electronic Arts*

Acknowledgements

"Shadowdance" Logo Design by Rob Wilcox

Deb Courtney, of Courtney Literary, for her words of wisdom

Charlie Potthast for her work on "By Virtue Fall" ad copy

John Dale for his expertise in flying

Penny Punnett, Nick Perakes, and Kris Blankenship
for their support of "By Virtue Fall"

Sheila Tekavec

A. K. Clarke Editing

Extra special thanks to Marcus Lowell for pushing me through

And to Christopher Smith for helping develop
"Shadowdance" in its infancy

Cover Acknowledgements

Model — Danielle Miller

Photography — Harry Wilkins Photography

Hair/Makeup — Jeptha Lee

Design — Eric Hernandez

Table of Contents

Introduction to the Master Edition

Greetings and salutations!

Yeah, I got a little George Lucas with this book too. Besides the cover change (had to keep the model the same!), I took the last chapter from the original version of "By Virtue Fall" and inserted it as the first chapter here. Flows better, gives a better start.

I've also added depth to the Gabriella Doran character, giving a bit of her origin. It was a spontaneous addition done in the editing process, culled from a deleted section of "By Virtue Fall."

Other than that, those of you who've read the previous edition will find cosmetic changes, but nothing that will throw you out of reading the next installment, "Illusion of Love," without reading this Master Edition.

Think of it as adding CGI to enhance the overall experience.

I'm also writing some short stories that tie into this book. Look for these materials at Shadowdancesaga.com in Winter 2016 in time for Christmas.

Gotta give ya time to read "For Her Sins" first.

And did I mention those short stories, like "A Reason to Live" (prequel to "By Virtue Fall"), will be free?

Hope you enjoy this enhanced version of the story, and thanks for following the "Shadowdance" action/ urban fantasy saga.

Measure One — Belly of the Beast

ORANIENBURG, GERMANY

DECEMBER 2013

Sahlu Tigray woke slowly.

He felt pain in the well-toned muscles of his back, arms, and legs. His clothing felt damp, presumably from the blood he'd shed from wounds. He felt movement and deduced he was in a car, specifically the trunk of one. He wasn't going anywhere except where the vehicle would take him. Even if he could escape, he didn't think his body was up for the challenge.

An indeterminable number of minutes later, Sahlu felt the movement cease. He heard car doors open and slam shut. There was a lock release sound; then light poured into his once dark world. It was too much for his tired eyes to take, and he shut them tight. Hands grabbed his arms, dragging him into the cold of winter.

It took Sahlu several moments to rouse himself out of his stupor. He felt his legs dragging across cold cobblestones, heard feet crunching across the snow. Sahlu slowly opened his eyes, squinting at the brightness of the day.

He recognized his "escorts" as two of the four MKDG thugs he had encountered on the U-Bahn late last night. He had stood against the men when they threatened violence toward a group of innocent students.

The encounter had not fared well for Sahlu. Though he was an experienced physical combatant, the odds were against him were he to battle four jacked up, racist thugs by himself. Sahlu used his magic, but in low, short bursts to hide it from the Uninitiated students' eyes.

He prayed those Uninitiated students had the sense to escape while the thugs beat him to within an inch of his life. He also prayed they had not seen the vulgar magic the leader of the MKDG thugs, the fifth man in the tunnels, had used to defeat him.

The students were already scared enough; there was no point in driving them insane with a vulgar display of magic.

Besides; the Shadowdance wouldn't be a secret war between supernatural creatures if the students saw any of it.

The thugs dragged Sahlu across a cobblestone road. The snow ahead was displaced by foot traffic. He heard what sounded like a large gate slamming shut behind him, chains wrapping around its steel bars.

His escorts followed two other men. Sahlu assumed one of the men, the taller of the two, was the leader from the tunnel. The second man was significantly shorter and struggled to keep up with his companion's determined march.

Both men wore long, black trench coats similar in style to the old Nazi SS officer garb. They stomped onward in stormtrooper-style boots. The taller man's uniform had the addition of the braided, silver and black shoulder boards of a *Reichsführer*, the Nazi equivalent of an American general of the Army.

It was the same rank held by Heinrich Himmler, commander of the Nazi paramilitary *Schutzstaffel*, or SS.

On both men's right biceps Sahlu saw the emblem of the MKDG: an upside down pentagram with a Nazi swastika resting between the two upturned points.

A repugnant group of Neo-Nazis, the MKDG had supposedly been destroyed when the Berlin Wall fell. Were these fools ideological successors or the real thing?

He'd have to inform his superiors at the *Ältestenrat*, should he survive this encounter.

"Just what do you hope to accomplish by capturing one of the *Ältestenrat?*" the shorter man asked his companion between gasps for breath.

Sahlu instantly recognized the sniveling voice of Trennan Lamar. His betrayal of the MKDG had led to their supposed demise. Why did this new incarnation trust him? As a member of the *Ältestenrat* council, Sahlu knew Lamar was a has-been, always begging for one thing or another in a pathetic attempt to retain whatever remained of his dignity.

He had also been Adriana Dupré's first victim upon her return to Berlin.

Maybe that connection was his true value.

"If you can defeat one council member," Lamar continued, "surely you have the power to defeat the rest. With Kleist gone —"

"If the *Ältestenrat* hadn't cut me out of the loop, I could have stopped the attack on the museum," the leader said. Lamar, too occupied with keeping up with the other man, did not refute his remark.

"Worse still," the leader continued, "Dupré is connected to three major breaks of the *Schattenfriede*. The *Ältestenrat* — even if they were going to leave me out — should have stopped her after the first. Kleist would still be alive. You would still have a full arm."

The taller man's words fueled Sahlu's suspicion. The man knew of the *Ältestenrat*, and of Adriana's actions in the city. The association left little doubt to the man's identity: Inspector Heinrich Reinhardt.

A Berlin *polizei* inspector, he was charged with investigating breaches of the *Schattenfriede*, the pact amongst Berlin's Initiated that forbade the public use of their supernatural powers and any act of aggression between Initiated factions.

Adriana had breached this pact in her brutal attack against Lamar at a Pankow district nightclub, an attack that had cost Lamar most of his right arm.

As the *Ältestenrat's* investigator, Reinhardt should have pursued Dupré. However, the *Ältestenrat* had stymied Reinhardt's efforts at Sahlu's request. He had made the request out of consideration for Makeda Arsi, a Knight of Vyntari and his estranged lover, who had some plan to use the ruthless assassin Dupré for the greater good of the Shadowdance.

Now Makeda and Adriana had disappeared, while Sahlu became the prisoner of Reinhardt and this new incarnation of MKDG racists.

He quickly remembered why he and Makeda were estranged.

Sahlu looked past Lamar and Reinhardt. The cobblestone road they traversed led to an open area bordered by a half-circle of stone wall, not taller than a man's knee. The road continued through the center of the half-circle.

Sahlu judged the area beyond the half-circle wall to be at least the length of a football pitch.

A stone wall not more than ten feet high and designed as a triangle enclosed the entire area. Its apex lay directly across from the entrance through which the MKDG thugs had led him.

An obelisk stood roughly thirty yards inside the outer wall's apex. Though Sahlu could not see it clearly from this distance, he knew it to have six rows of triangles, with three triangles across each column.

All who served the *Ältestenrat* knew the obelisk as a monument to the heroes of the Second World War, both those Initiated and Uninitiated, who had liberated this area from the Nazis and their Order of Haroth lackeys.

They also knew the triangles as the markings the Nazis assigned to the prisoners of this place — the Sachsenhausen concentration camp. Markings that were once symbols of hate had turned to symbols of respect and remembrance.

One of Sahlu's escorts bashed him on the top of his head, forcing his gaze back to the ground and ending his reconnaissance. He felt them turn on the cobblestone road and head toward the left.

"To allow the *Schattenfriede* to be breached so many times and in such rapid succession shows a lack of strength and cohesion," Reinhardt continued.

"I'm sure the *Ältestenrat* has its reasons for caution," Lamar suggested, baiting the inspector.

"This is not a time for caution," Reinhardt spat. "It is a time for decisive action. For too long the corporate greed of the foreigners and the Jews has corrupted our government and destroyed the world economy. Even the Zionist haven America cannot control their government in regards to spending and budget.

"They and the rest of Europe turn to Germany for salvation and expect our help without payment, without thought to what it would do to our growing economy. Why should we, the future of Europe and the world, risk our hard-earned capital and livelihood to bail out those not worthy of the sovereignty they're given?"

"And what does that have to do with the Shadowdance?" Lamar cut in.

Reinhardt glared at the smaller man. "If the *Ältestenrat* had not neutered the supernatural with their *Schattenfriede* and their Shadowdance, we could use these occult powers, these gifts, to defeat the enemy as our great Führer would have decades ago."

Sahlu was familiar with the type of anger fueling Reinhardt. It was an anger that smoldered over time, an anger needing a release. When stoked with a hatred for a particular other and fueled with dark magic,

Reinhardt's was an anger that another German exploited to turn a beleaguered nation into a powerful Reich.

Reinhardt led Lamar and Sahlu's escorts toward a barracks-style building. He grasped the barrack door's handle but did not open it. Instead, he turned to face Lamar. Sahlu almost got a glimpse of the man, but one of his escorts slammed his head down again.

"There are others who share our vision, Lamar. Others who are willing to do what is necessary to bring back the glory of the Third Reich, the glory of the German people."

Reinhardt opened the door and entered the barracks. Lamar followed, with the escorts dragging Sahlu in behind them. The MKDG had converted the rectangular hall into a meeting space. At its far side, a platform stood ready for presentations. A large banner bearing the MKDG insignia hung on the wall as a backdrop.

Between the flag and Sahlu's position stood thirty young men, all perfect Aryan specimens in their modified SS uniforms. As Reinhardt walked past them to the platform, the men thrust their arms forward in the traditional Nazi "*Sieg Heil*" salute.

Sahlu's escorts dragged him behind Reinhardt and forced him to his knees just before the platform. Lamar moved to Sahlu's side and sneered at the man. The MKDG thugs turned in lockstep to face Reinhardt. When the German looked upon his men to address them, he possessed a fiery passion.

"No longer should those with true power be held in check just to preserve some mindless status quo, or to avoid offending a potential consumer that fattens the pockets of Jews and foreigners. We will show them this power!"

Cries of approval from the men rang out.

Reinhardt became pensive, hatred welling up inside him. "But first, we have certain things to deal with."

"Dupré." Lamar spat, not hiding his hatred for the woman. The name drew howls of anger from the men. Reinhardt raised his hand for silence. The men obeyed.

"This…creature, Adriana Dupré," Reinhardt said with disgust, "betrayed our forefathers during World War Two. She has also broken the *Schattenfriede*! The *Ältestenrat* has failed to defend its one tenet, proving itself too weak to provide for the Fatherland, as we knew it would! It has fallen to us to show the entire Initiated world, the meaning of strength!

"We...the *Machtvollkommenheit durch Geheim*!"

Cries of "*Sieg Heil!*" rang out in the room.

Sahlu saw a smile of pride cross Lamar's face.

For the first time, Reinhardt turned to address Sahlu. Pointing an accusatory finger at him, Reinhardt added, "And this mongrel will be instrumental in the downfall of that which he foolishly chose to defend!"

More displays of excitement burst from the MKDG thugs, their enthusiastic hatred reaching a fevered pitch.

Sahlu realized that whatever the *Ältestenrat* had planned as punishment for him would be nothing compared to what the MKDG would do. Worse, they would subject Dupré, Makeda, and her Knights of Vyntari to that same pain —

...or they would quite possibly die in their attempt to resist.

Measure Two — One Last Thing Before Dawn

BERLIN, GERMANY

DECEMBER 2013

Adriana Dupré felt eyes on her.

Seated in the van's passenger area, she looked to her side and found Gabriella Doran staring at the stump that was Adriana's right arm. The blonde woman didn't stare in horror or even curiosity. She appeared to pity Adriana's loss.

Adriana glared back at Gabriella, her cold gray eyes eventually catching the other woman's vibrant blue ones. Gabriella went flush. She turned away and stared blankly out the van's frosted window, absently twirling a strand of her hair.

Turning from Gabriella, Adriana rubbed her stumped forearm, inspecting the other gashes and bruises on her small, lithe frame. The memory of the pain of the dark sorcerer's Hellfire searing through her forearm returned. It was a drastic physical injury; being a vampire, she could heal the wound in a few hours' time with some fresh blood.

She could not undo the emotional damage she'd suffered this night would not as easily.

She'd found Denson the garou, French for what an Uninitiated person would call a werewolf. He bore a grudge against her for her past transgressions during the *Abattage Terriblé* — the "Great Purge" of the early 19th century. It was not Adriana's finest hour. She had worked for the Daughters of Lilith, blindly slaughtering the garou, in particular, most of Denson's ancestors.

Adriana's meeting with Denson was interrupted by the arrival of the Hellfire-wielding dark sorcerer — Dwyer Strathan, the man with whom she'd made an ill-fated deal.

The bastard ordered his golem to slaughter Denson and his pack, all before Adriana could explain the truth behind her betrayal of his ancestors to Denson.

That truth was a burden weighing on Adriana, darkening her unlife and prompting her to vow to never harm another garou.

Strathan's interference condemned Adriana to continue carrying that burden.

There was also a matter of the missing Vyntari shards.

Adriana wondered why she had even considered her deal with Strathan. It had seemed simple enough: she gets the Vyntari shards for him, he gives her information on her missing sister Dominique.

In the end, Adriana lost the shards, lost Denson, and gained nothing on her sister.

Meanwhile, Strathan walked free.

Now Adriana's fate lay with these Knights of Vyntari, predicated on one agreement: their leader, Makeda Arsi, would help her find Strathan and allow Adriana to avenge Denson. If the Knights recovered the missing two Vyntari shards they were sworn to protect, so much the better for them.

This unholy alliance with Makeda and her Knights had landed Adriana in this van headed for Berlin's Mitte district and the Bebelplatz. From her time in Germany during the Second Great War, she remembered the Bebelplatz as a public square where Nazis had burned books.

Of greater relevance to their collective plight, the square housed a coffee shop owned by the Knights' Berlin contact.

Adriana looked to the van's front passenger seat and watched Makeda make the umpteenth call on her cellular phone. The African Knight had always been cool and collected, her skill as a tactician matched by her athletic prowess.

The vampire had to deal with both traits back in Berlin and almost lost to the woman.

Now, waiting thirty seconds for an answer that never came, her nerves frayed. Her finger dug into the phone's end button.

Impatiently, she dialed again.

"I suggest you think of another contact to phone," Adriana said. "Preferably one who can arrange transportation out of Berlin while being mindful to keep me out of the sun."

"You'd look good with a tan."

That came from the driver, Michael Freeman. Though he spoke directly to Adriana, Freeman didn't glance back at her. His focus remained on the road ahead. That he drove at all was a feat of magic:

Freeman was blind. The indigo-colored ethereal flames flaring from behind his sunglasses afforded him the ability to see.

Adriana believed Freeman used the sarcasm of a scared little boy to cover his lack of warrior spirit — not becoming a man probably in his late twenties. Tall and lanky, he was more tech nerd than a warrior like his two female companions.

The vampire thought back on her encounter with him and the other Knights earlier in Grunewald Forest, just before she dealt with Denson and Strathan. She had stabbed Freeman after using a magical relic to rob the Knights of their powers. Empathetic to grudges, Adriana would forgive his sarcasm.

For now.

"After the events of the past few nights," Makeda said, "the *Ältestenrat* will have no choice but to contain this situation themselves."

"The *Ältestenrat?*" Adriana asked.

"The governing body for the supernatural here in Berlin," Freeman replied. "All of the major Shadowdance players — Guardians of Faith, Knights of Vyntari, Order of Haroth, Sons of Cain and more — are members. They keep a very tight leash on supernatural activity in the city."

"My contact persuaded them to allow us to deal with you, Adriana," Makeda said. "So much has happened in the three days since...I need to know where we stand now."

"You need to know if this *Ältestenrat* is as eager to destroy you as they are me."

Makeda had no response, confirming Adriana's suspicion.

"Level with us, Praetor Arsi," Gabriella said with an Irish lilt. "Have we screwed up so badly that the *Ältestenrat* would sanction us?"

Adriana had first encountered Gabriella in an alley in Los Angeles just days before her arrival in Berlin. The Knight had used an ethereal sword to separate the vampire temporarily from the demon inside her. Had Adriana reacted one wit below her abilities, Gabriella would have finished her.

In Los Angeles, Gabriella had a fierce determination. Now her demeanor reminded Adriana of the times in her mortal youth when her younger, mischievous sister would get into trouble then brace for punishment.

"You have lost the Vyntari shards, allowed the slaughter of your garou allies, and failed to do whatever it is you intended to do to me," Adriana said.

"I can pull over right now and take care of that last one."

"Michael," Makeda scolded.

There was a brief silence until Freeman deadpanned, "We are so fucked aren't we?"

Gabriella leaned forward and punched Freeman in his arm, eliciting a yelp from the man. "Your language."

From her previous encounters with Gabriella and Freeman, Adriana surmised they often bickered like siblings. In her early thirties, Gabriella was the elder, but only by a few years. Freeman was only slightly older than Adriana; that is if she were actually twenty-two years old and not a centuries-old vampire.

"Perhaps, Praetor Arsi," Gabriella began, "it would be better if we went to the *Ältestenrat* —"

"And leave me at their mercy?" Adriana shouted. "You will do no such thing. You will lead me to Strathan —"

"Could you put your two thousand and three vendettas on hold for just a few damned minutes?" Freeman asked. "I mean, who in the hell is this Strathan you're bitching about, anyway?"

"Michael," Gabriella interjected. "Your language," she said again in a sterner tone. Freeman started to speak, but Makeda cut him off.

"That's enough from all of you," she insisted in a tone that rang of finality.

The group was silent for the remainder of the drive.

From outside the Bebelplatz coffee shop, all appeared to be in order. Adriana and the Knights found the front door unlocked, a troubling sign at this late hour. Upon entering, it became apparent that trouble was a severe understatement.

Vandals had completely trashed the inside of the coffee shop.

Not a single piece of furniture was left intact. Coffee and espresso machines were upended, their various components strewed about the main room. Christmas decorations were torn down and crushed, littering the floor.

The vandals had also torn the large menu board from its mounts behind the checkout counter. In its place, they had drawn an upside down pentagram. A swastika lay between its two uppermost points.

The vandals painted both the pentagram and swastika with blood.

A dagger pinned a piece of paper to the center of the pentagram. Though she professed no knowledge of arcane symbols, Adriana knew weapons. Without looking closely at the dagger, she knew it had the motto "My honor is loyalty" inscribed in German on the blade.

It was the motto and dagger of the Nazi Third Reich's SS officers.

"What the hell happened here?" Freeman asked.

This time, Gabriella didn't correct his vulgarity. The woman, like her fellow Knights, was too busy trying to comprehend the chaos that had befallen the establishment.

"Where are the cops?" Freeman continued. "I mean, how could this happen and no one hears or sees anything?"

"Some kind of silencing spell?" Gabriella asked, though her tone contradicted any confidence in her response. "The same kind of thing that kept us from seeing the damage from outside."

"Assuming your contact had magical wards over this place," Adriana interjected, "the vandals were obviously powerful enough to defeat them."

She allowed the implication to hang ominously in the room.

Makeda strode behind the counter and snatched the paper from the wall, tearing it. She had to hold it together with two hands to read it. Freeman moved to Makeda's side. Looking over her shoulder, he asked, "Uh, is that German?"

"Yes," Makeda replied through gritted teeth. Reading aloud she said, "'We have your ally at the place where the vampire betrayed the Reich. Bring the bitch to us if you would see him free.'" Makeda crumbled the paper in her fists. "Signed by the MKDG."

"Who?" Gabriella asked. "And what are they talking about?"

Freeman answered. "MKDG is short for some German babble meaning 'Superiority Through the Occult.'"

Off Gabriella's questioning gaze, he added, "Read about them from the Guardian digital archives on the flight to Germany. It was in the Berlin section, so…"

Makeda abruptly turned from the conversation and exited the room through a door marked "Employees Only." Gabriella and Freeman exchanged questioning looks. They started after her.

Adriana allowed Gabriella to pass. Before Freeman got by, the vampire grabbed his arm and used a martial arts technique that shot pain up his arm and to his shoulder. Freeman doubled over, which brought the taller man down to Adriana's level of just over five feet.

"Hey! I'm walking here!" Freeman protested. He tried to free himself from Adriana's grip, but she held firm.

"Tell me about this MKDG," she insisted.

Makeda entered the employee area, slamming the door behind her. It didn't matter who the MKDG were or what they believed. Only one thing mattered. The bastards had Sahlu, and it was —

"You need to talk to me, praetor."

The sound of Gabriella's Irish lilt interrupted Makeda's moment of reflection. She turned and saw the female Knight in the room, slowly closing the door behind her. Gabriella was Makeda's junior by nearly two decades but possessed wisdom beyond her age, though her modesty would lead her to deny this fact.

She could also empathize on a level that felt magical, though Makeda knew the ability was a non-magical gift the One Goddess had bestowed on Gabriella.

Makeda quickly turned away from her discipulus. She did not want Gabriella to see the rage and self-loathing in her expression.

"Thank you for your ear," Makeda said, "but I won't burden you or Freeman with my personal issues."

"It's about Sahlu and how much you care for him."

Makeda glanced at Gabriella. Nothing in Gabriella's tone or composure made Makeda think her statement was a judgment. Instead, Makeda felt as if she talked with a friend, one who truly cared for her. Makeda quickly looked away from her discipulus.

"You know Sahlu as my fellow tribesman from Oromia," she said. "But yes, he's much more than that." Makeda paused, letting the tension ease from her person as she allowed herself the comfort of

Gabriella's warmth. "I used our connection for selfish reasons. Now…now my selfishness may bring him harm."

"The Sahlu who taught me the *kamau nija* could handle himself," Gabriella said. "Besides, you work from a plan set before you by the One Goddess."

Makeda flinched.

Her plan had not come to her in a dream or during meditation, the usual methods of which the One Goddess sent her believers missions. Instead, Makeda had methodically devised her gambit to convert Adriana at the risk of the Vyntari shards. That was why Sahlu had so many reservations about her plan — besides the obvious possibility of losing the shards.

If she could have foreseen he would become a victim of her plan, that she would indeed lose the shards, would she have heeded his warnings?

Makeda hoped Gabriella had not noticed her moment of doubt. The woman continued as if she had not, moving to Makeda's side as she spoke.

"Back in Grunewald, Adriana neutralized our powers. You reminded us that the One Goddess would always be with us. You led us to a stalemate against a vampire assassin legendary for her skill who, by the way, retained her supernatural abilities."

Gabriella placed a gentle hand on Makeda's shoulder. "That was a test of faith. We passed it then. We'll pass this one too."

Makeda looked to Gabriella. She wished she could be as optimistic as her *discipulus*, but her mission had become a desperate gamble that may cost her more than she was willing to sacrifice.

It was wrong to hide it from Gabriella and Freeman, two people who trusted her so implicitly. But she did so to protect them from the potential retribution should the plan fail.

Much as it already was.

"We'd better not leave Freeman alone with Adriana," Gabriella said. "He's not as turn-the-other-cheek as the Goddess would like."

Makeda wanted to smile at Gabriella's attempt at humor, but couldn't find it within her. She did, however, nod in agreement. Gabriella returned to the shop's main room, leaving Makeda time alone to reflect.

Returning to the coffeehouse's main room, Gabriella found Freeman alone tapping away on his tablet computer. "Sachsenhausen, 1945," he said without raising his magically-enhanced eyes toward her.

"What are you talking about this time?" Gabriella asked.

"The Russians liberated Special Camp Number Seven at Sachsenhausen on April 22, 1945. What Uninitiated history books don't mention is the raid on April 21 by Guardians of Faith. Little Miss Murder said she was there." He shrugged.

"And here I thought she didn't look a day past half a century."

"I assume you mean Adriana," Makeda said, now joining her companions. Freeman nodded. She added, "And where is she now?"

"She figured she could handle the situation better on her own."

"And you let her go?" Gabriella asked.

"You think I'm gonna let the bitch who stabbed me join our Scooby Gang?"

"Michael, your language," Gabriella scolded.

"She didn't wound to kill," Makeda reminded.

"Well, she sure as hell wounded to hurt! Why did you even —"

"Do not question the praetor," Gabriella warned. "To question her is to question the One Goddess to whom all are faithful. And please...your language."

Freeman wanted to respond but thought better of it. Makeda was thankful Gabriella supported her. She had too much on her mind now to deal with a fissure between her allies.

Especially when she was its cause.

"Bottom line," Freeman said, "back at Sachsenhausen, Adriana was working for the Order. For whatever reason, she betrayed them, allowing the Guardians to take out the place — hence the 'vampire bitch betrayed the Reich' part of that note."

"But what does this have to do with the MKDG?" Gabriella asked

"Back in the war, Hitler dabbled in the occult, going so far as to enlist the Order of Haroth for some experiments at the Sachsenhausen camp. Well, imagine if the Nazis and the Order had a baby. It'd be the MKDG: all racist white supremacist with a dash of supernatural power. They believe if Adolf had gone full tilt boogie with the power of the occult, even America'd be goose-stepping to the Iron Cross right now.

"They pushed in that direction in the mid-eighties with some rather vulgar displays of magic. They only succeeded in forcing the creation of the *Ältestenrat*. That cabal shut the MKDG down. Or so they thought. Insert ominous music by Hans Zimmer here."

Makeda and Gabriella exchanged familiar knowing glances.

"Guess it's time to go do that hero thing, huh?" Freeman asked.

Measure Three — Into the Past

DECEMBER 2013

Located near the town of Oranienburg, the former Nazi camp at Sachsenhausen was a forty-minute drive northwest of Berlin. Now partially restored, the camp served as a living museum, a testament to the forty thousand people who died at the hands of the Nazis and the Soviet soldiers who had managed the concentration camp during World War II and after.

Makeda knew the MKDG were waiting for her and her fellow Knights. There remained one factor she could control — where their trap would spring. Makeda had Freeman parked the van near the railroad tracks northwest of the camp. The three Knights then cast the *Ibada ya Mawasiliano Kuimarishwa*, an Oromian spell that granted them telepathic communication.

The spell complete, they traversed the remaining distance to the camp on foot.

The Knights' Berlin haven was on the way to Sachsenhausen. They had stopped there and made a quick change into fresh uniforms before heading for the camp.

Freeman never really wore a uniform, per se. He picked clothes that, as he declared, "the cool kids wore," which consisted of a color-clashing hoodie-pants-sneakers combo more suited for hanging out in a dark basement geek love fest than fighting demons and monsters.

In the attempt to fight back the near freezing temperatures of the German winter, Freeman added a black denim jacket to his garb.

Gabriella's uniform was not something picked up at a Diesel store. She wore a white, hooded cloak over a white one-piece bodysuit that fitted her from neck to knee without diffusing any of her femininity. White boots with low heels and a set of gloves completed the outfit.

Two gray pouches, one on either thigh, broke up the bodysuit's monotony. Gabriella pulled her cloak closed against the cold.

Only Makeda acted as if immune to the weather, though she'd added a gray poncho to her usual uniform. It flowed down past her knees, with a split down the front middle to her stomach that revealed her wardrobe underneath.

She wore an earth-toned shirt adorned with several mystical markings similar to Egyptian hieroglyphs. Its long sleeves flowed down to a set of black gloves that just covered her wrists.

Makeda's pants were a similar color, made of denim and pressed into a pair of knee-high leather boots. Her head was exposed, her dark hair flowing down past her shoulders. Her Ogoun dagger hung in a sheath from her thick black belt, bouncing against her left hip.

The Knights passed through forested areas gradually losing the struggle against half-century old brick houses. The coming dawn would bring the awakening of the citizens in those houses.

The Knights needed to contain this affair before then or risk the Uninitiated seeing beyond the Veil of the Shadowdance.

"So here's some trivia for ya," Freeman muttered through chattering teeth. "Back in World War Two, Adriana rented herself out to the Order of Haroth as a bodyguard."

"Which explains her working with the Order to get the shards now," Gabriella said.

"Maybe not. See, the reason Adriana betrayed the Order and the Nazis was they were experimenting on werewolves."

"That makes two occasions on which Adriana, slayer of werewolves, balked at the thought of engaging in combat with or injuring werewolves," Makeda mused.

"What?" Gabriella asked.

"When I found Adriana in the forest, she was running away from Denson's werewolves."

"I figured she was out to finish Denson," Freeman said.

"On the contrary," Makeda said. "She had resigned to destruction at their hand. Until the Order's sorcerer, Strathan, arrived."

"You and Adriana mention this Strathan guy. There's this actor named Strathan —"

"I think it more important we figure out why he was even there," Gabriella cut in.

"He said he had a deal with Adriana to get the Vyntari shards. Slaughtering Denson and his pack was revenge for her reneging on that deal."

"She'll stab anybody in the back, won't she?" Freeman said.

Both the female Knights glared at him. He threw up his hands as a form of surrender. "Couldn't help myself," he said, then buried his gloved hands back in one of his many pockets.

"She betrayed cabals of evil, but preserved the werewolves," Gabriella said. "Perhaps, despite the legends, Adriana does know Good from Evil and would ultimately choose Good."

"Or," Freeman quickly rebutted, "she selfishly chooses her way as the highway over every other choice. And selfishness is next to Satan-liness or something like that. Which admittedly sounded a lot better in my head."

"Regardless," Makeda said with enough emphasis to end debate, "it is a safe assumption that the MKDG refer to this camp when they speak of the vampire's betrayal. With that in mind, Freeman, you have the information we need, yes?"

Freeman dug into a deep pants pocket; his thick winter gloves made the task more difficult. He eventually wrestled his tablet computer out and tapped the screen. It required a few tries, but he eventually pulled up a tourist's map of the Sachsenhausen camp on the display.

Gabriella and Makeda moved to Freeman's side as they continued their walk. He held up the tablet so the women could see.

"Found this on a website that had a travelogue," Freeman began. "Pretty darned informative for an amateur job. The camp is set up inside an isosceles triangle-shaped outer wall. I know, geometry. Never thought you'd use it —"

"Focus, Michael," Makeda insisted.

Freeman frowned but continued. "The camp's outer wall is an A-shape for those who flunked geometry. Its tip points north. Most of the upper section is a whole lot of nothing, just a bunch of memorials with a wide swath of open area.

"A path runs straight down the middle. In the center of the camp are two buildings, a kitchen and a laundry museum. The stuff that'll probably matter to us is in the southwest corner."

Freeman tried using his index finger to highlight the area on the screen's map but failed miserably. He succeeded when he used his thumb instead.

"Two long barracks, another smaller building to the west of them. Below that is an interior wall that separates the base camp from the prisoner section. There's also an officer's lounge outside of the bottom wall. But I'd put my money on the barracks or the buildings near it to stash a prisoner."

Gabriella pointed at another location on the map. "Are those guard towers?"

"Yep. Four total. Two halfway up the side walls and two just above those."

"The northern point of the camp is the most vulnerable," Makeda said, voicing the obvious conclusion of all three Knights.

"If I were a bad guy that's where I'd set my trap," Freeman warned. "Plenty of space to mow down an intruder between there and the barracks."

"Springing the trap will draw the enemy out into the open," Makeda replied. "Easier to deal with them, then move toward the barracks. Our search for Sahlu will begin there."

Gabriella and Freeman nodded in agreement, though Freeman didn't look too keen on this new adventure. He slid the tablet back into his pocket as they continued their march.

Minutes later, the Knights reached the edge of the wooded area. Beyond lay an open field divided in half by a rough but maintained dirt road. Sachsenhausen's outer wall lay on the other side of that field. Makeda stopped walking, her discipuli stopping a few respectful steps behind her.

"Michael will stay behind. Use your talents to find Sahlu." She turned to look at Freeman. "Which means you won't need your tablet anymore." She extended a hand toward Freeman.

He scowled like a petulant child. "Just be careful with my baby," he said while handing over the tablet.

"You be careful out here," Gabriella warned.

Freeman's expression broke into a bright, wide smile that belied his trepidation. "It's just me and nature, Gabriella! It's you two who'd better be careful!"

Makeda pressed Freeman's tablet against Gabriella's arm, gaining the woman's attention. "We will," she said. She motioned for Gabriella to take the tablet; the junior Knight dutifully accepted it.

To Freeman, Makeda said, "Time is not a luxury we enjoy. Get to work."

"Ah, you no fun, praetor!" Freeman lamented in a faux Chinese accent Makeda assumed was yet another allusion to a movie. He sat down and made a little pillow in the snow. Freeman then laid his head on the snow pillow and entered the trance state required for his Freemanvision power.

In addition to the gift of sight, Freeman's control of magic afforded him astral projection. Thus his soul could leave his body and project into the astral plane, moving about the mortal plane unseen by mortal senses. While on this astral plane, he could only see things. His other senses non-functional.

Hence "Freemanvision."

A drawback to his power was his lack of ability to communicate with those on the mortal plane. For that, he needed some form of telepathic communication, like the spell he and his Knights utilized. Thanks to a high level of creativity honed on tabletop role-playing games, Freeman's astral form could travel to any location he could recognize from memory or a picture.

Luckily, his research into the camp provided him with plenty of good pictures, so he had an idea of what to expect, allowing him to enter the camp by the laundry and kitchen museums. He could then move through the astral plane at the speed of thought.

An added benefit of Freemanvision was his ability to modify the objects in the astral plane to appear as an image of his choosing. For example, Freeman often made his female companions into anime versions of themselves, complete with the sprawling cloak for Gabriella that looked like something out of a Spawn comic book.

Freeman's power gave the camp surroundings a Gothic atmosphere, the dark concrete contrasting with the white snow. He threw in a gargoyle or three for good measure.

Stepping to the two museums, Freeman didn't see anything out of the ordinary. His astral form moved toward the barracks buildings.

"*All quiet on the western front,*" Freeman said to his companions via their telepathic link. "*Or am I on the southern front? You ladies took my map, so I don't —*"

"*What have you found?*" Makeda asked telepathically.

Freeman's astral form looked at the barracks. There were no doors, no point of entry. One of the barracks had several panes of glass in front of it, the barracks wall behind it recently burned. He frowned then continued past the barracks toward a nondescript, white stone building which, in his Freemanvision, showed the signs of decay and the aftereffects of war.

"*Checked the museums,*" Freeman reported. "*Locked tight, standard stuff. Barracks don't even have doors. 'Whole lot of nothing' vibe. Which, of course, means we're right where they want us.*"

His astral form, which he rendered as an anime-styled ninja, wandered into the camp's Pathology Building. It was a small building, not more than fifty feet across. Three concrete tables made for autopsies were spaced evenly across the center of the room. Shelves for pathology gear lined the back walls.

In Freemanvision, the room looked like the scene of a survival horror game, all dark shadows and decay. Freeman expected an attack by some evil living dead girl. He cautiously moved toward the back of the room to a flight of creepy, rotting stairs. An overhead sign identified the level below as the Corpse Room.

"Oh yeah. This just keeps getting better and better," Freeman mused.

Two goons with machine guns stood guard at the top of the stairs. Freeman presumed they were MKDG. His power made them appear as Nazi stormtroopers with midnight black uniforms cut in severe right angles. They were also bald with MKDG logos on their foreheads. As a tip to the occult, he gave them menacing red eyes.

Since the guards couldn't see his astral form, Freeman took great delight in waving his hands in front of their unknowing faces and telling them to suck on specific and private parts of his anatomy.

Gabriella would chastise him for his behavior, but since she wasn't around —

"*Stop doddering and hurry up!*" Gabriella shouted in Freeman's head via their telepathic link. He knew his companion couldn't see or hear what he was doing, but guilt caused him to halt the fun and games as if she could and did.

"*Who's doddering?*" Freeman asked. "*And who besides your ninety-year-old Irish grandmother even says 'doddering?'*"

"*Just find Sahlu,*" Makeda insisted.

Freeman couldn't read emotions through the telepathic link, but the terseness of his companions' thoughts reminded him of the seriousness of this mission.

He'd better make his efforts count.

Passing the oblivious guards, Freeman descended the stairs to the Corpse Room. It was nothing more than a basement, twice the size of the room above. He imagined (and instantly regretted doing so) the stench that must have permeated the room as all those bodies brought down from pathology sat awaiting autopsy or festered while Nazi soldiers found a means of disposal.

He noticed an ominous black glow emanating from something on the back wall. Approaching the anomaly, Freeman discovered an etching in the wall at the level one would place a door lock. He had no idea what the etching was but sensed the dark energy radiating from the image.

"*Makeda,*" Freeman began, "*head to the Pathology building. There's something I need your dagger to bust and —*"

Freeman didn't finish the thought, as his head suddenly snapped backward as if taking a blow. Before he could recover, his astral form buckled as if taking a sharp kick to his stomach.

While his astral form was moving inside the camp, Freeman's physical body remained in a trance in the woods outside the camp. Unfortunately, anything that happened to his physical form was felt by has astral form. It was an advanced warning system; if his body were too badly damaged, it would strand his astral form on that plane.

Freeman allowed himself a quick glimpse of his body's surroundings. He was under attack from two MKDG goons who looked like they could juggle Volkswagens and apparently had no moral misgivings about kicking a man when he's in a trance.

Despite intensive martial arts training from the Knights, Freeman disliked combat. He always thought of himself as a lover, not a fighter

— though, in truth, he preferred the role of research geek in an astral anime world to those of lover or fighter.

Unfortunately for him, it was time to return to the real world.

While Freeman did his astral reconnaissance, Makeda led Gabriella toward the northern side of the camp, eventually reaching the apex of the triangular outer wall. Gabriella referenced Freeman's tablet computer.

"According to the map," she began, "this is the site of several mass graves. Just on the other side of this wall is the open area Michael mentioned. It extends about a hundred yards to the barracks."

"And the Pathology Building," Makeda asked.

Gabriella consulted the tablet. "Just to the west of the barracks."

"We will find Sahlu there," Makeda said with certainty.

She studied the wall itself. At only ten feet high, she was confident they would easily launch themselves over, gaining momentum toward their target.

"*Find anything else, Michael?*" Makeda asked down the Knights' telepathic link.

No response.

Makeda turned to her companion. Gabriella looked down at the ground, her face a mask of anger. Makeda didn't understand until she followed Gabriella's gaze.

The skeletal remains of a human hand, decayed by decades of underground entombment, clawed its way through the frozen earth and to the surface. The gloomy smolder of a dark, ethereal fog emanated from the skeletal hand.

Drawing her Ogoun dagger from its holster, Makeda stepped forward and stabbed the reanimated hand. Arcs of shimmering blue ethereal energy radiated from the magical dagger's point of contact until they fully immersed the malignant object. The bolts purged the taint of dark magic from the skeleton. It shook once, fell still, and dissolved into ash.

The dark fog slowly wafted from the hand until it dissipated completely. Makeda withdrew her dagger and stood beside Gabriella.

A low rumbling behind her drew Makeda's attention. Both she and Gabriella looked at the source and saw a small mound of earth and snow break apart. Two more skeletal hands and the arms connected to them burst into the night air.

"You said this was a mass grave?" Makeda asked.

"For the fallen during and after World War Two," Gabriella said, her anger rising as she spoke. "People who have already suffered far more than their share."

Makeda thought of moving to an alternate route. However, when she looked back to the fields and the houses beyond, they were gone, replaced by a hazy, dark-hued dome covering the entire camp.

She recognized it as a mystical barrier blocking them from the Uninitiated world.

Makeda had seen its kind before; on the other side, the Uninitiated would see the camp as it had been moments before.

They would see none of the ensuing violence and destruction Makeda and her Knights would inevitably insight.

At the Knights' feet, more corpses pulled themselves from their unmarked graves. Makeda quickly lost count of how many hands scratched and clawed for the surface. She looked back to Gabriella. Her companion nodded silently, then took a few steps back and away from Makeda.

"May the One Goddess grant me the power to defeat these abominations!" Gabriella declared.

A tempest rose, Gabriella its center. Her cloak and hood flapped against the powerful winds, yet she appeared nonplussed as she held her hands before her.

A spark of ethereal, white flame danced above her hands. The blinding flame grew, transforming into a flat object just barely a foot in length. The flames spread, reaching a length of three feet. An ornate pommel and hilt emerged on one end. The other end became a point.

The object hovered in the air just above Gabriella's palms. She took the hilt in her right hand. The divine flames danced over the Ancient Roman-styled sword now fully formed in her hand: her *Spatha Perfidelis*, her Sword of the Faithful, the physical manifestation of her faith in the One Goddess. The tempest surrounding Gabriella dissipated.

Sword in hand, Gabriella assumed a combat kata. Holding her Ogoun dagger, Makeda mirrored Gabriella's pose. She then used her telepathic link to Freeman.

"Wherever you are, Michael, you had better hurry."

Measure Four — Assault on Special Camp No. 7

Freeman jolted out of his trance in time to take an uppercut to his jaw so forceful it propelled him backward. He landed hard on his side. Freeman would have preferred to stay there, but he heard his assailants' boots crushing snow on their path toward him.

Reaching into the pocket at his right thigh, Freeman drew his quarterstaff. He pressed two buttons, one at his thumb and the other at his pinky finger. The foot-long staff extended from both ends to six feet in length, locking into place just as the second MKDG thug launched an attack.

Freeman rolled, dodging a foot stomp. He swung his staff at the attacking thug's leg. It smashed the side of the man's knee. A bit of acrobatics vaulted Freeman out of the assailant's way just as the wounded thug lurched to the ground in obvious pain.

The maneuver bought Freeman enough time to reflect on the many bruises he would develop from this fight, as well as the smudges from the dirt and blood already staining the second Knight's outfit he'd donned in just a single evening.

"*Could use a little help here,*" Freeman said telepathically to his companions.

"*Little busy ourselves,*" Gabriella responded in kind.

Freeman would have to get out of this fix on his own. To that end, he relied on the one combat skill he excelled at — he ran away as fast as he could.

Makeda and Gabriella had trained in the African martial art of *kamau njia* — the Way of the Silent Warrior. The Way focused on transferring the energy from an opponent's attack back upon that opponent in a non-lethal attack. The intent was to immobilize your opponent without killing them. Makeda had learned the style as a child. In later years, she and Sahlu had educated Gabriella in the art.

The woman had proven a quick study.

In a general combat encounter, the two Knights instinctively fell into synch, one actively setting up the other for takedown blows and then alternating the pattern. Their enemies lost precious time trying to predict the evolving pattern of Makeda and Gabriella's attacks. This strategy was particularly effective during encounters in which their opponents outnumbered them.

Encounters just like this one.

The Knights' level of mastery went unappreciated by the attacking horde of zombie-like skeletons, whose sole combat instinct was to claw and bite living flesh.

Gabriella lost track of how many of the creatures she and Makeda had dispatched. She focused instead on which direction Makeda's attacks launched an opponent so she could cleave the foe with her *Spatha Perfidelis*, expelling the dark magic that animated the corpses.

Without that magic, the skeletons reverted to piles of decades-old ash.

Makeda slashed away with her dagger, occasionally throwing it into the air only to catch it as it fell and slash again. Gabriella used her cloak to disorient opponents, luring them into her *Spatha* or Makeda's dagger, which had the same ability to dispel dark magic.

Gabriella's mind drifted. She couldn't help imagining the atrocities exacted on the noble souls that once inhabited these bodies when they had lived, lives cruelly snuffed out by the forces of evil that had operated this camp.

Now those same souls tortured in life had become pawns of evil. Gabriella hoped that, should they survive this encounter, she could provide them the recompense and salvation their souls deserved.

A stinging bite to her arm brought Gabriella back to the immediate danger. Reacting swiftly, she decapitated the assailant, but its clenched teeth held the head firmly in place on her arm. Gabriella punched it off.

"*We have to make it over that wall!*" Makeda said to her discipulus.

"*There are too many of them!*" Gabriella replied. "*If we turn our backs even for a second —*"

"*If we time things correctly a second is all we'll need,*" Makeda insisted as she launched another skeleton into the arc of Gabriella's ethereal blade. "*When I say the word, charge the wall!*"

Makeda moved steadfastly through the swarm of skeletons. Gabriella followed with her back to Makeda's, protecting her partner's blind side. The women cut a path through the skeletons, bringing them both closer to the outer wall.

Gabriella watched as Makeda performed a maneuver that was not a martial attack but preparation for a spell. Blue ethereal energy sparked like electricity between Makeda's open arms. She thrust her arms forward. The energy blasted forward, pulverizing all the skeletons in its path but glancing harmlessly off the wall

"Gabriella, go!" Makeda shouted.

The younger Knight circled Makeda and ran down the path Makeda had cleared. Within a few feet of the wall, she lobbed her *Spatha Perfidelis* high up and over the wall.

Gabriella leaped at the top of the wall. Even Olympic gymnasts have difficulty jumping more than two feet vertically. With the help of a little ethereal magic, Gabriella easily cleared the four feet needed to grasp the wall's top. She twisted with a skill worthy of an Olympic gymnast, giving her the momentum to clear the wall and land safely on the opposite side.

She caught her *Spatha* in her right hand as it fell.

Gabriella's thoughts immediately turned to her praetor, who had not yet come over the wall. She knew that Makeda's energy field would have dissipated after firing. Had the skeletons regrouped and attacked?

Knowing Makeda's combat style, Gabriella envisioned her lashing out defensively at any skeletons pursuing her. But without an ally to clear the way, Makeda would lose the ability to maneuver.

Makeda must have sensed Gabriella's thoughts, for she said telepathically, "*Stop worrying and move to the Pathology building!*"

Overriding her instinct to aid her companion, Gabriella acted immediately and followed orders. She scanned the area, assessing her location at the end of a wide-open field that led to the main camp.

About seventy yards away, two gravel paths ran south through the center of what was the prisoner area and toward the camp's main gate. A pair of long barracks bordered each path on the east and west.

Three-quarters of the way down, a three-foot high, curved wall shielded the last expanse of ground before the gatehouse entrance. From her brief glance at Freeman's tablet earlier, she knew this area to be the Appellplatz.

Two longer barracks were on the western side of Appellplatz.

It was all as Freeman had briefed them. But which of these buildings was the Pathology building again?

At the start of the fracas with the skeletons, Gabriella had stored Freeman's tablet computer in a thigh pouch. She reached for the device now — only to find it gone, fallen through a hole in the pouch presumably torn by one of the creatures.

"*Michael!*" Gabriella shouted telepathically. "*I lost your tablet! Which building do I want?*"

No response.

Gabriella called for Michael again, becoming pensive when she didn't receive an answer.

She was about to try again when he finally replied, "*Kinda getting my Jesse Owens on here!*"

"*Move towards the entrance to the camp,*" Makeda urged Gabriella. "*And mind the watchtowers.*"

As if seeing them for the first time, Gabriella looked to one of the four watchtowers strategically located along the outer walls. Just as she did, two MKDG thugs rose from behind the guardrail, aiming assault rifles at her.

She looked to the tower closest to her on the western side of the camp and saw two more MKDG thugs, also with assault rifles.

With the Knights, Gabriella had survived all manner of demons, vampires, and supernatural horrors. She wasn't about to let four man-made yet barbarous weapons bring about her demise.

Gabriella broke into a sprint, staying close to the western wall. Her tactic neutralized the threat of the gunmen in the closer tower, but bursts of bullets from the men in the eastern tower rained down around her.

"As you formed to cleave the darkness," Gabriella said aloud, "may you now disperse and safeguard against it!" She released her *Spatha*. It transformed into a brilliant, fluid flame that transformed into ethereal, white-flaming armor.

What few bullets reached their target burned harmlessly into the armor.

Suddenly, the shooting stopped.

Gabriella grew up with two gun-loving brothers. Though she never liked the things, she had learned about them. The MKDG gunmen were firing in burst mode and not succeeding in harming their target. She reasoned they'd stopped firing long enough to switch their rifles to fully automatic mode.

Gabriella could concentrate enough to block the limited number of bullets from a burst; in automatic mode, gunfire would come too heavily for her magical armor to block.

She was halfway down the western wall, past the first of the two towers. Another forty yards ahead lay the row of barracks buildings along the west side. They were perpendicular to the gunmen's line of fire and would provide cover —

If she could reach them.

Inevitably, the barrage of automatic fire rained upon Gabriella. The constant barrage weakened her concentration, in turn weakening her ethereal armor. The shock thrust her against the outer wall. Her concentration wavered for a split second. That was all the time needed for a single bullet to penetrate her shield and clip her leg.

Gabriella stumbled, giving the men in the eastern tower enough time to correct their aim and finish her. She made a furtive glance toward the triangle apex, praying that if this were her last breath, Makeda would complete the mission without her.

The thugs in the tower took aim.

A burst of dark blue energy rose violently in the shape of a dome from Makeda's side of the outer wall. Skeletal fragments exploded, forming a cloud of dust and debris. Distracted, the thugs in the tower held their fire, looking to the new potential threat.

Makeda rose into the air above the wall. A gleaming ethereal suit of blue armor covered her.

Through her pain, Gabriella's eyes widened at the sight before her. She stole a glance at the eastern tower and saw the men there take aim at her praetor.

Before the MKDG fired any weapons, Makeda transformed into a blue streak that raced toward Gabriella. The streak swept up the Irish Knight, rushing her away from the area. When she was able to focus her thoughts and energy, Gabriella realized she was now safely behind the two buildings bordering the center path to the main gate.

Makeda sat beside Gabriella, her mystical armor dissipating into a blue steam and floating away on the cold winter breeze. Gashes in the fabric of her uniform revealed wounds inflicted during the strenuous battle with the undead skeletons. Her shoulders slumped, her breathing came in deep inhalations.

It dawned on Gabriella that the blue color of her praetor's armor meant she had used personal magic and not that of the One Goddess to get as far as she had. Her fatigue stemmed from the expenditure.

Makeda's moment of fatigue quickly passed, once again replaced by the well-composed expression of a determined woman who would not concede defeat.

"I can recharge you, praetor," Gabriella said aloud, no longer utilizing their telepathic link.

Bullets ricocheted against the walls of the buildings as the men in the towers unleashed a storm of lead death. Unfortunately for the gunmen, the barracks buildings completely shielded the female Knights. However, Sahlu was trapped somewhere in the camp, possibly near death.

The Knights would have to break cover to free him.

Then the gunmen would take them.

Ignoring Gabriella's offer for healing, Makeda reached around her back. "You dropped this," she said, handing Freeman's tablet to Gabriella. "Michael told us to go to the Pathology building."

The younger Knight studied the tablet. "Blessed Goddess! I was almost there!"

Makeda stared at Gabriella. The blonde Knight noticed her superior's curiosity. "The Pathology building was just at the south end of the west wall."

Makeda stole a glance around the southern corner of the building they used for cover. She saw the two longer barracks on the southwest side of the building.

Machine gun fire pelted the wall above her head. Concrete chips fell into her hair. She pulled back around and looked to Gabriella.

"I see the two barracks," she said.

"Just on the other side is Pathology," Gabriella told her.

"Our best route is to travel along that circular wall ahead in the Appellplatz. We can use it for cover as we move to the barracks."

"Or you can do that superhero thing, fly up and clear the towers," Gabriella suggested.

"My power is too weak for that now," Makeda replied wearily.

Gabriella fought to contain an "I told you it was no good using personal magic" speech. She'd delivered it several times before; it was not her place to insist. Rather, Makeda had to come to that realization on her own as any child of the One Goddess must.

Makeda thought for a moment. The sound of bullets shattering concrete surrounded them. "We'll have to give them another target," she suggested. "But my magic is weak."

"You can use the power of the One Goddess to —"

"Not this time, Gabriella."

The Irish Knight noted her praetor's solemn expression. Makeda extended a hand to Gabriella, who did not hesitate to take that hand in hers. Both women closed their eyes in concentration, ignoring the sporadic gunfire trying to draw them out.

Makeda extended her free hand toward the triangle's apex of the camp's outer walls, the area from which she and Gabriella had just barely escaped.

"May we two of the Faith join our power for the good of all," she said.

A dark blue ethereal smoke appeared around Makeda's arm. A similar white smoke appeared around Gabriella's. The two clouds moved down the women's arms, swirling around their hands and merging to form a lighter blue cloud that expanded to encompass both women.

At the apex of the triangular wall, that same blend of smoke manifested around several individual stones in the wall. Moments later, those stones began shaking themselves free of the wall.

The two MKDG bruisers who had ambushed Freeman were still in pursuit. The one without the knee injury was gaining on him. The pain in Freeman's battered body slowed him down, but the hope of not ending up a Mortal Kombat-style fatality at the hands of the MKDG spurred him on.

His zigzagging path led him to the edge of the woods. Up ahead he saw what he remembered as the Strasse der Nationnen, the main road leading to the tourist entrance at the southernmost part of the camp. His magically endowed vision revealed one major problem: a magical barrier engulfing the entire camp.

"Nice of them to pull up the welcome mat," Freeman said.

In a rare moment of blind faith, he ran full tilt toward the barrier. At the last moment, Freeman threw up his hands in front of his face as his momentum thrust him into the barrier. Mentally, he prepared to crash hard against solid material.

To his total astonishment, he passed through the barrier.

Freeman stumbled, lost his footing, and fell to the ground, rolling a short distance in the same direction.

When he finally stopped himself, his gaze went immediately back to the barrier. It remained intact. He then ran his hands over his body, discovering no new wounds.

"Maybe there is a One Goddess," Freeman muttered.

He looked around and found himself near the gate that allowed entrance to the officers' area of the camp, which doubled as the tourist entrance.

Gunfire immediately assaulted his ears, something he hadn't heard on the other side of the barrier.

Then it dawned on him that he hadn't heard from Gabriella or Makeda in the last few minutes. He could only imagine what they were going through.

On second thought, he figured he'd rather not. Besides, he had his problems. His assailants passed through the barrier and were lumbering straight toward him.

Freeman leaped up and sprinted directly at the closed and presumably locked gate. As he ran, he held his quarterstaff in front of him like a pole-vaulter. Just as Freeman's staff hit the ground a few feet in front of the gate, the goon on the good legs leaped at him.

The MKDG goon grasped space as Freeman's staff propelled him up and over the closed gate. His landing on the other side was less than graceful, but since the gate was between him and the goons, Freeman accepted the situation as a win for the good guys.

The Knight sat up and looked at the bumbling MKDG idiots on the other side of the gate. With a smile, he stood and dusted himself off, but quickly winced from the wound on his side.

In a poor attempt to play off his pain, Freeman stood up straight and then stuck his tongue out at the men. He also wiggled his hands beside his ears.

"I was the Atari Track and Field champion, bitches!" Freeman taunted.

After fiercely displaying a middle finger (of which Freeman knew Gabriella would not approve, but she wasn't here), he turned from the gate —

...and tripped over something on the ground.

After landing flat on his face, Freeman lay there for a moment, thinking this a great place to sleep until dawn. Dreading Gabriella's inevitable nagging, he ultimately pushed himself upward.

Now on his knees, Freeman got a glimpse of the object that had tripped him — a fallen MKDG thug. His throat was slit; his skin was the pale white of the snow around him.

Curiously, there was very little blood near the man or any flowing from his wound.

It was the last thought Freeman had before a booted foot kicked him in the face, knocking him unconscious.

Measure Five — Delusions of Grandeur

The Green Monster building sat just outside the southern wall of the Sachsenhausen camp. Across a dirt road, a small iron gate within the stone outer wall marked the original entrance to the officers' area. During the Second Great War, the Monster had housed a casino and luxury dining for Nazi officers.

Today, the Sachsenhausen museum's curators barred tourists from the Monster's interior.

Heinrich Reinhardt and his MKDG soldiers were neither tourists nor men who let little things like "rules" stand in their way to victory.

Under cover of darkness and well-placed bribes, Reinhardt's MKDG had established a base of operations in the Monster. It didn't meet the lofty standards their predecessors had set, but it served their purposes for this night.

Reinhardt and his soldiers also cast two spells in preparation for this night's events. The first spell summoned dark energies that reanimated the skeletons of Jewish and Russian prisoners who had died at the camp during and after the Second Great War.

These reanimated corpses would serve as the first line of aggression against the Knights of Vyntari and their vampire bitch ally, Adriana Dupré.

The second spell was an illusion that would shield the entire camp, giving the outward appearance that all was well within. Reinhardt and his men could advance their campaign of revenge without interference from the Uninitiated.

Several MKDG soldiers stood at the ready in the Monster with Reinhardt. Like him, all were perfect Aryan specimens: fair hair and blue eyes, square jaws, long noble faces, and athletic physiques underneath the standard uniform of their organization.

Reinhardt sat at a table in the center of the room. A bottle of liquor and Kummel klop meatballs with spaetzle sat ready to eat.

He looked at his companion, Lamar, seated across from him. A decrepit old man in an ill-fitting Nazi SS uniform, Lamar hunched over his meatballs like a prisoner hesitantly eating his last meal.

Time and guilt had beaten Lamar down. He was a cruel parody of himself, wasting his later years with under-aged girls, parlor magic tricks and endless nights of decadence and debauchery.

Reinhardt felt it was beneath the old man, who had fought alongside Reinhardt's grandfather during World War II, leading the occult faction within Hitler's Nazi command.

"I do not question your loyalty to the cause," Lamar said, bringing Reinhardt back from his thoughts.

"You question my interest in a feeble old man?" Reinhardt asked.

The remark drew a scowl from Lamar. He rose from his seat, a struggle for the wizened senior who had last been at the Sachsenhausen camp in 1945.

"Just hours ago, you played the role of inspector for the Berlin *polizei*," Lamar said. "In truth, you were a mere puppet for the *Ältestenrat*, charged with investigating any breach in the city's *Schattenfriede*."

Reinhardt laughed.

"The so-called Shadow Pact," he said. "Created by a group of fossils afraid of their own power!"

"A pact that you have now breached," Lamar countered. "Do you think those fossils will allow your actions to go unanswered?"

Reinhardt slammed his hand down with such force that his fork bounced from his plate and onto the damask tablecloth, soiling it with sauce. "They broke the pact first!"

Reinhardt's men tensed, wondering if they would be required to remove the old man from the room. Sensing the rising tension, Reinhardt caught his lead man's eye and made a subtle motion with his hand, diffusing the situation.

Lamar must also have sensed the mood, for he now spoke in a less confrontational tone. "And how do you figure that?"

Reinhardt retrieved his fork and stabbed another meatball. "You should relax. Eat. These are not as good as my father's, too little seasoning." He devoured his food, talking as he chewed. "He used a special spice not usual for —"

"Taking the *neger* Tigray will work in luring the Knights to you," Lamar said, "but it will also put the *Ältestenrat* on alert."

Reinhardt continued to eat, but his grip on his fork tightened. It was out of respect for Lamar's past alliance with his grandfather that he allowed the man a seat at his table. Lamar's line of questioning reminded Reinhardt that he should instead slay the man for his betrayal that led to the *Ältestenrat* and the *Schattenfriede*.

"They will want to know what happened to him," Lamar continued, his tone drawing close to hysteria. "They will find us eventually and —"

"The *Ältestenrat* is weak!"

Reinhardt's outburst silenced Lamar. Reinhardt stopped eating and closed his eyes, trying hard to hold back his anger. After a few moments, he opened his eyes and looked to Lamar. He motioned to the stump that was Lamar's right arm. "Your injury at Dupré's hand is a sign of their weakness. For them to let that go unchallenged..."

Lamar held the stump that was his right arm close to his body like a child would a cherished stuffed doll, one they didn't want someone to snatch away. Reinhardt was right: if the *Ältestenrat* had honored their *Schattenfriede* and eliminated Dupré soon after the incident at Club Five by Five, all this would be unnecessary.

Lamar still wouldn't have a hand.

The old man turned away from the table and paced. Reinhardt continued eating. "The *Schattenfriede* suppressed the natural power of the Initiated as if that power was shameful," he said between bites. "Long before this evening, I grew weary of that suppression."

Looking to Lamar, Reinhardt saw that his words had little effect on the old man.

He added, "You were there when Hitler's Reich fell."

Lamar stopped pacing. Reinhardt continued.

"You saw what happens when we let others suppress who we can truly be, what —"

The distant sound of gunfire from the main camp silenced the men in the Monster. Lamar looked to Reinhardt, who in turn looked to one of his men with a radio. The man picked up his radio, shouted questions into the device and waited.

The radio squawked to life as the sound of gunfire continued. Reinhardt and Lamar looked expectantly at the radioman. The soldier raised his radio to his ear and listened. After a few moments, he stepped to Reinhardt and gave a full on "*Sieg Heil!*" complete with raised right arm.

Reinhardt acknowledged the man with a nod.

"The Knights have evaded the skeletons and entered the main camp," the underling reported. "The soldiers on watch have them pinned down near the kitchen and laundry barracks."

Reinhardt looked to Lamar and saw fear in the man's eyes. He stood from the table and approached Lamar, putting a firm hand on the old man's shoulder. "Listen," he said.

The gunfire continued, coming faster now. Reinhardt smiled. "The Knights' defeat against the true might of the Fourth Reich is inevitable," he said. The MKDG leader patted the older man's shoulder heartily and then moved back to the table.

"Come! Drink!" he suggested.

Reinhardt picked up the liquor bottle. "*König Alkohol* — the Demon's drink," he explained. "My grandfather Matthias rescued this liquor from Nazi vaults. It was his intent to pass the supernaturally charged elixir down the generations, saving it for when the Nazi party rose to power once again."

"I remember Matthias," Lamar said. "He was a good soldier. A good German."

Reinhardt removed the bottle's wax seal and twisted its cork free. A black vapor escaped. He held the bottle to his nose, inhaling the vapor, savoring it. Looking back to Lamar, he smiled broadly, as the mystical fumes intoxicated him.

"Surely there is no better time to drink and celebrate our certain victory."

Lamar studied Reinhardt for a brief moment. Then he turned soberly and shuffled to the window that looked out to the old officer's gate.

"Relax, Lamar," the MKDG leader said with full confidence despite his sullen expression. "The Knights are under control. If the vampire does not show by dawn, we will extract the information about her from one of the Knights or the *Ältestenrat*'s *neger*."

Reinhardt poured the preternatural beverage into a glass.

"The *Ältestenrat* will be unable to deny our power and efficiency. They will cede their power to stronger leadership — the MKDG — or be crushed by their weakness."

Reinhardt held his glass aloft. "And that, Lamar, will merely be the beginning. *Beifall!*"

"I admire your fervor," Lamar said. "Yet, a similar confidence sent an army on an ill-fated mission into the winter fields of Russia. I trust you recall?"

Reinhardt, who had set the edge of the glass to his lips, hesitated before drinking. A scowl darkened his expression.

"When Dupré is dead and the *Ältestenrat* destroyed," Lamar insisted, "I will be the first to celebrate your success, Herr Reinhardt. Until then —"

Off Lamar's sudden end of speech, Reinhardt lowered his glass. The old man appeared transfixed on something beyond the window in the December snow.

"Did you post men at the officer's gate?" Lamar asked, fear creeping into his words.

Reinhardt returned his glass, the liquor inside untouched, to the table. "Two men are posted at the gate. Four more are patrolling the area between that gate and the camp entrance."

Lamar continued to stare into the night as if prolonged exposure would afford him night vision. His look of worry spread to Reinhardt, who moved so that he stood directly behind and to Lamar's side. He too peered through the thin glass panes.

Reinhardt could almost feel the winter's chill through the stone and glass, reminding him of his grandfather's stories of hardship from the dark period of Third Reich history Lamar had referenced. He saw the officer's gate, but there were no men standing guard outside it.

Lamar's eyes narrowed. In a low tone, he asked, "Do you see something, old man?"

Lamar studied the scene beyond the window. He started to shake his head, then stopped abruptly. Reinhardt followed his gaze.

One of the shadows beyond the closed gate moved.

With Gabriella's help, Makeda pulled down a semi-truck sized section of the outer wall. A horde of skeletons scrambled through, swarming the camp like bees from a broken hive.

The MKDG gunmen in the watchtowers predictably turned their guns on the skeletons, mowing them down with machine gun fire. The fallen skeletons littered the ground with ash and bone.

"*Michael*," Makeda said telepathically.

No response.

"Freeman is down," Gabriella surmised aloud.

Ignoring the danger of that possibility, Makeda referred to the tablet. "We sprint down this center path to the short wall ahead," she said. "That will serve as cover until we reach the barracks near pathology."

"We just have to get past two watchtowers to make it," Gabriella said.

Both Gabriella and Makeda looked back down the path toward the sanctuary of the wall and saw a further complication. Eight members of the MKDG entered through the now open gate.

Compared to the men in the towers, these soldiers were stripped down for physical combat. Despite the cold of the Berlin winter, they wore only earth gray khakis, brown turtleneck shirts and communication headsets.

A black substance swathed the soldiers' hands. Makeda instantly recognized the substance as magical in nature.

These soldiers were Initiated and versed in dark magic.

Makeda and Gabriella exchanged knowing glances. The younger Knight summoned her ethereal *Spatha*. "This will be a much greater challenge than beating back skeletons," she said. She sounded excited in the face of such a dire challenge.

Realizing the necessity of maintaining the cover the barracks provided, the Knights waited for their attackers to come to their position. Four combatants moved in to engage the Knights while their brethren maneuvered to flanking positions.

As Makeda engaged the two men who came for her, she kept two of the flanking MKDG goons in her line of sight.

The effort paid off.

As she dodged the blows of the two front men, Makeda set herself up for an attack against one of those on her flank. The thrusting punch to the soldier's solar plexus should have caused the man to crumble.

Instead, the soldier held firm and smiled with smug satisfaction.

He countered with a swing of his own that Makeda barely dodged. As strands of the ethereal black substance attached to the soldier's hand whisked past her nose, Makeda felt the cold darkness emanating from it.

The Knight used her martial skill to leap away from her combatants, putting some space between them.

"*Their magical enhancement extends to their entire bodies*," Makeda telepathically told Gabriella. "*Our blades should help us there.*"

Thankfully, Gabriella fared better on her side. Flourishes of her cloak distracted her two main assailants while she maneuvered toward the men at her flank.

Without taking her eyes off the thugs, Gabriella spun her ethereal sword from a forward to a backward position and thrust behind her. Her *Spatha* caught an MKDG bruiser through his chest.

Gabriella's weapon did no physical damage to the perforated soldier. Where the sword pierced flesh, dark energy shot from the soldier's body as would blood. The energy dissipated, as did the energy sheath surrounding him.

"The One Goddess is still with us," Gabriella yelled to her mentor.

"*Perhaps with you*," Makeda thought, careful to keep the comment to herself despite their telepathic link.

"*Change combatants!*" Makeda ordered.

In a maneuver practiced to the point of becoming instinctive, Gabriella and Makeda feinted before their current opponents and then swapped those same opponents with their fellow Knight. The MKDG soldiers lost precious seconds as they adjusted to the new scenario.

By then Gabriella's *Spatha Perfidelis* had already run through two more MKDG soldiers, dispelling their magical auras and draining them of their supernatural strength and resilience. Well-placed kicks from Makeda rendered the other disempowered soldier unconscious.

Makeda spared a glance at Gabriella. The young woman moved with an accomplished grace that had developed over years of passionate dedication for her mission.

It almost made Makeda regret deceiving so valiant and loyal a warrior.

Reinhardt led three men from the Monster through the officers' gate, across the common area and to the gate that allowed access to the camp proper. They found the corpses of the four soldiers he'd assigned to patrol the area scattered about, their throats slit. There was no blood in the area.

Lamar had warned Reinhardt not to underestimate the vampire. He now understood why.

Reinhardt looked through the open gate and saw eight of his men engaged with two of the Knights of Vyntari. The men were losing, several of them already struck down in the melee.

In the distance behind them, he saw the skeletons invading the base. His men in the towers used their weaponry to hold the skeletons at bay, deflecting focus from the Knights of Vyntari.

Reinhardt activated the radio headset he'd acquired before leaving the Green Monster. "Ignore the skeletons," he ordered. "Concentrate on the Knights. Once they are incapacitated, all troops converge on the Pathology building."

He turned to the men with him. "Retrieve the packages from the Monster."

The men saluted and turned to follow their orders.

Reinhardt took another moment to glare at his enemies. He then removed a satchel from over his shoulder. Reaching inside, he withdrew a decades-old skeletal arm that glowed with a dark ethereal light. Reinhardt broke the bone in two.

A thick black mist wafted from the pieces and dissipated. The bone itself turned into dusty ash that fell from his hand and littered the snow.

Reinhardt headed for the Pathology building.

Two more MKDG soldiers fell to Gabriella and Makeda's cooperative assault. The remaining four changed tactics, dodging the Knights' blows instead of using parry-attack maneuvers. Their actions pulled the Knights perilously close to stepping beyond the safety of the barracks buildings.

"*They're at least leading in the direction we want to go,*" Gabriella observed telepathically to Makeda, who started to respond but stopped short. In her peripheral vision, she saw the skeletons inexplicably turn to dust and ash.

"*The skeletons are down. The gunmen will now refocus on their primary targets,*" Makeda informed Gabriella between her feint and attack combo on one of the MKDG soldiers. "*They are drawing us into their line of fire.*"

Gabriella continued her assault against the remaining MKDG soldiers, but managed to reply, "*But they won't shoot their own men, will they?*"

"*Press through these men and get us to the Pathology building.*"

"*As you wish, praetor.*"

Makeda could sense the excitement in Gabriella's thoughts as she leaped into the air and swung her flaming sword at the MKDG thugs. They predictably dodged away from her, but inadvertently left her an opening down the path toward the main gate.

Gabriella skillfully landed on her good leg.

Both Knights seized the opportunity and charged down the open path. Makeda got in a good kick to one of the thugs on the way through.

Two other MKDG thugs rushed alongside the Knights; one grabbed Gabriella's cloak. She brought her good leg up and around the cloak. Bending her knee, she pulled the cloak toward her, in turn pulling the MKDG bruiser off balance.

Gabriella swung her *Spatha Perfidelis* through the bruiser as he fought to regain his balance. She then spun around the man, preparing a downward blow with her hands to finish him.

Suddenly, the soldier shook violently as bullets pierced his torso. He fell away from Gabriella, releasing her cloak as he went down.

The action answered Gabriella's earlier question: the MKDG thugs were expendable.

Makeda knew her discipulus all too well. Her tough exterior belied the sentimental woman underneath. Despite the evil she had seen as a Knight of Vyntari, she still showed dismay when confronted by new evil.

Any hesitation caused by that dismay could get them killed.

"Keep moving!" Makeda shouted.

Thankfully, Gabriella responded immediately. The blonde woman began a zigzagging, acrobatic course toward the safety of the Appellplatz walls and, ultimately, the Pathology Building.

Makeda followed Gabriella, watching her struggle valiantly against the pain in her wounded leg. She prayed the One Goddess whom she had disappointed would remain with Gabriella and see her through.

Measure Six — A Dead Man's Plea

Freeman came to with a violent jolt — promptly bashing his head against something hard. Scowling while rubbing his second head wound of the evening, he felt around and identified his latest attacker as a porcelain toilet.

"Bitch kicked me and left me in a shitter!" Thinking it over, Freeman shrugged. "Guess I should be happy she didn't stab me again." His eyes flared with ethereal flame. Looking into the toilet bowl, Freeman sighed. "Least they flushed."

Reaching out telepathically, Freeman thought to his fellow Knights: "*Makeda. Gabby. If you're listening, we have a vampire bat in our belfry.*"

"*Scan the Pathology Building,*" came Makeda's response.

Freeman acknowledged the command. Getting as comfortable as he could in a bathroom stall, he entered his trance state. Freemanvision returned him to the Pathology Building's Corpse Room.

The two guards once at the top of the stairs now sprawled on the floor, their torsos slashed to ribbons and their throats slit. Again, the blood that should have been everywhere was minimal.

I can only imagine why, Freeman thought.

His astral form descended the stairs and approached the back wall. Someone had desecrated the etching there. On a hunch, he bent to one knee, taking a closer look at the dusty ground in front of the etching's wall.

Several male boot prints marched up to the wall, then disappeared. A closer look revealed what Freeman had expected — a single pair of female boots. Allowing the image of the Corpse Room to swirl and dissipate, Freeman pulled himself out of his trance and returned to the cold tile of the bathroom floor.

"*Found our bloodsucker,*" he reported to his allies. "*But you'd better have a plan for getting through a secret door in the wall.*"

No response came; Freeman figured they were busy busting the MKDG trap. Better them than him, though he hoped they weren't in too much trouble. He pushed against the bathroom stall to help get to his feet, lamenting his tired, bruised body. *"Next time I'm playing lookout from the van,"* Freeman thought.

"We'll discuss that later, Michael," Makeda replied telepathically.

Freeman would have thought an "oops," but he'd already let one errant thought slip through.

"Make your way to Pathology," Makeda continued. *"We will meet you there. And do mind the soldiers."*

"Do mind the soldiers!" Freeman said, mocking Makeda's African accent. He rubbed his face with his palm. "Could have stuck to the paper and dice fantasy. But oh no! You had to go and find the real thing!" he mumbled as he headed out of the building.

Machine gun fire cut down two of the three remaining MKDG soldiers. Gabriella and Makeda came within yards of the sanctuary teased by the curved wall of the Appellplatz.

Unfortunately, Gabriella's wound got the better of her. She stumbled to a knee, allowing the remaining MKDG soldier to catch up to her. The soldier grabbed one of Gabriella's arms. He pulled her up, attempting to fling her into the path of the towers' guns.

To the soldier's surprise, Gabriella used her martial arts skill to reverse his maneuver. Bullets slammed against the soldier's magical shielding. They didn't penetrate, but they hammered painfully into the man's back, pressing him into Gabriella. The two fell, with Gabriella the first to hit the ground.

"Gabriella!"

The blonde Knight stole a glance at Makeda. From the safety of the Appellplatz wall, she extended a hand to Gabriella but was too far away to reach her. Instead, a faint blue ethereal ooze launched from Makeda's hand.

It reached its full length halfway toward Gabriella.

Gabriella aimed her *Spatha* in the direction of Makeda's power. White flames extended from the *Spatha* and latched on to Makeda's ooze. Makeda pulled the ooze, dragging Gabriella and the MKDG soldier on top of the Knight to her.

Meanwhile, bullets assaulted the soldier. Gabriella almost regretted the pain on his face but figured it fair justice for his evil.

Once the blue ooze had reached Makeda, Gabriella contracted her flames, completing her pull to safety. Gabriella pushed the weakened soldier away from her and continued her roll to the safety of the wall. Bullets peppered the wall but did no harm to the two Knights on the other side.

"Why are you even bothering with personal magic?" Gabriella asked Makeda.

The last MKDG thug crawled toward the wall. Makeda pushed Gabriella behind her and lunged forward, leading with her Ogoun dagger. She stabbed the MKDG thug, shattering his protective magic. Makeda then punched him repeatedly in the jaw, eventually rendering him unconscious.

Bullets tore through the fallen man's torso. Gabriella grabbed Makeda's poncho and pulled her back behind the wall. The two Knights looked to one another. Makeda gave a silent nod of thanks. She then pointed to Gabriella's leg wound. "You'd better do something about that."

Gabriella closed her eyes and held her *Spatha* in her open palms. The *Spatha* dissolved into pure ethereal flames engulfing her hands. She pressed those flames to the wound on her leg. They melted into her wound, creating an x-ray-like view of the wound. Gabriella watched as the flames repaired torn ligaments and muscle.

When the healing was complete, Gabriella transformed the flames into a body sheath. She smiled in anticipation as she looked to Makeda. "Ready when you are, Praetor Arsi."

Makeda nodded in acknowledgment and then led the charge along the curved wall toward the Pathology building.

"Damn her!"

In the Pathology building, Reinhardt's face flushed to crimson as he looked upon the two dead men he'd left to protect the Corpse Room's secret chamber. Again the slit throats with lacerations on their torsos and the lack of blood.

He stepped over the dead men and descended the stairs toward the wall with the etching. Three other MKDG soldiers followed at a respectable distance. "*Umgestaltung*," he commanded. He looked to the wall as if expecting something, his anger rising.

"*Umgestaltung!*" he shouted.

Then he noticed the etching.

Blade marks defaced it; its ebony glow had faded. Having worked with the Nazis, Dupré must have known the magical phrase that opened the door. With all the other magical preparations, Reinhardt had neglected to change the phrase. He never anticipated Dupré getting this far.

Again he had underestimated her.

The desecration had destroyed the magic controlling the door, locking it shut. She had made sure no one would follow her in.

"Get me into that room!" Reinhardt commanded.

The three MKDG soldiers set down the satchels they had retrieved from the Green Monster. They withdrew several brick-sized mounds of what appeared to be clay but were not.

They were plastic explosives.

As the men set to work planting the explosives in a door shape on the wall, Reinhardt reached into his satchel. He withdrew a large skull. It resembled that of a human but was nearly twice the size. It had an elongated nose and mouth, more of a snout line with vicious looking fangs.

Reinhardt said another phrase in German.

The skull emitted a sinister, ebony glow.

Adriana stood at the bottom of the narrow stairs beyond the secret door. A vast room lay before her. She knew the room as the former laboratory for *Projekt: Erwachen der Tier* — Project: Awaken the Beast.

In the spring of 1945, Hitler's Reich crumbled around him. Allied forces marched toward Berlin on both its eastern and western fronts. One of Hitler's last hopes for victory lay in this project. He'd given the project over to members of the Order of Haroth. The sorcerers led the project not because they shared the Nazis' philosophies of hate, but for the freedom to practice their magical arts and the experimentation on human subjects Nazi fascism allowed.

Adriana's job as a bodyguard for the Order's leader Malachi Thorne and his assistant, Trennan Lamar, afforded her knowledge of the project's existence, but not its purpose.

Though the Order kept her in the dark about the project, they made no effort to hide the secret door's password from her. She never did see the inside of the laboratory.

One fateful night, Thorne's lack of trust toward Adriana nearly got him slaughtered.

On that night, a test subject escaped and attacked the camp.

That test subject was a female garou.

Thorne and his minions had escaped the lab into the Corpse Room where Adriana was waiting. He ordered Adriana to kill the beast. Unknown to him, Adriana had sworn to do no harm to the garou after what she had done to their numbers as a Daughter of Lilith. Instead of destroying the garou, she had helped her escape and took her to the Guardians of Faith and their Allied partners.

In April of 1945, a Guardian-led Allied assault team raided Sachsenhausen. The Order's sorcerers and their Nazi lackeys put up a valiant yet ultimately futile fight. The Russian army raided the camp the next day, never knowing of the project or the supernatural beings that had occupied the laboratory.

Adriana and the Guardians had ensured Project: Awaken the Beast would never make it to fruition, much less the history books.

Owing to the MKDG leader's desire for retribution within a historical narrative, Adriana deduced this space as the best spot to hide a prisoner.

Oil lamps illuminated the tomb-like, rectangular room, confirming Adriana's suspicion of the laboratory having become a prison. To her left and right, the shells of glass cabinets lined the walls, their contents long ago spilled upon the ground and absorbed into the fractured and scorched concrete floor.

Tables, once solid slabs of concrete and tile, were now crushed, broken and strewn across the open area that had served as the operating theater. Scorch marks from mystical fire and lightning discolored the tiles and walls. Bullet holes and claw strikes further conveyed the battle that had occurred in the room.

Moving through the operating theater, Adriana approached the remnants of the lower half of a wall that ran the length of the room opposite the stairs. Shards of broken glass protruded from the wall, alluding to the upper half of the wall having been protective glass that allowed a view into a hallway on the other side.

Beyond that hallway lay the main attractions of the laboratory: holding cells for captive humans and garou. Like the rest of the laboratory, the decay brought on by time reduced the cell area and its connecting hallway to dusty rubble and memories.

A stirring of shadow in the dim oil light caught Adriana's attention. As she focused on that location, blood flowed into her eyes, changing the whites to a deep red: the physical manifestation of her blood vision.

Inanimate objects appeared as cold shades of black and blue, allowing her to see anything with blood in its system — like the man chained to a cell wall as though he were another of the Reich's human test subjects.

Adriana noted the dim luminance of the man's blood.

Dispelling the blood from her eyes brought back her normal vision. She then moved through the wreckage and to the prisoner's cell.

Adriana had spent thirty years working for the Daughters of Lilith. In those years, she had become acquainted with a variety of forms of torture to the point that she could discern the torturer's intent from the marks left on the subject.

The MKDG had carved and beaten their African prisoner as if he were a worthless piece of meat; his wounds inflicted out of amusement and with a great deal of hatred.

To Adriana's astonishment, the man miraculously opened the one eye that injuries had not swollen shut. That eye looked Adriana up and down as she approached. She suddenly became conscious of her appearance.

In such a hurry to finish this business with the MKDG, Adriana had left the Knights, retrieved her motorcycle and driven to Sachsenhausen. She still wore the torn and bloodied clothes from her struggle with Strathan and the garou back in Grunewald Forest.

Blood from the MKDG soldiers she had killed for sustenance further stained those clothes. Adriana's severed right hand remained a work in progress, merely half a palm with no fingers or thumb.

The only effort she'd made regarding her appearance was to tie her shoulder-length, dark brown hair back into a ponytail.

"And you must be Adriana Dupré," the African prisoner said. From the halted rasp in the man's voice, Adriana inferred he didn't have long before this cell became his tomb.

"If you know who I am, then you know why I am here."

"Yes," the man Adriana deduced to be Sahlu replied. "But... Makeda?"

"Where is the third shard?"

Despite all the MKDG bastards had done to him, Sahlu exhibited no anger, no rage as Adriana felt she would in his situation. His battered face and downturned lips projected a deep sadness. It reminded her of the disappointment Makeda had shown for her when she had turned her blade on Freeman.

She hated that her actions drew such feelings. Yet what could she expect from the Righteous, those who saw redemption as something that was actually attainable? Adriana knew better; she knew her life was damned and expected no salvation other than the satisfaction of revenge.

Sahlu would tell her where to find the shard. Then, she would find Strathan and extract that revenge.

"Do not waste what precious little breath is left you," she said.

Guilt tightened the muscles in Adriana's chest. She usually issued that statement as a warning before assassinating a target. In this instance, she meant it as an empathetic suggestion, as if her melancholy for the unnecessary deaths of Denson and the garou had expanded to include this man.

"You doubt this path Makeda offers you," Sahlu said, the strain of speech evident in his voice.

Adriana looked at the broken walls, the shattered glass — anything to avoid meeting Sahlu's one-eyed gaze of disappointment. "This is not a conversation I wish to have."

"Then why are you here, Adriana?"

Adriana cast a sideways glance at Sahlu. His condition deteriorated with every breath, yet he continued devoting the little time he had left to a woman most would rather see destroyed.

"I need you to tell me where I can find the third shard. Then I will find Strathan."

"You want to find Strathan? Pick up a gossip rag."

Adriana once again turned her eyes away from Sahlu. He was correct in the ease with which she could find Strathan. Hollywood bad boy actors were always in the news in some way.

Perhaps the Knights' righteousness had affected Adriana more than she would admit.

Was she here for the shard?

For revenge?

Or to rescue this poor soul because it was the right thing to do?

It then occurred to Adriana that had the Knights followed Adriana's path of vengeance they would simply end her accursed existence. Yet at every turn, they chose instead to take injury upon themselves rather than allow it to befall her.

Initially, Adriana thought their tactics merely the foolishness of the Righteous. In hindsight, she realized that had she tempered her violence, Denson and his pack might be alive. All of the Navarre garou might still be alive.

"What has your vendetta gained you?" Sahlu asked.

Adriana focused her attention back on Sahlu. A scowl marred her expression, but it faded in light of the man's condition. Adriana moved closer to him. "You do not have time for this," she said, desperation on the edge of her voice.

Then an explosion rocked the entire laboratory.

Adriana moved to the front of the cell to look back across the operating theater. Parts of the secret door through which she had entered rained down upon the age-old debris, propelling a cloud of dust that obscured the already dimly lit room.

MKDG soldiers would soon enter the laboratory in an attempt to either contain or destroy her.

"You are correct, Adriana," the dying man behind her confirmed. She turned back to him as he added, "We no longer have the time."

Adriana moved back to Sahlu. The tone of his next words carried an earnestness even Adriana's frozen heart could not ignore.

"Go with Makeda to Oromia. There you will go back to the moment that made you. Make again the decision that set your current path. Or, perhaps...choose another."

Adriana watched as the man Makeda knew as Sahlu Tigray closed his one good eye. A single tear fell from that eye, the only sign of pain he allowed himself to show. He then sagged in his chains as the life he once lived slipped away from him.

Anger welled in Adriana. This time, it was not for the evil done to her, but for the waste of this man Sahlu, a man who no doubt had been a noble warrior. Adriana shed tears for the man. They were not human tears of water, but a vampire's tears of blood.

The obvious choice now would be to say to Hell with Makeda's path. Adriana should return to Los Angeles, where Strathan would inevitably surface. She knew that path. It held no surprises for her, only for those she would see dead.

But Sahlu prophesied about returning to "the moment that made her" intrigued Adriana. What had he meant, and why would she find this moment with Makeda in this Oromia place?

Her thoughts were interrupted when the earring covering the back of her left ear began to vibrate.

Measure Seven — Fall of the Fourth Reich

During the time of the *Abattage Terriblé*, Adriana had acquired an enchanted earring that would vibrate upon proximity with garou, whether they be in human or wolf form.

That earring now issued its warning.

From her numerous encounters with the garou, Adriana had learned to identify their various howls. When they first encountered an enemy, they issued a challenge that curdled the blood and drove away the faint of heart.

In contrast, the howl Adriana heard now was a sorrowful release born of great pain. It was more like the howl born of a dead garou's family than an attacking predator.

Through the smoke and debris, Adriana saw a creature floating above the stairs. It had the appearance of a wolf but was larger, more menacing. Adriana recognized it as a garou, but this creature possessed an ethereal presence like the flames that surrounded Gabriella. However, this creature's ethereal flames were a darker hue.

A garou was a lethal creature. This creature was not a true garou, but its spirit in the form of a wraith. That made the creature much more deadly.

The garou-wraith's eyes focused with laser precision on Adriana. Its lips curled into a snarl, revealing a set of teeth that could rend flesh from bone with the efficiency of a butcher's cleaver.

It unleashed another howl.

It then sprang forward.

Though the creature gave the illusion of traversing the ground, it made no contact with the concrete as it stalked toward Adriana. Its rate of movement varied; the creature would bound across an area, then suddenly disappear, only to reappear almost instantly in a new location and closer to Adriana.

The wraith's erratic movement complicated Adriana's attempt to time its approach making her defensive options more difficult to execute. She had to time each move to the millisecond or risk being torn limb from limb by the creature's talon-like claws.

Adriana backed into the shadows of Sahlu's cell, using her preternatural powers to expand those shadows, extending her hiding space.

The keen eyes of a natural garou could not pierce the supernaturally aided shadows. Adriana knew this much from her days in the *Abattage*. But she had never encountered this creature before. She had no real idea of its abilities.

The garou-wraith stopped abruptly at the jagged bars at the front of the cell. It scanned the interior with the eyes of a natural predator — but made no attempt to enter.

The shadows served their purpose. However, the creature blocked Adriana's escape.

Having lost sight of the vampire, the garou-wraith unleashed its sorrowful howl again. It then sniffed at the stale air of the decaying laboratory.

Adriana knew its sense of smell could penetrate the shadows' obfuscation, assuming the wraith possessed that sense. In answer to her thought, the garou-wraith floated into the cell, its nose still sniffing at the air.

It walked toward Sahlu, brushing its snout against him, taking in the scent of death. The creature stood far enough away from the cell exit that Adriana could slip past the beast.

She cautiously edged around toward the cell's opposite side —

The garou-wraith's head snapped away from Sahlu. It sniffed the air again. Adriana froze in place. The creature looked directly at Adriana's position. It could not see her, but it had to know she was there. It leaped at Adriana, its jaws yearning for flesh.

Adriana spun to her right and out of the wraith's path. It came up short, just missing its target.

Adriana shivered at the cold emanating from the creature as it passed behind her. As turned, she dashed out of the cell and into the hallway.

The garou-wraith charged after its prey, continuing its erratic movement during the pursuit.

Adriana sprinted over the shattered glass in the hallway and to the half wall separating the cells from the operating theater. She vaulted the wall —

Just as automatic weapon fire exploded around her. Bullets pierced Adriana's supernaturally animated flesh. The vampire went down but rolled to safety behind one of the ruined experimentation tables.

That safety was merely a matter of perception.

Adriana saw the garou-wraith in her periphery stalking toward her position. As it pounced at her, she rolled to lay prone on the floor. The garou floated over her.

The creature should have smashed against the table and landed near Adriana. To her dismay, it became insubstantial and sailed through the table, disappearing from view.

Now the vampire faced two problems from the garou-wraith: she had no idea where it lay hidden, and since it could go through solid objects, it could attack her at will without her knowledge, without her capability to mount a defense.

There was also the matter of the machine guns.

Adriana moved to a crouching position and propelled herself across the opening between her and the next dilapidated table. Bullets chipped pieces from the table she had used as cover as well as the floor between the tables.

She made it without further injury. Adriana took a quick look around the table's corner. She had just enough time to count three MKDG gunmen standing halfway down the stairs before bullets pelted the side of the table.

Shards of broken concrete sprayed across her face.

Better that than a bullet.

Taking a moment to check her wounds, Adriana found that the gunmen had clipped her side. It was merely a flesh wound and easy enough to heal with her blood magic.

Adriana wouldn't have the time.

A low growl to her side grabbed her attention. She looked and saw the garou-wraith's head passing halfway through the table she had previously used for cover.

Its eyes, glowing pools of hatred, fixed upon her.

Then the wraith's head receded into the table and disappeared.

Adriana's options were limited. She didn't waste time debating them. Instead, she lurched across the space between her and another table.

Her timing was perfect. The creature bounded through the table she had just used for cover. Its jaws snapped shut, having anticipated tearing into Adriana's flesh. Instead, it tasted disappointment. Its claws raked across the concrete where Adriana's body had once been.

More bullets flew, again missing their target.

Adriana, meanwhile, had maneuvered herself closer to the gunmen. At this rate, she would be bouncing between tables well past the sunrise. What good was an escape if it resulted in her destruction by the rays of the sun? She looked back to the wraith.

It had disappeared.

Adriana needed another tactic.

The garou-wraith suddenly appeared and leaped at her again.

"What kept you?" Freeman asked while twirling his quarterstaff.

Makeda and Gabriella joined him outside of the Pathology building.

"Raining lead, zombie apocalypse," Gabriella replied.

Freeman, mouth agape, looked around as if he were surprised. "Was that a funny?" he asked. "Did Gabriella Doran make a funny?"

"No," she replied. "We were literally dodging bullets and fighting zombies."

"And I missed that excitement?" Freeman said with enough sarcasm to convey his relief that he had indeed missed the excitement. He stopped twirling his staff and pounded one end of it on the ground with all the authority of Moses parting the Red Sea.

Makeda grabbed his arm and turned him to face her. "Focus, Michael. Where is —"

The Knights heard the explosion, felt its concussive force rattle the walls even this far removed from its epicenter. The Knights spared a glance at one another. Gabriella nodded. She held up her hand. Her white ethereal flames engulfed her hand.

The Knights entered the Pathology building.

Smoke billowed up the stairs from the Corpse Room below. Gabriella's light cut through the rising smoke. Makeda moved toward the stairs. Gabriella followed.

"Um, shouldn't we be running away from explosions?" Freeman said. "I can look ahead with the ol'—"

"Come on!" Gabriella chided. She turned her head to flash Freeman a scolding glance.

By doing so, she missed the bolt of dark-hued, ethereal energy that slammed into Makeda. Gabriella did see her praetor fly off her feet and back into the Pathology room. Her landing was neither graceful nor pleasant.

Thankfully, she missed the center autopsy table.

Just as Gabriella turned back to the stairs, another bolt flew toward her. She dove to the side. The bolt came so close she felt the cold emanating from the evil that spawned it. Gabriella ended her evasive maneuver with a roll that brought her to Freeman's side.

Both Freeman and Gabriella looked to the stairs.

A man in an old Nazi SS uniform emerged from the smoke and darkness. His demeanor was that of a demon rising from Hell. Dark energy flowed from his body like ethereal steam.

"Hell of an entrance... pun intended," Freeman said, his fists clenched in a nervous death grip around his quarterstaff.

"In preparation for your exit," the newcomer said in English with an accent right out of a Hollywood Nazi movie.

"Care to try a fair fight?" Makeda said while rising to her feet.

"You are beneath me, *neger*," the newcomer snarled. "You don't deserve the right of a fair fight."

"Works for me," Gabriella said.

"Gabriella, wait!" Makeda yelled.

Her warning came too late.

The blonde Knight launched herself at the newcomer. As she moved, the flame on her hand transformed into her *Spatha*. The newcomer dodged the flaming sword and punched Gabriella in her stomach. The Knight buckled over.

The bruiser raised his other hand to slam it down on the back of Gabriella's neck in what would have been a killing blow.

It never connected.

Makeda's leg lashed out and hooked the soldier's forearm before he could do Gabriella harm. She wrapped the back of her knee about his forearm. Using his arm as a fulcrum, she spun around and into the air. Makeda's knee smashed the man in the face, forcing him to stumble back and away from the female Knights.

Makeda landed on her feet. The Nazi bruiser quickly regained his composure. He squared off against the two Knights.

Infuriated, the bruiser fired another bolt of dark energy. Makeda dived forward under the bolt and rolled. She came up with a boot to his midsection, forcing him backward again. He slammed into a set of shelving, crushing it. Wood and glass fell around him.

Makeda got to her feet and kicked at the neo-Nazi. He blocked the attack then followed up with several of his own. Makeda parried them and prepared to dodge what she thought would be a punch from a mallet-like right hand to her stomach.

Instead, the thug grabbed Makeda's forearm and held on tight. She maneuvered to protect against a potential throw, but that was not his intent.

Ethereal steam rose from where the newcomer gripped Makeda's arm. The damage he inflicted appeared on her face. The lines grew deeper around her eyes. Her vibrant, raven-colored hair grayed. Her skin tightened.

Freeman thrust his staff at the neo-Nazi's face. The man easily dodged the blow without losing his hold on Makeda. With Freeman now nearby, he was able to kick the Knight in his thigh.

Freeman's leg buckled. He fell to one knee, now an easy target. The neo-Nazi gave him a swift kick to his head.

Freeman landed on the floor in a heap.

The German returned his attention to Makeda, who had crumpled to her knees. Looking up, she could clearly see her attacker's face.

Blind hatred consumed him.

A flash of light blinded Makeda.

She quickly surmised the flash to have been Gabriella's *Spatha Perfidelis*. In the next moment, Makeda was free of the bruiser's grip. With that release, the drain on her essence ceased. Unfortunately, that did not reverse her prematurely advanced age.

Makeda looked to her attacker. Gabriella stood near him, her *Spatha* finishing an arc that swung clean through his torso. The *Spatha* did no physical harm but disrupted his mystical underpinnings. The shock had forced him to release Makeda.

Gabriella continued her assault with a roundhouse kick to the man's face. The German assailant parried her leg, pushing it away so forcefully he threw Gabriella off balance. She slammed stomach first into one of the autopsy tables, her free hand grabbing its edge so she didn't fall.

Before she could catch her breath, the man grabbed her in a bear hug with her back against his chest.

The German was a head taller than Gabriella's near six feet in height. He looked down at her lecherously. "Why do you carry on with these inferiors, *fräulien*? You are of good breeding stock, and should be at the side of a proper Aryan such as myself."

Gabriella rammed her head backward. Reinhardt moved his head aside, dodging her attempt to butt him in the face. He squeezed harder. Gabriella's shut her eyes tight against the pain. Her lungs ached for air.

When she opened her eyes, they exposed her determination.

Gabriella's *Spatha* transformed from a sword into a tight sheath of flame encompassing the Knight's body. This sheath pressed against the German's hold. He put up a respectable fight, but his hold proved no match for the physical manifestation of Gabriella's faith.

She kicked against the table with both feet, pushing the German backward. He landed on his back. His hold on Gabriella broke. The Knight rolled away from him, coming up against a wall near the stairs.

It took her a moment to catch her breath. In that time, the German moved to a kneeling position. He squared off with Gabriella.

"Don't let the blonde hair and blue eyes fool you, Adolf," the Knight said.

Breaking his hold didn't wipe the sneer off the German's face.

"And a fighter as well, eh?" he said as he got to his feet. "You most definitely deserve a place at Heinrich Reinhardt's side."

Gabriella moved into a combat stance while sizing up her opponent. He filled out his Nazi uniform with a full set of muscles, and he knew how to use them.

With her smaller stature, a prolonged assault would end in her defeat. She'd either have to end this quickly or buy the time for her companions to aid her.

"Reinhardt, huh?" Gabriella said. "You're the leader of this misguided set of jokers?"

The German's sneer widened into a full-fledged smile.

"Figures." Gabriella flipped her cloak so that it hung behind her and out of the way. Her sheath of ethereal flame flickered about her. "You stink of arrogance," she said as a final taunt.

The Knight charged the German. Her first attack was a feint; Reinhardt fell for it. Gabriella's real attack, an upswing of her hand, connected with the underside of Reinhardt's jaw. It merely annoyed him, not hurting him. Gabriella used her boot for that.

Both of them.

The German and the female Knight exchanged a flurry of blows. He used brute force. She answered with feints, acrobatic dodges around the tables and carefully placed strikes.

In the end, Gabriella used a martial throw to send Reinhardt across the room. He slowly rose to his knees, shaking his head in stunned confusion.

Gabriella seized the opportunity to look to her wounded praetor. She reached an ethereal-flamed hand toward Makeda — but Makeda grabbed her wrist and stopped her.

"Thank you, Gabriella," Makeda managed in a weak voice over strained vocal chords. "But don't let down your guard."

She motioned to something behind Gabriela. The younger Knight quickly followed Makeda's gaze. Reinhardt had gathered himself and once again stood tall. He cut an imposing figure, made worse by his sinister laugh.

"Yes, you are a very competent warrior," he declared. "It will be unfortunate to lose such a fine Aryan specimen."

Reinhardt cracked the bones in his neck. He then took up a fighting stance, beckoning to Gabriella. She looked past Reinhardt — and smiled.

"I told you not to let my appearance fool you," she said. "One other thing."

Gabriella pointed at something behind Reinhardt. At first, he didn't fall for it. Then he slowly cocked his head to one side.

"Two can play that sneaky stuff, Toht!" declared Freeman. He had recovered from the earlier assault and stood behind Reinhardt. Freeman swung his staff at Reinhardt —

The German caught the staff.

Freeman gulped but didn't release his hold. Reinhardt grabbed the staff with both hands and pulled, yanking Freeman over the top of the table on the far end and to a position on the ground in front of him. Reinhardt held the staff out horizontally at waist level.

Gabriella launched herself at Reinhardt. She leaped above Freeman, landing with one foot on the staff. She kicked out with the other foot, connecting with Reinhardt's forehead.

The German released the staff and stumbled backward into the table. He rolled away from it. Hitting the wall behind him stopped his momentum.

The blonde Knight landed on the floor with the staff between her feet. She scooped her foot under the staff, kicked it into the air and caught it. Freeman shuffled up next to her.

"Next time," Gabriella advised, "strike first. Then talk."

"Now you tell me," Freeman said.

"You bitch!" Reinhardt said.

Freeman and Gabriella both looked at Reinhardt. He was back on his feet and looking for a fight.

"I'm not a bitch," Gabriella said emphatically. She launched a flurry of strikes with Freeman's staff against Reinhardt, bashing the German repeatedly from varying angles, intent on keeping him off balance. She threw her cloak and a few kicks into the mix, compounding Reinhardt's confusion.

Eventually, she used the staff to trip the German, bringing the man to his knees.

"By the way," she began.

Reinhardt spat blood, then looked at Gabriella. His eyes showed defiance.

"I'm Irish, ya racist prick."

The German lunged at the female Knight.

Gabriella sidestepped his charge, draping her cloak across his head and shoulders with one hand like a matador against a charging bull. She threw the staff into the air and with her newly freed hand disconnected the cloak's clasp.

With her foot, she tripped Reinhardt. He stumbled. Gabriella used the cloak to drive him head first into the side of the center concrete table.

Reinhardt went to the ground, her cloak obscuring his view and covering his upper torso.

The staff came down into Gabriella's outstretched hand.

"And another thing," Gabriella said as Reinhardt scrambled to free himself from her cloak. "The next time you want to use the innocent dead as pawns of evil —"

Reinhardt removed the cloak in time to see Gabriella swing the staff at him. It stopped millimeters from his temple.

She moved the staff to Reinhardt's chin and raised his head, forcing him to meet her gaze.

"Remember the mercy I showed you this day," the Knight declared. "Show the same to the dead."

Reinhardt's lips moved to retort, but Freeman kicked him in the shoulder, sending him stomach-first to the floor. Gabriella straddled him. She grabbed her cloak and used it to bind Reinhardt's arms behind his back.

The German struggled.

Freeman slapped his elbow then slammed it into the back of Reinhardt's head. While the man was stunned, Gabriella moved to one side. She then grabbed the man's feet to bind them with his arms in her cloak.

Freeman continued hitting Reinhardt with the palms of his hands, distracting him while Gabriella finished hog-tying him.

Her job done, Gabriella stood up. Freeman joined her.

"Gobshite," Gabriella said with contempt.

"Gabriella!" Freeman said. When she looked at him, he said, "Your language!"

Gabriella shook her head. She moved from Reinhardt to Makeda. Freeman was still looking at her rodeo work.

"Where'd a city girl get mad cowgirl skills, anyway?"

Gabriella knelt down to Makeda. "Growing up with two hooligan Irish brothers," she deadpanned.

Measure Eight — Reflection

Adriana remembered the StG 44 assault rifle from her days in the Second Great War. It had been the answer to the Russian submachine guns, matching them in power and surpassing them with the range of a German rifle.

She also remembered that it fired 600 rounds a minute on full automatic. At that rate of fire, and at such close range, one didn't need to aim to hit a target. One merely sprayed the room and let the sheer volume of ammunition do the heavy lifting.

That made the weapon nearly impossible to dodge even with supernatural speed and acrobatic skill.

Luckily, the gunmen fired in bursts.

Adriana's luck was about to run out.

The weapons had ceased firing for the moment. Then Adriana heard the telltale click of the men switching their weapons over to full auto. She took the opportunity to move.

Try as she did to avoid them, bullets from the guns inevitably tore through parts of her body. She'd nearly spent all the blood in her system, either magically by maintaining her supernatural speed or by natural loss through wounds.

Despite these challenges, Adriana finally reached her destination — a few stairs down from the three MKDG thugs.

Bloodied and exhausted, Adriana crashed to her knees before them, her head hanging low as her unkempt hair covered her face.

The thugs trained their guns on her. If they fired now, there wouldn't be enough left of Adriana for her to heal even if she had the blood within her to perform such magic.

"For someone with such a fierce reputation of dealing out death," one of the thugs began in his native German, "you don't seem so tough."

"What do you expect from a French whore?" another thug quipped.

One of the men stomped down to Adriana's position and grabbed a handful of her hair, pulling her head back sharply. He probably expected to see her beaten expression.

Instead, the MKDG thug saw Adriana's smile — and her vibrating earring.

To their utter shock, she spoke in perfect German, "You Nazis were always too arrogant."

The thug pulling Adriana's hair looked to his companions. Neither of them understood how she could be so confident.

The growl of the approaching garou-wraith provided a very strong clue.

The thugs looked past Adriana in time to see the wraith leaping toward them. They had no time to do anything —

Except die.

Up in Pathology, the Knights had heard gunshots and a woefully melancholy howling coming from the levels below. Freeman wanted to check things out in Freemanvision, but Gabriella had insisted he remain focused here in the real world.

Someone had to stand guard in case someone else tried to ambush them while she tended to Makeda.

"You took pretty good care of the last guy that tried that," Freeman had replied while indicating Reinhardt.

The subdued Nazi wannabe lay in a corner bound by Gabriella's cloak. A stern look from Gabriella had ended the argument Freeman had wanted before it started.

Gabriella sat with the preternaturally aged Makeda. The African woman tried to speak, but a coughing fit interrupted her words. Gabriella rested Makeda's head in her lap, as she had done for Freeman when tending his wounds back in Grunewald.

Eventually, Makeda's coughing ceased.

"Don't bother to heal me," she said in a haggard voice reflecting her forced age. "Save your energy for whatever is in the next room."

The ominous sounds of rapidly firing machine guns and the howls of a wolf made that prospect something Freeman could do without.

"Whatever is in that room we'll face together," Gabriella replied.

Freeman stood watch, though his watching both his partners and the activity beyond the Corpse Room's secret door divided his attention.

Gabriella raised a hand, willed it to ignite with her white, ethereal flame. Makeda feebly raised a hand to stop her.

"If you try to heal me," Makeda wheezed. She paused to take several breaths, then said, "It may cost you more than the One Goddess can provide."

Gabriella's expression conferred dismay. It broke Makeda's heart. The younger Knight lowered her flame-quenched hand to touch Makeda's head.

Her hand never touched Makeda's flesh.

A dark film materialized on the Knight's leader, blocking Gabriella's flames. She concentrated, willing her flames to spread, forming a cocoon about Makeda's entire body.

The dark film oozed like a living liquid, preventing Gabriella's flames from reaching Makeda's skin and blocking their healing power.

The Irish Knight closed her eyes as she deepened her concentration. The aura of flame surrounding Makeda grew brighter. Freeman had to shield his preternaturally enhanced eyes. The dark, living liquid on Makeda's skin hardened and then cracked.

Gabriella's flames seeped through those cracks, making contact with Makeda's aged skin.

Where there was contact, the skin softened, slowly regaining its supple quality. Her hair returned to its former condition.

The strain of the effort showed in Gabriella's furrowed brow, in the slump of her shoulders.

In time, the flames burned away the dark shell, continuing their work on Makeda and returning her to her appropriate age. Then they withdrew to Gabriella's hand and dissipated into steam. Freeman moved to Gabriella's side and caught her before she fell to the floor.

"Thought the One Goddess's power was inexhaustible," he said.

"It is," Gabriella replied weakly. "My ability to focus it is not. I just need a moment."

Looking at her, Freeman thought she'd need more than that. He glanced over at Reinhardt and saw a satchel lying on the ground near him. Freeman's gaze turned to Makeda, who slowly sat up. "Think you can hold her, praetor?"

Makeda nodded. She moved to support Gabriella. It was the infirm holding the infirm, but Freeman had to follow his hunch.

He moved to the satchel, picked it up and reached inside. He pulled out what appeared to be the skull of a wolf, though one that was much larger and far more menacing than an average wolf.

"I think I can buy us that moment Gabriella needs," Freeman said. "Or at least take care of one of our problems down below."

Freeman bounced the skull in the palm of his hand and smiled. He tossed it a bit higher than before then watched it fall.

From her observation of the garou-wraith, Adriana deduced it would have to stay substantial to attack her.

She made a point to get out of its way.

Adriana grabbed the hand holding her head, twisting it as she fell to the ground. Her maneuver pulled the thug directly into the path of the garou-wraith. She looked back and saw the garou-wraith's front claws inches from the thug.

Adriana's only regret was that she would not see the horrified faces of the other MKDG men as the wraith cut into them.

There came a mournful howl —

…then silence.

No further howls.

No claws rending flesh.

No screams as internal organs became external.

Adriana looked up, only to find the garou-wraith gone. The three thugs looked to one another in surprise, and then down at Adriana. She shared their surprise.

"Did I get it mommy?" came a voice from the room upstairs.

Adriana recognized the sniveling sarcasm. The male Knight Freeman had arrived and somehow eliminated the garou wraith. The other two Knights were no doubt with him.

Seizing on the confusion of the moment, Adriana vaulted to her feet, at the same time reaching behind her. Her still viable left hand grabbed at the scabbard on her back. One of her legendary *Fukushuu* blades met her hand.

The MKDG thugs raised their weapons —

Adriana slashed the outer thigh of the MKDG thug closest to her. As he started to fall, Adriana used her preternatural speed to move up the steps to the other two thugs.

The first thug fell to his knee.

Adriana's blade stabbed the second thug in the stomach.

The first thug fell forward.

Adriana dragged her blade up, eviscerating the second thug.

The first thug extended a hand to break his fall.

Adriana arched her blade downward, slashing the throat of the third thug.

The first thug landed on his hand but rolled to one side.

Adriana came back down the stairs.

The first thug landed on his back.

Adriana thrust her blade downward, stabbing the first thug in the forehead.

Their complete shock and horror registered in the expressions of all three thugs.

The third MKDG thug tried to talk, but his severed spinal cord blocked his windpipe. He spun as he fell, shooting blood back up the stairs. The blood of the others showered Adriana.

The vampire withdrew her blade. She used her right forearm to wipe the blood from her face, resisting the strong urge to replenish herself.

"Really! Do you have to kill everybody?" Freeman asked from the top of the stairs.

In a practiced motion so fast it was nothing more than a blur, Adriana returned her blade to its scabbard. Freeman blinked as if he'd missed it.

Adriana looked to him and said, "Well, I have not killed you."

"I knew you weren't as bad as the legends say!" Freeman said, descending the stairs.

"I have not killed you — yet," Adriana added.

Freeman gave her an incredulous look. "Better check yourself, lady. I may be more of a lover, but I have the serious skills of —"

Freeman's foot slipped on some blood. His leg went out from under him, and he landed on his butt with a splat. He then skidded down several stairs, stopping when he bumped into one of the corpses.

Adriana looked disapprovingly at Freeman. "You were saying, Knight?"

Freeman scowled. He rolled over and attempted to push up with his arms, but his hands slipped on more blood; he chest-planted, splattering his face in the process. "Ugh!" He started spitting. "I think I got some in my mouth!"

Adriana shook her head.

"Pull yourself together, the both of you," a woman said.

Adriana recognized the African Knight's voice. She looked up the stairs to see Makeda descending. The two exchanged a brief glance before Adriana looked away.

Gabriella followed her master. She was sans cloak and looked as if the slightest nudge would send her to her knees. The Knight placed a hand on the wall to steady herself.

Freeman finally got to his feet and stood next to Adriana. He looked down to the vampire, who stood half a foot shorter than him. After a brief moment, Freeman grabbed Adriana's non-bloodied arm and used her sleeve to wipe the blood from his face.

"Least you're good for something," he said.

Adriana snatched her arm away and snarled, revealing her fangs to Freeman.

"We need to get moving," Makeda said. She passed Freeman and Adriana, adding, "The MKDG soldiers in the towers will make their way here." She continued to the laboratory level.

Gabriella joined Freeman and Adriana. She looked disapprovingly at the fallen thugs, then back at Adriana. "We really need to talk about your methods," she said.

The vampire made no show of emotion.

Stepping over the fallen MKDG thugs, Gabriella continued toward the laboratory to join Makeda. Freeman followed.

Amid the eerie shadows cast by the dim light of the oil lamps, Freeman contemplated the room as an archeologist would a newly discovered lost kingdom. Gabriella leaned against one of the broken tables for support.

"Do you have any idea how important a find this is?" Freeman asked with the tone of one in rapture. "I mean, you read the stories about Awaken the Beast, but this… this is the literal belly of the —"

"Stay focused, Michael," Makeda insisted as she scanned the room. "We have to find…"

She paused as if noticing something. Concerned, she moved quickly through the debris and toward the hallway separating the main laboratory from the holding cells beyond.

"You waste your time, Knight," Adriana said.

Makeda stopped but did not immediately turn to face Adriana.

"He isn't here?" she asked, her voice cracking with emotion.

Adriana was silent.

Gabriella turned to look at the vampire; her face was a dispassionate mask.

"What do you know, Adriana?" she asked.

Adriana gave no answer but dropped her gaze to the ground. Gabriella looked to Freeman. He looked expectantly at Adriana.

Their praetor moved to the cell area.

"Makeda."

The Knight stopped at the sound of Adriana's voice. It was not a challenge, but an empathetic warning.

"All you will find there is death."

The subordinate Knights exchanged looks of concern. Makeda paused briefly but ultimately continued into the cell area.

Rage.

It had consumed Adriana Dupré, driving her to the murderous path she had chosen.

Makeda had hoped to persuade Adriana to choose a more productive way. She had initiated this plan before she realized how persuasive rage could be; before she saw the man who had been her confidant and lover chained to a wall and beaten to death.

As she stalked across the laboratory toward Adriana, Makeda saw the alarm on the faces of her discipuli. Normally, their alarm would give her pause.

Makeda was beyond normal now.

Gabriella moved to intercept her.

It was at her peril.

"What has happened, praetor?" Gabriella asked.

"Sahlu is dead!" Makeda said, her voice barely above a whisper but containing an edge.

Gabriella accepted the news with shock but recovered quickly in the light of Makeda's uncharacteristic anger. Makeda would have been proud had Gabriella not been in her way.

"He died at the hands of these Nazi zealots," the junior Knight insisted.

"So says the vampire with a history of betrayal!" Makeda barked.

Adriana stood beyond Makeda's two companions, halfway up the stairs.

"Adriana came back to help us," Gabriella insisted. "Even when she attacked Michael —"

Makeda waved a hand at Gabriella. Makeda's magic became an invisible force that swept the woman out of her path and slammed her against the nearby wall. Makeda continued at Dupré.

The vampire hadn't so much as blinked.

Her funeral, Makeda thought.

Drawing her Ogoun dagger, Makeda made the final strides to striking distance. Freeman stood just to the side, but he never posed any threat to her in combat. The show of force against Gabriella should intimidate him to inaction.

Makeda raised her dagger. Adriana remained defiant but made no motion toward defense. Makeda brought the dagger down squarely at Dupré's heart —

Freeman's quarterstaff caught Makeda's arm, stopping the blow. He used the advantage of leverage to spin Makeda's arm away from Dupré, then to stab Makeda in the stomach with the blunt end of the staff. She hunched slightly as she stumbled away from Freeman and Adriana.

Before Makeda could recover, Freeman spun his staff and swept Makeda's legs out from under her. She quickly rolled to a defensive position at the bottom of the stairs, several feet away from her attacker.

Freeman stood in front of Dupré, his back to the vampire and his staff ready to defend against the woman who had taught him how to use it.

"Whatever happened to Sahlu," Freeman said in as righteous a voice as he could muster, "this is not going to bring him back. It damn sure isn't going to help us move on."

As Makeda glared at Freeman, he suddenly shook his head. "I don't know what's worse — the fact I just said that or the fact I just protected the bitch who stabbed me from my suddenly homicidal praetor!"

"Praetor Arsi! Remember yourself!" Gabriella insisted.

Makeda had put Gabriella down hard, much harder than necessary. Yet when Makeda looked to her, she saw the woman standing defiantly. Like her fellow Knight Freeman, she intended to defend that which she believed to be right.

It made Makeda think back on her lessons during the trials of becoming a Knight of Vyntari, the lessons she had learned alongside the man she had found murdered in a dank, decaying cell.

"Think, praetor!" Gabriella continued. "What purpose would it serve Adriana to kill Sahlu? Especially after having fought alongside the Righteous, both tonight and decades ago in this very place?"

"Give or take a few severed heads," Freeman muttered. Gabriella shot him a stern look. He shrugged, mouthing a silent "Sorry."

Gabriella cautiously approached Makeda. "Right now, praetor, you're letting rage take hold, as Adriana has done for all these years. But when she had the opportunity to kill Michael, she held back that anger. Just as you need to do."

Makeda stood. Her grip tightened on her dagger's hilt. Freeman adjusted his position. Adriana watched in silence. Gabriella spoke in a softer tone.

"I know you loved him, Makeda."

Makeda's head tilted slightly downward in acknowledgment of the junior Knight's words. It was enough to encourage Gabriella to continue.

"I know you're devastated. You couldn't be at Sahlu's side when he passed. But Adriana had nothing to do with his death. Perhaps she can even convey a final message from him to you."

Gabriella looked to Adriana. The vampire remained impassive, oblivious to the Knight's stare.

"Adriana?" Gabriella asked.

The vampire looked to the blonde Knight, who urged her own with a look. Adriana looked back to Makeda. The senior Knight's head hung low, but she didn't look as if she were a threat.

Freeman leaned back to whisper to Adriana, "This is the part where you say something soothing."

Adriana bit her lip. Eventually, she said, "He died a warrior's death, showing no pain."

Makeda's grip on her dagger loosened. It slipped from her fingers and clattered to the floor. A tear landed softly on the ground beside it. The others in the room gave her this moment of silence.

"So now the discipuli become the praetors," Makeda said, her voice choked by shame.

"No," Gabriella responded. She walked over and picked up Makeda's dagger. Taking Makeda's hand, she pressed the hilt into her palm. "We're simply reminding you of the noble praetor you are."

The blonde Knight of Vyntari had humiliated Reinhardt by binding him in her cloak. He did not take humiliation well. Nor did he need his limbs to extract a quick revenge.

The Knights had gone into the laboratory presumably to deal with the vampire. While their eyes were away from him, Reinhardt began to chant.

Measure Nine — A Prayer for the Dead

"You should be this valiant against evil, Michael," Makeda told Freeman as she slid her Ogoun dagger back into its sheath.

"Fighting evil is about saving me," he replied. "Right now I'm more concerned with saving you. That's a hell of a lot more important."

Freeman's newfound courage forced a weak smile to break through Makeda's melancholy. She looked down, turning her face away from the others. She couldn't bear to see the reactions of her discipuli.

Worse, she couldn't bear to meet Adriana's eyes.

In her moment of fury, Makeda had finally understood the centuries of anguish and pain Adriana had endured.

Several months ago, Makeda had met with Illyana Dakanova, Adriana's vampire "mother." Makeda needed to know how to get Adriana to this point. Illyana had hesitated in answering. She knew then what Makeda had realized now.

Everything she had done up until this point had been wrong.

Stealing one of the Vyntari shards, lying to her discipuli and Sahlu, manipulating Adriana; she had behaved no better than Thorne, Strathan, the hateful German Reinhardt or any other evil she sought to defeat.

Unfortunately, Makeda could not stop the juggernaut she had unleashed back on Mount Kanchenjunga. At best, she could hope the potentially positive results of her gambit outweighed the damage she had done.

Makeda felt the touch of a hand on her shoulder. She started but calmed when she realized the touch had come from Gabriella. Sparing her a glance, Makeda saw no malice in the woman's expression. Instead, love and respect for her praetor reigned.

"We all have moments of doubt," Gabriella said. She smiled. "But if you bash me like that again, may the One Goddess help you."

Makeda allowed her smile to take over. She embraced her discipulus.

"Um, ladies — Namaste, one love, and all that good stuff," Freeman said. "But we're in mixed company. Don't want to tarnish the badass image."

Gabriella and Makeda broke their embrace and looked past Freeman to Adriana. Makeda suppressed her guilt and finally met the vampire's gaze.

To her credit, Adriana's expression was free of malice; she displayed her usual stalwart, impassive mask. When she spoke, her tone carried that same indifference, with just a slight edge brought on by pain that Makeda now understood.

"You know I did not kill him," Adriana said.

Makeda, shamed once more, nodded.

"Pathetic," Adriana continued, "how one so virtuous could so easily be swayed to evil."

"And how, just as easily, one sworn to evil could become one of the Righteous," Makeda countered.

Adriana's lips curled into a snarl, then parted as if to speak. No words came. Instead, the vampire looked to the other Knights. Makeda followed Adriana's gaze. Her discipuli stood their ground, patiently awaiting word from their praetor. Adriana would find no quarter there.

The vampire's expression became passive once more; her gaze returned to Makeda. "Before he died —"

Makeda flinched at Adriana's words. Noticing how her tone had negatively affected Makeda, Adriana softened her voice. "Your man said I should follow you to Oromia, where I could go back to the moment that made me."

"What does that even mean?" Freeman asked no one in particular.

Adriana descended the stairs and approached Makeda. "Makeda Arsi," Adriana said in a tone that brought everyone's attention back to her. "You will take me to this Oromia. I will deal with Strathan. This insanity will end."

Adriana stopped in front of Makeda. The leader of the three Knights slowly nodded. She started to speak but paused. Her body shivered. She glanced at her discipuli. Whatever she had felt, she could read in their expressions that they had felt it too.

All three Knights knew the sudden chilling sensation signified a sinister and malignant presence creeping through the environment. As silent confirmation, shadows crept up from the ground, darkening the lit areas of the laboratory.

"Well, we're not doing this," Freeman said. "And those three guys" — referring to the dead men on the stairs — "don't have the voice for it."

The Knights reflected. "Reinhardt," they said in unison.

Adriana looked to each of the Knights. "You berated me for killing my enemies."

"The Righteous don't kill," Freeman replied, conviction in his voice.

"Instead, they may be killed," Adriana said, matching Freeman's conviction.

Freeman frowned. The vampire had a point. He looked to Gabriella. "Thought you grew up hog tying your two brothers."

"They never got out," she insisted.

"The sorcerer does not need his limbs to chant," Adriana said, her voice sounding as if it were moving away from the three Knights. They looked at the vampire.

She had disappeared, the only sign of her having been there a trail of her bloody boot prints heading up the stairs.

"Now I know how Commissioner Gordon feels," Freeman muttered.

"What?" Gabriella asked.

"Gordon. From 'Batman.' Every time he and —"

"Prepare for your enemy!" Makeda commanded. Her air of authority and confidence had returned.

Gabriella and Freeman immediately moved into the formation, standing back to back with Makeda and forming a defensive triangle against the imminent preternatural threat.

A cold wall of darkness moved before the Knights, cutting them off from the stairs. A section of it splintered, forming a snarling mouth filled with tiny, dagger-like teeth.

The darkness continued up the walls, dimming the lantern light and plunging the room into a supernatural lack of light.

Freeman leaned toward Gabriella, while his eyes remained on the living wall of darkness. "Can't your *Spatha* —"

Gabriella held her hand before her face. A spark of ethereal flame burst from her palm, but she could not sustain it. "As Praetor Arsi warned, I am too weak to manifest my connection to the One Goddess."

The dark entity continued to splinter into fragments. These fragments morphed into humanoid shapes that came to resemble fallen Nazi and Order of Haroth members.

All of them looked menacing, though severely damaged from violent ends.

All of them looked ready to eviscerate the Knights.

A sea of shadow-like wraiths surrounded the three Knights of Vyntari. They braced themselves for combat, but with Gabriella's weakened state and Freeman's limited combat skills, this would be an uphill battle at best.

The wraiths moved on the Knights —

Then, just as quickly, they stopped, shrieking as if they were in pain. The Knights all covered their ears, barely able to withstand the high-pitched noise.

They watched as the wraiths retreated, whimpering and yelping as they vanished into the darkness. Natural light returned.

A repetitive thumping sound coming from the stairs drew the Knights' attention.

Reinhardt's severed head bounced down the stairs and landed at their feet, his garish expression of surprise frozen for eternity.

Moments later, Adriana appeared at the top of the stairs. Her skin was so pale it was nearly translucent. Her shoulders slouched; her first attempt at sliding her bloodied sword into its scabbard missed.

"Can we go now?" she demanded more than asked.

Lamar had waited long enough.

Twenty minutes ago, the soldiers from the watchtowers had returned to the Monster looking for direction. As Reinhardt did not respond to numerous radio checks, Lamar had sent them to the Pathology building with orders to kill anyone not a soldier of the MKDG.

They had yet to return.

Lamar cautiously cracked open the entrance door to the Green Monster and took a quick glance outside. The light of the risen sun illuminated the area well enough to squelch any chance of an interloper — particularly a vampire — hiding nearby.

Seeing nothing out of the ordinary, Lamar risked opening the door and stepping outside for a further look.

Nothing.

Popping back inside the Monster, Lamar moved to the table at which Reinhardt had sat and grabbed a set of keys. Spotting the bottle of *König Alkohol*, Lamar decided to salvage it as well. He then returned to the exit, opened the door —

...and rammed his forehead into the end of a quarterstaff.

The collision sent Lamar backward. He landed hard on the floor. The bottle of *König Alkohol* fell from his grasp, shattering upon the concrete beside him. A dark mist drifted from the liquid as it burned its way into the floor.

Lamar wasted no time mourning the loss. Instead, he looked to the man entering the room.

This man was young, dressed in some fashion Lamar assumed was relevant to today's youth. Blood covered the outfit, though it didn't appear to be his. He held the staff with which he had struck Lamar. The man looked rather proud of himself behind his smirk and sunglasses. Ethereal flames shone from behind the glasses.

He must be one of the Knights of Vyntari Reinhardt and his men were supposed to have killed. Perhaps the MKDG soldiers were busy destroying the other Knights; this one may have simply outflanked them.

The woman who entered after the staff-wielding man dashed Lamar's hopes. Possibly Aryan, she wore a white jumpsuit that had fared far worse than the man's blood-soaked outfit. Blood stained the woman's thigh, though no visible wound lay under the torn material of her bodysuit

The male Knight knelt beside the spilled *König Alkohol*. "What a waste," he commented. "But as the Reich goes and all."

The woman moved to a position near Lamar. The male Knight moved to stand with her, and they both gazed down at him.

"None of this was my idea!" Lamar insisted in the Knight's native English.

"You are neither smart nor brave enough to have planned this, Lamar."

Terror gripped the aged German as he instantly recognized the newcomer's voice.

Adriana Dupré had not only survived but had also succeeded in finding him again.

She stood in the doorway behind the Knights. A white cloak covered her from head to toe, yet parts of her extremities still smoldered from exposure to the sun. Once inside, Adriana closed the door behind her. Turning to Lamar, she dropped back the cloak's hood and joined the others standing over him.

Adriana looked as if she had not fed. Her right hand was merely a fingerless palm. The hint of a smile bled onto Lamar's lips as he savored that irony. Then again, Lamar knew the vampire was still a threat even in a weakened state.

The blonde spoke. "Our car is too far away for our present company" — she motioned to the vampire — "to reach. Give us the keys and the location of yours."

Lamar quickly dug into his pocket and produced the keys. He threw them on the floor before the trio of would-be heroes. "We parked on the east side of the camp!"

"We came in from the west. 'Splains why we didn't see them," the male commented. He picked up the keys and handed them to the blonde. "You ladies mind driving? My eyes are kinda tired."

She took the keys and headed toward the door. "I'll take care of that thing, then get the car."

"We need to be gone before your *Ältestenrat* arrives," Adriana insisted.

Nearly out the door, the woman said, "The fallen souls tormented here have waited decades for salvation. We can wait the few minutes it takes to give it to them."

Gabriella strode onto the northern clearing just inside the now shattered apex of the camp's outer wall. Looking at the litter of ash and skeletal remains, she felt a deep sense of grief.

The atrocities the Jewish prisoners had suffered at the hands of Hitler's camp guards were reprehensible, as were the atrocities Stalin's Russian troops had perpetrated on the defeated Nazis interned here after the war.

Admittedly, she had difficulty sympathizing for a Nazi. But the One Goddess would not condone mistreatment of the enemy, no matter how vile that enemy's actions may have been.

This group of neo-Nazi sorcerers only two generations removed from Hitler's evil tortured the dead souls further by using them for their nefarious plans.

That riled her to her core.

Gabriella closed her eyes. She focused inward, driving thoughts of the previous night from her memory, shoving aside images of the horrors that occurred on these grounds in the not so distant past. She replaced those thoughts with ones of her family, of her time training with the Knights. Warmth filled her heart. Then she spoke the words.

"May the One Goddess who watches over us all rid these poor souls of the evil that stains them. May She embrace these lost souls and take them into her warmth, and may She dispel all the malevolence infesting these grounds."

Gabriella suddenly felt a surge of magical energy. Her head snapped back; her eyes went heavenward. She manifested a smile born of pure joy. As she levitated from the ground, she realized the One Goddess had heard her prayer.

She would use the Knight as a vessel for Her love.

Makeda emerged from the Pathology building, having spent a few final moments with Sahlu. She headed toward the camp's entrance gate. Before she reached it, a flash of light caught her eye. Makeda turned in its direction and found herself looking out toward the open area near the destroyed apex of the outer wall's triangle.

Gabriella was the source of the light. Her sheath of ethereal white flames had burst to life about her. Its glow intensified as Makeda watched. The sheath flowed outward, its flames expanding across the grounds, amplified by the love of the One Goddess. Makeda shielded her eyes from the glow that was as brilliant as the heart of a distant star.

That splash of light dissolved into individual slivers. Their intensity dimmed, allowing Makeda to view them. They assumed vaguely human forms. There were tens of thousands. Makeda realized these lights were the souls of the people who had suffered and died here.

One soul near her caught her attention. It was more fully human than the rest. Makeda assumed this was due to its more recent death.

The soul before her was that of Sahlu Tigray.

The two exchanged no words, communicating through their expressions of respect and love for one another. Makeda could have sworn she saw just the slightest nod of approval from Sahlu. She felt the warmth from his light. Drawn to it, Makeda slowly walked toward him. She extended her arm, reaching for him.

Their hands were but inches apart.

Before she could touch him, Sahlu rose up into the air with the rest of the souls. Makeda watched him go, his image transforming into pure light as it raced toward Heaven. The collection of souls smashed against something solid. Makeda remembered the shield the MKDG had erected surrounding the camp.

In the next instant, she witnessed a shimmer in the sky. The trapped souls, once momentarily halted, now continued upward, disappearing into the clouds. The rays of the rising sun slipped through the clouds like a sign of the One Goddess's acceptance of her fallen children.

The preternatural lights gone, Makeda looked back to Gabriella. She knelt, presumably giving a final prayer for the dead. Makeda could not be more proud of her discipulus and would later thank her for the final moment she had given her with Sahlu.

Now the sun's rays stretched over the horizon. The magical shield the MKDG had raised to hide the camp from prying Uninitiated eyes had fallen. No disturbing noise had escaped the camp to rouse suspicions, but the destruction of the outer wall was visible to all. The Uninitiated keepers of the camp-turned-museum would ask questions.

Best that the parties responsible weren't here when they arrived.

"You saw what almost happened when you left the Nazi leader alive," Adriana insisted.

"We could have handled that," Makeda countered.

Now in the Green Monster, Makeda stood toe-to-toe with the vampire, though she did hover a few inches above the girl. "The *Ältestenrat* will soon learn of Sahlu's disappearance if they haven't already. The note left at Sahlu's shop will lead them here. They can deal with Lamar."

"He will give us away," Adriana countered.

"By telling them what?"

"Exactly!" Lamar interjected. The Knights had bound him to a chair at the table. Freeman sat opposite him and was hard at work on what remained of his damaged tablet computer. Gabriella had not yet returned.

"I know nothing of your plans!" Lamar continued.

"Any information he gives them —" Adriana began.

"As long as you're with us," Makeda began, "you do not kill."

"Except for those last couple of guards from the watchtowers," Freeman muttered. Makeda strode across the room and punched Freeman in the arm. "Ouch! Now I gotta get it from you too?"

Makeda glared at Freeman. He went back to his tablet.

"Then perhaps I should leave you," Adriana said.

Makeda paused and stared at the woman. "You do what you must. But this discussion is over," she declared with an air of finality that silenced the Frenchwoman. Adriana took a seat at the table with Lamar and Freeman.

Adriana stepped past Lamar, smacking him in the head with her good left hand as she went. Lamar let out a very unmanly yelp.

"Adriana!" Makeda said.

The vampire looked to Makeda and shrugged. "He still lives."

Freeman and Makeda exchanged glances. Makeda motioned to Freeman's wreck of a tablet. "You have our route, Michael?" she asked.

"It may take a little longer to get to Berlin-Tegel 'cause I'm sending us on back roads," Freeman said. "Best to keep out of the spotlight I reckon."

Makeda nodded. "True, but lean toward expediency. Give me exact times, and I'll establish a path from there."

"If Sahlu was your contact here," Adriana began, "how exactly are you getting us to Oromia?"

Makeda looked to Adriana. "Sahlu was a trusted contact, but he wasn't my only one."

The door to the room opened. Gabriella entered. She looked completely re-energized.

"Our chariot awaits," she declared triumphantly.

Makeda stood and moved toward the door. Freeman followed. Gabriella put her hand on the doorknob but turned back to Adriana before opening the door. "My cloak's on the table. Put it on. We'll get the trunk open."

Adriana tilted her head slightly, unsure of what she had just heard. "The trunk?"

Measure Ten — The Myth of Transcendence

The sun had fully risen, washing away all traces of darkness from the night before.

The Knights and their vampire companion had relieved the MKDG men of their vehicle and used it to escape the Sachsenhausen camp. Makeda made a phone call that she finished just as Gabriella pulled their newly acquired transportation up to the van, which they'd hidden hours before when they'd arrived.

The team quickly retrieved their belongings from the van and continued their journey in the new vehicle.

Following Freeman's directions, Makeda instructed Gabriella to drive them to the Adrema Hotel near the Berlin-Tegel Airport. Once there, they drove into the outside self–parking lot as to avoid any curious valets or hotel guests in the front lobby — particularly considering their physical appearance and cargo.

Freeman approached the trunk before leaving. "We're just going to get cleaned up," he whispered to Adriana. "With all this sun out here, ya might just wanna sleep it off 'til we get to the airport."

Adriana kicked the inside of the trunk. The resulting thump startled Freeman. His companions looked at him, barely containing their amusement at his frightened reaction. "You got a reservation or something?" he asked as a means of changing the subject.

Stifling a chuckle, Makeda said, "A room with a magical key code awaits. There's a service entrance around the back."

Makeda led her discipuli through back halls and to a room where civilian business suits, toiletries, and spare Knight uniforms awaited them.

The female Knights took individual turns in the shower first, leaving Freeman for last so that they could change away from his prying eyes.

They were a team, yes, and Freeman respected his partners. But, as Gabriella would often point out, he retained the perverted mind of a fifteen-year-old boy. No need to tempt him.

"Thanks for using up all the hot water," Freeman yelled sarcastically over the shower spray so that his companions could hear him through the cracked open bathroom door. "Now it's the perfect temperature to reinforce hypothermia!"

"Hurry, Michael," Makeda said. "The longer we delay, the more we risk being discovered."

"And if we mess up the flight plans at Berlin-Tegel," Freeman countered, "an *Ältestenrat* watchdog is sure to flag it and us."

Gabriella stepped into her pants. "Flights change all the time," she said.

The shower turned off. "Can I come out now?" Freeman asked.

Makeda, now dressed in a nondescript blouse and pants, tied her hair back in a ponytail. "We are decent."

A few moments later, Freeman stepped out of the bathroom wrapped in an expensive cotton robe. He used a towel to dry his dark hair. His eyes lacked the telltale signs of his powers, exposing his empty eye sockets. "You weren't supposed to be decent," he quipped.

Gabriella, dressed in a dark-hued pantsuit, walked behind Freeman and popped him on the back of the head.

"Hey!" he yelped. "So uncalled for!"

"Your juvenile behavior is uncalled for," Gabriella retorted, rolling her eyes. "And please wear your sunglasses. Your eyes are…unnerving."

"Says the woman who faced down a mucus-demon in Toronto."

Makeda grabbed a hanging wardrobe bag from a closet. She took one of Freeman's hands and placed the bag's hanger within.

"Do hurry and make yourself presentable," she insisted.

"I don't think we have that much time," Gabriella said.

Freeman stuck out his tongue in the direction of Gabriella's voice. He then took the bag with him back to the bathroom, extending a hand in front of him to ensure he didn't run into anything. He closed the door behind him.

When he emerged minutes later, he wore a tailored suit. Its shirt sleeves required cufflinks, which he hadn't quite conquered. Indigo-hued ethereal flames danced in his eye sockets behind a set of designer, business-appropriate sunglasses.

"And regarding your pre–uncalled-for head slap question, Gabriella, flights change all the time, but they keep a closer eye private flights," he said while fighting the left cufflink and sleeve. "I assume we're not flying commercial."

Makeda stepped over to Freeman and helped him with his cufflinks. "A private plane belonging to Cameron Ventures will take us out."

"Seth Cameron?" Gabriella asked incredulously. "The philanthropist?"

"Whose family money comes from steel, glass, and the banking industry, yes," Makeda answered, finishing with Freeman's first cufflink and moving to the second.

"Is he…?"

"Initiated?" Makeda said. "As a Guardian of Faith he worked alongside Adriana in liberating Sachsenhausen." She let this knowledge bomb settle before adding, "He's kept an interest in Berlin's supernatural community ever since."

"An interest you exploited," Freeman said.

"You're not the only one who did their research on Berlin," Makeda replied while finishing Freeman's second cufflink.

"So are we on his personal jet or one of the ones he uses to smuggle stuff around?" Freeman asked.

"What?" Gabriella asked.

"The reason the Guardians probably don't parade Cameron around as a hero is the U. S. Department of Justice thinks he's a big time mobster," Freeman explained.

"Remember the nature of the Shadowdance," Makeda said. "Nothing is what it seems."

"Maybe," Gabriella began, "but which side of Cameron can we trust?"

Freeman moved to a mirror near the exit. "Whichever one gets us out of Germany, I suppose." He gave a very disapproving glare at his reflection.

Gabriella came up behind him and straightened his collar.

"You almost look like an adult," she told him.

"More like I'm going to parochial school in an outfit made for an eighties yuppie movie!"

"Well, it's better than my Catholic school outfit."

"You were a Catholic school girl?"

"Four years at the Jo." Freeman's look of confusion prompted Gabriella to add, "The Josephinum Academy back home in Chi-town."

Then she caught his expression of amazement. Her eyes narrowed suspiciously.

"Don't even," she warned.

"Let's move, people," Makeda said. She scooped up the car keys from the nearby dresser and tossed them to Gabriella, who deftly caught them one-handed. "I'd rather not cause further discomfort for our companion in the trunk."

Back in the hotel parking lot, Freeman beat on the trunk of their acquired car. "You okay in there?"

Adriana yelled a muffled stream of French Freeman construed as vulgarity. "What's that? You want out? Well, let me just open this up —"

Gabriella punched Freeman's arm as she walked past him toward the driver's side of the car. He frowned.

"Again, totally uncalled for!" he said.

Gabriella glanced at him then got into the driver's seat.

Rubbing his arm, Freeman took a seat in the back with their belongings. He let the ethereal flames in his eye sockets evaporate and lounged back. Makeda joined Gabriella up front. Moments later, the three and their trunk-riding companion were away.

At the Berlin-Tegel Airport's security checkpoint, Makeda presented another item she had acquired at the hotel — papers that allowed them to pass through security to the private hangar and its waiting Cessna CJ3.

Gabriella drove into the hangar and parked in an area well away from the sunlight slipping through the open doors. The plane was on the other side of the hangar, lined up to drive out to the tarmac. Once the Knights were out of the car, Gabriella opened the trunk.

The first thing she saw was Adriana's scornful expression. "Do I ride inside the passenger cabin or stashed with the cargo?" the vampire asked while climbing from the trunk.

Gabriella noted that Adriana had healed her right hand to a full thumb and several small fingers. She must have used the blood "donated" by the MKDG thugs she defeated.

Freeman, his eye sockets devoid of their indigo flames, began removing baggage from the passenger seat he just exited. "We can leave you here," he told Adriana.

The vampire liked that option less.

Makeda grabbed two bags. "The plane is fully fueled and ready to go," she said. "Cameron's contacts —"

"Cameron?" Adriana asked. "Seth Cameron?"

Freeman turned his head in Adriana's direction. "Yeah. Just found out he was a friend of yours."

"Is he behind your little crusade?" Adriana asked, visibly annoyed.

"He only knows we need out of Berlin," Makeda explained.

"And why has he not sold you out to this *Ältestenrat* group?"

Gabriella and Freeman looked to Makeda. The vampire did raise a legitimate concern.

Unfazed by the question, Makeda responded, "Because when I added that I'm trying to help you curb your violence, he said he owed you for the Millennium Massacre."

Adriana remembered that time, when she had saved Cameron from assassination at the hands of the Daughters of Lilith under their newest leader, Fatale. "He repaid that debt when he sent me after the Daughters in Paris," she said.

"Well, I guess he just really likes you," Makeda said. She took her bags and headed toward the waiting plane. Freeman and Gabriella picked up the rest of the bags and followed her.

"Cameron's contacts set us up with a flight plan to Addis Ababa," the lead Knight explained, finishing her earlier thought. "It's not exactly the one we'll use, but it will get us in the air."

"Aren't we missing one other little thing?" Freeman asked.

The female Knights remained quiet. Adriana, bringing up the rear in their walk to the plane, gave voice to Freeman's implication. "Who is flying this plane?"

Makeda carried her bags to the plane's cargo section and set them down. "You used to fly with your father, didn't you Michael?"

Joining Makeda, Freeman said, "I flew right seat a couple of times in my teens, yeah. But that was a decade ago."

Makeda smiled and turned to Freeman, placing an assuring hand on his shoulder. "You'll be fine. It's like riding a bike."

Freeman threw up his hands. "I always fell off my bike! And why are we always making the blind man transportation guy?"

"Ready the plane, Michael," Makeda insisted.

With a frown, Freeman ignited the indigo flames behind his sunglasses. Placing his bags with Makeda's, he began a walk around the plane, making a careful examination of the fuselage.

Gabriella opened a bag and pulled out an additional women's business pantsuit. She offered it to Adriana. Met with a disparaging look, Gabriella shrugged and said, "You want to travel covered in blood? Fine. But you kind of smell like death."

Adriana crossed her arms and looked to the female Knight. Unlike them, she had no change of clothes and had remained in the battle-worn outfit from her encounter with Denson's garou.

The vampire hesitated for a moment. With a frown, she removed her jacket and dropped it to the ground. She started for her tattered shirt, but Gabriella put a hand on her arm.

"You may want to wait until we're on the plane," she said.

"Why would she want to do that?" Freeman asked.

Gabriella and Adriana looked to Freeman. He peered around the side of the plane and had the expression of a dog in heat, his gaze locked expectantly on Adriana. Makeda strode to his side and yanked his arm so that he turned away from the other women. He snapped back to reality.

"Shouldn't you finish the maintenance check?" she said.

Freeman frowned. "You no fun, Praetor Makeda," he said in a mock Chinese accent. He snuck a final peek at Adriana before walking to the other side of the plane to continue his inspection.

Gabriella pulled on the latch to the cargo section. It didn't budge. Upon closer investigation, she saw a little slit that served as the lock to the latch. "Did someone leave a key?" Gabriella asked.

"I was told it would be unlocked," Makeda replied.

She joined Freeman on the other side of the plane. He ran his hand along the fuselage until he found the object of his search — the small slit that was the lock for the cabin door latch. He pulled on the latch.

It didn't budge.

Freeman's shoulders sank. He turned to Makeda.

"On average it costs about ten grand to maintain this thing and another two grand to rent it for just fifty hours a year," Freeman said. "You don't want to know what it costs to own it."

Makeda raised her arms while shrugging her shoulders, a sign that she neither understood Freeman's rant or even cared.

Freeman sighed. "In other words, you don't just leave the door open. All your 'we can do it ourselves, give us privacy, thank you' shooed away anyone who may have had the key."

"Well I'm sure I can just go to security," Makeda began.

"Yeah. And then explain the living dead girl who's not on the passenger list."

Makeda's lips twisted in frustration. Freeman looked back at the lock through his magical vision. Tapping the lock with his finger, he said, "I'm gonna need your dagger."

Makeda walked to the plane's cargo hold. Digging into one of her bags on the ground, she retrieved her Ogoun dagger. She walked back to Freeman and handed it to him. He gently placed the tip of the dagger into the lock of the plane.

"What are you doing?" Makeda asked.

"Once my old man left his key at security," Freeman said. "I didn't feel like waiting for him to go get it, so I used my pocket knife to —" Freeman's hand slipped. The dagger fell out of the lock. He shrugged, then reapplied the dagger to the lock.

Suddenly, Adriana pushed Freeman away from the lock.

"Hey!" he exclaimed as Adriana snatched the dagger from his hand.

Adriana jammed the dagger into the lock and then yanked hard on the door latch.

Something within the plane's door snapped. The door popped slightly open. Adriana pulled it down then unfolded the stairs on the back of the door, allowing access to the plane's interior. The vampire tossed the dagger back to Makeda. "Can we go now?" she asked before climbing aboard.

Makeda's gaze followed Adriana up the stairs. She then looked to Freeman, registering the look of pure horror in his expression. The senior Knight shook her head. "Gabriella. We'll bring the bags inside."

Makeda walked past Freeman, heading toward the other side of the plane. She stopped when she realized he hadn't moved, his expression remaining unchanged. Makeda patted him hard on his shoulder. Still no change. "You have a plane to fly, Michael."

She stood at Freeman's side for a moment. He eventually shook his head. Makeda nodded, then moved to help Gabriella with the bags.

"Well let's just hope that Little Miss Impulsive hasn't wrecked the damned plane!" Freeman yelled.

Out of consideration for their vampire passenger, the Knights of Vyntari shut all the plane's window blinds to keep out the morning sun. Adriana had cleaned up and changed into the pantsuit. She now sat on the floor at the rear of the plane.

She had ripped out the light above her, despite Freeman's protests, allowing the shadows to envelop her as she absently toyed with her medallion on its slender chain.

Despite her efforts at solitude, Adriana noticed Gabriella continually glancing in her direction. Initially, she ignored the girl. An hour into the flight, the action became obnoxious.

"What do you want?" Adriana asked in an exasperated tone without looking at her.

"I've never seen someone so consumed by hatred and rage," Gabriella said.

Adriana slowly looked up at the blonde Knight. Her disdainful glare caused the woman to flinch, but it did not wilt the Knight's look of compassion. Baffled by the Knight, the vampire turned her gaze away.

"You Knights believe everyone is good at heart, that everyone can be redeemed."

"It is the way of the One Goddess," Gabriella replied. "As long as you turn to the Goodness within and fight the Evil without —"

"Your Goddess is wrong."

Adriana paused long enough to ensure Gabriella made no retort. She then added, "Sometimes a person wanders too far away from your Goodness. Then, there is no turning back."

"That simply isn't true."

Adriana narrowed her eyes and focused on Gabriella's face.

"How old are you, little girl?"

Gabriella frowned at the question. She probably never thought of herself as a "little girl," but when compared to the 243-year-old vampire, the words rang true. Judging from the Knight's scornful expression, she didn't appreciate the insult tied to the question.

"Thirty-two," Gabriella eventually replied.

"Think of the evil you have witnessed in those thirty-two years," Adriana said. She paused, felt the self-hatred welling inside her. She released it through the hard edge of her words.

"Now imagine witnessing that for over two centuries. Worse, imagine that you are the cause of that evil, an evil that included murdering nearly every single person in your entire bloodline."

Gabriella took that in. She started to speak but caught herself. She closed her eyes. Adriana thought the woman in prayer. After a moment, Gabriella marshaled the courage to respond, "Freeman told me the legend —"

"It is not some damned legend!" Adriana shouted. "It is my life!"

"Yes, it is your life!" Gabriella opened her eyes and met Adriana's rage with a level of calm that further irritated Adriana.

The Knight rose from her seat, approaching Adriana in a crouch due to the plane's low ceiling. She eventually sat on the floor opposite the vampire. When she spoke again, it was in the same annoyingly calm tone.

Adriana turned away from her.

"When I was sixteen, a friend of mine got pregnant. She wanted an abortion but being Catholic I tried everything to talk her out of it. When that didn't work, I simply turned my back on her." Gabriella paused for a moment, probably looking for some reaction from Adriana.

The vampire was determined not to give her one. The Knight continued anyway.

"You were Catholic before you became a vampire?"

Yes, Adriana thought, but she wasn't going to contribute to the Knight's banal story.

"You understand the devotion to Scripture, to what the Church says is right or wrong," the Knight continued as if Adriana had answered "yes." "In that situation, I did what the Church said was right, though I felt in my heart that not helping my friend was wrong."

"Whoa, Gabby!" Freeman said from the cockpit. The plane had no wall or door separating that area from the rest of the plane. "That's pretty heavy —"

"Michael, please," Makeda interrupted from her cabin seat. Freeman, his eyes alight with his magical flames, glanced into the cabin. He saw Makeda shake her head. Freeman turned his attention back to flying.

Gabriella prattled on.

"When you were with the Daughters, you were trapped in a similar situation. Do what the organization says — kill. But your Catholic upbringing, your life as a pianist and singer, they weren't in synch with the life of an assassin. Ultimately, your better soul rebelled against the violence."

Adriana flashed a glance at Gabriella, who maintained her annoyingly earnest and compassionate expression.

The vampire couldn't bear to look at her.

"My friend..." Gabriella stopped abruptly. Adriana heard the girl's sniffle. She looked to the blonde Knight again. Tears developed in the woman's eyes.

"My friend, having nowhere to turn, tried to abort the pregnancy herself," Gabriella said, her voice choked with emotion. "It nearly killed her. So much...blood."

The lines of anger on Adriana's face dulled. She blinked, staring at the woman before her who was baring her soul to a stranger.

"That's the first time my healing powers manifested," Gabriella continued. "I saved my friend's life, but not the child within her."

"What is your point?" Adriana asked.

It was a few moments before Gabriella answered.

"When the Church learned of what I claimed to have done, they didn't see it as a miracle. Instead, I had used demonic power to cover up a mortal sin. What should have been a gift I was told was a curse. How could I continue my faith when I was the embodiment of all my faith abhorred?"

"And yet," Adriana interjected, "you are here now. Using your power."

"Because Makeda Arsi showed me a different path."

Adriana stared at Gabriella. She glanced at Makeda, who silently listened to the conversation from her seat. Adriana looked back to Gabriella.

"Makeda showed me that my power was a blessing from the One Goddess," Gabriella said. "She and the Knights showed me that the Church was infallible because it came from Man. The love of the One Goddess was something higher, and that was the source of my miracle.

"The Goddess, working through Praetor Arsi, gave me a home." Gabriella gently touched Adriana's arm. "They can do the same for you, Adriana."

The vampire leaned back against the fuselage, pulling away from Gabriella's touch. She closed her eyes, absently reached for her medallion, moving it through her fingers as if it were a Catholic Rosary.

Gabriella remained silent, allowing Adriana time to think.

"You used your power for good," the vampire eventually said. "I used mine to slaughter my family."

"You didn't know who they were," Gabriella insisted.

Adriana's eyes opened, her expression changing from sorrow to rage in a heartbeat. "I blindly followed the orders of people I knew to be evil!"

Gabriella pulled away from the vampire as if the girl had bared her fangs at her. Adriana closed her eyes again. Nearly a minute passed in silence. When Adriana spoke again, her tone returned to one of melancholy.

"All I can hope for in this world is the chance to destroy those who made me what I am."

"And what are you?"

Adriana recognized Makeda's voice asking the question. She didn't bother to answer. She just wanted this all to stop so —

"Back in Grunewald you said you were a Navarre," Makeda prodded.

"That's fucking impossible!" Freeman yelled from the cockpit. Adriana silently acknowledged the inevitability that he'd join in.

"Michael, your language!" Gabriella chided.

"A lie that big deserves language!" Freeman shouted back.

"Is it really that unbelievable?" Makeda asked. "Adriana says she killed her bloodline. During the Great Purge, she killed werewolves." Makeda extended her hands in a 'ta-da' motion.

"Wait," Gabriella said. "Are you trying to say that Adriana's family were werewolves? And who are the Navarre?"

"Did you read anything about this mission?" Freeman asked with a touch of disappointment in his voice.

"I knew we faced a formidable combatant in Adriana," Gabriella responded. "I didn't think we'd be having a conversation about her life. Now could you just answer —"

"The Navarre were the first garou, the *Sangs Purs*," Adriana answered in a voice just above a whisper. "What you know as werewolves. I share their blood."

Gabriella blinked in astonishment.

"Yeah, right," Freeman said. "Adriana the vampire cannot be a Navarre because the Navarre are werewolves and a werewolf cannot become a vampire!"

"Unless," Adriana said, a bit louder than before, "that garou does not possess the *Cadeau de Transcedence*."

"Ah yes!" Freeman said. "The Gift of Transcendence, often more crudely translated as the Gift of Change. I can't wait to hear how hundreds of years of legend that all werewolves can shapeshift is a lie."

Adriana sat in silence. She had wanted to tell Denson this story, but the demon sorcerer Strathan had stolen that opportunity.

Exposing her family's secret to these three Knights didn't matter, for what could they do with the knowledge? Anyone endangered by the revelation was probably already slaughtered, either at her hand or the hand of someone she enabled, despite her release of the last Navarre back in Illinois.

"In the early eighteenth century," Adriana began, "the Navarre pack split in two. Those who left — those who longed for a life outside of the violence of the Shadowdance — took the name, Dupré.

"They later found a sympathetic sorcerer who cast a spell cleansing them of the *Cadeau*. They hoped the lack of supernatural power would put them outside the Shadowdance."

Freeman made a big show of sniffing the air.

The other Knights looked at him as if he had lost it.

"What are you doing?" Gabriella asked.

"I think we have a methane leak," Freeman responded.

"What?" Makeda said with a hint of alarm.

"It smells like bullshit in here!"

Makeda relaxed, but a frown settled on her face. "Think, Michael," she said. "Imagine if enemies of the Navarre knew that not only was there dissension in the ranks of the *Sangs Purs*, but that Navarre existed who could not defend themselves with their Gift?"

Following Makeda's logic, Gabriella added, "Their enemies would slaughter those without the Gift regardless of their involvement in the Shadowdance. The Navarre who could change would now have to defend their brethren all while doing their created duty of staving off the vampires."

"Wait a minute," Freeman said. "Let's back up to that whole thing about werewolves not changing."

Makeda and Gabriella looked to Adriana. The vampire remained silent, her focus elsewhere.

"Perhaps the idea that all werewolves can change was a myth perpetuated to protect those who couldn't," Gabriella deduced. "Those werewolves Adriana killed during her reign of terror... they died protecting that secret and the secret of the Navarre."

Adriana remained silent.

Memories she'd rather not remember flooded her mind. She wanted to change the subject, to end the conversation, but that wouldn't banish the memories. They would plague her until the day of her final death.

"She still killed people for fun, man!" Freeman yelled in some weird Hispanic accent. "Just 'cause she was duped don't make her a saint or somet'ing!"

"That is enough, Michael," Makeda suggested in a firm tone.

"The hell it is!" Freeman shouted. Gabriella tried to correct Freeman's use of language, but he ignored her and continued. "If Little Miss Murder here's trying to give me a reason not to throw her skinny little stabbed-me-in-the-back ass out of this plane —"

Adriana heard Makeda move toward the cockpit. "Where is the autopilot button?" she asked calmly.

"Makeda," Freeman began with an air of the incredulous. "You have me flying at a little over two hundred feet to stay below German radar. There's some weather just to the east, heading in our direction.

The slightest bump and we get a close-up view of Munich. I am not gonna put my faith in a machine!"

"Then you'd best concentrate on your flying and leave Adriana to Gabriella and me."

Adriana could not see Freeman but imagined him frowning at Makeda's roundabout 'shut the hell up and fly' command. Finally looking around the cabin, Adriana watched Makeda move to the seat closest to her and Gabriella. She raised the armrest and turned in the stationary chair to face the women.

"Michael is a good man at heart," Makeda explained politely, "but sometimes his thirst for knowledge is a bit...overwhelming."

The group was silent for a moment.

"You asked me what I am," Adriana finally said. "I am a killer. That is why I am going to find Strathan and kill him. That is what I do. That is what I am. And that is the only reason I am on this plane with you now."

Adriana drilled her point home with a stare at each female Knight that was void of any emotion. Gabriella was the first to look away.

"Strathan?" Freeman called from the cockpit. "You mentioned him before. You're not talking about —"

"Fly the plane, Michael," Makeda said. She turned back to Adriana. "Have you already forgotten what Sahlu said to you before he passed?"

Adriana had not forgotten.

Return to the moment that made her.

There was also the factor of Makeda's knowledge of another Navarre. Adriana was lying to herself if she denied that played a factor in her continuing with the Knights.

"Perhaps you should focus on that," Makeda continued, "something positive. And not your usual crusade toward self-destruction."

Gabriella cut in with, "And I'd like to point out that you've had several opportunities to kill us and other innocents. You didn't."

"Except that pop star!" Freeman interjected. "She must have been a werewolf."

Adriana's fangs extended from her gums as she glared at Freeman in the cockpit. "I said I do not —"

"Ignore him," Gabriella insisted. Adriana looked to the Irish Knight, but her fangs did not recede. Gabriella continued, more earnest this time.

"The One Goddess says there is the potential for Good in all. I have faith that even you —"

In the time it took Gabriella to think her next word, Adriana had the girl by the throat and pinned to the floor of the cabin. Adriana's fangs stopped an inch from Gabriella's exposed neck.

"Even me? A creature bound to darkness and violence?" Adriana asked.

The vampire rose so she could stare into the Irish Knight's eyes, driving her next words into Gabriella's soul. "Just remember how close to death your faith brought you," she whispered.

To her credit, Gabriella did not flinch, yet Adriana could see the fear in the woman's eyes.

"Adriana!" Makeda called.

"Hey!" Freeman said. "Don't make me come back there!"

Her message imparted, Adriana returned to her position on the floor in the blink of an eye. She lowered her head between her knees, closing her eyes and her mind to the Knights of Vyntari. Adriana pulled the shadows in around her, finding comfort in the physical darkness that was her metaphorical home.

Measure Eleven — Learning to Fly

"Uh oh."

Makeda moved from the cabin to the copilot's seat. "What is it, Michael?"

"Well, a slight miscalculation," Freeman said uneasily. "Flying below the radar was a good idea, seeing as we're kinda on the run and all. But flying this low has burned more fuel than I thought it would. Always sucked at math…"

Makeda took this in. "So what do you suggest?"

"We can float on fumes to Florence, or the west side of the Mediterranean. Depends on whether you'd like to refuel or swim to Oromia."

"Is this based on further bad math?"

Freeman shot Makeda a fierce look. "Actually, we have a much more immediate problem. When Little Miss Stab-A-Brother broke into the plane, she must have damaged the seals in the door. The cabin pressure is off, and the air's gonna get pretty thin in here when we fly over the Alps."

"There are oxygen masks."

"But not enough oxygen for the trip, for sure not enough for all of us." Makeda stared at him, a questioning look on her face. Freeman added, "I noticed on a previous flight log the oxygen was supposed to be restocked. But there's no follow-up report saying that anyone did it. We were rushing, and I didn't consider the need for it."

Makeda sat quietly, contemplating their situation.

"I told you it's been a decade since —"

"It's alright, Michael. Just remember your meditative training at Mount Kanchenjunga." She stood up and headed toward the back of the plane. Freeman called after her.

"If we do the trance thing, who's gonna fly the plane?"

"The one among us who doesn't need to breathe."

"Tell me again why this is necessary?" Adriana asked aloud. She sat in the pilot's seat. Her good left hand had a white-knuckled grip on the U-shaped yoke. Her damaged right hand rested on the other side of the yoke, its still-reforming fingers barely wrapping around the handle.

"*I can't hear you,*" Freeman thought in her mind. "*Look next to you.*"

Adriana looked to the co-pilot's seat. Freeman sat there, deep in a trance. Glancing back into the cabin, Adriana saw Makeda and Gabriella doing the same.

"*I'm in my little Freemanvision zone,*" he continued. "*Makeda's spell allows me to talk with you via telepathy, but essentially my body's tranced out. And I didn't pay the full Freemanvision bill, so I can't hear you unless you think it.*"

"*What is this Freemanvision?*" Adriana thought. He didn't answer at first. Adriana glanced at the Knight; his trance gave nothing away.

"*Let's just say it's a second sight type thing,*" he finally responded. "*Too complicated to go into. Besides, you've got other priorities right now. Like dodging the mountain ahead of you.*"

"*So you can see me right now.*"

"*For argument's sake, yes, though I'm using my power to manipulate your appearance to give you much better breasts.*"

"What?" Adriana shouted curtly.

"*Kill him,*" the demon within Adriana hissed.

"*Whoa!*" Freeman thought back to Adriana. "*Who's in there with you? Is that? Wait… it's true that vampires have demons inside them?*"

"*Yes,*" Adriana thought back to Freeman. "*Keeping it in check requires a great deal of effort. Do not provoke it. Or me.*"

"*Uh, right. What say we get back to the flying part of our trip, 'kay?*"

Adriana instinctively nodded her head. Her grip tightened on the yoke. With what little had reformed of her right hand she made a failed attempt to adjust her seatbelt harness. She could never get it just right over her petite frame.

Looking out the front window, Adriana thankfully saw mostly clear skies ahead. The plane rapidly sliced through what few wisps of clouds it did encounter.

Direct sunlight was not a factor compromising Adriana's safety as the sun was positioned behind them and to the east.

"*Do as I say and you're gonna be right as rain,*" Freeman thought to Adriana.

Adriana cast a sideways glance at Freeman. "*What is it I have to do?*" she replied telepathically.

"*How'd you learn to be such a badass if you can't remember simple instructions? Pull back for up, forward for down. Leave the throttle where it is. You'll have a hard enough time flying in all the downdrafts.*"

"*Downdrafts?*"

The plane suddenly jerked hard and downward. The yoked pulled from Adriana's hand.

"*Pull up! Pull up!*" Freeman thought.

Adriana could imagine him diving for the yoke, unable to grip it from his other world. She reached forward, grabbed the yoke with her one hand and pulled.

It fought her, refusing to yield to her efforts.

Adriana looped her arms around the yoke, throwing a foot against the front panel for good measure. Her Herculean effort paid off as the plane responded. Its sudden decent ceased, eventually leveling off. Adriana settled back in her seat, her hand in a death grip on the yoke.

"*Whatever you do,*" Freeman though to her, "*do not take your hand off the yoke! You do that, we die!*"

Adriana looked to Freeman; in his trance, he remained cool and oblivious to his surroundings. She envied the sleeping Knight.

"*Now pay attention,*" Freeman continued. "*We're hitting the leeward side of the mountains and flying low. The winds will press down hard — hence the downdrafts — so you'll be doing a lot of pulling back just to keep level.*"

Adding a dash of sarcasm, Freeman said, "*Figure a girl who can rip the lock off a plane door can handle it. Which, by the way, is part of the reason you have to do this.*"

"*You just hate me,*" Adriana countered.

"*Yes, but where we're going, we'll be fourteen thousand feet high. Now that normally wouldn't be a problem but — oh yeah! When you jimmied the lock, you messed up the plane's pressurization. Anything over fourteen thousand feet and we'll lose cabin pressure, which means we lose oxygen. You'd be the only thing that'd live up there. So unless you know how to phase us Kitty Pryde-style through a mountain —*"

"How did you survive this long without getting your tongue cut out?"

"How did you survive this long period?"

Adriana started to reply, but another downdraft hit the plane. As it started to go, Adriana pulled hard on the yoke. The plane didn't immediately react, and she worried that it wouldn't.

As she pulled desperately on the yoke, the plane eventually righted and started to climb.

"Gentle, Vampirella," Freeman thought. *"There's another catch. See that little dial right in front of you? Below the blue and brown one? That's the altimeter. Ya gotta keep that at a relative two hundred feet to the ground."*

"Why?"

"We gotta stay below German and Italian radar. Which means blending in with the ground clutter. Lucky you, we're just flying over a mountain range and not, say, through downtown Florence."

Adriana pushed forward on the yoke, leveling the plane close to the number Freeman recommended. *"Who cares if radar spots us?"* she asked.

"Well, between the lack of a transponder ID and the registered flight plan we're illegally off-course from, not to mention flying into a sovereign nation's airspace without permission, I'm thinking whoever spots us may just save you the trouble of learning to fly. They'll just shoot us the hell down."

Adriana took this in, almost regretting her curiosity over what Sahlu had called "returning to the time that made her" in Oromia. A cliché came to mind, one she never thought she'd exemplify.

"Once you're over the mountains, mind the inevitable updrafts. Be ready to push forward on the yoke."

Adriana used her stub of a right hand to point at a red light, presently not lit, next to the altimeter. *"What's this?"*

"If that light comes on, you're about to crash into something," Freeman warned. *"I'd advise changing course."*

"How will I know where I am?" Adriana asked.

"See that dial with the plane drawn in it? That's the heading indicator. Go south, little lady. And whatever you do, don't turn too hard. Hell, don't turn at all if you can help it."

With that, Freeman went silent, leaving an agitated Adriana to fend for herself.

She stared out the front window. Everything came at her so quickly, but she had no training in how to react to this situation. This foreign task of flying required her to relax, concentrate and act simultaneously.

Either she gets it right or splatters herself and the Knights against a mountain.

Adriana became aware of something else. Before, when she had stared the prospect of final death in the face, she had welcomed it. She felt she deserved it.

Now, with the promise of knowledge in Oromia, the promise of avenging her garou kin, Adriana felt a desire…a need to continue.

The plane jerked downward. Adriana reacted faster than before. Noting the rush of the ground toward the nose of the aircraft, she pulled back on the yoke, imagining herself scaling up the side of the mountain.

"*You learn quick, grasshopper,*" Freeman chimed.

Adriana ignored the Knight and focused on her task, dedicating her will to something she did have experience in — survival.

A little over a half hour later, Freeman slowly woke from his trance. He looked to Adriana. She was a few shades paler (if that were possible), from her experience in the pilot's chair.

"I am done here," she said aloud. "The rest is yours."

Freeman smiled as he watched Adriana fumble her way out of her seatbelt. She abruptly stood, almost falling over before steadying herself on the co-pilot chair. Freeman stifled a laugh. Adriana snarled at him.

The trip over the Alps had stressed the vampire. It must have been hell fighting those downdrafts, but Adriana had done it.

If she hadn't tried to fake kill him back in Grunewald Forest last night, Freeman would have been impressed.

Suddenly, the radio burst to life in a barrage of Italian. Freeman didn't speak the language, so he had no idea what they were saying, but the tone and urgency suggested bad news.

The fact that someone was talking to them at all meant that person knew the plane was there. He glanced at the altimeter; they were flying at several thousand feet above the two or three hundred required to stay out of Italian radar.

"Didn't I say to keep it under two hundred feet?" Freeman yelled at Adriana as he slid over to the pilot's seat.

"I got us over the mountains," Adriana said in a deadpan that barely masked her frayed nerves.

Adriana turned from Freeman to move into the main cabin. Freeman threw the plane into a forty-five-degree angled dive. Taken by surprise, Adriana lost her footing and fell backward into the back of the co-pilot's chair.

Freeman heard Gabriella and Makeda fumbling around in the rear of the plane. "Better buckle up! We're in for a bumpy ride," he announced with more than a hint of derision.

Adriana pulled herself around and into the co-pilot's seat. She threw out her good left hand to avoid slamming into the instrument panel. She struggled to strap in with her one good hand.

"What are you doing up there?" Gabriella yelled.

"Hear that Italian over the radio?" Freeman responded. "I'm gonna guess they're not rolling out the red carpet. Time to play hide and not get found!"

Freeman kept a steady, ethereal flame-laced eye on the altimeter, watching as its dial rapidly spun, matching the plane's rate of descent.

Adriana looked out the front window. The plane burst through a layer of clouds. Below, the hills of northern Italy loomed, filling the cockpit's view.

Freeman watched Adriana's expression of anger and annoyance change to one of fear, despite her best effort to hide it. He pressed forward on the yoke with one hand and the throttle on the other.

The vampire looked at him as if he were insane.

Freeman, his eyes now on Adriana and not the plane's instruments, smiled.

"Don't worry," he said, not bothering to conceal his arrogance. "This is a controlled dive. Kind of like the controlled way you put a blade in me."

"Still bitter?" Adriana replied. She attempted to sound tough, but the wavering of her voice cut through her false bravado to the unease beneath. "I thought your Goddess insisted you forgive."

"Makeda has faith in you. Goddess knows why, but she thinks you can do some good."

"Can we discuss this after you pull up?" she suggested, insecurity tainting her voice.

Freeman continued to look at Adriana, paying no attention to the instruments or the rapidly approaching Italian countryside. "I'm willing to bury the hatchet with you... as long as it's not in my back. Again."

"Pull up."

"But if you deviate from the path of Good for even a heartbeat I'll —"

Adriana reached forward and grabbed the co-pilot's yoke. Freeman reached across to grab her arm, stopping her.

"Careful," he said in a voice so casual it was sure to annoy the vampire.

Freeman pulled back on the throttle then pulled back gently on the yoke. The plane leveled out at just over two hundred feet.

"It's not like a downdraft. You pull back hard at that speed, you're gonna get an up close and personal view of the Italian countryside just before your eyes go through your ass."

Adriana unstrapped from the chair and stood. She stumbled, grabbing the pilot's chair to steady herself.

"I just hope I am there to see it when someone knocks every last bit of bluster out of you," she hissed.

"And I hope I'm there when you finally realize you're more than just a murderous bitch, take that vengeance stick out of your uptight French ass, and, I don't know, maybe even get laid or something else that would indicate you have any emotions at all!"

Reading the intensity of her anger, Freeman braced for a hit.

Thankfully, the hit never came.

"I just contacted Cameron's agent in Libya," Makeda said while returning the airphone back to its cradle in the arm of her chair. "He'll arrange a refueling stop in Florence as another Cameron charter flight, but we'll have to move quickly before the Italian *polizia* discover our ruse."

"He better have a good plan," Freeman said from the cockpit, "'cause the *polizia* are probably already swarming the major airports to monitor incoming flights."

"Is your tablet up to the task of reprogramming the plane's transponder?" Makeda asked.

"If I ever get the chance to repair it after what you ladies did to it at Sachsenhausen," Freeman replied curtly, making sure the words conveyed his irritation.

Makeda moved to the cockpit and slipped into the co-pilot's seat next to Freeman. "I can keep the plane on course. You've got thirty minutes to take care of things before we approach the flight pattern my contact established."

Freeman grimaced. "You want me to fix my tablet with what amounts to chewing gum and a jeweler's screwdriver, then link to the plane's computer, change the transponder code and make it convincing enough to fool Italian law enforcement? In a half hour?"

"Is that a problem?" Makeda asked.

Freeman burst into a beaming smile. "About time you gave me a real challenge!" He practically leaped from the pilot's seat and into the cabin. He grabbed his bag from underneath one of the passenger seats and wasted no time pulling out the battered tablet computer along with some small tools, setting to work on repairs.

"And how does all of this get us to Oromia?" Adriana asked from her vigil in the rear of the plane.

"From Florence, we fly to Tripoli," Makeda began, "where Cameron's man has arranged transportation to Addis Ababa aboard a cargo plane."

"I trust that trip will be less eventful," Adriana quipped.

"Hopefully yes. Ground transportation from Addis Ababa should have us in Oromia late tomorrow evening."

"Giving Strathan a full day to get to Oromia and the shard before we arrive."

Makeda allowed herself a smile. "Don't worry. My people can handle one dark sorcerer for a day. The shard is in safe hands."

"As it was with Denson?" Adriana asked.

"Says the girl who provoked Denson to get involved in the first place," Freeman said while tinkering with a soldering iron.

Adriana fell silent.

"And just who the heck is this Strathan guy?" Freeman asked. "Only Strathan I know is that douchebag actor in the shitty 'Tampa Vice' remake. Do you mean to tell me —" an idea hit Freeman. He looked to Gabriella.

"Wait a minute. Just who did Makeda have you spy on in Los Angeles when I went to give the tech to that contact of hers?"

Gabriella moved from her position. "Just promise me if we have to fight him you won't get star struck," she said on her way to join Makeda in the cockpit.

Freeman frowned, then set to work on his tablet.

Gabriella slid into the pilot's chair.

"Care for a lesson?" Makeda asked.

"I wouldn't trust myself with something this big."

"Said the woman who has fought countless demons and temperamental vampires," Makeda teased. Gabriella frowned at Makeda's response then looked out the window.

"Something troubling you, discipulus?"

Gabriella hesitated before answering. She looked back, staring down the aisle at Adriana. The vampire appeared lost in thought. Turning back to Makeda, Gabriela whispered, "I don't doubt you, Praetor Arsi, but I have to ask."

Makeda cast a glance at Gabriella. The girl looked out the window again, her fingers absently drumming on the arm of her chair.

"In Madrid, we encountered an angel who forsook its duties to Heaven for the love of a mortal, only to be rejected by that mortal. It then used dark magic to force the mortal to return its love. We stopped it, but the angel would not repent. We cut it down."

"I was there."

"Yes…" Gabriella again looked to the rear of the plane. She turned back to Makeda and said, "Adriana has done far worse than the angel we ended. She counters every moment of potential redemption with some morally questionable act.

"Again, no disrespect, praetor, but why take the chance on her? Why is she so special?"

Makeda knew the question would come; never did she think Gabriella would be the one to ask it.

Gabriella would follow Makeda out of faith, regardless of the reason for her choice of Adriana as a champion. That, Makeda knew, was the very definition of faith, a concept even Makeda questioned.

Out of respect for Gabriella's faith, both to the One Goddess and Makeda, the Knight deserved an answer.

Unfortunately, Makeda could not give her one.

At least, she could not give her the real one.

Measure Twelve — Dream Deferred

An enraged Dwyer Strathan threw open the handcrafted oak door to his bedroom with such force it almost flew off its golden hinges. Had the valuable antique broken into pieces suitable only for kindling, Strathan wouldn't have cared.

Though he did enjoy his expensive, luxurious lifestyle, material possessions held little value for him.

No, Dwyer Strathan found true meaning and worth in the ruthless acquisition of his expensive, luxurious lifestyle and material possessions.

Storming into the gilded room, he growled an ancient, magical phrase. A man-sized rift opened in the air in front of him, revealing a closet-like space. Within that space, an ornate lacquered box one could hold in the palms of their hands rested on a waist-high pedestal. The bones of once mortal villains now damned to an eternity in Hell comprised the pedestal.

Strathan yanked two chains from around his neck. Amulets containing the Vyntari shards were attached to the chains. He opened the lacquered box, tossed the amulets inside the box's padded black silk interior and turned away.

The amulets clattered against something.

Startled by the sound, Strathan peered into his hellish safe deposit box and noticed two polished orbs lying next to the amulets.

"Thought I gave those away," Strathan said in a gravelly voice that hinted strongly of whiskey, cigarettes, and his Irish heritage. Curiosity sapping a bit of his rage, he picked up the orbs and spun them both in the palm of his left hand.

Holding them at eye level, Strathan studied their clear exterior to see the inconstant murky substance mysteriously trapped within.

"Can I play with your balls?" came a woman's husky voice with a slight Spanish accent.

A smile crawled across Strathan's lips, melting away his remaining rage. He turned toward the sound of the voice and stared at his immaculate four-post bed, an antique from the 18th century. Beams of moonlight shone through ornate French doors and illuminated the female who beckoned — Valentina Lorena.

She lay on her stomach, her elbows bent with chin propped in her hands. The soft, ebony sheets barely covered her naked body contrasted with her pale skin and bleached-to-platinum blonde hair. She watched Strathan intently.

"You of all lasses don't have ta ask permission for that," Strathan answered.

Moving toward the dresser, he uttered a second ancient phrase. The dimensional rift closed. The dark mage placed the orbs on his dresser, then removed his belt and pants on his way to the bed.

Valentina moved to her knees in anticipation of Strathan's arrival. The sheet slid down her lithe form and onto the bed. The curves of her breasts, larger than a girl of her small frame and stature should have yet remarkably real, caught Dwyer's attention.

His gaze continued leisurely down her body, pausing at her slender, rounded hips.

Reaching the bed, Strathan took Valentina's face in his hands and pulled her close, stopping short of kissing her. "I don't need your mouth quite this high for what I have in mind," he instructed.

Valentina blinked, then smiled coyly. Her hands moved down the toned muscles of his chest and abdomen. Strathan utilized powerful, Hell-born magic to maintain the illusion that he was a late twenties Hollywood bad boy. A magical tooth held everything in place. The musculature was mostly a gift from that, but he also spent the requisite days in the gym punching a heavy bag.

How else was he going to meet all those sexy female trainers?

Strathan closed his eyes in anticipation as Valentina grasped his member with fingers that had played many an instrument, musical and otherwise. He anticipated her skilled tongue — but nothing happened.

The sorcerer opened his eyes and looked down at Valentina. Though reassured by the general girth of his member, Strathan knew the lack of a full erection wouldn't do for her. "We'll just have to work on that, lass," he murmured and moved to kiss her lips. She turned her head, giving Strathan only her neck to nuzzle.

"Just the sight of my bare flesh used to be all you needed," Valentina lamented.

"It'll come." Strathan worked Valentina's neck with his lips, his teeth and tongue. One hand cradled her face; the other moved to caress her breast.

"Perhaps too soon," she whispered.

Strathan pulled away from Valentina. His hand holding her face moved to cup her delicate chin. He looked into her eyes and found a blue sea of indifference. It took tremendous willpower for him to maintain his physical ardor under her cool gaze. He stepped away from her.

"Well maybe if you used that tongue for something other than lashing my ego —"

"Or maybe if you'd get over whatever's pissing you off," she countered.

Strathan frowned.

Normally, his conversations with women went no further than idle banter, ending with the question of what position the woman would like to be in when she climaxed. Anything more complicated killed his libido. Strathan always found himself capable of much more with Valentina.

It was as if she were some twisted kindred spirit.

She shared his love of illusion, evident in her masquerade as an eighteen-year-old pop star. Not a bad gig for a vampire from nineteenth century Spain who used her supernaturally gifted voice to manipulate the emotions of her audiences.

Strathan guessed that he and Valentina's respective levels of magical power were nearly equal (though, he conceded to himself that without the added power bestowed upon him by his infernal master, she might even be more powerful than him).

If they ever combined forces for anything besides sex and badmouthing the competition, they'd be an unstoppable force.

This simple fact compelled him to halt his sexual advances and take a seat on the bed next to Valentina.

"Met with Taylor earlier," Strathan began. Off Valentina's questioning look he added, "He fills in as the Los Angeles leader of the Order while I'm not around." The information did not excite the vampire. She respectfully remained silent, opting to lie on her side next to Strathan.

He didn't let it bother him that she seemed more interested in his one thousand thread count, Egyptian, Pima cotton sheets than his words.

"I had sent your girl Adriana to find these two Vyntari shards."

Valentina's eyes came alive. "*The* Vyntari shards?"

Strathan quizzically studied the vampire vixen in his bed. "Yeah. What're they ta you?"

Sitting up on her haunches, Valentina faced Strathan, her excitement palpable. "You really don't pay attention to the Shadowdance, do you?"

"What? You my old lady now?"

"The Vyntari shards are what this stupid Dance is about, Dwyer. They're supposedly lost, or at least —" she finished in a subdued but mocking tone of disbelief, "hidden for all eternity!"

"Some bloke found one o' them and delivered it ta me," Strathan stated with little sense of reverence for the legend. "Same bloke also sent me directions for findin' two more shards and information I could use to draw in Adriana."

Valentina turned her head slightly to one side, one dark eyebrow raised in disbelief. "Somebody just gave all this to you?"

Strathan wasn't sure if her question came from doubt or jealousy — not that he cared either way.

"Sure did. I got an idea who, but don't worry yer pretty bleached head over it. That I got Adriana to get me one of the other shards…that's the tits."

"So you only have two of them?"

Strathan saw the lust for something other than him in Valentina's eyes. It reminded him of the reason he and Valentina could never really work together. As soon as she recognized a greater prize than his company, their camaraderie would end so she could pursue and obtain the newest object of her desire.

If that meant destroying her former partner, so be it.

Valentina's needs were simple.

"Ya can add. Bully fer you," he said, returning to his cocksure, dismissive manner.

Valentina must have sensed his suspicion. Her eyes left him to stare at the floor. She began playing with a lock of hair. "What are you going to do with the shards?" she asked, trying to sound only casually curious.

"I was gonna use 'em to barter my way the hell outta this bloody Order."

"Didn't work, did it?" Valentina hissed.

Strathan studied the vampire before leaving his bed to pace. She paid him no attention. "Taylor gave me some crap about how only two stones were worthless."

Valentina dismissed Strathan's remark with a flip of her hair, letting it flow back over her shoulder and cover her bare breasts. He had seen her dismiss many an underling with that same move. He'd also seen her dismiss underlings by tearing their throats out.

Since he still drew breath, Strathan figured he was still in the conversation. He moved back to the bed and sat with Valentina, pushing her shoulders so she lay on her back.

"Going for something kinky?" Valentina purred, though Strathan felt tension rather than surrender in the muscles of her slender shoulders.

He gently ran the back of his hand down Valentina's cheek, working hard not to be distracted by the softness of her skin. "You pass your time studying all things supernatural. I'm bettin' ya know somethin' I should."

"About?"

"About the shards, ya silly bird," he cajoled, running his finger delicately over Valentina's luscious, wet lips. "What's so bad about only two?"

She took Strathan's hand in hers and moved it to her other cheek. "Maybe you should be more curious as to why the Order wants the shards in the first place."

Turning her head slightly, Valentina traced the lifeline in his palm with the tip of her tongue. When she finished, she added, "Or have you forgotten all your studies with the Order?"

Suddenly Strathan's hand latched onto Valentina's throat.

She choked out a laugh.

"What are you going to do?" she asked. "Strangle someone who doesn't need breath?"

"Enough feckin' me 'round, Val," Strathan hissed. "Tell me what ya know!"

Strathan's flash of anger did nothing to quell Valentina's humor. He should have expected it wouldn't. The vampire in his grasp knew damned well he wasn't about to kill her. Another pop star dying under mysterious circumstances within three days would be a bit of a strain on the Uninitiated psyche, drawing unwanted attention even his ego could do without.

Despite what Strathan said, he still respected the Veil of the Shadowdance, the unofficial but mutually agreed upon decision to keep the Uninitiated in the dark about the supernatural.

Valentina also knew how fond Strathan was of her. He wasn't opposed to violence, but not over something this trivial — or that didn't culminate in an orgasm.

Strathan released Valentina. He walked casually over to the dresser. He picked up his boxer shorts, sliding into them along the way. Even with his back to the vampire, he could feel her eyes probing him, probably accompanied by a smug grin. Ignoring her, Strathan picked up the mercurial orbs, twirling them in the palm of his left hand.

"Seriously, Dwyer. How did you rise so high in the Order without knowing their most basic precepts?" Valentina asked in a matter-of-fact tone that Strathan did not appreciate. He spun around to address the vampire. Any glimpse of the playful, girlish pop star was completely gone from her expression now.

"Those precepts are a sham!" he said. "All that mumbo jumbo about some true God they believe in and the unbelievers who follow the One False Goddess! Who cares about all that when there's power to be had?"

"Spoken like a true unbeliever," she affirmed with more than a hint of snark.

"Just because a couple of the Vyntari shards popped up doesn't mean we're on the verge of bringing back the Order's god."

"Finding any shard is worthy of reflection," Valentina stated with the full wisdom of all her two-hundred-plus years. "That someone just handed one to you begs extreme caution, especially if their next move was to suggest entrusting them to Adriana Dupré."

"Feckin' 'ell, Val! Spare me the 'I told you so' lecture, would ya?"

"It needs to be said," a wheezing male voice interrupted from the closed French doors leading to the balcony. Valentina turned her attention toward it. Strathan merely shook his head, for he recognized the voice as well as the slight echo therein.

"You could at least knock fer feck's sake," Strathan chided.

Measure Thirteen — Of Masters and Men

"You could be more faithful to your studies," the familiar male voice scolded.

Strathan's eyes narrowed to hateful slits as he looked toward the French doors. Where moonlight once entered the room, now there was a pitch-black void. Slowly, the image of a man materialized within that space, stretching across dimensions to appear before them.

The man was a few inches' shy of six feet tall, though he stood with a hunch that made him appear shorter. Time had added a few pounds to his middle, had thinned and grayed his hair.

The skin on his face was hardened, each wrinkle a crevice carved by deceit and strife. He wore a suit so crisp he could have mixed in with any high society crowd.

Valentina sat up on the bed, returning to a seductive pose without bothering to cover her nudity from the stranger. "Dwyer, darling, I don't think we've been properly introduced," she said, hungrily eyeing the visitor.

"You don't wanna know this guy, Val," Strathan said slowly and with purpose. "He'll string you along with hopes of power, use ya, abuse ya, then use ya again when he gets the chance."

The image was a projection of the man who had dragged Strathan from the gutters of Kilkenny, Ireland. The man who had mentored him in magic and lured him into the Shadowdance.

Strathan would never forget and always loathe the man who put him on the Order's leash.

"Course, ya can always pay back the betrayal," Strathan added, turning fully to the image. "He's used to it. Aren't ya Malachi?"

"Really?" Valentina purred. Strathan had rarely seen her so impressed. "Malachi Thorne. Second in command to the founder of the Order of Haroth."

Thorne's projection was impressed by her recognition. It turned its attention to Valentina. Bowing like a Victorian gentleman, it said, "I am he."

"This projection…impressive you're so clear from presumably so far away," Valentina said. "I mean, you're still in exile after that betrayal during World War II, right? Dupré's handiwork, if I recall the histories correctly."

Thorne's projection turned to Strathan. "This girl seems well educated in our ways, Dwyer. A much better choice than your usual whores."

"She's a bloodsucker," Strathan spat.

"A vampire," Valentina corrected with a hint of attitude. "One with a great deal of knowledge of the Shadowdance." Thorne's projection turned back to Valentina, who continued to practice her wiles. "For example, I know the power of the Vyntari shards comes in threes, with a total of three sets completing the collection."

Strathan threw up his hands, careful to keep the orbs intact. "Oh, the trouble with trilogies! But can't somebody else find the last of this set and let me be done with it?"

"Think of what you're asking, Dwyer," Valentina insisted. "You want out of the premier group dedicated to the Shadowdance. Think of all the contacts within the Shadowdance you have, the knowledge — or, rather, lack thereof."

"Stuff it, Val," Strathan replied in a huff.

Valentina smiled wistfully. "Seriously, Dwyer. You simply know too much. That's why no one has ever left the Order. Not alive, anyway. For them to make such an exception, they would expect something of equal value. Two shards? Whatever. But three?"

"That was always your fundamental flaw, Dwyer," Thorne's projection intoned. "Forever performing the least you can to accomplish your goals, always working below your potential."

"Oh, screw this!" Strathan growled. "They don't want the shards I got? Fine! I'll throw 'em out and leave anyway!"

The expression on the Thorne projection's face darkened. "Will you?"

Strathan gripped the orbs tightly as a sharp pain ripped through every cell of his nervous system. It felt as if his body were on fire.

He remembered the feeling.

Strathan had spent decades mastering the Dark Arts under Thorne's direct tutelage, an honor rarely bestowed upon a neophyte to the Order. Despite Strathan's disregard of the Order's theocratic beliefs, his attraction to magic and power was undeniable. Strathan had the potential for great power; Malachi was determined to bend Strathan's power to the will of the Order.

During his initiation ceremony, Strathan was set alight with mystical fire. Nothing could have prepared Strathan for the searing pain afflicted upon him then. He was equally unprepared for the pain Thorne now generated from wherever his true form lay hidden.

Strathan was a powerful sorcerer; his power was nothing in the shadow of his master.

Strathan's grip tightened to the point that he cracked one of the orbs' glass shell.

Thinking back to that initiation, Strathan remembered the meditations that afforded him the control necessary to deaden his pain. He didn't submit to Thorne and the Order then; he would not do so now. His anger built in direct correlation to the pain. It felt as if the pain had continued for minutes, for hours.

In reality, it lasted all of a few seconds.

"Your threshold for pain is as impressive as always," Thorne's projection said. "It is expected, as you were given more than any disciple before you, just as you are receiving more now. One might imagine that you enjoy it."

"Piss...off..." Strathan hissed through gritted teeth. So overcome by the magical pain, he didn't notice the glass of the broken orb cutting into his palm, nor did he notice infernally hot steam escaping the orb.

From his periphery, Strathan watched Valentina rise from the bed, using the sheets to cover herself. She spoke to Thorne's image, but Strathan couldn't focus on the words. It took every ounce of focus to prevent his master's power from killing him.

Then the pain stopped as abruptly as it had begun.

Strathan stumbled and should have fallen to his knees, but he forced himself to hold his ground. He would not falter before Thorne and Valentina. His hands clenched; he felt something squirming in the hand that held the orbs but did not loosen his grip.

The anger he used to fight the pain focused like a laser at his master Thorne.

"Yes, this girl is much better suited to you, Dwyer," Thorne said, though Strathan barely registered the words. "She understands what is at stake in the Shadowdance, and is willing to fight for our great cause. You could learn much from her."

The squirming in Strathan's hand churned like it demanded release. He held it tight. "She's willing ta fight for *her* great cause," he corrected.

"We want the same thing — dominance in the Shadowdance," Valentina said. "What's the harm in helping one another, hmm?"

Strathan could feel the metaphorical dagger sliding into his back. He never trusted a girl, and he trusted Thorne less. He silently cursed the idiot who had saddled him with the Vyntari shards for placing him in this situation, then shook his head ruefully.

No.

The true source of his frustration was Adriana Dupré.

If she had honored the deal they'd struck and retrieved both shards, Taylor would have accepted three shards and set him free. Thorne would have never invaded his home this night.

Should he ever see Adriana Dupré again...

"I know where the third shard is," Strathan spat. "I'll get the feckin' thing."

"You will notify me upon your return," Thorne's projection said. "I will work your deal with Taylor."

"Oh, so you'll be coming out of hiding fer this?" Strathan said. "I'm impressed, old man! Should I book a table at Spago or Avalon?"

He looked to Thorne's projection. It withheld any words and simply faded from view, plunging the space it once occupied back into darkness. Moonlight soon pierced that darkness, restoring the room to its natural setting.

The projection's light had barely faded before the sheet-clad Valentina rushed to Strathan's side. "You're not really planning on giving him the shards, are you?"

Strathan ignored her words. He raised his clenched left hand. Blood slipped through his fingers and down his forearm. He opened his hand, the shards of glass buried in the flesh of his palm making this a painful maneuver, and the unmolested orb fell and landed softly on the embroidered carpet.

Strathan's blood landed next to it, and a plasma-like substance landed next to the blood. It melted through the carpet, revealing the limestone floor beneath.

The plasma spread from the broken orb and mixed with Strathan's dripping blood. Inexplicably, the plasma gained mass, expanding to engulf his entire hand and trailing down his forearm.

The plasma burned Strathan's flesh, yet the pain did not compare to what Thorne had inflicted. Strathan laughed. It wasn't the laugh of a sane man. His struggle entranced Valentina, who made no twitch of fear or revulsion.

She did wisely take a few steps away from him.

A portion of the plasma mass pulled away from Strathan.

It morphed into the head of a small demon.

The creature's jaw-like appendage gaped open in a silent scream. As it struggled to pull its plasma-ooze form loose from Strathan, the sorcerer's pain increased. He addressed the demon.

"Denizen of Hell! As I have released you from your prison, I command you to perform my desire! Give me your demonic form to use as a weapon against the Light!"

Strathan closed his hand into a fist and concentrated. His body trembled with the effort to contain the pain caused by the struggling plasma demon. Soon, its head melted back into plasma and transformed into a leathery hide that slowly crawled up Strathan's left arm and shoulder.

Deadly barbs thrust from the hide. Strathan opened his hand. The plasma leather extended each finger into a talon capable of rending flesh from bone.

Strathan forced a smile of satisfaction to his lips. "Still... works..."

Fingers touched Strathan's cheek. He looked down, registering a face before him but was unable to focus on it as the plasma demon demanded his attention. Strathan closed his fist as best he could, talons digging into the plasma on his forearm. The new pain focused him. He looked back to the face and recognized Valentina.

He also recognized her look of lust.

Strathan was unsure if that lust was for him...or for the power he wielded.

Valentina touched Strathan's demon-enhanced arm. Steam rose from the point of contact. She immediately pulled her hand away and placed the burnt finger into her mouth, her tongue languidly moving over it. Her eyes met Strathan's, who returned her dark lust.

The vampire draped her arms around Strathan's neck. She stood on her tiptoes yet still barely reached her lips to the taller man's ear. In a breathy, seductive voice she said, "Save it for Dupré."

She released the dark mage and walked away from him. She let the bed sheet slip from her grasp, exposing her perfectly curved ass.

Strathan strode forward, grabbed Valentina's arm with his non-demon hand and spun her around. Before she could protest, the demon hand gripped her throat. The smell of burning flesh permeated the air.

"You may not breathe," Strathan said with a voice spawned from the depths of Hell, "but if I were to squeeze your throat and pop off yer head, you'd be destroyed just the same."

Though Valentina did well to contain any fear she may have felt, Strathan could see in the vampire's expression that she did not doubt his words. He threw Valentina across the room and onto the bed.

Valentina landed hard, the lush mattress and bedding cushioning her fall. His rough treatment served only to arouse her desire for him further. She turned to Strathan, legs spread and beckoning.

"Quit showing off," she cooed. "Let me help you relax before your trip."

Strathan stared at Valentina. The corner of his lips curled into a wry smile.

"Your task complete, demon, I release you to the Hell from which you came," Strathan commanded.

Another rift in the fabric of reality opened before him, providing a view of Hell. The demon hide peeled from Strathan as if the rift sucked the material from his flesh. The demon's head appeared. It gave a silent scream of protest before the rift dragged the creature into Hell and snapped shut.

Strathan fell to his knees. His struggle against first Thorne and then the demon's magic had drained him, but he would not let it defeat him. It was his time now, and that bitch on the bed would help him set things right.

He'd just have to watch his neck around her.

Strathan struggled to his feet. As he approached Valentina, she used her vampire power to heal the third-degree burn on her neck. Her gaze moved down Strathan's body, stopping at his hips.

She smiled widely, obviously pleased with his new mood.

"Looks like you've gotten over our little tiff," she said.

"You have no idea the things I'm gonna do to ya, girl," Strathan promised.

As he moved onto the bed and hungrily pressed his mouth to Valentina's, he couldn't decide if he meant the phrase for her —

Or for Adriana Dupré.

Measure Fourteen — A Change of Scenery

OROMIA

DECEMBER 2013

Biblical scholars believe that the Garden of Eden, the mythic place their holy book declares as the birthplace of Man and Woman, was located in the Middle East near the Tigris and Euphrates rivers. They would be surprised to learn that, not only does the place actually exist, but it is actually in Ethiopia's Oromia region.

However, Uninitiated scholars would never find their Eden, for magic hid it from their eyes.

Under the protection of that magic, the Agazyan tribe has thrived over the millennia, using traditions initiated by Adam himself to maintain this paradise as it existed at the time of Man's birth.

As an Agazyan boy of fifteen years, Tekle knew a simple life. Mornings brought household chores or a few hours learning the harvest. He would marvel in grasslands covered by fields of wheat and maize; their serene beauty disturbed only by the occasional gurgles of the stream, its source the great Web River, that bisected the grasslands.

Afternoons brought lessons in the Agazyan traditions. Some days the boys practiced the martial art *kamau njia*, and combat with *quiyana* and slingshot, while the girls learned cooking or caring for the young. On other days, the roles would reverse.

When not involved with these studies, the village mothers used playacting and theater to educate the children in Agazyan history, the tribe's philosophy, and how it related to the world here and beyond their idyllic sanctuary.

These tales energized young Tekle.

Sometimes, when he should have been playing *kib-kib* or *pero* with the other children, he'd find a secluded area in the forest just beyond the grasslands. There he would relive the tales, wielding a custom-made spear against imaginary historical foes and their attempts to disrupt the Agazyans' peaceful coexistence with the land.

During today's forest trip, Tekle practiced the movements seen in Agazyan religious rituals that tapped their greatest strength — communal magic. Each Agazyan held part of their tribe's magic within them. Individually they were strong; together, they could defend against the most powerful dark magic.

To use this communal magic, select individuals become the focus of the tribe's magic. Tekle's family held prominence in the role of magical foci. He longed to continue the tradition himself.

Tekle caught a glimpse of the sun hanging low in the sky and cut short his daydreams of glory. His father had assigned him the task of gathering ritual supplies for an event this evening. Failure in the task would surely play against the fruition of Tekle's goals.

He had brought his mule into the forest with him, the ritual items safely stored in a bag thrown over its back. Still reliving his heroic fantasies, Tekle ran up on the mule from behind, vaulting onto its back. The force of his landing got the mule's attention. A slap on its rear convinced it to move forward.

Tekle directed the mule with a tug on its mane, turning it away from the forest and toward a wide dirt path leading back to the village.

Only Agazyan feet and their beasts of burden had traversed the few miles between the lower forest and the Agazyan village above. It had been this way for thousands of years.

As Tekle continued his trek, the forest's juniper trees' needled pines gave way to a treeless, sloping area of exposed soil, tussock herbs, and grasses. The men of the village worked the fields, preparing the winter soil for the coming planting season.

The grassland soil gave way to barren rock. The Agazyan village rose up from this rock and dirt plateau. The dirt road Tekle traversed widened. Wooden huts with thatched roofs lined the road ahead.

Other trails to similarly fashioned huts branched away from the main road, several dozens in all. Agazyan children of all ages played while adult females socialized or moved about completing various chores.

Halfway through the village, the distant churning of the Web River beckoned Tekle further. A trek through the rest of the village and another stretch of juniper trees sprouting from the mountain's volcanic rock would take him there.

Thirty minutes later, Tekle took in the view beyond the trees. It always stole his breath.

A lake of pure blue water washed over the rocky earth at the edge of the juniper forest. The powerful Web River plunged into the lake from a plateau half a mile up the side of the great Mount Batu. Near the shore, a long-horned nyala family drank from the water. White-collared pigeons competed with thick-billed ravens for dominance of the skies.

Tekle sat in awe of this oasis teeming with life. Yet he knew he must move on.

Pulling his mule's mane and prodding it with a heel to its stomach, Tekle steered the beast around the lake toward a jutting area of rock to the side of the waterfall. There, he followed a steep, winding trail up the side of the mountain and to another plateau just below the top of the fall. A four-foot rock wall protected the mule and his rider from plummeting down into the lake below.

The falling water was close enough to the path to send a soft spray upon Tekle's skin. The sound of the fall was nearly deafening, but Tekle had grown accustomed to it. To him, it was the lullaby of a caring mother.

Behind the fall was a wall of volcanic rock. To the Uninitiated, this plateau was no more than a place with a wondrous view, the last stop of their tour of Agazyan wonders. However, all tribesmen knew the sacred phrase that would unlock the secrets beyond the rock wall.

Tekle spoke the phrase now.

"*Afkonigkennis.*"

A large section of the rock wall shimmered and then disappeared, revealing a deeper area of the existing plateau. Several other mules were present, a sign that others were here ahead of Tekle. He dismounted his mule and pulled down the bag he had secured over the beast's back. It crashed to the ground, its weight nearly pulling the young boy over with it.

Dragging the bag, the boy crossed the plateau, walking toward a tunnel carved through the rock. This tunnel, wide enough for two adults to walk shoulder to shoulder, ended at two wooden doors. The tranquil waterfall sound faded as he continued deeper into the mountain.

Once in front of the doors, Tekle released the bag. He paused for a moment to catch his breath, dragging his arm across his forehead to remove the sweat from his brow. After a few moments more, Tekle gently pressed against one of the two doors.

The door stuck.

He gingerly applied more pressure, but it still would not budge. Tekle knew that sometimes the doors required some force to open, but didn't want to appear as an intruder to those on the other side. He tried the door once more —

Someone snatched the door open from the other side. Tekle fell into the next room. Looking up from his prone position, he recognized several of the adult tribesmen. They paused briefly from their various tasks and looked over at Tekle, amused expressions on their faces. He heard more than a few stifled laughs.

A male voice to his side scolded him in his native Agazyan tongue. "Laughter and shame are what you deserve for entering the *galma* during preparations, Tekle."

The boy recognized the voice his father, Mehari.

Tekle jumped to his feet. Mehari stood before him. Tekle's short stature only emphasized his father's warrior physique, despite the man's middle age. The boy believed he had seen his father's stern expression more than he'd ever seen a smile, a laugh, or anything else for that matter.

"I am delivering the items you asked for, father," the boy explained.

"Then where are they?" Mehari asked.

A look of embarrassment crossed Tekle's face. He turned from his father and to the *galma* entrance tunnel. He grabbed the bag and tried lifting it. He got it a few inches off the rock floor before it crashed back down. This time, the men in the *galma* did not hide their laughter. Tekle's embarrassment turned into frustration.

Determined to show his worth, Tekle dragged the bag into the *galma* and placed it at his father's feet. Sweat fell heavily from his brow. His breathing was ragged. Yet he'd completed his assignment.

Mehari easily picked up the bag with one hand and hefted it over his broad shoulder. "I told you to drop them off with the mules outside, did I not?"

Unable to meet his father's scolding glare, Tekle's attention drifted to the rest of the room — the *galma* sanctuary.

The room was a natural cave within Mount Batu, formed out of the mountain's volcanic rock. His ancestors had carved symbols in their ancient Agazyan language on the walls. Torches spaced at intervals between the symbols provided illumination when the sun went down.

An opening high up in the side of one wall served as a vent for the torches' smoke. Light from the setting sun entered through that same opening, bathing the altar across from the entrance in its glow.

The altar itself was nothing special, merely a dais of volcanic rock set before a large area of ground. Behind the altar, a raised —

A loud and uncomfortable smack to the side of his head brought Tekle out of his reverie. He looked up at his father, the culprit behind the smack. "You have seen enough, Tekle," his father said in his authoritarian tone. "It is time for you to go."

Night had fallen in Oromia. Normally this would be a time for stillness, a time to rest and regroup before the chores and adventures of the coming day.

On this night, however, the Agazyan tribe was anything but still.

Numbering at a little over one hundred men, women, and children, they had assembled in the *galma* to participate in their most sacred ritual, the *Dalaga*.

The area in front of the altar was a large circle fifty feet in diameter and two feet lower than that of the *galma* floor proper. Illustrations commemorating moments in Agazyan history decorated the circular area.

A small ramp connected the dais with this recessed area.

Within the lower circle, twelve musicians played a variety of instruments, from kettle gourds to bamboo-framed balafons with its wooden keys to doumbeks drums. Percussive beats drove the music.

The bulk of the tribe sat on the upper edge of the recessed circle. Some sang with the musicians' song. Others danced nearby, their movements in perfect sync with the music. The overwhelming sense of hope and joy in the sanctuary was so strong that it could touch even the most hardened heart.

Sitting with the others outside the circle, Tekle looked to the raised area just behind the altar. His father and an elderly man who looked barely alive sat in this position of honor.

Both men wore ceremonial robes of black, red, and white in horizontal stripes from top to bottom. These colors represented those Agazyan yet to enter active life, those within active life, and those who had passed through active life respectively.

The elderly man complimented his robes with a turban of identical colors. Tekle knew this man as the *Qaallu*. He was the spiritual center of the Agazyan tribe, honored with the ability to communicate with the tribe's god, *Waaqa*. The *Qaallu* held sway in all spiritual and moral matters, interpreting the will of *Waaqa*.

Mehari had earned his position of honor as the tribe's leader, the *Abba Gadaa*, through a democratic election. The *Abba Gadaa* held an eight-year term of service. The tribe so trusted Mehari that he'd held this position for nearly three times that long.

Though the two leaders did not move to the rhythm of the music, Tekle could see the pride in their eyes. It warmed him to feel that same pride within himself.

He looked at the two men and two women flanking his father and the *Qaallu*. They were athletically built like his father and bore the tattooed markings of the *täkälakay*, the tribe's best warriors. In the history of the Agazyan, no threat had ever bested these warriors.

Tekle then saw the *Qaallu* close his eyes. Mehari took notice as well. He raised his hand so that his open palm faced the lowered circle. The leader of the musicians acknowledged the motion with a bow to her *Abba Gadaa* seemingly choreographed to the dancing.

The musicians drove their music into a final cadence, pushing their tribesmen to the limits of exhilaration.

Mehari quickly closed his fingers into a fist. The music stopped in the same instant. He lowered his hand. The musicians gathered their instruments and moved from the circle to an area at the perimeter of the raised section. The remaining tribesmen gathered and sat behind them.

The sanctuary, whose inhabitants had just been so boisterous and active, became as still and silent as a tomb. The *Qaallu*, eyes still closed, picked up a scepter, his *bokku*. He used it to push himself to his feet. He shuffled the few steps to the altar and then opened his eyes.

The remaining Agazyan, Tekle included, silently bowed their heads in prayer.

"My brethren," the *Qaallu* began. "We come here tonight in celebration of the Goodness that comes from *Waaqa*, the Goodness that is *Waaqa*. You felt it in your song, in your dance. It is time to share that feeling with our allies who know *Waaqa* as the One Goddess.

"May these feelings of Goodness aid us in our struggle against the Darkness, the Darkness that threatens to engulf the world that *Waaqa* has made for us."

The *Qaallu* lowered his head. Relying on his *bokku*, he descended the slope leading into the recessed circle and walked to its center. Once there, he resumed his sleep-like trance, his *bokku* held before him, its well-worn base resting on the floor supporting his minimal weight.

The musicians started to play. The tune was somber, in sharp contrast to their earlier performance. The melody lulled the tribe into a meditative state.

The *Qaallu* swayed in time with the music. Suddenly, he moved effortlessly into a highly technical, rhythmic dance in time with the somber musical chords. He made the movements more fluid than what one would expect for a man of his advanced years dressed in a heavy robe.

An emerald haze of ethereal light formed about the *Qaallu*. Tekle could hardly contain his excitement, for this signaled the next phase of the *Dalaga*, one that always fascinated him. This part of the ceremony reminded Tekle how special the Agazyan were.

As the *Qaallu* continued his dance, the ground beneath him started to glow softly. The illustrations and hieroglyphs illuminated with similar light.

Tekle looked around him, mesmerized by the radiant images.

His fellow tribesmen were as deep in a trance as their *Qaallu*. Tekle had done the same for fifteen years. This time, things would be different. He would watch the transformation before him.

At least, that was his intention.

Tekle glanced to the raised area behind the altar and caught his father's disapproving eye. Mehari signaled for Tekle to close his eyes, and he did so in a hurry. Far be it for him to gain his father's ire by destroying the communal bond and disrupting the ritual.

An indeterminable time later, a forceful percussive sound brought the music to an end. Tekle stole a glance just in time to realize the sound had come not from a drum, but from the *Qaallu* slamming his *bokku* into the center of the lowered circle.

The transformation was complete.

Once, the lowered circle had been solid volcanic rock. Now, the rock was gone. The *Qaallu* remained in his trance and embraced by his emerald sheath of light. He levitated at the level where the lower floor would normally rest.

That floor was gone.

A shadowy representation of the Agazyan village lay a mile beneath what should have been the surface of the lowered circle floor.

The *Qaallu* spoke.

"Thank you, *Waaqa*, for hearing our call and blessing us with this vision of the *ekeraa*, Your world for the souls who have passed through active life.

"May it be Your will that none here shall make passage to your *ekeraa* this night, none save she who must find her way."

"May it be the will of *Waaqa*," the Agazyan tribesmen said in unison.

The *Qaallu* opened his eyes.

Still floating above the *ekeraa*, he turned to face Mehari without moving his feet. He nodded to Mehari, who then presented the bag Tekle brought to the *galma* earlier in the day. It was less full than before, much of its contents removed for the ritual.

The boy's excitement and pride rose as his father reached into the bag. Tekle had not looked into his parcel; like his tribesmen, he would see the item Mehari withdrew for the first time.

The item was a small, nondescript box. A metal clasp that had no discernible means of being unlatched sealed it. Mehari stood and moved to the edge of the glowing circle. Kneeling and bowing his head in reverence, he presented the box to the *Qaallu*.

Tekle's eyes widened, his heart pounding in his chest. This exchange had never occurred at a *dalaga* before, and he had been a part of making it happen.

The *Qaallu* raised his arm, extending a closed fist. He opened his fist, palm downward. The clasp on the box broke free. The *Qaallu* turned his palm upward, and the box opened.

An item floated from inside the box and hovered above it. Shrouded in a green aura that matched the *Qaallu*'s sheath, the item was an amulet of bronze, in its center a single red crystal. A thin gold chain extended from the amulet, dangling within the green, ethereal cloud of magic.

Tekle had no idea what significance this item had, but even as a novice in the use of magic he could sense the waves of darkness that flowed from the crystal shard. He was transfixed as he watched it pass, unaided, through the air and into the *Qaallu*'s open palm.

"I hold before you an instrument of great evil," the *Qaallu* warned. "*Waaqa*, I ask that you hold this instrument in your *ekeraa*, the great land where all things that were go to rest."

"May it be the will of *Waaqa*," the Agazyans intoned in unison.

The *Qaallu* began to turn his open palm. The amulet's chain slid out of his palm. Gravity took hold, dragging the chain toward the portal at his feet. Then the amulet itself began to slide on the elderly man's hand, following the chain down.

"Don't even feckin' think about it, old man!" came an Irish brogue from the entrance of the *galma*.

Measure Fifteen — Evil in the House of Waaqa

LOS ANGELES

FIVE HOURS EARLIER

Strathan woke suddenly from a stupor.

The relentless strain of a Valentina Lorena pop song blasted from his cellphone. He turned and raised his head, looking in the direction of the annoyance. His shoes, his socks, his pants, his silk boxers formed a trail leading from the bed, across the bedroom and to a burnt area of carpet. His phone lay near the blackened carpet.

A few more bars of the song and the phone abruptly went silent.

Strathan dropped his head back to the bed and met bare mattress. Reaching next to him within the tangle of sheets, Strathan came up empty. Valentina had ridden him raw and left.

Again.

Sitting up on the bed, he noticed the mess he and Valentina had made of the sheets. There was plenty of sweat, other bodily fluids and some blood, mostly his from her biting.

Kinky thing fucking a vampire, though Strathan had done much worse with even Uninitiated girls.

Though they were uninitiated to the supernatural, they damn sure were initiated to the kink.

The morning sun bled in through the French doors, letting him know he needed to get a move-on. Thorne and Valentina were expecting him to get the last of the three Vyntari shards, and he'd best not disappoint.

Then again, fuck 'em.

Thorne wanted the shard so he could continue his cult's crusade of bringing back their shadow god Yahweh, trapped within the nine Vyntari shards.

Valentina wanted it for who knows what, but probably something selfish.

Why in the hell should he do something for them, when what he really wanted was Dupré's head on a stake? He could pull that off simply by calling up her handler, that Rutger guy, and setting her up again. No need to pursue that damned shard. He could bury the other two shards, sell them to the highest bidder, whatever.

Better yet, why not set the entire supernatural community against Adriana — most of it was already — with the two shards as the reward? Yeah. That sounds about right.

Inspired, Strathan got out of bed and headed to the bathroom. Might as well wash up and get the ball rolling.

Any thoughts he had of getting out of his deal with Val and Thorne evaporated when Strathan looked to the bathroom mirror. Valentina had left him a message:

"Get your ass after the last Vyntari shard."

She'd written it in his blood.

Whenever Valentina was over, she had Strathan cover all the mirrors. A vampire's reflection was always that of their inner demon; Valentina hated the reminder of looking so ugly despite her actions solidifying that ugliness.

Having to look at her demon self in the mirror while writing the message probably pissed Valentina off to no end. The vampire was willing to push that aside to ensure Strathan did as she desired. It looked like his day wasn't going to be as simple as he had hoped.

OROMIA

DECEMBER 2013

If there was one thing Dwyer Strathan knew as well as magic, it was how to make an entrance. That ability (and, admittedly, his magic) opened many a door in Hollywood and many a pair of legs in his bedroom. It worked to perfection here in this sacred, makeshift temple inside the volcanic rock of a mountain.

The tribesmen stopped their ritual, turning almost in unison to see Strathan striding from the entrance toward the inner circle. When he reached the outer ring of tribesmen, he pointed a finger from each hand at the tribesmen. He then thrust both fingers apart from one another in a horizontal pattern.

Invisible magic did the physical lifting of parting the sea of primitives before him without him sullying his hands.

Across the circle, a man who would have been a brute of a boxer rose quickly to his feet in reaction to Strahan's intrusion. His demeanor and location pegged him as the leader. He barked something probably directed at Strathan, but in a rash of gibberish the dark sorcerer assumed was his native language.

"Can it, Kunta," Strathan said. He raised his free hand to the man and used magical force to push him back into his seat. "I don't even know what the feck yer sayin'."

The man looked more offended than before — if that were possible.

Like Strathan gave a damn.

He turned his attention first to the old man in the center of the circle, then down at the spectacle beneath him. Strathan whistled.

"I'm impressed," he said. "Didn't think old farts like you had this kinda magic in ya." He shrugged. "Then again, out here in the middle a feckin' nowhere, what else ya gotta do but learn stuff?"

Strathan's eyes lost their humor as they focused laser-like on the amulet in the old man's hand. Pointing at it, he said, "That belongs ta me. Hand it over, and maybe I won't kill the lot a' ya."

A boy — he couldn't have been older than fifteen or sixteen — stood up and faced Strathan. "That belongs to the Agazyan!" the boy declared in English tinged with a thick African accent.

Both the boy's defiance and his grasp of the English language surprised Strathan, but not enough to discourage his quest. "Sit, Ubu, sit." He waved a hand at the boy. The African lad struggled against the invisible force pressing against his shoulders.

He refused to go down.

Annoyed, Strathan put a little more effort into his magic. The boy struggled against the preternatural weight pressing down on him. The effort brought sweat to his brow despite the cool night air. He eventually succumbed and stumbled to a kneeling position. Though his body went down, the boy's face exhibited defiance.

Bully for him.

"Your powers of Darkness hold little sway here in the *galma* of *Waaqa*."

Strathan, his magic still focused on the boy, turned to see the old man in the circle's center addressing him. Not only were his words in English, but also in a matter-of-fact tone that bordered on a condescending dismissal.

Strathan hated condescension.

"He speaks! In a language I understand!" he cracked, hiding his frustration behind sarcasm.

"Though we remain outside your world," the old man explained, "we are not ignorant of your ways."

A smirk crept its way onto Strathan's face. Glancing at the boy, he saw him push up to a standing position. Strathan felt his magical grip on the boy weakening. Maybe the old man was on to something?

Strathan would have to finish this quickly or, because of the stifling of his magic, suffer the wrath of these primitives.

"Fine," he snorted. Strathan released his magical grip on the boy, who stumbled a bit from exhaustion. Another villager moved to his side to support him.

Strathan opened his palm and extended his hand toward the amulet. The old man did nothing to oppose the action. The amulet's chain pulled fiercely toward Strathan, though the amulet remained in the old man's upturned palm.

Then, slowly, the chain lowered back to a position dangling from the old man's hand. Strathan tried harder to pull the amulet to him, but it did not move.

The dark sorcerer threw up his arms in frustration.

"Bloody effin' Hell!" he exclaimed.

Strathan leaped from the raised area down into the lower circle.

Bolts of electricity shot from the point of contact between Strathan's feet and the invisible floor that was now a dimensional portal. A great wind nearly drowned out Strathan's anguished scream as it blew him up into the air.

The tribesmen watched as the wind carried Strathan over their heads back toward the sanctuary's entrance and slammed him onto the ground.

It took Strathan a few moments to gather himself. When he did, he sat up, wincing at the pain in his back. He would definitely have to look up that little Asian massage girl when he got back to L.A.

Right now he had a more pressing concern. He needed that amulet and the Vyntari shard it held, but after that display of resistance and his lack of magical power, he couldn't fathom a way to get to the old man.

His dilemma soon became moot. As Strathan and the tribe watched, the old man turned his outstretched hand so the palm faced downward. The amulet slid from his palm and dropped in what to Strathan looked like slow motion.

The amulet hit the portal's surface, passed through with little consequence, and drifted down to the ethereal village below.

"Good job Fecky the ninth!" Strathan said while getting to his feet. "Now ya gotta go down there and get —"

"Your coveted shard is in the *ekeraa*," the old man interrupted. "No living thing may enter the *ekeraa*, for it is the land of those whose spirits have passed on."

"Oh really?" Strathan replied, a snarl forming on his lips.

Tekle had no idea of this intruder's identity nor how he had found the sacred *galma*. He did know the man was evil. Tekle's destiny, like that of his father and aunt before him, required him to stand against evil.

Though the fear of death crossed Tekle's mind, like a true Agazyan warrior, he did not let that fear deter him. He stood up to the evil man, addressing him in his language. The man unleashed his evil magic upon him, but Tekle found the strength to resist where his father had not.

After the righteous magic of the *ekeraa* had thrown the evil man across the room, Tekle was emboldened to make his next move, crossing through his peers to intercept the evil man.

The man got to his feet near the entrance, dusting himself off after his expulsion from the *ekeraa* portal. Tekle stalked toward him.

"Back for more, squirt?" the man asked with an air of arrogance.

"Your powers are gone, Evil One," Tekle declared. He picked up his pace, preparing for a physical attack.

"Wait, Tekle!" Mehari demanded from his position at the circle's edge.

Tekle heard the command from his father, but he did not heed it. He knew he must remove this evil from the sacred *galma*. Success would prove his worthiness as an heir to the Arsi lineage.

More importantly, it would make his father proud.

Tekle charged.

Just before the point of contact, Tekle fell into a slide aimed at the man's legs. The evil man easily sidestepped Tekle's attack. He reached down and grabbed Tekle by his throat. "This is cute, kid, but don't make me —"

Tekle's foot shot upwards, catching the sorcerer on the inside of his thigh. The sorcerer yelped in pain, releasing his hold on Tekle and stumbling to one knee.

The boy quickly found his footing.

He followed up his initial assault with several well-placed punches and kicks. The sorcerer stumbled backward, eventually falling onto his back.

It was just as Tekle had practiced in the forest. Finally, his day had come. He imagined his tribesmen cheering him on. But when he looked back to them, Tekle saw that they were noticeably somber. He figured they reserved their applause for his final triumph.

Turning back to the evil intruder, Tekle proclaimed in the man's language, "Do you see what happens to evil here, dark sorcerer?"

The man got to his feet, still limping from the blow to his inner thigh. "Wait 'til ya see what happens to punk ass, wannabe heroes."

With a fierce battle cry, Tekle launched another attack. The dark sorcerer dodged Tekle's initial blow, then delivered a massive punch of his own, connecting with Tekle's chest. The boy felt the wind rush out of him. He fell to the ground gasping for air.

Still trying to draw breath, Tekle felt the dark sorcerer pick him up with an arm locked around his throat. "Move against me, and I snap the little bastard's neck!" he yelled while dragging Tekle toward the circle.

Tekle swung his arms at the man but lacked the strength to have any noticeable effect. It was all he could do to pull air into his lungs.

The tribe parted so the evil man could stand at the edge of the circle directly across from the *Qaallu* and, further back, Tekle's father. "So you won't go in there for the shard, huh? Then how about this?"

Tekle felt himself yanked around. He saw horror in his father's eyes.

Then —

Strathan snapped the primitive punk's neck. He then unceremoniously threw him to the portal. Strathan watched as the boy's corpse passed through the portal's membrane and floated down toward the ground within the underworld village.

Looking back at the natives, he noticed them growing restless.

Luckily, the old man raised his hands and uttered some jungle gibberish. The tribe stood their ground, though Strathan wasn't sure the mumbo jumbo would work on the boxer. The muscles on the man's well-defined arms could get no tighter. He looked as if he would murder Strathan if given a chance.

Strathan figured he could take the boxer in a fair fight, but also figured that once a fight broke out, "fair" would go the way of the punk ass kid he just dispatched.

"Now then," Strathan began as he wiped his hands together in a mock attempt to clean them. "I'll keep breaking necks until someone goes in after my shard. Got it?" He pointed at the old man.

"You seem able ta control the bunch. Make one of 'em go get my property, eh?"

"You bastard!" the boxer yelled in a language Strathan understood and in words he heard from fathers, boyfriends, and husbands.

The old guy said something in his primitive tongue. Gone was the high flung gravitas of an Oracle. A stern, commanding voice had replaced it. Whatever he said convinced the boxer to hold his ground.

"Good job," Strathan teased. "You teach him to sit, roll over, all that shite too?"

The old man ignored him. Instead, he held both his arms skyward and then brought them down to cross his chest. The portal beneath him flashed once, blinding all around.

When Strathan's vision cleared, he saw the portal ripple under the old man's feet. Then the floor returned to stone.

The boxer shouted something in primitive gibberish to the old man. "I cannot," the old man replied so that Strathan could understand him. "My powers are too weak to re-open the portal so soon."

The old man's gaze fell squarely on Strathan. No anger, no fear, no remorse clouded his expression. The dark sorcerer read disappointment. "No living creature may enter the *ekeraa*," the old man repeated.

Strathan frowned incredulously. Then an idea occurred to him. "No living creature ya say?" His frown melted into a sinister smile. He reached into a pocket and withdrew his cell phone. "You guys haven't put upwards against mobiles, have ya?"

Strathan looked at his phone. He smiled, then turned back to the boxer.

"Full bars."

Strathan dialed.

Measure Sixteen — The Prodigal Daughter Returns

Adriana couldn't withstand the harsh punishment for much longer. She'd spent her blood magic. Maintaining something as simple as her grip on her *Fukushuu* blades became a struggle of Herculean proportions, the act of using them against her foes even more so.

Not that it mattered.

Every time she swung at a new foe, a different one attacked from another side. She also struggled against blurred vision brought on by exhaustion and too many blows to the head; she couldn't see the enemy as they closed in around her.

The forest canopy admitted little or no light to the snow-covered clearing. What light trickled through was absorbed in preternatural shadow.

Adriana swung at another foe, but in her weakened state overextended. Thrown off balance, she stumbled to one knee. A set of claws slashed across her back, adding to the coat of blood and torn flesh already there. Adriana drove one of her blades into the dirt and leaned against it to steady herself.

"This would be a good death," she reasoned aloud.

"Oh no, Adriana."

She recognized the female's child-like voice. Adriana had learned to loathe that voice, the voice of her former master, the leader of the Daughters of Lilith.

Cytheria.

"You have caused far too much pain in this world to be allowed a simple death, my sweet nightingale," she said.

Shapes emerged from the shadows all around Adriana. Through a battered haze, she made them out to be human aggressors — at least, humanoid. Looking closer, Adriana realized the identities of her attackers.

They were all her victims: human prey from her earliest days as a vampire; Navarre garou she had butchered; Daughter of Lilith assassins she had destroyed in her quest for vengeance. They were all here, in various states of ruin and decay. They wanted their pound of flesh from Adriana.

In her weakened state, they would have it.

A hand grabbed a handful of Adriana's disheveled hair and pulled her head backward, exposing her delicate, pale throat. Adriana looked up at her aggressor: a frightfully thin man with leathery skin and a jagged-toothed sneer. He bounced a rotting peach in his free hand, inches from Adriana's face.

She instantly recognized him.

"I was gonna have a bite o' this peach, but reckon I found something juicier for ol' Yarok!"

The man, Yarok, tossed the peach aside. He then locked his other hand around Adriana's throat. She struggled, but other victims grabbed her arms, holding her in place, bringing her to her knees. Yarok kissed Adriana, muffling the vampire's screams of rejection. He used his tongue to part her lips, then pressed further, prying her mouth open.

Yarok jerked his head, and Adriana grimaced in complete agony. He pulled away from her —

In his teeth, he held Adriana's tongue.

Yarok released Adriana and receded into the shadows.

Adriana fell forward, a small torrent of blood oozing from her injured mouth, practically the last blood in her system. Only the hands of her victims kept her from falling to the ground.

"You were always too mouthy," said a different female voice.

You cannot be here, Adriana thought. *Not now. Not with her.*

The vampire struggled to look in the direction of the voice, but could not muster the strength to raise her head. A pair of feet wearing ballet shoes danced into her line of sight. The ballerina did a pirouette once, twice, and then ended in a *croisé* in front of Adriana.

She must have bent at the waist, for she came into Adriana's line of sight with her upper body parallel to the ground, looking sideways at the vampire. A set of angry brown eyes glared at her. Adriana had last seen those eyes in a living girl just before the revolution in France.

Back then, the girl was eleven years old.

When Adriana saw her again, the girl, this ballerina, was twenty-one. She would remain at that age for the rest of her unlife. Cytheria had turned the girl into a vampire, one with a desire for vengeance against Adriana the same as she bore Cytheria.

This girl was Dominique — Adriana's baby sister.

"Your mouth always got you into trouble with father," Dominque said. "I think that's the real reason he sent you away to Austria, away from me."

Dominique sat down on her haunches in front of Adriana. As she stared at her sister, tears of blood streamed down Dominique's face. "And when Cytheria came for me, you weren't there to stop her. To help me. To save me."

Dominique's anger returned in a flash. She slapped Adriana with a strong backhand. Adriana's captors released her. She fell, her face smashing into the dirt. She lay there for a time, bloodied and bruised. Her body ached. She waited for the killing blow that would end her miserable existence. She welcomed it.

A man's boot kicked Adriana in the shoulder, rolling her onto her back. She looked up through bruised eyelids to see Dominique standing over her.

Dwyer Strathan stood behind Dominique, his arm around her waist as a man would hold his lover. The smile on the bastard's face was pure malevolence.

"Oh, we're gonna have a right spot of fun with you, Adriana," Strathan said. He snapped the fingers of his free hand. Hellfire enveloped his hand. "But first, get a load of what I'm gonna do to yer wee lil' sis!"

Adriana struggled to raise her arm in a feeble attempt to stop Strathan.

It was as pointless as it was pitiful.

Strathan's flaming hand grabbed Dominique's face. Her flesh burned, the putrid smell flooding Adriana's battered nostrils. Melting flesh sliding from her skull and down her throat choked Dominique's anguished scream.

"Now you've lost her twice!" Strathan said.

Adriana tried to scream —

She woke with a start.

Disoriented, Adriana scrambled up but found herself restrained by something cutting diagonally across her torso. A hand touched her shoulder. Reflexively she grabbed it and twisted it in a self-defense hold.

"Calm yourself, Adriana!" a woman yelled. Her voice barely contained her surprise at the sudden pain brought by Adriana's attack.

Adriana shook her head to clear the cobwebs. Looking around, she realized she sat in the rear of an off-road vehicle. The restraint was a seatbelt. The hand she still twisted belonged to Knight of Vyntari Makeda Arsi, who sat in the rear seat next to her.

"Don't make me come back there!" Freeman said from the front passenger seat. Gabriella drove.

Adriana released Makeda's hand. The Knight Praetor shook it to get the blood flowing again. The vampire then realized she'd grabbed Makeda with her right hand. It had fully healed during her sleep, thanks to the animal blood Makeda's contact had prepared for her when they landed in Tripoli.

The vampire flexed her fingers, making sure everything worked properly. The effort had cost her a lot of her blood reserves. She couldn't use any of her supernatural abilities until she fed again.

Adriana wasn't sure when that would ever happen, not in the foreseeable future, anyway.

She thought back to the events that had transpired after their episode in the Alps. Freeman had succeeded in whatever techno-magic he needed to get them in and out of Florence. From there, they flew to their rendezvous in Tripoli.

Makeda's contact had procured them a flight in a much less comfortable Cameron-owned cargo plane transporting construction materials to Addis Ababa, the capital city of Ethiopia.

The contact also had a change of clothing for the Knights and Adriana, something modern with a touch of local color. The package contained their traditional Knight uniforms, as well as something close to Adriana's typical garb.

A careful transfer from the plane to this rundown vehicle had taken place at dusk. The entourage continued toward their final destination, a village hidden in the Oromian wilderness.

"How long until dawn?" Adriana asked.

"We've still got several hours despite the roundabout journey," Makeda replied. "We had to use back roads and double back a few times to make sure no one followed us."

In response to the vampire's questioning look, she added, "The tribe we're going to see, the Agazyans, have secluded themselves from much of the world. I intend to honor their wishes and maintain their secrecy."

Adriana frowned. "More Shadowdance garbage."

"Actually, it's more real world than that. The Agazyan tribe has kept to themselves, only occasionally emerging to defend their lands against other tribes or local supernatural evils.

However, the late 19th century ushered in heavy European colonialism. With the Europeans came supernatural aggressors like the Order of Haroth.

"The Agazyan fought these enemies in kind, aiding in the eventual withdrawal of the European colonialists from Ethiopia by the turn of the century. Their duty done, the Agazyan returned to hiding, waiting to be called again."

"And if someone finds them, so what?" Adriana questioned. "They seem capable of defending themselves."

"The present conflict in Ethiopia between the government and the Oromo Liberation Front is very different. The OLF charge the Ethiopian government with rigging the 2005 election and intimidating Oromians into following their rule, jailing the opposition."

"And this affects the tribe how?" Adriana asked.

"Let me guess," Freeman chimed in. "When the government gets too violent, the Agazyan step in."

"Actually, no," Makeda corrected. "The OLF are not saints either. They plot and execute terrorist attacks against the national government and coerced tribes to fall in with them. With both sides committing acts of evil, the Agazyan remain neutral, hoping the Uninitiated will first help themselves."

The conversation continued, but Adriana zoned out.

Without warning, she felt a dull ache throughout her body. She could feel the demon within tightening its grip upon her soul. The ache turned into a piercing pain in what would have been Adriana's heart. She became lost in the misery, brought out only by the gentle touch of Makeda's hand to her shoulder.

"What's wrong?" Makeda asked.

It took Adriana a moment to consider. She eventually replied, "I have a sense of... foreboding. The demon within wishes to go no further."

"What's with you centuries-old types?" Freeman interjected. "It's all 'great disturbance in the Force' and stuff. You can't just say 'I'm scared' like the rest of us?"

Gabriella took up the defense. "That's not it, Michael. We're approaching the Agazyan village. Its *galma* stands on sacred ground, enhanced by the communal faith the Agazyan have for their god *Waaqa*."

Freeman playfully hit himself on his forehead. "Duh! Vampires don't like holy ground, do they, Little Miss Murder?"

Gabriella punched Freeman on the arm. The hit wasn't playful; neither was the yelp that came from Freeman in response to it. "Respect, Michael," Gabriella warned. "Though she feigned taking your life, she may one day save it. Oh, wait! She already did by flying us over the Alps."

She accompanied the scolding sarcasm with a glare. Freeman remained appropriately chastised. Adriana silently thanked Gabriella for her support.

"We'll park just a mile south of the village, in the grasslands," Makeda said. "The walk to the village should allow Adriana enough time to prepare herself."

To Adriana, she added, "As much as you despise the Daughters, remember their training regarding places of faith."

"They resisted the power of faith via an annual ritual. I have not undergone that ritual in over a century," Adriana spat in sudden anger. Said anger was not hers, but that of the demon fighting for control. She did her best to reign it in.

Freeman chimed in with, "No disrespect, but let's really think about this for a sec. How's this girl supposed to help us save the world when she can't even set foot on the playing field?"

Makeda studied Adriana. The vampire fought back a series of shakes as she stared out the window. "She will be fine," Makeda said.

"Sure. Right," Freeman mocked. "Cuz she did so well against Gabby's sacred *Spatha Perfidelis*. Walking into a sacred temple? No problem!"

If Makeda or Gabriella had any doubt, they hid it well.

Adriana wasn't as convincing.

Strathan rolled two new demon orbs in the palm of his hand. It gave him something to do while he languished in the primitives' sanctuary. His cell phone had died several hours ago, so no Angry Birds or Plenty of Fish.

At least the primitives brought me food, he thought.

The hospitality didn't surprise Strathan. Though the primitives saw him as the Evil White Man, they were still the Good Guys. They had moral obligations, particularly in the line of sight of their god.

Strathan was just thankful he'd conjured the demon's tooth installed in his molar. It served as the focus for the spell creating his illusion of youth. Without it, with this place jamming his powers, he would already look his century or so of age. Going all elderly David Lo Pan wouldn't have been a cool look.

The boxer now sat stoically in his place near the altar. His only departure from observing Strathan came when he stepped out to change into some warrior garb. His new threads showed off his muscular arms and chest while covering his lower body in pants made of animal skins.

Hell — the guy stared at Strathan even while eating the meals the other primitives brought him.

That costume change was nearly a day ago.

Since then, it's been just the two of them in here. Even when other tribesmen brought food, the boxer never let them stay, taking all the glory of watching Strathan for himself. The guy wasn't much for conversation, either.

Probably had something to do with killing the kid on his watch.

Luckily, the old guy's last instructions were to leave Strathan intact. Boxer wasn't at all happy about it, but he abided the rules.

Sight of God and all.

Strathan noticed the boxer's killer stare finally leave him for the entrance of the sanctuary. His expression got even angrier if that were possible. Curious what could piss off the boxer more than him, Strathan looked to the entrance.

A black babe entered, followed by a blonde looker and another young male pup. The ladies wore garb Strathan thought came straight out of a comic book. He found it particularly disappointing that the ladies' costumes lacked any good sexual overtones. With bodies like those, they'd totally missed an opportunity.

The kid wore more modern fashions, stuff this generation's youth would consider hip-swank. It allowed him room for movement in battle should it come to that.

"The cavalry has finally arrived!" Strathan declared with a triumphant flourish of his arms. "You all do speak English, right? I'm fed up with hearing the claptrap crap from these monkeys."

The male spoke first. "And me without my autograph book!"

"Don't be too impressed," the blonde girl began. "He's a leader in our nemesis organization."

Strathan stood, bowing slightly. "That may be, lass," he said. He ambled over to the girl, making sure to turn the charm up to eleven despite what must have been a haggard appearance on his part. He pocketed his demon orbs along the way.

The male Knight moved away from the trio, opting to lean against the nearby wall.

Stopping in front of the female Knights, Strathan added, "But I can be right nice when allowed."

The blonde's full lips narrowed into a scowl. "Can we beat this *gurrier* senseless, Praetor Arsi?" she asked her female partner.

"*Gurrier?*" Strathan said. "You been hangin' out with yer Irish grandma or somethin'?"

"Grandfather, actually," the blonde corrected. Her eyes showed fierce resistance.

"I encountered him in Berlin, in Grunewald," the Black babe answered.

Strathan snapped his fingers in recognition. "That's right!" he said, only now remembering. "You kicked me around a bit before sending me away... but not empty handed."

He watched the black babe for a reaction to the words he left unspoken, words that would reveal how this Knight of Vyntari allowed him to leave with one of the Vyntari shards.

"Whatever," the little guy interjected from his position at the wall, his arms folded across his chest in a show of disbelief. "So you here to adopt a baby for a girlfriend, Strathan? Though you and Valentina never struck me as the parenting types."

"I suspect I'm here same as you," Strathan replied. "I want the third Vyntari shard."

"Bad boy Hollywood star seeking an ancient relic?" Freeman said. "What, you looking to fill Harrison Ford's fedora? Should I be tweeting about this to TMZ?"

Strathan glared at the boy. "Oh, you're a right can a piss ain't ya, kid?" he said. Turning back to the black babe, he hooked a thumb behind him, pointing to the circle on the floor.

"The old guy dumped my shard into some portal thingee that —" and here Strathan raised his arms, shaking his hands and mocking the old man — "'no living creature may enter!'"

The sorcerer pointed at the three newcomers. "You three know someone who can enter, but either you lost her..."

Arsi's gaze left Strathan and went to the boxer behind him. Strathan watched her expression change from hard-nosed to surprise. He moved back into Arsi's line of sight. An indignant scowl instantly replaced her look of surprise.

"Or maybe you know what rock she's hidin' under," Strathan finished.

Suddenly, an invisible force constricted Strathan's torso. That same force catapulted him off the ground, propelling him through the air over the circle, the altar, the area in which the boxer sat, and slammed him against the far wall of the sanctuary.

It took a few moments for Strathan to clear his head and catch his breath. In those moments, tentacles of volcanic rock broke from the wall. They snared his arms and legs, hauling him into the surface of the wall.

The boxer quickly stood. "Makeda Arsi!" he yelled.

Strathan looked to Makeda. Her hand raised in his direction. When she lowered her hand, the wall reverted to inert rock. Strathan remained embedded in the wall, with only his head, torso and thighs visible.

"Just because the Agazyan do not condone violence in the temple does not mean I won't deliver it," she declared.

The young lad walked over to stand next to Makeda. He looked approvingly at Strathan. "Jabba would be proud," he quipped.

The boxer stormed around the circle and right up to Makeda, though he didn't wait until he got there to spew his venom.

Too bad he's saying it all in his primitive language, Strathan thought. *Bet it's a right love fest.*

Measure Seventeen — Not Worthy

"What a brilliant plan you devised, Makeda!" Mehari fumed in his native Agazyan tongue as he stood before the senior Knight of Vyntari. "I can see the Good it will bring to the Agazyan... and your world outside!"

Makeda maintained her stern expression, fighting the urge to retaliate verbally. At least she had matured that much since her younger days. Mehari would not bait her into an argument, not at such a crucial time.

"Where is the *Qaallu*?" Makeda asked in an even tone, matching Mehari's choice to speak in the Agazyan tongue.

"He is resting!" Mehari replied indignantly. "We opened the portal to the *ekeraa* at your request, Makeda, despite this being outside of the normal cycle. The strain of focusing the necessary elements exhausted him!"

"I'm not sure what you're saying..." Gabriella said in English, trying her best to use an innocent tone to defuse the situation.

Mehari turned to her. Speaking in English, he said, "This is not your struggle, woman!"

Gabriella's expression soured. Makeda knew her as a staunch believer in equality for women, never backing down from the opportunity to defend that position. She knew her brother wasn't a sexist, but throwing the 'woman' at the end of his dismissal of her junior Knight didn't help.

However, this was not the time or place for grandstanding.

Thankfully, Freeman stepped up before Gabriella could utter a word. "Oh contraire!" he began. "Remember, Mehari; we're the good guys! When it comes to who gets to save people, we're equal opportunity!"

"But you are useless to my son unless you are dead!" Mehari insisted.

This statement stopped Freeman cold. Confused, Gabriella started to ask a question. With a curt shake of her head, Makeda signaled for the girl to hold her tongue. Makeda then looked back to her brother Mehari.

"I have planned for this contingency," she said matter-of-factly.

Mehari shook his head. "Contingency?" he asked. He turned away from Makeda, pacing, trying to take this in. "My son —" Mehari whirled and pointed at Makeda. "Your nephew — is dead…and you call that contingency?"

Makeda spared a glance at her discipuli. They were horrified by the news of Tekle's death. Both Knights knew the boy from their time studying martial arts here. Thankfully, they remained silent.

Mehari approached Makeda, moving so close she had no choice but to face him. "Would you implement a plan that endangered your loved ones?" he asked.

If Mehari knew Sahlu's fate, his rage would know no bounds. He was liable to do something that would disrupt her plan, inadvertently destroying everything Makeda had worked for thus far. Both Tekle and Sahlu's deaths would be tragic wastes of life. She had to see her plan through if solely to honor their sacrifices.

Frustrated, Mehari turned from Makeda. "Your exposure to the world outside the Agazyan has corrupted you, my sister. It has perverted your sense of duty, pushed you away from the grace of *Waaqa*. And now you bring this…" — Mehari motioned toward Strathan — "evil upon your tribe, upon your family. All to save a world that has not made itself worthy of being saved!"

Makeda listened in silence, doing her best to remain calm.

"I have served with Praetor Arsi for over a decade now," Gabriella said. Despite her agitation, she maintained a respectful, yet forceful tone. Makeda saw in her discipulus the pure righteousness she would never attain.

She prayed the foulness of her methods would never tarnish Gabriella.

"Though her methods may not exactly adhere to the tenants of the One Goddess," at this Gabriella gave Makeda a sideways glance, "not once in those years did Praetor Arsi commit an act of overt evil, despite what others may have thought of her actions."

Like lightning, Mehari turned on Gabriella, his tone just as electric. He spoke in English. "So then you accept that Makeda planned for that evil animal to murder my son?"

Gabriella opened her mouth to speak but found no words to utter. She and Freeman turned to Makeda, their eyes pleading for an explanation their praetor was not inclined to provide.

Mehari refocused his anger on his sister. "The only reason the sorcerer lives is that the *Qaallu* insists upon it. Again, at your request, Makeda."

A new voice broke in, asking, "Are you quite finished?"

The voice came from the entrance to the *galma*. All eyes turned toward it.

Adriana pressed her right hand against the wall of the tunnel just outside the sanctuary proper. Without the support, the vampire looked as if she would succumb to the demon's fear and fall to her knees. If Adriana had overcome the demon long enough to reach this point...

A chorus of "Here she comes, Miss America" rang out. Makeda and her Knights looked to Strathan to see him singing, changing "America" to "France" in his rendition.

Suddenly, in mid-sentence, Strathan's voice simply disappeared. His lips continued to move, but the sound wasn't there. Freeman and Gabriella looked at Strathan, then at each other. Makeda and Mehari were too busy staring one another down.

The Knight *discipuli* looked to Adriana. She had slumped against the tunnel wall and looked even more pale than normal.

"You do that?" Freeman asked Adriana.

She gave a weak nod of her head.

Freeman looked back to Strathan. He continued to rant, but no sound escaped his mouth. Freeman nodded. "Nice! I'd heard vampires could control sound, make 'em all stealthy. Didn't know you could hone it in on a particular person."

Gabriella took a step toward Adriana. Makeda stopped her. When Gabriella looked to her praetor, Makeda said, "She must take these steps alone."

The younger Knight hesitated but nodded in understanding. She looked back to Adriana. The vampire started shivering. She slid to the ground, her back to the wall.

"...your best shot at —" The sound of Strathan's voice returned as suddenly as it had disappeared. He even seemed surprised. "That was just damn bizarre, but ya can't hold me down." Looking at his bonds, Strathan added, "mentally anyway."

"Speaking of mental," Freeman began, "why'd you do that 'Caesar' movie? Or 'Tampa Vice?' Talk about the suck factor!"

"Angelina begged me to do 'Caesar,' among other things," Strathan replied with a lecherous wink. "As for the other, who doesn't want to spend some time in at Mons Venus?"

Gabriella flashed Freeman a questioning stare. Freeman waved her off with a "You don't want to know" expression.

"But let's not change the subject, eh?" Strathan continued. "Your boss Arsi there seems to have thrown in her lot with Adriana. But now your best shot at victory can't even set foot —"

Strathan stopped talking, this time because he saw something that shocked him. Following his gaze, the Knights and Mehari turned to see Adriana at the entrance. She'd turned, now facing the wall. She pushed up with her arms, rising on unsteady legs.

Adriana stood to her full height, fighting to remain standing. A few tense moments later, she took a hesitant step, crossing the threshold and entering the sanctuary.

Makeda knew that holy artifacts themselves were not repulsive to a vampire; they were merely a focus for the wielder's faith in a protective, loving, righteous Supreme Being.

In the *galma*, that focus represented the communal faith in the Supreme Being. The demon within condemns the vampire to walk the earth committing evil. Those actions damn the vampire to a life devoid of the love of a Supreme Being, a life outside communal faith and love.

Thus the source of the vampire's repulsion to holy artifacts.

Adriana Dupré struggled valiantly against that repulsion with every beleaguered step that brought her further into the *galma* sanctuary. Makeda could only imagine what memories of hope and love Adriana used to resist the pull of the demon within her to flee this sacred place.

Unfortunately, those memories failed to sustain her.

Adriana faltered, falling to one knee. Gabriella moved to join Adriana, but Makeda again held her arm. Gabriella started to speak, but Makeda's expression urged her to remain silent. Satisfied the junior Knight would not interfere, Makeda let her go. Gabriella turned to address Adriana.

"You've made it this far," the Knight said in a sympathetic tone.

Adriana looked at Gabriella. Even from a distance, Makeda saw the fear and regret in the vampire's eyes, the tears of blood that streaked her pale skin.

"I do not deserve this," Adriana stammered. She rose and stumbled back toward the tunnel. Soon, she was gone.

Makeda started after Adriana. Mehari grabbed her arm, breaking her reverie. She turned on him and met his gaze. Makeda had expected to see Mehari's anger.

Instead, his expression relayed a tragic disappointment, similar to what she had shown Adriana back in the Berlin forest after she had stabbed Freeman.

Even in her most guarded moment, Makeda could not deny the pain she felt beneath her brother's judgment. Masking her emotions, she yanked her arm from Mehari and strode quickly toward the entrance.

"Hey, Makeda!" Strathan called. She stopped and looked over her shoulder at the sorcerer. In his best Edward G. Robinson impression, he asked, "Where's your messiah now?"

The dark sorcerer's laughter haunted the praetor as she exited the *galma*.

Adriana made it only a few steps beyond the *galma's* entrance and into the tunnel before falling to her knees. Upon impact, her body convulsed in a dry heave; blood spat from her mouth. She struggled to her feet, stumbling a few more yards before falling again near the mouth of the tunnel.

The vampire heard the water roaring just beyond the plateau area. Its promise of tranquility did not raise her spirits. Rolling to her side, Adriana curled into a fetal position, her body shivering.

The powers of love and faith held by the *galma* forced all of Adriana's sins to invade her mind. Through it all, Adriana realized she could not blame her evil solely on the demon bound to her by the *B'akhza D'eab* ritual, the demon that had co-opted her body and memories so many centuries ago.

Committing those acts of evil were Adriana's decisions alone. Those decisions left only violence for Adriana to love; the destruction of those she felt had done her wrong was the only hope she would ever know.

If that were all Adriana had, she truly had nothing at all.

Faced with this reality, Adriana welcomed a permanent end to her misery. Yet Makeda must have other plans for her; the vampire heard the woman's determination in the deliberate fall of her footsteps as she approached.

"What do you want from me?" she muttered, not bothering to look at the Knight.

"I want you to become what you are!" Makeda replied.

"I am a killer," Adriana gave as a weak reply.

She didn't expect the kick to her shoulder that rolled her onto her back. Makeda dropped to one knee and grabbed Adriana's medallion. The chain held as Makeda pulled the vampire up to look her in the eye.

"You have killed, but you are *not* a killer!" Makeda insisted. "You are a young woman demoralized through extraordinary circumstances!"

From her tone, Adriana could not decide whether Makeda directed her anger toward her for failing or toward herself for attempting this lunacy of saving a vampire's soul.

"I betrayed my family," she said.

Makeda grabbed Adriana's chin with her free hand, turning the vampire back to face her. "I know the things you did! The very fact that you feel remorse proves you're not the detached killer you've condemned yourself to be!"

Adriana looked at Makeda as if the woman had said something that never had occurred to her. Her despondency faded. The Knight released Adriana, dropping her to the ground. While the Knight stood, the vampire buried her face in her arms.

Fortunately, Makeda knew enough to let Adriana have her moment. When she inevitably spoke again, the African dialed back her frustration.

"Ask yourself this," Makeda began. "Would a killer seek to avenge those they had killed?"

The weakened vampire looked to the Knight. When she spoke, her voice was choked by her exasperation. "I don't know. I don't even care anymore. About any of it."

"Yes you do," Makeda said, her anger flaring temporarily. She paused to regain control. "Otherwise, you would not have entered the *galma*."

"I did it to kill Strathan."

"If you really wanted to avenge those you erroneously slew," Makeda said, "you could have simply killed yourself."

Adriana stared impassively at Makeda. The idea of destroying herself had never occurred to her. She then realized that her crusade of vengeance was never about those she had killed. It was about avenging the hurt Adriana felt, lashing out at the world before it could hurt her again.

"When the Daughters found you," Makeda continued, "you were confused, without purpose. They gave you a purpose — to kill. But that was not in your nature."

"I just happened to be very good at it."

The side of Makeda's boot connected squarely with Adriana's jaw. The vampire rolled backward, slamming against the tunnel wall. She blinked several times, her hand moving to her jaw to ensure it was still attached. Confident that it was, she pressed against the tunnel wall and sat up, facing Makeda.

The Knight had moved beyond the tunnel and to the plateau area. She sat with her legs crossed in front of the rock wall that prevented travelers from falling into the lake below.

Makeda chanted in her native tongue.

As Adriana stumbled toward her, the chanting ceased.

"And you kicked me because?" Adriana asked.

"To knock some sense into you," Makeda replied. She stood and faced Adriana. Her expression maintained a dull level of frustration. "You've stopped whining, so I assume it worked."

Adriana stopped in front of Makeda. The Knight held out her arms and cradled Adriana's face between her hands. The vampire's bloodstained eyes met the Knight's gaze.

The sorcerer Knight chanted again. When she finished, she moved her hands away, using her thumbs to wipe clear the twin trails of blood staining Adriana's cheeks. Makeda smeared the blood on the palms of her hands.

Turning her back on the vampire, Makeda waved her right hand in front of her as if wiping dirt from a window. Adriana stared in awe as Makeda's hand erased the reality before them like chalk from a chalkboard.

The window she created revealed a scene of two teenaged female hands playing furiously upon a piano. Adriana quickly perceived the image as a first person point-of-view — her point of view, from a memory of days long past.

Adriana watched as a younger version of herself finished playing and turned away from the piano. She took in the lavish sights of the room, a parlor decorated in a style she remembered from the Paris of her childhood back in the late 1700s. Before her point of view turned completely away from the piano, something slammed into her.

Rather, someone.

Her younger self watched the rambunctious form of her eight-year-old sister Dominique. The young girl embraced her older sister with a passion and love Adriana had long since forgotten.

Adriana now recognized the scene before her as the parlor in her family's Parisian mansion. The year was 1786.

A young woman just sixteen years old, Adriana was finally home after a three-year stay in Vienna with her uncle Joseph II, the Holy Roman Emperor. Her aunt Marie Antoinette had arranged for the trip to Vienna. She also beseeched her childhood friend Wolfgang Mozart to teach the little nightingale Adriana all he knew of music.

In those three short years, Adriana's skill as both a pianist and a singer had blossomed.

Little Dominique, whom Adriana had rarely seen in all that time, expressed intense admiration for her big sister's skill. No sound accompanied the image before her, but as Adriana saw Dominique through the eyes of her past self, she clearly remembered the words on Dominique's lips.

"I want to grow up to be just like you, Adi!"

A sob choked Adriana. She turned away from the image, but it proved no help. These were her memories; she could never escape them.

"Why are you showing me this?" Adriana asked.

"Why did you choose this moment to remember?" Makeda countered.

All Adriana could focus on were Dominique's words.

"I want to grow up to be just like you, Adi!"

Dominique had succeeded.

She had become a killer.

Just like her sister.

"I cannot change any of this," Adriana said.

"No, you can't," Makeda challenged. "But, as I've said, you can rise from it and do something positive within the Shadowdance."

Adriana remained silent.

Makeda chanted a few words in Agazyan and then wiped her hands across the image from Adriana's memories. The image disappeared; reality restored itself.

"Strathan thinks you'll enter the *ekeraa* and retrieve the shard," Makeda said.

"Then I should not do it," Adriana replied.

"But if you refuse, you won't return to the moment that made you."

Adriana looked to Makeda. Upon seeing the woman's earnest expression, Adriana shook her head. "Another manipulation." The very thing that got Adriana into the Shadowdance.

"Actually, all of that is secondary."

That surprised Adriana. Makeda continued.

"While you are in the *ekeraa*, you will retrieve the boy's, Tekle's, soul and lead it back to the world of the living."

Makeda stared her words home. She then turned from Adriana and headed back to the *galma*.

"Why me?" Adriana asked.

The Knight stopped a few yards away from Adriana. She looked over her shoulder at the vampire. "As a creature dead, you are the only one who can."

Measure Eighteen — Fare Thee Well

When Makeda returned to the *galma*, Gabriella stood just outside the circle on the floor and near the altar. She held her *Spatha Perfidelis* like a spear, ready to hurl it at Strathan. He smiled like a very amused Cheshire Cat despite his seemingly inferior position embedded in the wall above the altar.

Freeman stood behind Gabriella, restraining his fellow Knight's hand.

"Gabby, I thought 'Tampa Vice' sucked too," Freeman said, "but one shitty movie's no reason to obliterate the guy. We'd have to go after ninety percent of Hollywood if we did that!"

"This is not a time for levity," she chastised while trying to push him away.

"This is the perfect time!"

Gabriella used a martial arts maneuver to fling Freeman to the side. She turned back to face Strathan, only to find Mehari standing in her way.

"Despite your leader's careless example, you are not to initiate violence within the sacred *galma*," Mehari insisted. His stern look expressed his intent to put a stop to the Knights' disrespectful antics. The tenseness of his muscles alluded to his willingness to use violence to stop more violence.

Freeman grabbed both of Gabriella's arms and spun her around so that her back was to Strathan. He became her focus. The male Knight spoke rapidly, not knowing if he'd get it all out before Gabriella shook herself free again.

"Look. The chief's son — our boss's nephew — was murdered and thrown into an underworld, the bastard who did it is embedded in a wall, but we can't otherwise touch him. Who knows where the two Vyntari amulets are that we, 'Defenders of the Amulets,' have lost?

"And here's the kicker: our only hope for making all this right rests in the efforts of a vampire who's done nothing but betray everyone she's ever known!"

Freeman paused to catch his breath. Gabriella and Mehari stared at him, both impressed and bewildered with his delivery. He eventually added, "If we don't laugh at the absurdity of this situation, we're gonna kill ourselves for being dumb enough to have gotten into it!"

Makeda approached the two Knights.

"And this sibling spat is because of?" she asked.

Gabriella shook Freeman's hands off her arms and pointed her *Spatha* at Strathan. "That —"

"Your language, Gabriella," Freeman whispered as a mock warning.

The Irish Knight glanced at Freeman then closed her eyes for several moments. Makeda watched the snarl in her disciplus' expression dissolve to something more neutral. When she opened her eyes, however, the hint of anger remained despite her calmer tone.

"Strathan's cell phone rang," she said. "Michael answered it."

"It was Valentina Lorena!" Freeman said with a little too much glee. "Not every day a guy gets to hear that luscious voice —"

"She was returning Strathan's phone call from last night," Gabriella finished while sending a reprimanding glare at Freeman.

"By the way," Freeman said, turning to Mehari, "how do you guys even have cell reception way out here?"

"Though the Agazyan prefer the old ways to modern technology," Mehari said, "we are not ignorant of it. Seth Cameron has provided us with communication tech, hidden by the same magic that hides our location from Uninitiated eyes."

"You mean you coulda hooked me up with a TV?" Strathan shouted.

The others ignored him.

"Didn't think to invest in a signal jammer or scrambler, did you?" Freeman asked Mehari.

Mehari's silence confirmed Freeman's suspicion.

"Anyway," Gabriella said loudly enough to draw everyone's attention back to her. "On a hunch, we checked Strathan's call list."

"A bevy of beautiful babes, I must say," Freeman interjected.

"Except one number with a local international code," Gabriella said, completely ignoring Freeman's interjection.

"This is going somewhere?" Makeda asked, masking what she could of her impatience.

Gabriella's tone became grave. "Strathan called the Ethiopian government and let them trace his signal. He told them he was at an OLF base. This village."

Makeda could not conceal a look of genuine surprise. She recovered quickly. "I will get us through this."

"How exactly are you going to do that?" Mehari exclaimed. "Can you withstand an army? Because that is surely what will come!"

"Don't you guys have a history of taking on Big Bads?" Freeman asked.

Mehari turned on Freeman quickly and with an angry glare that easily intimidated the young Knight. "We fight on our terms," Mehari explained. "Your praetor's little game with the vampire has given the enemy the advantage."

"I will get us through this," Makeda repeated.

Mehari berated her with a barrage of Agazyan.

Both Freeman and Strathan yelled for him to shut up then looked to one another in disbelief of their common concern.

"That better be the last time we agree on anything," Freeman said.

"Except that we both wanna diddle your little blonde friend there," Strathan replied. He winked at Gabriella. She snarled in return, raising her *Spatha*. Freeman quickly grabbed her arm and forced it back down.

"Don't mind him, Gabby," Freeman said.

Content Gabriella would stay her weapon, Freeman turned to Makeda. "Seriously, though. I'll go on record as saying this whole crusade with Adriana was a schmucked up idea. We're beyond that now, but this whole village is about to go the way of the Tusken Raiders after killing Anakin's mom. So let's focus people!"

Freeman and Gabriella looked expectantly at Makeda. Mehari was still angry but remained silent. Makeda took that as a sign that she could speak freely without receiving another verbal assault.

"I acknowledge that I have no right to ask this of you, Mehari," she began. "But to defend the tribe, we will need your best —"

"Have you forgotten all of your *kamau njia* Makeda?" Mehari questioned. He referred to the tribe's martial combat style. Though it is indeed the Way of the Silent Warrior, the art specified learning the tactics of the warrior as a last defense. The student should rely more on the nature of peace, harmony and spirituality.

Makeda had done nothing but attack her enemies. Their counterattack now endangered all that she loved, almost all that she had left, considering. Had she miscalculated so badly?

"There is a bright side ta all this," Strathan chided. The Knights and Mehari acknowledged the sorcerer as he spoke. "It took that bitch vampire a century to muck up her life. It only took the three of you a little under a week! Bravo for your efficiency."

Makeda raised her hand toward Strathan, but Gabriella caught her by the wrist. Praetor looked to discipulus and noticed her glance toward the *galma* entrance.

"This isn't over yet," Gabriella said softly.

Makeda followed the younger Knight's gaze.

Adriana stood at the entrance. She had not yet crossed the threshold into the sanctuary. Her expression was calm, but she was shivering.

"This is worse than that *Twilight* series!" Strathan said. "Face it! If the first one sucked, why would ya think the second one —"

Adriana took a single step into the sanctuary.

Strathan stopped talking, his mouth open. Mehari remained visibly skeptical. Gabriella smiled warmly. Whatever Freeman felt he kept to himself.

Each labored step suggested the battle between Adriana's will and her demon's desire to turn back. Yet the vampire continued forward, determined to win. She soon stood trembling at the edge of the inner circle. Her gaze fell to Makeda.

Meeting Adriana's gaze, the senior Knight saw the terror in the vampire's eyes. She also saw something else replacing the girl's usual rage. That something, Makeda felt, could be a flicker of a desire to live.

"You started this, Makeda Arsi," Adriana said through gritted teeth. "But I shall finish it."

It was rare that anyone outside of the *Qaallu* performed the Dalaga ritual dance. In this extraordinary circumstance, it fell to

Makeda. Only she had both the knowledge of the ritual dance and the magical aptitude to complete it.

As the emerald glow of the One Goddess's power embraced her, she remembered the swell of power available when using the energy of a sacred area as opposed to the power one found within oneself.

It felt good.

It felt right.

Makeda finished the last steps of the dance. The lower circle beneath Makeda began to glow. Moments later, the *ekeraa* came into view. The Knight opened her eyes to look upon the *galma*.

The Agazyan tribe had returned and had resumed their places about the inner circle, offering their share of communal magic, its focus Makeda.

The *Qaallu*, still weak from his earlier performance, sat at the raised area behind the altar. Mehari stood at his side. Makeda saw the nearly imperceptible smile the *Qaallu* wore. It lightened her heart, though she didn't feel she deserved his pride.

Mehari's only testimony to his approval came in a slight nod. Her brother never displayed much in the way of emotion, other than occasional (but often deserved) anger; what little emotion he showed Makeda now spoke volumes.

Mehari dismissed the tribe while he and the *Qaallu* decided on the best course of action. As the Agazyans exited, Makeda looked to the wall behind the altar area.

Strathan remained embedded in the wall like an insect on display. Figuring it best not to show him the power of the Agazyan, she had cast a spell that had put him to sleep.

"Got a little update for ya, boss."

The Knight Praetor turned to the sound of Freeman's voice and found him and Gabriella at the edge of the circle. She joined her fellow Knights, her emerald sheath evaporating as she progressed from the center of the portal. Freeman held up the Frankenstein-like mess of wires and circuitry that was his repaired tablet computer.

Makeda saw a map of the area on the tablet's fractured screen. A red dot accented a particular point on the map northwest of the village's position on Mount Batu. The words "ETA 1 hour, twenty minutes" glowed in green next to the dot.

"That's how much time we've got before the government's soldier boys get here," Freeman explained.

"Your skill with technology never fails to amaze, Michael," Makeda said approvingly.

Freeman smiled a sly smile. "Chloe O'Brian's got nothing on me."

"Who?" Gabriella asked.

"You need to watch a little more TV, Gabby," Freeman replied. "Besides *Charmed*, I mean."

"Gabriella. And I'm two seasons into *The Good Wife* —"

"Now is not the time," Makeda gently reminded her discipuli. They respectfully ended their banter.

"So what happens now?" Gabriella asked.

Makeda's gaze drifted elsewhere. The two Knights followed her gaze to see Adriana sitting at the entrance to the sanctuary. She had buried her face in her knees, wrapping her arms around her legs.

When Makeda had started the ritual, Adriana had a minor shiver. Since that time, the intensity of the shiver had increased. Makeda predicted the girl needed all her mental fortitude just to keep her from running screaming out of the room.

Makeda stepped off the portal and approached Adriana.

"Entering your *ekeraa*," Adriana began as Makeda stopped before her. "Will it hurt?"

In her centuries as a vampire, Adriana Dupré had undergone no end of mutilations due to violence, up to and including the pain of rebirth as a vampire. Now she feared the potential for pain while crossing into an underworld.

If the stakes weren't so dire, Makeda would have laughed. Instead, she reined in her emotions, displaying a mask of seriousness.

"You are a creature dead," Makeda replied. "There will be no pain for you."

Adriana thought on this. "What is this *ekeraa*?"

"The place where the dead undergoes a final journey before reaching the higher planes of existence. Perhaps Sahlu anticipated your journey."

Adriana contemplated Makeda's words. After a short time, she moved to rise. It was rough going; Makeda helped her to her feet. The vampire looked past the Knight and to the glowing circle.

An old human instinct rose in her as she took a deep, though unnecessary, breath.

Makeda studied Adriana. Her resolve remained intact; the usually hardened lines of her face had softened, giving the Knight a glimpse of what that nightingale from 18th century France may have looked like.

The African Knight escorted the French vampire toward the enchanted circle. Adriana stopped before the other two Knights of Vyntari. Gabriella gave Adriana a look of encouragement. Freeman's skepticism had not abated. Adriana focused on him.

"What I did to you," she began.

"Totally sucked," Freeman finished for her.

"But you didn't hit anything vital," Gabriella interjected. "It was as if you only wanted Freeman out of the way, not dead. We had plenty of time to save him, even without our powers."

"Of course, we didn't know that then," Freeman added.

Adriana gave no reaction.

Freeman still wasn't buying it.

"You never explained why you did that," Gabriella added.

Freeman waved Gabriella off. "Who cares? I want to capture this moment in its entirety because I've never had someone apologize for trying not to kill me before!"

The male Knight crossed his arms across his chest and looked expectantly to Adriana. The vampire returned his stare for a moment. Her gaze soon drifted to the floor as she hurriedly said, "I'm sorry I didn't kill you and save you all this trouble."

Avoiding his gaze, she moved past the Knights and toward the glowing circle.

Beaming with pride, Freeman began, "Apology — wait a minute! What the hell's that supposed to mean?"

Gabriella placed a reassuring hand on Freeman's forearm. "At least she made the effort."

"'I'm sorry I didn't kill you?'" Freeman shouted. "That's not an apology! That's like saying, 'Too bad you're not dead!'"

The female Knight flashed the scolding look her male partner knew so well. Freeman let the conversation drop.

Adriana stood at the edge of the circle and its glowing dimensional portal. Makeda moved past her and to the circle's epicenter.

"Are you ready, Adriana?" she asked.

"Can one ever be ready for anything involving the Shadowdance?" Adriana replied.

"No," Makeda said with a slight smile. "But acknowledging that means you are ready enough."

Adriana watched Makeda raise her arms to the heavens.

"Oh humble *Waaqa*," she began. "Allow this creature who knows Death's hold to enter into your rapture for the once living. Aid her on her quest to find the one who does not belong in your realm and for the evil that has poisoned it. Return them safely to this world.

"We pray to you for this, *Waaqa*."

Makeda motioned for Adriana to step forward. Adriana nodded, but a hand firmly grabbed her arm. Turning, Adriana learned the hand belonged to Mehari.

"My sister has deemed you worthy of this task, vampire," Mehari grudgingly admitted. "I believe her trust misplaced, her methods corrupt. But you are the only hope my son has."

Mehari looked as if he had more to say, but his struggle to maintain his stoic disposition precluded any further words. Adriana met his gaze and nodded. Mehari released Adriana's arm.

Makeda watched Adriana turn from Mehari and back toward the glowing circle. She gingerly took a step onto the portal.

It was as if the vampire had stepped on solid ground, yet she could see the *ekeraa* version of the Agazyan village far below. Despite the trembling caused by the demon within, Adriana made her way across the portal, stopping at a position just before Makeda.

"Find yourself, and you will find all else that you seek," Makeda advised.

Adriana began to speak, but Makeda placed her palm on Adriana's forehead, her fingers pointed skyward. The vampire remained silent.

"May *Waaqa* watch over you," the African Knight said. She then pressed downward on Adriana's head.

Slowly the vampire's feet slipped through what was formerly the stone floor and further into the *ekeraa* below. As she passed through, her sneakers and pants transformed into the laced, knee-high boots that were standard for her assassin wardrobe.

With Adriana's descent begun, Makeda had no need to press further. She stood and watched Adriana's continuing descent and transformation into her assassin's clothing.

Moments later, the vampire had moved completely beyond the portal's membrane, floating into the unknown encounter waiting for her in the *ekeraa*.

The intensity of the portal's glow increased to the point that those left behind had to look away.

A flash denoted its closing.

The circle returned to stone.

Adriana's journey had begun.

Measure Nineteen — Birthplace of a Legend

Adriana landed on the *ekeraā's* ground as gently as she had descended. During that descent, her wardrobe had completed the transformation into a pristine version of the uniform she wore while an assassin: laced, knee-high boots, dark pants, a leather jacket with far too many buckles and drawstrings, a halter top, and her family medallion.

She also retained her *Fukushuu* blades in their back scabbards.

The realm itself was one of eternal night, with the glow of an unseen moon illuminating the village. The dead souls of the Agazyan inhabited the area as shadows of their living selves.

Boys in their teens practiced the martial art *kamau njia*, and combat with *quiyana* and slingshot. Women both old and young acted out some play for younger children. Adult males carried farm tools as if heading for the fields.

Adriana assumed these were their usual activities had they still been alive.

It made her wonder: when she rid herself of the demon that made her a vampire, when her soul finally passed on to an underworld such as this, what life would she be doomed to for all eternity? Would it be that of an 18th-century pianist? A loving sister? A violent assassin?

A tortured soul?

Unease gripped Adriana, similar to the tension she felt upon first entering the *galma*. She looked to the souls around her. As they were oblivious to her presence, she moved close to a few of them.

The tension grew more unbearable the closer she came, but she had to know.

Upon closer observance, Adriana realized these souls… smiled. They carried on in a jovial fashion emanating a profound sense of joy like the sense of faith and community flowing through the *galma*. The sensation felt unfamiliar to Adriana.

The good feelings passed over her in waves, drowning her in a strangely stifling euphoria. She did not deserve such warmth; she didn't know how to accept it.

Stepping away from the joyous souls, Adriana refocused on her mission, hoping to finish it and find a way out of the *ekeraa* before the sensations all around her crippled her and the demon within.

As Strathan had wrongfully forced the boy into the *ekeraa*, Adriana went on the belief that he would not exhibit the same sense of joy as those who truly belonged here. She posited further that the boy would not participate in the daily rituals. Instead, he would want to be alone, something Adriana understood all too well.

As the Agazyans were a communal group, Adriana further reasoned the souls would not let the boy wallow in his misery. They would take him somewhere to raise his spirits.

She could think of no better place for that than the *galma*, which surely had a representation here in the *ekeraa*. To this end, Adriana followed the same path toward the *galma* here in the *ekeraa* as she would have in the real world.

As she neared the outskirts of the *ekeraa* version of the village, Adriana noted a lack of Agazyan souls in the area. At the edge of the village and the thicket of trees, she found a clue as to why.

A dense shadow obscured what should be the continuance of the path into the trees beyond, as if the creator of this *ekeraa*, the one the Agazyan called *Waaqa*, did not want the *ekeraa* souls to venture from its confines.

Adriana had sacrificed too much and pressed too hard to allow this shadow to constrain her efforts. She had not taken more than a step toward it when a voice resonated from behind her. To her surprise, it spoke in her native tongue.

"Are you here for the child?"

The voice, a thunderclap in its intensity, caused Adriana to wince. She turned, expecting to find the source of the voice, but saw nothing.

"I am here for the child, yes," Adriana replied to the disembodied voice. "But I am not accustomed to talking to people I cannot see."

"I am the *kake-guie*, spirit guide to the souls of the *ekeraa*," the voice boomed. Still wincing at the voice's volume, Adriana checked her ears to make sure they did not bleed.

Nothing yet, but she remained unsure how much longer she could go without damage. The potential injury made her wonder if her vampire ability to heal damage would function in this realm.

The voice, this *kake-guie*, continued.

"Only a warrior may lay eyes on me." The *kake-guie* remained silent for a moment, but then added, "Though I acknowledge your valiant nature."

Adriana scoffed at this as she continued to look for a physical manifestation of the *kake-guie*. "I assure you, I am not valiant."

"Yet here you are in the *ekeraa*, to rescue a child to whom you owe no allegiance."

"My reasons are not so benevolent. I am here for the Vyntari shard as well. I am merely the only one who can accomplish both tasks."

"And do you understand why?"

Adriana had no response. Frustrated by her search for the shapeless *kake-guie*, Adriana turned back to the mass of shadow at the edge of town. "My answers lie beyond this village."

"You will find no answers there, Adriana Dupré."

That the *kake-guie* knew her name surprised Adriana, though upon reflection she figured it should not. As it is the guide to the souls of the *ekeraa*, the *kake-guie* should know all who entered. It also made sense that it should know the location of all within the *ekeraa*.

In hindsight, the *kake-guie*'s knowledge of her also explained its use of the French language to address her.

"Honor your responsibility as a guide and lead me to the boy," Adriana demanded of the air about her.

Her words met silence. She found no reason to remain. She turned to the shadow mass before her. "If you will not honor your responsibility, stay out of the way as I honor mine."

"I sense in you an element making you uniquely suited for this quest," the bodiless voice intoned. "Until you identify this element within yourself, you will never find the boy."

Once I find myself, then I will find all that I seek, Adriana mused, thinking back to Makeda's words. "If my answers do not lie beyond the village, then where should I look?"

"The one place you refuse to look, for fear of seeing your true self. I shall release the burden preventing your search. The rest, I leave to you."

Adriana started to ask another question. She did not see the *kake-guie* materialize behind her. It took the appearance of an African man who stood seven feet tall. Muscles rippled across his black as night skin. Ceremonial warrior's garb draped over his shoulders and mid-section. A large buffalo head rose from his shoulders, giving him the appearance of a minotaur.

He pinched the area on the back of Adriana's neck at the top of her spine and pulled. Between his fingers, he held the ethereal form of the demon residing within Adriana, the demon that made her a vampire.

Adriana screamed bloody murder.

The demon howled a wretched sound in kind.

As the demon emerged from Adriana's body, it solidified into its hideous form. Tentacles flailed; what passed for arms grasped for purchase on Adriana's body but could not manage a grip. In all, the demon proved far larger than Adriana, but could not escape the *kake-guie*'s grasp.

The *kake-guie* pulled the demon forcefully from Adriana. The vampire fell to the ground unconscious.

The *kake-guie* raised his free hand and created a ball of light and then forced the demon into it. The demon's form compressed, becoming imprisoned within the spherical cage. The demon raked its talons and slammed its tentacles against the container's membrane, but could not create the friction necessary for escape.

The *kake-guie* released the ball of light. It floated in the air at his side with the demon contained within. He looked to Adriana's unconscious form.

"Now," the *kake-guie* boomed, "you are ready. Prove your worthiness, or face damnation at your hand."

Freeman looked up from his tablet. Mehari and Makeda were off in a corner of the *galma* conferring in heated exchanges. Gabriella sat near the altar praying. Freeman figured she was asking for the strength to resist beating the crap out of Strathan, though she ought to pray for an intervention to help combat the Ethiopian government's army when they came riding into town.

"Okay, sending Adriana along was cool and all, but we need to face reality," he said.

Mehari and Makeda looked at him expectantly. Gabriella had not turned to face Freeman, but he could tell from the slight rise of her chin that he had her attention. He continued.

"Adriana's a smart girl. Soon as she figures out she can stay there indefinitely and absolved of all her sins, our girl ain't gonna come back to help our piddly asses."

"She had best complete her mission," Mehari interjected.

"Whether she does or not," Freeman continued, "that's still secondary. Hell, it may be better if she didn't."

This thought brought a scowl from Mehari. He glared at Makeda, who held a stoic reaction.

Freeman quickly added, "There's no safer place for the Vyntari shard than a place living villains can't go. But that still takes a backseat to the fact that we have an army on the way that'll bring enough firepower to make us all citizens of the *ekeraa*."

Makeda stepped away from Mehari and toward Freeman. "Mehari and I have discussed that."

"I hope that discussion doesn't involve the four of us taking on an army," Freeman said. "Cause that'd be stupid."

"We have the *täkälakay* at our disposal," Makeda replied. "On their ground, they can mount a formidable defense."

"Oh they're good and all," Freeman agreed, "but I think this time we may need a bit of an edge. I've got an idea you can thank Mel Brooks for."

Mehari, Makeda, and Gabriella looked to one another, none of them understanding the pop culture reference. That the Knight least likely to enter a fight had devised a plan to fight an army was inconceivable to them, but the smile on Freeman's face begged for an explanation.

Adriana woke to the feel of cold, hard stone against her face. Her every muscle ached. She pressed up from her prone position to a seated one. She then looked herself over.

Dirt and grime smeared her flesh, bruised from wounds she did not remember, pale and malnourished from a lack of nutrition. Dirt clung to the tattered commoner's dress she wore that looked as if it hadn't seen a washbasin in weeks.

It all fit her environs: a trash-strewn, wood-tiled street trapped between rows of two-story buildings that were as defeated by the elements as the street beneath her. A horse and carriage would barely fit down the street, a side alley in some misbegotten town of old.

A more populous thoroughfare lay a brisk walk away. An oil lamp illuminated the occasional traveler passing the intersection. No one crossing the intersection paid attention to anything happening within the alley. The lamp did little to illuminate the alley itself; the buildings strangled what little moonlight penetrated the darkness.

Adriana recognized her location — St. Petersburg, Russia, 1791.

She thought further back to 1789, during the revolution in France. Illyana Dakanova, a Russian émigré, had found Adriana on the streets. The Mob seeking to overthrow the monarchy hunted Adriana for her familial relation to the queen. Illyana rescued the innocent girl and spirited her away to St. Petersburg.

The young noblewoman came to know the Russian as a surrogate mother. They lived together for a year, though Adriana received little indoctrination to the culture around her. She needed no money, for Illyana had a mysteriously endless supply.

And then Illyana disappeared, leaving Adriana to fend for herself in a foreign city, where she didn't know its language or its customs. Despite Illyana's perceived deep coffers, the money had run out within a few months.

Adriana was reduced to scavenging on the streets.

She had not been this alone since losing contact with her parents and sister back in 1789 before Illyana had found her. She was a girl just turned twenty who had lived an otherwise sheltered life in the palaces of Versailles and Hofburg. Adriana had no concept of how to fend for herself in such conditions.

Somehow, she had survived.

Could she do so again?

"Why am I here?" she demanded of the space around her, unsure if she should expect an answer.

"This is where the legend of Adriana Dupré began," the now all too familiar thundering voice of the *kake-guie* answered.

Adriana did not respond. She forced herself to her feet and proceeded down the filthy alley, headed toward the lit street beyond. She planned on ignoring the guide.

Unfortunately, she could not.

"Your royal blood allowed passage into the finest chateaus and palaces throughout Europe," the *kake-guie* intoned. "Yet you found yourself here."

"I survived," Adriana muttered. She continued toward the intersection and the lamp, but with each step, they seemed to move further away from her.

"And for what purpose?" the *kake-guie* continued. "To become a butcher of your own blood? How many have you murdered for no reason other than to sate your lust for violence?"

Adriana stopped. "What I did with my life should have no bearing on saving this boy!"

Finally silence from the *kake-guie*.

At first, its lack of rebuttal pleased Adriana. However, the absence of the spirit guide only meant she now had to fend for herself.

Again.

Adriana looked to the streetlamp. Impossibly, it had come no closer despite her walk. Turning, she looked back to the darkness of the alley.

Return to the moment that made you. Once you find yourself, you will find the answers you seek.

Adriana turned from the comfort of the streetlamp and ventured into the isolated alley. Suddenly, a sharp pain gripped her stomach, forcing Adriana to bend over. She recognized the pain as one of hunger. Unlike the hunger for blood that drove the demon within her to frenzy, this hunger weakened her.

Adriana's stomach tightened to the point of physical pain.

Stricken by the weakness and hunger, Adriana stumbled toward the side of one of the buildings. She just managed to extend her arm to the wall, steadying herself before she fell. Breathing came in short gasps; her heart raced, blood thundered in her head.

Wait.

Breathing? A beating heart? Hunger for food?

A vampire did not need such things.

Searching within herself, Adriana expected to hear the demon calling to her. Instead, she heard...

Silence.

She tried to pull the shadows in around her and extend her fang-like canine teeth.

Both attempts failed.

Adriana accepted the only possibility. Her hunger now was not for the sustenance of a vampire, but the sustenance of a human being. Somehow, someway, she was no longer a vampire.

The *ekeraa* had turned her into a mortal, just as she had been in St. Petersburg hundreds of years ago.

Sahlu Tigray had said she must go back to the moment that made her and confront the demon that haunts her.

Adriana now understood.

This was one of the last nights she had been mortal. This was the night she made a fateful decision, took a fateful action.

Fighting her mortal body's fatigue, Adriana continued down the alley, her hand pressed to the wall, steadying her. She had no blood vision, no heightened sense of hearing or smell to aid her through the darkness and, ultimately, to safe passage.

Adriana tripped over a pile of debris, stumbling away from the wall and onto the wood tiled street. Something dislodged from the debris rolled away from her, across the street and through a sliver of moonlight. In that light, Adriana caught a glimpse of the object.

Her eyes widened, her stomach knotted. Desperate, Adriana crawled as quickly as she could toward the object, scraping her arms and knees and further tearing what remained of her dress.

Capturing the item, she held it up to the light to confirm her earlier vision.

Adriana held a single, untarnished peach.

Famished, she moved to devour it.

A kick to her shoulder knocked her back onto the street. Her prized peach fell from her grasp, its skin untouched by her teeth. Scrambling, she searched for the peach, finally seeing it. The peach had rolled to a stop at the feet of a man in ragged shoes.

Adriana's gaze crawled up the man's thin, bowed legs, but she could only make out a silhouette with the pale light of the unseen moon behind him. Yet Adriana recognized the thin frame. She imagined the leathery skin and the jagged-toothed sneer that hung in the darkness beneath eyes searing with spite.

Though she did not know him back then, Adriana knew now and would forever remember this man — Yarok.

He muttered something in Russian as he reached down for the peach. A French émigré, Adriana had no idea what he had said, but she knew one thing: that fruit belonged to her. She told Yarok as much, but the language barrier prevented understanding.

She suspected that, although he didn't understand her words, he would understand her intent.

Yarok replied with mocking laughter.

Adriana had learned a small amount of the Russian language from Illyana. She tried what she knew. It drew only more laughter. Yarok then did the unthinkable —

He bit down into the peach.

A rage worthy of the demon she'd lost welled inside Adriana.

Measure Twenty — Confronting the Demon

The slop and slurp of Yarok's mouth around his first bite of peach thundered in Adriana's ears. Despair tightened like a fist upon her rapidly beating heart. She cried out in a flurry of French, none of it anything she would say in her parents' parlor. Her eyes locked on the peach, which Yarok crammed greedily into his mouth.

Adriana leaped to her feet, charging the peach-eating man.

Yarok easily stepped aside, giving Adriana a little shove as she passed.

She instinctively thrust her arms forward, preparing to break her fall. Her right hand landed on a broken bottle, the glass piercing her palm. She ignored the pain even as blood dripped from the wound. Her attention returned to what remained of the peach.

Yarok chomped away merrily. It seemed as if more of the peach flew from his ravaging mouth than went into his stomach. Adriana charged him again. He threw up a hand and shoved her aside. She crashed into another pile of debris.

The peach thief never stopped sucking and nibbling, gnawing the peach down to the craggy seed in its center. He turned away from Adriana as she pulled herself out of the debris. Yarok carelessly threw the pit over his shoulder.

It bounced once, twice, and landed in front of Adriana, who by now had struggled to all fours.

Something ignited within the girl. Familiar feelings rose like flames within her. They pushed aside the hunger and despair. They embraced her, warmed her. They urged her to pick up the broken bottle lying just a few feet from her bloodied hand.

Adriana slowly crawled back to the shattered bottle. She stood, the bottle's unbroken neck gripped tightly in her bleeding fist. Adriana raised the bottle, ready to drive it into Yarok's back —

In that instant, Adriana caught a glimpse of a warped reflection in the bottle. It appeared as what she could only describe as a monster standing down the alley behind her. She turned toward the source of the reflection.

A girl stood a few yards down the alley. She was younger than Adriana, with a lean, athletic body. The leering smile of her blood red lips set against her inhumanly pale face marred her beauty.

"Don't stop on my account," the girl said in exquisite French while playing with a lock of her flowing amber hair. Though she had the face of a teen, her voice sounded like that of a younger child. "This is my favorite part."

Adriana stared at the girl. She slowly lowered the fractured bottle. "I know you," she said, though unable to place the girl in her memories.

Suddenly, Adriana gripped her head as if assaulted with an intolerable headache. She endured it. A sea of memories assaulted her, their focus the girl before her. The memories dragged Adriana back to her mortal life, back to the palace at Versailles in 1786.

In that memory, she sat with Dominique for a portrait painting in the garden. Domi was restless. She ran off to meet…

This girl.

Adriana remembered the girl as the teenaged daughter of her father's American business partner. The girl had what Adriana saw as an obsession with Dominique. Adriana's parents dismissed her concern, claiming it born of jealousy; while Adriana studied music in Vienna with Mozart, the girl filled the void left by the older sister.

Adriana fell to her knees as more memories of her sister hammered her psyche.

In those memories, the image of Dominique transformed from the innocent eight-year-old Adriana had left in Versailles to the vengeful twenty-one-year-old who had stabbed her in Orléans.

Orléans.

The girl in the alley had been in Orléans and Versailles. She had corrupted Dominique, just as she had corrupted Adriana. She now recognized the girl as the Mistress of the Daughters of Lilith.

"Cytheria," Adriana spat, hatred coloring the name.

She freed herself from her memories, looking at Cytheria with more than a glint of murderous intent. "You manipulated me. Even here. Even now."

The girl, Cytheria, broadened her smile as if she were about to laugh. "Wrong, little nightingale," she cooed. "This moment belongs to you and you alone. You chose to kill Yarok in a violent act born of the rage you know oh so well. You chose the life of violence that followed.

"The only thing I did?" Here Cytheria's smile eroded to a harsh snarl. She titled her head down, drawing the shadows about her. Now all Adriana could see was a hint of fang and the girl's pale green eyes. "All I did was wait."

Adriana felt a sharp pain in her hand. Looking down, she realized she had unconsciously tightened her grip on the bottle's neck. It had shattered in her hand, cutting her skin, which in turn shed more blood. Looking at her wound, then the fallen glass, Adriana realized how simple, how ordinary the glass was.

It was instrumental in this life-altering moment.

Adriana screamed, releasing the tension building inside her. She slumped down to all fours, her arms shaking, barely able to keep her upper body off the rugged cobblestones. Blood oozed from her hand, mixing with the grime of the street.

Behind her, feet scraped across the wooden street tiles.

"Do not waste what precious little breath is left you."

Yarok spoke the words, this time in Adriana's native French. He wanted her to understand. The words resonated within Adriana. She had spoken those words to every soul Adriana the assassin had condemned to death. She had not realized she stole the words from the evil that had destroyed Adriana, the nightingale.

No.

She'd stolen the words from the evil that had brought out the evil within herself.

With those words, she had spread the evil born in this alley.

Adriana now understood how this was the birthplace of the Adriana Dupré of legend, how this was the moment that made her.

Both Denson, her garou kin, and Cytheria, the woman who had helped destroy the Dupré sisters, were correct. Adriana had chosen this life of violence.

Makeda had also been correct.

Adriana could choose to free herself from that life of violence. She would have to make that choice here, now.

Do not waste what precious little breath is left you.

From behind her, Yarok maintained his spiteful taunts. "What're ya gonna do with that glass, *mon chéri?*" His pronunciation of the

French term of endearment was as pitiful as his use of it was inappropriate. "You gonna stick ol' Yarok?"

Adriana looked over her shoulder at Yarok. Her expression was the mask of rage she would wear from this point forward if she let history repeat itself, if she murdered this man in cold blood over nothing more than a peach.

Yarok's cocksure expression morphed into one of fear as Adriana picked up a shard of glass and threw it.

Surprise overcame Cytheria as the glass lodged in her forehead. That surprise gave way to anger as a trail of blood cut through the symmetry of her otherwise perfect facial features.

"That wasn't very nice," Cytheria said.

"You deserve worse," Adriana said. "But that is not who I am. Not anymore."

Cytheria grunted in disgust. Her image dissolved into a dark silhouette that fell away in splintering slivers of darkness until nothing remained.

Adriana turned back to Yarok.

He watched her with trepidation. Slowly, Adriana stood and stalked toward him, stopping so closely in front of him that she could detect the sweet aroma of the peach on his breath. She looked up to the taller man, her eyes meeting his.

"You should go," she said with the patience of an animal trainer holding back a fierce beast.

Yarok looked at Adriana for a long moment. Then he turned and walked toward the lighted end of the alley, stopping more than once to glance over his shoulder at her.

As he arrived at the intersection with the street, he too turned into a silhouette and splintered, disappearing piece by piece.

Adriana took a deep breath. She slumped to her knees and gave into the sobs that wracked her body. Tears came next. When they fell, they were not the drops of blood from a vampire, but the salt water tears of a human.

"Very good, Adriana Dupré," said the stentorian voice of the *kake-guie*.

Adriana looked around her. To her surprise, she stood in the *ekeraa* version of the village. But now, the village was bathed in sunlight. Adriana's gaze went to her hands, then her hands to her face. Despite the sun, her skin did not burn.

It was the first sunlight Adriana had seen without danger in over two hundred years. It warmed her, made her feel comfortable.

Adriana then realized she now wore her assassin's outfit, but it was in pristine condition. Her hand, once bloodied by the broken glass, had healed. Her *Fukushuu* blades were in the scabbards on her back. She regretted that. They were the tools of murder and revenge; she no longer held either in her heart.

Something fell against Adriana's leg. She looked down to see a young boy in a fetal position. He shook violently. Adriana assumed this was the boy she sought, Tekle. She knelt down to him, placing a hand on his shoulder. The boy reacted to the touch but did not otherwise acknowledge Adriana's presence.

"I will take you home," Adriana whispered.

"Before you choose to leave, Adriana Dupré, know this," the formless *kake-guie* began. "As a creature dead and with the path of redemption ahead, you are welcome to take your rightful place here in the *ekeraa*."

Adriana considered this.

She had wanted death. Now she had it. And yet, she felt her life was not finished. Not yet.

Adriana helped Tekle to his feet, moving one of his arms over her shoulder and placing her arm around his waist to hold him up. "How do I leave this place?"

Though she could not see the *kake-guie*, Adriana felt his eyes upon her. "You have impressed me, Adriana Dupré," he finally admitted. "You are well suited for the role you must play within the Shadowdance. However, I leave you with a final warning.

"When you leave the *ekeraa*, the demon that makes you a vampire will haunt you. It will find you. It will do its best to ensure your total damnation."

This last did not faze Adriana. "Have you anything else?"

"Until the demon finds you, you will retain your two hundred and thirty-nine years of knowledge, but your mortal form will be that of the nightingale you are now, with no supernatural abilities."

Again, Adriana considered the *kake-guie*'s words. Unconsciously, her hand returned to the medallion about her neck. The words she spoke next had come from the Knight Gabriella, who had spoken them back in Grunewald when Adriana had used dark magic to depower the Knights.

Then, Adriana did not comprehend the meaning of the words. She said the words now with total understanding.

"Battling adversity without one's powers is the true sign of faith, a true sign of strength. Is it not?"

Strathan slowly woke from the magically induced sleep the black bitch had used to shut him up. He remained embedded in the wall; at least it gave him a good view of the area.

The boxer and all the other primitives had left. The three Knights sat in a meditation circle in the center of the lowered circle. Lost in their trance, they were oblivious to him. They probably figured that even if he woke up, the drain on his powers and his position on the wall would be enough to neuter him.

Unfortunately for the Knights, Strathan was a rather virile opponent. At least, that virility had gained him several allies, one in particular that would come in very handy.

"You owe me, Dwyer," a female voice with a pronounced Spanish accent said.

Strathan looked to the entrance of the *galma*. There he saw the form of a woman. To him, though, she was an absolute angel. In reality, she was a devil of a vampire in the form of Valentina Lorena.

Strathan had made two phone calls the day he had invaded this sanctuary: first to the Ethiopian government, the second to the pop diva. During the call to Val, he had explained how to open the dimensional portal through Hell, where to meet him and a particular item to bring with her.

Knowing her curiosity for supernatural knowledge, he figured she'd hook him up.

He figured right.

The trip through Hell had done a number on Valentina's hair; frizzy curls swirled around her face and shoulders. As she entered the *galma*, she pulled it all back, struggling to get her once again dark mane into a ponytail.

The basic hairstyle clashed with the postmodern and revealing wardrobe Strathan recognized from their trip to Milan last month.

"You gonna have trouble walking into a holy place?" Strathan asked.

Valentina waved a dismissive hand. "That crap? Just a state of mind affecting the weak or the guilty. But your little trip through Hell? Vampires don't like heat and flames. And you made me do it twice."

She stopped some distance from Strathan, tilting her head to one side and glaring at him. A wisp of hair fell across her face, cutting into her veil of anger. She brushed it aside, still maintaining her indignant stance.

"I had better get those shards," she said.

"Aw, I do appreciate ya going through Hell for me," Strathan replied. "Twice."

To avoid Strathan's silly grin, she turned her attention to the Knights.

"What about those three?" she asked.

"Leave 'em," Strathan said. From her expression, he could tell that wasn't the answer she wanted to hear.

"The faith-holy thing may not bug ya, lass, but the depowering evil will. We'd get one, maybe two of the gooders, but the third'd put us out faster than a couple shots o' my uncle's home brew whiskey."

"Then how is your spell going to work if —"

"It'll work if ya do it quick." Valentina stared at him blankly until Strathan added, "Like now, love."

"Remember, you owe me," she said as she reached into her Louis Vuitton purse and pulled out her iPhone.

"And I won't even treat ya like a scabber when ya ask," he said. Valentina looked at him with a raised eyebrow. Strathan clarified, "Within reason, o' course."

Valentina swiped a finger across the touchscreen on her phone. Strathan cast a glance at the Knights. They were still busy doing whatever it was they were doing and oblivious to him and Val.

"Okay," Valentina announced.

Strathan's eyes quickly turned back to her.

With another flip of her hair to keep it from in front of her face, Valentina held the iPhone in front of her and read aloud words in an ancient tongue. When she finished, she looked to Strathan.

His position remained unchanged.

"I never was good with arcane languages," Valentina said with all the concern of a fox for a hen.

"Well, why didn't you get the pronunciations from one of the wiz kids?" Strathan blasted at the vampire.

Valentina responded with a glare and a twitch of her neck. "I did!" Her glare evaporated as quickly as it had appeared, giving way to the shy eyes of embarrassment. "Not like I wrote it down phonetically."

"Oh for feck's sake!" Strathan exclaimed.

Angered, he tugged at his stone restraints.

Something shifted.

Strathan looked to his restraints. Another tug.

He felt the stone closest to his arm give. Closing his eyes, Strathan summoned whatever darkness the *galma* would allow him. The act complete, Strathan gave a final strong pull with both arms and legs.

The stone holding him became fluid. It lost its grip. Gravity did the rest, bringing Strathan unceremoniously to the ground.

Valentina stood over Strathan. She paid more attention to returning her phone to her purse than to Strathan's discomfort. "So you'll do anything for me now?"

Strathan pressed himself up to a standing position. He did his best to shake the dust from his Armani suit which, despite the effort, was ruined now. "Can we discuss that later, love?" he said.

Valentina licked her glossy red lips and went from sultry to pouty in an instant. Strathan loved both looks on her, but he knew this performance was a prelude to a demand he'd have to honor unless he wanted to face the vampire's ample wrath.

"I want the shards," Valentina demanded, digging a perfectly manicured nail into his chest as she spoke.

Strathan took Valentina's chin in his hand and leaned down to kiss the shorter woman's forehead. "They're going to Thorne so he can get me outta the Shawshank that's the Order of Haroth."

Valentina opened her mouth to protest. Strathan put a finger to her lips, silencing her. "But I'll be sure to find where he goes so you can snag 'em after. Best I can do."

A smile crept onto Valentina's lips. She ran her tongue along his finger, pulling it into her mouth. She wrapped her lips around it, gently sucking on the finger. Her eyes never left Strathan's.

Valentina slowly pulled back, releasing Strathan's finger. She then looked over her shoulder at the Knights. "Last chance," she said while snuggling up to Strathan, pulling his arm around her waist.

A playful lust filled her eye. "I've never defiled a holy place with the blood of the righteous."

"I spent the last of my power getting off that wall. And I may need the goodie goods later if Dupré comes back all grrr! Argghh!" Strathan kissed Valentina quickly. "Now ya need to pull a legger."

Valentina played with the collar of Strathan's dust-covered shirt. "Why should you have all the fun?"

Strathan gently pushed Valentina away from him, turned her around and playfully spanked her, nudging her toward the exit. "Your time's coming."

Valentina hit Strathan with a glance that would seduce the Pope.

"I'll be waiting, lover."

"Then again," the sorcerer thought aloud, "I can think of another way we can defile this place before ya go."

Measure Twenty-One — Use Your Illusion

Not all acts of cruelty are a result of the Shadowdance or the Initiated.

In June and November of 2005, Ethiopian government police violently clashed with protesters of that year's May election. In the process, the government's forces killed 193 protesters — civilians who merely spoke out against what they felt was a corrupt government and its bogus election.

Calls of government abuse were not a one-time incident.

Meanwhile, in 2009 the government banned their main opposition, the Oromian Liberation Front (OLF), as a terrorist group with links to al-Qaeda.

The accusation had little to no evidence to support it. In October of 2013, Human Rights Watch issued a press release claiming acts of torture committed against anti-government rebels at the Maekelawi Police Station.

It thus made sense that when an Irishman claiming to be an American military advisor called the Ethiopian National Defense Force (ENDF) with information on a possible OLF terrorist base, the ENDF scrambled a team to investigate.

Standard protocol was to wait for American surveillance drones from the Arba Minch airport to confirm the information. However, the Irish advisor created a sense of urgency by describing the location as the launch pad for an imminent al-Qaeda-supported dirty bomb attack.

This information was enough to urge the ENDF to defy protocol and immediately deploy a military detachment to eliminate the terrorist camp.

Bathed in the light of the moon, five M113 armored personnel carriers barreled through an area of grassland that appeared as if it had remained uninhabited for centuries.

The tall strands went on seemingly forever up the side of Mount Batu, giving the commander in the lead vehicle the impression that they were on a wild goose chase — or heading into a trap.

Then his vehicle slammed into several juniper trees that suddenly materialized from nothing.

The commander ordered his convoy to an immediate halt, then issued two men to exit the vehicle and inspect the damage. Meanwhile, the commander checked with his navigator.

The GPS coordinates given by the Irish advisor had led them through land that their maps and surveillance data showed as nothing but endless grassland like the area the convoy had previously traversed.

The men outside reported back that the vehicle had taken minimal damage, nothing that would stop the convoy. The commander stepped out of the vehicle to assess the damage personally. He also wanted to get a better look at the road ahead.

His vehicles could cleave a path through the trees, but he worried over what other surprises lay ahead.

The commander's second informed him of whisperings of magic among the men. Ethiopians were a superstitious lot, and these trees did appear from thin air.

The commander immediately took to the radio and barked stern words against such worries, though he admitted to himself that something had to explain the sudden appearance of an entire forest.

He discarded such thoughts, focusing instead on the very real possibility of thousands of his fellow Ethiopians dying horrible deaths from radioactive waste and explosions if they did not stop this potential dirty bomb.

Returning to his vehicle, the commander ordered the mission to continue.

Minutes later, the juniper forest yielded to a volcanic plane, upon which the terrorists' wooden huts lay. The village appeared tranquil in the dead of night; no one moved about and only the light of the moon illuminated the area.

The rumble of the convoy destroyed that tranquility and would surely alert the terrorists within.

That was acceptable, even desired. Like the American military the Ethiopians so revered, the powerful engines of the Ethiopian war machine should and would instill fear. They would use brute force to decimate their enemies.

Three carriers continued down the main path through the carnage. One of the carriers stopped in the middle of the village. Its rear compartments lowered in a strain of hydraulics.

Eleven Ethiopian soldiers wearing body armor and brandishing AK-47 assault rifles deployed from the rear of the carrier. They maneuvered in practiced patterns, intent upon bringing the fight to the terrorists man to man.

The two other carriers continued to the far side of the main road, cutting off the exit. Again, soldiers deployed.

Back at the village's entrance, the rear two carriers stopped and deployed their troops.

Soldiers manned the fifty caliber machine guns mounted on the top of the M113 carriers. They fired upon the huts' roofs. Wood and grass splintered in a volley of heated lead. Anyone inside would surely flee the carnage.

Curiously, no one did.

At the far end of the village, the Ethiopian commander stepped from his carrier and acknowledged his pride in his soldiers' efficiency. They had taken all of a few minutes to execute the raid and assume control of the village. One thought struck him —he had not seen a single point of resistance.

For that matter, there was no one in the village, terrorist or otherwise.

The commander reached for his radio. Panicked chatter met his ear. He listened for a moment, straining to decipher the radio's cacophony over the gunfire and... he couldn't quite make out the noise, but it sounded like the thunder of... hooves.

He returned his radio to its holster, drew his binoculars and aimed them at the village entrance.

Two explosions seared the commander's eyes.

He tore the binoculars away, his free hand rubbing the blindness from his eyes. As he recovered, the impossible sounds he had heard over the radio met his ears unaided.

Finally looking up, he saw something his brain did not want to believe.

A crash of rhinos rammed the M113 at the village center, hurling the metal hulk aside like the commander would swat an annoying fly. As the carrier overturned, an explosion tore it apart, transforming it into a burning metal husk. The rhinos continued their stampede through the village, scattering soldiers amongst the toppling huts.

Soldiers fired at the animals. The attacks merely angered the behemoths and did nothing to stem their charge. More rhinos added to the crash faster than bullets could slow the ones ahead of them.

Fear consuming him to his core, the commander reached for his radio. His shaking hands barely kept their grip on it as he ordered his men to regroup on the mountainside of the village. He then raced back to his carrier and leaped inside the rear. Without waiting for his soldiers, he smacked the controls that closed the rear compartment.

As the rear panel closed, panicked soldiers hurled themselves within its jaw, some barely making it inside the carrier. The commander moved to the front of the carrier and ordered the drivers to get moving. The carrier, barely full with its contingent of soldiers, lurched forward.

The remaining carrier followed. Soldiers on foot dove atop the two carriers, holding on for all they were worth.

The rhinos fell into pursuit. Speeding beyond the edge of the village, the commander saw no signs of the rhinoceros' stampede slowing. They continued to come from all directions. It was as if...

Yes.

The rhinos were herding the soldiers out of the village and toward the mountain. No rational explanation existed for this; even if the terrorists were hiding in the mountains and preparing an ambush, they could not control beasts in this manner, unless if by some... magic...

Another thought occurred to the commander — rhinos weren't even native to this part of the country anymore.

Native or no, controllable or no, the commander had seen firsthand what the rhinos could do. The commander hammered his driver with the binoculars he'd failed to put away while ordering faster movement toward the mountain, hoping to find safety in the same place he suspected the terrorists were hiding.

Unfortunately, the commander's path of escape ran out.

The carrier driver screamed while pointing out the viewport ahead. This moment marked the second time that night the commander failed to believe what his eyes showed him —

A cliff.

In a panic, the driver stomped his brake pedal as if trying to push it through the floorboard. This would have saved the carrier from the long fall over the cliff, had the carrier behind him also seen the hazard and reacted in kind.

Unfortunately, the lead carrier blocked the view of the other.

The commander's carrier skidded along the volcanic rock and toward the edge of the cliff. The carrier behind it failed to stop, ramming it from behind. Both carriers and men flew in all directions, headed for the same landing in the waters hundreds of feet below.

"Thank-yous are welcome, but kisses work so much better!"

Freeman beamed as he came out of the trance required for the implementation of his master plan.

Gabriella came out of the trance seconds after Freeman. "I admit I had my reservations," she said.

He feigned shock. "You doubted me?" Freeman dropped the act, admitting, "Well, I had my doubts too."

"So now we just assist the *täkälakay* with the cleanup and —" Gabriella began, but then she caught a glimpse of Makeda. The woman had exited the trance, not to excitement but frustration. She stared at the area behind the altar.

"What's up, boss?" Freeman asked without looking at the wall. "We just saved our part of the world, and you look like your cat went missing."

"Our cat has gone missing," Makeda replied, hoping there wasn't too much edge to her voice.

Her discipuli's eyes immediately went to the spot on the wall where Strathan had once hung.

He was no longer there.

"This just keeps getting better and better," Freeman lamented.

Gabriella moved to the scene of Strathan's escape. She picked up some of the fallen stone from the wall, examined it. Though it was solid, it looked as if it had poured itself from the wall and splatted upon the ground.

Freeman moved to her side. "See anything interesting?" he asked.

"The stone was weakened before it was broken," Gabriella said.

Freeman glanced at the altar. Something there caught his eye. He moved closer to investigate.

"Dark magic doesn't work in here," Gabriella said.

"It does for a short time before it is dampened," Makeda corrected.

"I think I know who helped him out," Freeman said.

"Who?" Gabriella asked.

"Well I can't say who exactly, but I can unequivocally say she's got a great ass print."

Makeda's expression immediately turned to one of disgust. Gabriella became confused.

"What in the world are you —" she began. Then she caught Makeda's expression. "Wait. You mean…"

Gabriella looked to Freeman. His expression clued her in to the truth. "That's disgusting!" she yelled.

"That's so Dwyer Strathan," Freeman said. "The tabloids said there was this one time in Rome when he —"

Ignoring Freeman, Gabriella turned to Makeda. Approaching her praetor, she asked, "If Strathan had an accomplice in here, why didn't they kill us when they had the chance?"

"The accomplice used their power on the releasing spell," Makeda speculated. "In that weakened state, we would have defeated them."

"So Strathan has a partner here and they're probably waiting outside where their powers work so they can kill us."

Makeda nodded.

Freeman joined his fellow Knights. "This isn't going to be pretty, is it?"

"For Strathan?" Makeda asked. Her eyes narrowed in determination. "No."

Strathan had to admit that shagging Valentina on the altar of a holy place proved quite the thrill. Luckily, the Knights' meditation vigil had continued long enough for them to finish. Getting literally caught with your pants down by the enemy was the very definition of awkward.

His lust sated for the moment, Strathan walked out to the plateau with Valentina. There, he opened the portal to the Hell dimension. It felt good, the rush of power he'd missed while inside the sanctuary. He sent Val on her way and waited for the Knights.

Strathan took a long, deep breath. He immediately began coughing. He mumbled some curse against the clean mountain air. Reaching into the pocket of his ruined pants, Strathan pulled out his platinum cigarette case.

With expert precision, he clicked it open and used his thumb to kick up a single cigarette far enough for him to pull it free with his lips.

He snapped the fingers of his other hand and smiled as his thumb ignited with a muddy, red-colored flame. He used the flame to light the cigarette, inhaling deeply.

Strathan burned a good ash while shaking his thumb to extinguish the flame. He closed the cigarette case and returned it to his pocket.

After a few moments, Strathan took the cigarette from his mouth and allowed himself a beaming smile he usually reserved for post coitus.

After taking in a few more deep drags, he felt the nicotine kick in and muttered, "Now that's a pleasant feel in the ol' lungs."

While enjoying his cig, Strathan glanced at the trail of volcanic rock that ran up the side of the mountain to the plateau on which he stood. Despite the roar of the waterfall coming from overhead and beyond, Strathan could hear something that sounded like a motorcade, accompanied by something damn near to those old Wilhelm yells you heard when people fall in Hollywood movies.

Strathan walked to the edge of the plateau and leaned over the guard wall. Looking down to the lake below, he spied what appeared to be army clods splashing around like lemmings in the lake. Some managed to swim; some flailed as if drowning. Two armored vehicles had collided and crashed down as well.

Looking to the edge of the cliff that overlooked the lake revealed a series of deep tread marks marring the ground.

Wait, Strathan thought. *I don't remember any cliff.*

The instigators of the clown car pile-up in the lake were back in what was left of the cliff's surrounding underbrush. A crash of rhinos — easily two score of them — had torn a swath through the underbrush leading to the lake.

Strathan could only guess the army clods had met the rhinos at the village and ran away like little virgin girls scared of prom night sex. The crash now stood grazing, the military men forgotten.

That ain't right either, he thought.

Strathan made his way down the trail, which ended on the cliff near the wreckage of the tank-like vehicle. He looked to the tank, then back to the men in the water.

Closing his eyes, Strathan wiped his hand across them from top to bottom. Sparks of muddy red flame passed before his eyelids.

They disappeared as he lowered his hand.

When he opened his eyes again, the world before him shimmered like a mirage. When the world came back into focus, Strathan frowned in disgust.

The rhinos had disappeared. No cliff existed before the lake. Instead, the lake calmly splashed against the level area of volcanic rock and sand just a few yards from his position.

Meanwhile, the army clods sloshed around in water merely a few feet deep.

So this is what those meddling Knights were up to.

Strathan decided against dispelling the Knight's grand illusion for the soldiers. Uninitiated sods deserved their fate. Instead, he concentrated on how he'd deal with the Knights should they decide to feck with him.

On cue, he heard footsteps on the rock trail behind him. Not bothering to look in that direction, Strathan opted instead for another drag on his cigarette.

"Not bad, really," he complimented. "Even I almost missed it."

"I stole it from you Order of Haroth scumbags," replied a voice Strathan recognized as that snot-nosed, twenty-something Knight of Vyntari guy, Freeman.

Strathan turned. The black babe, Makeda, led the other two Knights down the trail and to a position opposite Strathan on the rocky beach.

"Least something good came out of my time with you," Freeman added.

The dark sorcerer took a long drag on his cigarette. He watched all three Knights. Makeda's fist tightened around the dagger she wore at her side. The blonde appeared to whisper something while she glared at him fiercely.

Freeman's flaming eyes behind his designer sunglasses gave him a bit of scrapper cred, but his hands shook like a man who did not want to see combat.

"I said I almost missed it," Strathan insisted while he did his best to keep the cigarette smoke in his lungs. He looked straight at Freeman. "You were in the Order, huh?"

"Until Makeda helped me see the error of my youth, yeah," Freeman replied.

"Well, maybe ya shoulda hung around, practiced a bit harder. Become a proper dark mage." Strathan took a final drag on his cigarette. Withholding the smoke, he added, "Then ya could do somethin' like this."

Strathan exhaled.

Like a dragon, flame fired from Strathan's mouth, straight at the three Knights.

Measure Twenty-Two — While You Were Away

Makeda reacted as quickly as she had back in Grunewald Forest. Her hand waved in front of her, palm open. Strathan's flame smashed against a blue field of ethereal magic projected from Makeda's hand.

The flames splayed out revealing the shield's curved form protecting all three Knights., all of whom could feel the intense heat of the Hell-inspired flames despite their magical protection.

The flames disappeared into the night's air, and the heat lasted only a few seconds before dissipating.

Then the Knights learned that Strathan had disappeared too.

"That's it?" Freeman yelled. "The Big Baddy comes up with smoke and mirrors for a cheap disappearing act?"

"I imagine that's only part of his plan," Gabriella said.

Makeda turned away from Strathan's last position to look at the Ethiopian soldiers. Her discipuli did the same. The soldiers no longer splashed about nor swam for what they had perceived as the distant shore. Instead, they looked at their surroundings as if for the first time.

Several soldiers spotted the Knights standing nearby. As they pointed at them, their conversations came in angered bursts of their Amharic language. So agitated, these soldiers gathered the attention of their brethren, all pointing at the Knights and then shouting commands to one another.

Some searched the water, presumably for their fallen weapons. Others began a strategic formation through which to engage the Knights.

"Strathan dispelled our illusion," Gabriella said.

"Not that simple," Makeda corrected. "He cast an illusion of his own." Off the questioning looks from her discipuli she explained, "I gather from their conversation those soldiers think we're a squad of OLF soldiers."

"Better and better, I tell ya," Freeman lamented. He pulled his quarterstaff from its thigh holster and extended it.

"These men came here for war," Makeda said. "We will be forced to give it to them."

Bold words, but Makeda knew the odds were heavily against them. Unlike the wretched zombies or the MKDG thugs she and Gabriella had combatted in Germany, these soldiers were Uninitiated adversaries. Casting the illusion would merely confuse the soldiers; using vulgar magic to defeat them would reveal the Shadowdance.

The Knights must rely solely on their physical skills against nearly two dozen trained soldiers.

"Draw your flames behind your sunglasses, or you will be useless to us," Makeda warned Freeman.

"But that kinda concentration takes away from what little fighting skills I have," he lamented. Nevertheless, he did as his praetor commanded.

"We can't just let Strathan run free," Gabriella said as she moved into a battle kata.

"He hasn't gone far," Makeda said. "He still wants the shard."

As Makeda drew her Ogoun dagger, she realized that no cavalry was forthcoming. Mehari and his *täkälakay* warriors had led the other Agazyans to a hidden location away from the village. There they would remain, protected, until Makeda contacted them to assure their safe return and mop up the soldiers.

There was also the matter of Adriana.

While the Knights dealt with this threat, she would return from her spirit quest only to meet Strathan, the man she had sworn to kill — the man who would undoubtedly take great pleasure in killing her.

The stone circle on the floor of the *galma* rippled then emitted its customary dark light. The *ekeraa* materialized below, but with a difference this time. Now a flight of stairs ascended toward the stone floor in the *galma*. Adriana, Tekle in tow, moved up the stairs.

Adriana rose out of the membrane that was once the stone floor and ascended the last of the *ekeraa* steps. As she crossed the membrane, her assassin's clothing transformed into a light-hued dress. The sleeves clung to her arms; its bottom skirt fluttered over her feet, a sash circled her waist. Her hair, full of bounce and shine, cascaded down past her shoulders. Her lips were full and rosy; her cheeks pink with the radiance of life.

Adriana's metamorphic return to the nightingale she was before St. Petersburg, before her life-changing choice, was complete.

Immediately after she and Tekle achieved the level of the stone floor, the *ekeraa* light and image rippled out of existence. Adriana now stood upon the normal stone surface. She gently laid Tekle down on the floor and knelt beside him.

"Do not fear, little one," she said in a sympathetic tone she remembered from her days with her sister, before the horrors of the Shadowdance. That she could recall and utilize the tone surprised her. It made a difference, seeing the world through the eyes of care and concern instead of rage and vengeance.

She then noticed something in the boy's hand — the chain attached to the Vyntari amulet. Adriana picked up the amulet, tearing it free of the chain. She stared in disgust at the object that had caused the pain of so many. The vampire threw it away from her.

Dwyer Strathan, a cigarette dangling precariously from his lips, caught it.

While looking at the amulet, he said, "'bout time you made it back."

Adriana rose to face Strathan, who stood just on the edge of the circle, his back facing the *galma* entrance. It annoyed Adriana that Strathan's concern favored the jewel and not any threat from her.

"And baby makes three," Strathan quipped. He slipped the shard into his empty pants pocket and then heard a clanking on the floor. Looking at the pocket, he realized it had a hole in it. He glanced at Adriana. She wore an annoying smirk.

Frowning, Strathan bent down and picked up the shard. He checked his other pants pocket. His cigarette case was still there — no hole. He slipped the amulet inside and turned his attention back to the vampire.

Adriana noticed Strathan looking her over as a butcher would a piece of meat. Self-conscious, she pulled up the front of her dress, covering the last bit of cleavage. Her hand brushed against her medallion. She took it in hand, looked down at it.

Remembering her sister, she gathered the emotional strength she would need to confront this bastard sorcerer.

"Nice dress," Strathan said while nodding his approval. "Very turn of the 18th century." He hopped down the few feet from the circle's edge and walked toward Adriana and Tekle. Adriana's muscles tensed in preparation for the inevitable fight.

"Gotta hand it to ya, lass. Ya really do come through in a pinch. Ya sure ya don't wanna… you know… partner up or somethin'?"

Adriana stared coldly at Strathan. He shrugged at her reaction. "Val probably couldn't stand the competition anyway."

She wanted to hit Strathan, to punch that smugly arrogant expression from his face. Had she done that, however, she would have learned nothing from her time in the *ekeraa*.

Adriana turned from Strathan and helped Tekle up, throwing his languid arm over her shoulder. She moved toward the stairs leading out of the circle and toward the *galma's* entrance.

"What? No kiss? Not even a punch or three?" Strathan called after her.

"You are less than meaningless to me."

Adriana didn't look back to see Strathan's reaction. She had learned in the *ekeraa* not to allow rage and anger to cloud her judgment. She would try not to make that mistake again.

"Seriously. We can't end it like this," Strathan practically begged. "There's supposed ta be a big fight, mano a womano, with CGI effects and shite!"

Adriana paid no heed to Strathan's taunts. She continued toward the entrance. Once outside, she would find Gabriella and get the girl to help the young boy. Then she would —

Strathan grabbed Adriana's shoulder from behind. Instinctively she reached for one of her *Fukushuu* blades. She met only air; her blades were left behind in the *ekeraa*, a reminder to leave her rage behind as well.

But she needed Strathan out of the way.

The fingers of her free hand balled into a fist. Turning to face Strathan, Adriana brought that fist around. It connected full force with Strathan's jaw. The dark sorcerer stumbled away from her, more out of shock at the sharp blow than any real pain.

So much for the nonviolent approach.

"Now that's the spirit!" Strathan said.

"This boy needs help," Adriana replied, pulling Tekle back up so she could manage him. "Let me get that for him. Then we can engage in whatever childish act of violence you desire."

Strathan's face lit up with a grin that would make Alice's Cheshire Cat jealous. Adriana immediately regretted her choice of words. Strathan stopped to think for a moment. He shook his head.

"Nah. I'm not gonna let ya banjax me moment o' climax."

Strathan moved forward and knocked Tekle out of Adriana's arms. Adriana brought her hand up to hit Strathan again, but he caught her arm in his hand. He jerked her toward him, wrapping his other arm around her waist. Strathan pinned her to his body in a lover's embrace, leaned in and kissed Adriana full on the lips.

The former vampire struggled but could not break the sorcerer's grasp. Strathan eventually broke the kiss himself. Adriana gasped and then spat in the attempt to rid herself of Strathan's filth, her anger matched by her disgust.

"Kinda takes your breath away, doesn't it?" Strathan teased. Suddenly, his expression became serious. He studied Adriana's face before saying, "Of course, a vampire's not supposed ta have breath to take away."

Adriana thrust her knee squarely into Strathan's groin.

With a guttural moan, he released Adriana and stumbled to one knee. "Oh for feck's sake!" he spat through clenched teeth, failing miserably to conceal his pain. "The best the big bad Adriana Dupré has is a kick to the yarbles?"

Adriana grabbed her skirt at thigh height and pulled it upwards. Her legs free, she lashed out with a kick. It connected with Strathan's face. He fell backward, crashing onto his back. His head smacked hard against the stone floor. A slew of expletives rained from his mouth.

She looked to the wall. "You like playing with fire, do you not?" she asked.

Strathan rolled over on all fours. The knee shot still pained him. "I'd prefer to play with a pair of diddies," he said. "Think you can manage —"

Adriana smashed a flaming torch across Strathan's head.

The dark sorcerer fell over onto his side. Flames singed the side of his head where he had been struck but quickly burnt out.

Adriana hit Strathan again. He writhed in pain, struggling to parry her blows and fight potential fires at the same time.

As she bombarded Strathan with more blows from the torch, Adriana felt herself slipping back into that abyss of hate and rage.

Perhaps it would be best to put him down now, so that he causes no more harm, she thought.

The Adriana Dupré of legend would not hesitate to do so.

The Adriana Dupré who had returned from the *ekeraa*, who had earned a second chance, now understood that the path of vengeance began with thoughts such as these, and ended in self-destruction.

Adriana stopped her assault mid-swing. Her arms shook. She suddenly dropped the torch as if its flames had lapped at her hands. She backed away from Strathan, who knotted himself into a ball at her feet. Adriana closed her eyes and inhaled, practically gulping in air to fill her lungs.

When she opened her eyes, Adriana looked to Tekle. If it were possible, she thought he looked worse than when she had dragged him from the *ekeraa*.

"That boy needs help," Adriana insisted. She looked back to Strathan. "I will waste no more time on you, sorcerer."

Again Strathan rose to all fours. Blood flowed from several blows to his head. Bruises would mar his movie star good looks. Adriana stifled her urge to smile at the justice in that.

She turned from Strathan, intending to return to the boy.

This was her first mistake of the night.

Strathan released a guttural yell born of deep-seated rage. Before Adriana could turn, he slammed into her. The two crashed to the ground, Strathan on top. He turned Adriana around so she was on her back. He raised his fist, ready to deliver a blow.

"Much trouble as you've caused me, bitch, you'll make time."

The Knights had made a good show of things, taking down half of the soldiers before a hail of automatic gunfire forced them to take cover behind the closest armored carrier. Makeda ended up behind the second one in the line. She glanced at her discipuli; they hid behind the one closer to the soldiers.

"Ain't gonna last long if we don't even the odds on those guns!" Freeman yelled over the racket of soldiers' chatter and machine gun fire.

"And I'm not getting shot twice in forty-eight hours!" Gabriella added.

Makeda lamented that they had not recharged the spell that allowed them telepathic communication. The speed of thought could make the difference in this combat. She would have to trade strategy for speed.

"Form up behind me!" Makeda commanded. "I will use my shield to protect us!"

"But if we use magic," Gabriella said, "that will break the Veil before the Uninitiated!"

"Freeman will use his magic to make my shield look like a broken piece of this tank!"

"Cuz that's so easy to do while I'm trying to see!" Freeman yelled back.

"Then stop seeing and cast the illusion!" Makeda said.

Freeman, who never liked fighting in the first place, allowed the flames about his eyes to dissipate. Then he focused his magical energy around Makeda. She manifested the blue energy that would work as a shield.

Freeman made that energy look like a large scale replica of Captain America's shield. Makeda frowned at the reference and looked to Freeman. He shrugged.

In the heat of battle, Makeda had no choice but to go with it.

Gabriella dashed from her position of hiding and dove behind Makeda. With the Irish girl at her back, Makeda moved forward.

Bullets immediately impacted the shield; indentations appeared at those junctures, but the shield held. Makeda pressed through the seeming wall of bullets and toward the soldiers.

More bullets impacted the shield. As they did, it began to warp. Makeda's magic had held against Strathan's flame, but that was but a short blast of energy.

The sustained physical assault soundly tested Makeda's mental control of her personal magic.

Still, the Knights advanced on the soldiers, walking on a path that wouldn't allow for a flanking maneuver from the soldiers.

"When in range," Makeda yelled, "move out and attack the closest soldiers!"

"Even if we take the fight to them," Gabriella said, "in their state of mind they probably won't give much care to the whole friendly fire thing!"

Makeda ignored Gabriella's warning and focused on her shield. It held, but she could feel the strain. The soldiers slowly retreated from her as she advanced; the Knights would have to run to catch even the closest soldiers.

At that point, her shield would not provide enough surface area to protect both her and Gabriella.

Then they would see if Gabriella's observation was correct.

As if hearing Makeda's thoughts, Gabriella said, "If we're to do this we should just —"

Before the Knights could act, a rain of small stones fell from the nearby treetops. The stones weren't enough to hurt, but they succeeded at their throwers' goal — to distract.

Makeda should have realized that her brother's pride would not allow him to leave the defense of his village to his sister. Instead of sticking to the plan, he had left his *täkälakay* in hiding.

The Knights' cavalry had arrived.

Reacting to the new assault, the soldiers divided their firepower between the Knights and the unseen assailants in the trees. Makeda saw an opportunity she could not miss.

"Now!" she commanded.

Gabriella ran from behind Makeda and, with speed enhanced by magic, crossed the distance between them and the closest soldiers. Using her *kamau njia* skills, she disarmed two soldiers and then engaged them in hand-to-hand combat.

Several of the *täkälakay* descended from the trees and entered the melee. Others remained in the trees, launching more stones from slingshots, picking off soldiers on the extremities of the battle or defending their brethren from enemy attacks they may not have noticed otherwise.

This time, the stones were more precise, doing real damage and taking down their targets.

It would be a difficult battle, but now the Knights had a better chance for victory.

Makeda prayed Adriana could hold out until they arrived.

Measure Twenty-Three — Victory in Death

Having returned from the *ekeraa*, Adriana was a normal mortal lacking her supernatural powers. However, she retained the very mortal fighting prowess she had learned as a vampire assassin.

As Strathan's fist came down to pummel her face, Adriana struck the elbow of the arm Strathan used to hold himself above her. This maneuver shifted the line of his shoulders, which in turn altered the trajectory of his punching fist.

The dark sorcerer yelled in pain as his fist bashed the stone next to Adriana's head.

With the sorcerer off balance, Adriana rolled the man off her. She scampered to her feet. The length of her dress made the task more difficult. Strathan was on his knees and one hand, favoring the sore hand.

"Feckin' cunt!" he yelled.

Strathan got to his feet, clutching his injured hand.

"All right! Enough of this trick-acting shite!" he yelled, quickly losing his Hollywood bad boy cool. He pointed at Adriana with his undamaged hand. "You 'n me!" Strathan now pointed to the ground in front of him. "Right here! Right feckin' now!"

Adriana slowly pulled up her skirt and used a fingernail to begin a small tear. "Let me get the boy to —"

Anger drove Strathan like a locomotive toward Adriana. In five quick steps, he was in front of her and in striking range. He lashed out with a left hook.

Adriana easily spun away and avoided the blow. At the same time, she alleviated the problem of her dress by tearing it away just above the knee.

Strathan stepped toward Adriana, this time leading with a right cross. Adriana ensnared Strathan's arm in the section of fabric she'd torn away from her dress. She pulled him forward and off balance, throwing her leg out to tangle his.

The dark sorcerer fell to the floor. Adriana whipped her torn skirt free of Strathan's arm.

"Do you really want me to continue this humiliation?" Adriana asked.

Her words only made Strathan angrier. He spied something to his side. Too late Adriana realized he was in the range of the torch she had used to batter him.

She moved forward but was too slow to stop the sorcerer. Scurrying to his feet, Strathan scooped up the torch. Adriana skidded to a halt a few yards away from him.

Strathan smiled.

He threw the torch at Adriana. Kicking out a leg, she deflected the torch away from her and out of harm's way. She then realized the torch was a distraction. Strathan charged into her, knocking her to the ground but retaining his footing.

Adriana felt Strathan's foot stomp her leg. He continued his assault by kicking her in the stomach, then across her face.

"Doesn't feel so good, does it, ya bibe?"

As a vampire, Adriana would use the blood in her system to replenish her strength, to heal any wounds that befell her. The blood would also help mask any pain she felt from her wounds.

As the mortal nightingale, she could not use her blood in such a manner. Instead, she watched as her blood splattered on the stone floor of the *galma*. Her body had never withstood such extreme punishment without immediate relief.

Adriana tired quickly, but she refused to let her rage push her through.

Strathan abruptly stopped his assault and circled Adriana like a pensive cat. "You tryin' ta let me off easy?" he yelled. "What happened to all the super speed? The flashy blades?"

Adriana forced herself to her knees and spat blood. Her breathing came in heaving gasps. "You are not worthy of my talents," she said, hoping the boldness of her words would help disguise her lack of those abilities.

"And you're not gonna win without 'em! C'mon, Dupré! Give me your all or…"

Adriana forced control of her breathing. She spared a glance at Tekle, strewn unconscious on the *galma* floor. He reminded her of her new purpose and her need to defeat the menace that stood before her. She inhaled, again controlling her breathing to contain the rage within.

That was her second mistake.

Strathan now stood directly over her. She craned her neck to look up at him. With the bruises and burns beneath his torn shirt and the cuts to his face, he looked almost as bad as she was sure she did. In his expression, Adriana observed the rage that had driven her for so long.

Seeing it directed at her was a shock that nearly took Adriana out of the moment.

Then Strathan tilted his head just a bit. The hint of a smile broke through his rage.

"When I said that kiss earlier took yer breath away, I was just feckin' 'round," Strathan said. "But it looks like it really did."

Adriana attempted to rise, but Strathan stomped on her back, forcing her down on her stomach. He kicked her onto her back and knelt beside her.

"If ya can breathe," Strathan said, "you can die."

His hands locked around Adriana's throat.

The dark sorcerer continued to speak, but his voice sounded much farther away than it should have, as if Adriana were underwater. The sensation triggered another memory within Adriana, something primordial — the sensation of drowning.

No.

The loss of sound hadn't triggered the sensation of drowning. That had a completely different cause, one that after two hundred years had become foreign to Adriana, but now became a pivotal factor in her survival.

Adriana couldn't breathe.

Instinctively, Adriana's hands clawed at Strathan's hands, his arms, anything to release the pressure from her throat, to taste the stale air of the *galma*.

She failed.

Her instinctual need to breathe supplanted every other thought. She felt it worse than her vampire need for blood. The need for air drove her into a blind frenzy.

Adriana felt herself kicking, pressing against Strathan with her hands and arms, though it felt like it was happening so far away. Sounds receded. She saw his lips move, issue a final taunting phrase.

She could not hear him.

She closed her eyes, preferring darkness to the sight of Strathan so close to her.

Adriana ravaged her mind to find one maneuver that would free her. Yet her need for air, the need to breathe so alarmed her newly mortal senses she could not think strategically.

Adriana could not think at all.

Memories of her past, of the pain she had inflicted, assaulted Adriana. Her guilt unbearable as her mind raced away from her, she opened her eyes.

Strathan met her gaze as he lay upon her at arms' length. His Cheshire Cat smile would haunt Adriana for the few moments remaining in her life.

Suddenly, the pressure on her throat lessened. Sound raced back to her ears, only to deliver the threatening voice of her attacker, her murderer.

"Adriana Dupré," Strathan declared with an air of finality, "Adieu."

A small amount of air passed her lips, found its way to her lungs.

It was a false hope.

Adriana felt a renewed pressure on her throat. The protestations of her limbs slowed. Her lungs burned within her chest. One thought pressed through her clouded mind, through the pain of memory, through the desperation of her body failing her.

This would be an honorable death…but I do not want to die.

Makeda landed a solid kick to the midsection of an Ethiopian soldier. He doubled over and splashed into the lake water. She looked around.

Freeman, his illusion-casting duties complete, had joined the battle and had dispatched another soldier. Gabriella pulled her defeated soldier out of the water and dragged him to the shore so that he would not drown.

The *täkälakay* had rounded up the other defeated yet still conscious Ethiopian soldiers near the shore.

This battle won, Makeda and her Knights' fate now resided inside the *galma*. She used her Ogoun dagger to reflect moonlight into the eyes of her discipuli. Having gained their attention, she motioned for them to follow her. Makeda moved up the stone path leading to the *galma*, her Knights close on her heels.

The *galma* sanctuary was much darker than when they had last been inside. Makeda noticed several of the torches had either been extinguished or removed from their position.

Moonlight from the opening above bathed the lowered circle so integral to the *Dalaga* ritual.

Dwyer Strathan stood just outside the circle. He held Adriana by the throat, practically waving her around like a ragdoll. The girl did not resist, did not move in any way, as if —

"Strathan!" Makeda yelled, capturing the dark sorcerer's attention.

Pure, menacing glee filled his expression.

"Remember this day!" Strathan proclaimed to the Knights, who, under the circumstances, had halted their advance. "You'll be able to say you were there when Dwyer Strathan did what nobody else in the Shadowdance could! The day Dwyer Strathan killed Adriana Dupré!"

Strathan threw Adriana to the ground as if she were so much rubbish. He then flashed his hands to the Knights.

"And I did it with my bare hands!"

"You lie!" Gabriella spat.

Freeman quickly added, "Don't worry about it, Gabby! Vampires don't breathe, so he couldn't have strangled her. Adriana's just playing possum and is about to kick Strathan's movie star butt all the way back to Hollywood."

"Yeah, vampires don't breathe," Strathan acknowledged. "But vampires who come back from the underworld as mortals do!"

Gabriella had summoned her *Spatha Perfidelis* on the way down the tunnel to the *galma* entrance. Her grip on the holy weapon's hilt tightened. "Praetor Arsi, may we beat the lies out of this man now?" she asked.

Makeda gave no answer. Her gaze fell to the floor as to avoid the questioning glances she expected from her discipuli.

"Praetor?" Gabriella asked, her voice wavering.

"I'm afraid he speaks the truth," Makeda said. "Only dead souls may enter the *ekeraa*. Only living souls may leave."

Silence befell the sanctuary as the other Knights processed this information.

Freeman turned to Makeda. "Wait a minute. If Dupré came back mortal, what happened to the demon inside her?"

Gabriella also looked to Makeda for an answer.

None came.

"Doesn't matter," Strathan interjected. He strode triumphantly toward Makeda and her Knights. "She put up a fight, good as she could without the vampire stuff. But in the end, Adriana Dupré was just another worthless skank —"

"She was trying to change!" Gabriella shouted. "She felt remorse for all the evil she'd done and was trying to make amends!"

"Pray your One Goddess takes that into consideration," Strathan countered. He now stood before the Knights and pointed to Freeman and Gabriella. "You two kids seem pretty bright. How do you work with somebody who's straight out lyin' to ya?"

Freeman looked to Strathan. "I know you're going somewhere with this. I for one don't want on that crazy train of thought."

"Seriously," Strathan continued. "Did you honestly think that crazy bitch could change her ways? And even if she did, she'd still be uncontrollable and totally untrustworthy."

The Knights gave no reaction.

Strathan looked behind him at Adriana's corpse. "But I guess that's what made her a legend." Turning back to the Knights, he added with a smile, "Past tense, of course."

Gabriella moved to attack Strathan with her *Spatha*. Makeda extended an arm, blocking the junior Knight's advance. She did not make eye contact with her *discipulus*.

"If you've got a point, Strathan, you'd better make it quick," Freeman said. "Makeda can't hold Gabby back forever, and you're kinda impotent here."

Strathan broke into a smile. "That's not what Valentina said —"

Freeman threw up his hands. "Stop! Don't need that mental image!"

"What do you want?" Gabriella yelled.

The dark sorcerer dropped the teasing banter for a straight out accusatory tone backed with a bit of anger. Pointing a finger at Makeda, he said, "Your boss here led you on a fool's crusade to save a vampire. And you failed! In the process, you gave me and those the Shadowdance calls evil the shards, the advantage we need to wipe you goody two-shoes Knights off the playing field!

"Without anything to show for yourselves, just how long do you think your bosses are gonna let the three of you exist?"

The Knights stood in silence. Strathan ran his fingers through his hair, then turned his back on them. He suddenly threw up a hand as if remembering something. When he turned back to the Knights, his mocking mood had returned.

"And I almost forgot the best part! Makeda didn't even give you two Muppets the big picture!"

"You've done enough here," Makeda warned.

"No, Makeda," Strathan said. "This one is all you. I mean, if you had told your kids that you sent me the first shard…"

Here Strathan paused long enough to see the younger Knights' dumbfounded expressions.

"Then you suggested using Adriana to find the others," he continued. "Hell, if they or your Knight leaders had known your real plan, they'd have shut you down at the start!"

Makeda's gaze remained on Strathan. She felt the stares from her discipuli, but could not bear to return them now. She knew they would learn the truth of her crusade one day, but she didn't want it to be this way, not from the villain with whom she had made what she had hoped would remain an anonymous alliance.

Not when she was so close to success.

Strathan moved right up to Makeda. "You've lied to and manipulated your fellow Knights, your tribe of primitives and Adriana, all for your selfish little plan. Way I see it…" Strathan ran a finger gently down the side of Makeda's face, "you're not that far from being a force of evil yourself."

Makeda stared hard at Strathan. The man smiled, pleased with himself. Makeda longed to knock that smile off his Hollywood famous leading-man face, but she knew this was not the time.

Strathan stepped around Makeda and her Knights and headed toward the exit.

Gabriella stormed after Strathan, but Freeman caught her arm. She turned on him, anger bleeding from her in waves. "Let the bastard go," Freeman suggested, his first words since Strathan's accusation against Makeda. "We're not the ones who should get to bring his sorry butt to justice anyway."

Strathan looked over his shoulder and laughed at the Knights. He turned back to the entrance and left.

Makeda dodged the watchful eyes of her discipuli and checked on Tekle, who lay in a heap near the stone circle. Despite his hardship, he appeared intact. On the ground near his hand, Makeda saw the thin silver chain that once attached to the last Vyntari shard.

Makeda allowed herself a smile.

She now turned to address her discipuli. Gabriella had moved to Adriana, placing the girl's upper body in her lap. Gabriella spoke her healing prayer to the One Goddess. At its completion, ethereal flames engulfed her hands.

"Leave her, Gabriella," Makeda instructed, approaching her discipulus.

"No," Gabriella said with uncharacteristic defiance. It barely obscured the hurt in the girl's expression, the waver of uncertainty in her tone. "I can save her! The One Goddess let her return from the *ekeraa* for a reason!"

Freeman kneeled beside Gabriella. "It's not necessary," he said.

"What do you mean it's —"

Freeman gently took Gabriella's flaming hand in his. He looked her in the eye. From Makeda's position, still approaching her discipuli, she could see a resolve in Freeman's expression hinting at some hidden knowledge.

He understood.

"Have faith, Gabriella," Freeman said with a smile.

The Irish Knight held her healing hand at the ready, her eyes turning from Freeman to lock on Adriana's lifeless form. Something in Freeman's demeanor must have gotten to the girl.

She silently dispelled the ethereal flames and used the same hand to stroke Adriana's hair much as a mother would a sleeping child.

"After all she's been through, all she tried to accomplish," Gabriella murmured.

Makeda met her discipuli. "For too long I have kept you both misinformed," she said. "Yet you remained faithful to me, going so far as to believe in the possibility of the redemption of even Adriana Dupré."

"You got a lot of 'splainin' ta do, Lucy," Freeman cut in with a faux Cuban accent. "To us, and especially the *Concilium*. And redemption or no," he continued while looking down at the former vampire, "Adriana will probably still be a pain in the ass."

"You speak of her as if…" Gabriella fell silent. She looked to Makeda. "What is it you're not telling me?"

"You might want to let her go and get out of the way," Freeman suggested.

The blonde Knight looked to Freeman as if the man had just spoken gibberish. She looked to Makeda, who extended a hand to assist Gabriella to her feet.

Makeda said calmly, "Adriana's story is far from over."

Measure Twenty-Four — Ghost

JUNE 2014

The Chinese-themed architecture of TCL's Chinese Theater (formerly Mann's, formerly Grauman's) contrasted with the surrounding modern architecture. That contrast made it a mainstay of the Hollywood Boulevard tourist trail since its opening in 1927.

The legendary "Walk of Fame," the sequence of foot and handprints of Hollywood's elite immortalized in the cement of the Boulevard, began at the front of the theater.

The central building was three stories high. Pagoda-style roofing topped the building, pushing it up another ninety feet. Two other buildings served as bookends to the central theater. They shared the Chinese architecture with mini pagodas erected on their fronts. They were also adorned with two spires each that reached the height of the central pagoda.

Altogether, the building looked like something a monk would live in at the top of some remote mountain location.

The marquees on the two side buildings announced the premiere of the new Michael Mann-directed cop thriller, "In Deep." One marquee displayed the rugged, macho, gun-wielding image of star Mark Wahlsen. The other featured the suave image of his co-star, bad boy Dwyer Strathan.

A red carpet ran from the theater's center set of double doors to meet the five-lane Boulevard. A single lane directly in front of the theater remained open for traffic.

At that spot, three-gun spotlights flanked either side of the wide red carpet, shining light into the heavens, so the gods knew that reel stars — Hollywood's stars — were out this evening.

The next lane over was used as a buffer between the stars and a line of police barricades.

Despite the record late June heat and the strangling level of smog, celebrity worshippers, sightseers, the curious, and the ever-present paparazzi formed a mob just beyond the police barricade. The ear-splitting screams were those of witnesses to new messiahs recently born to the Earth.

Staccato bursts of light from paparazzi cameras assaulted the celebrity demigods as they arrived in their chariot-like stretched limos. Everyone wanted a piece of them, but only red carpet reporter Lauren Kahler got them for a few brief moments before they entered the theater.

Those in the entertainment business (and some in the news end of the media) regarded reporters like Lauren as little more than parasites earning their livings feeding on the stardom of those they covered. There was some truth to that, but Lauren didn't think of herself that way.

She considered herself a journalist with credentials on the level of Lara Logan (minus the shoddy fact-checking) or Anderson Cooper. A failed relationship had brought her from New York's hard news to LA's extremism and celebrity. She landed at KTLA5 as the entertainment reporter — a glorified TV hostess and gossip columnist rolled into one.

Her network had bartered their way into the exclusive right to conduct the red carpet interviews for tonight's event. Lauren stood near the spotlights waiting for the next celebrity arrival. Her dress played a bit skimpy for the pomp of the event, but she wanted the attention. In this market, looks mattered.

As her male colleagues joked, she had a body better suited for porn than television news. Her advantage was that her parts were all natural, including the blonde hair. She kept it that way so that her guests at the mic — particularly the male ones — underestimated her.

Then her Master of Arts in Journalism from Columbia University would get her the answers she wanted.

Unfortunately, reporting events like this didn't demonstrate her true potential, but at least she was in the game. It wouldn't take long for Lauren to get the attention she felt she deserved. She'd have Anderson's job before she was thirty.

The event had started around seven when the evening sun had just begun setting, which allowed for a live feed to the network's evening entertainment show. It was almost eight thirty now; the sun had long since slipped down below the horizon, and the network had begun prime time fare. The movie was supposed to have started a half hour ago, but the evening's program was on hold awaiting the arrival of the second half of the marquee — Strathan.

Lauren had never had the displeasure of interviewing him. She'd heard campfire stories about him and his lecherous ways. That was nothing she needed.

What she did need was a story that would pull her out of the shadows of celebrities and into the spotlight. Maybe she could needle something out of Strathan, take him down a peg and get some inside scoop.

That is, if he ever showed up.

Strathan hated movie premieres.

He'd have played to his bad boy image and skipped this one, but the studio's suits, his manager, his agent, and even his damned lawyer had warned him against it. They had also warned him against messing with his co-star and creating more tabloid fodder.

Tonight they all wanted to see a united front between him and Wahlsen for the good of the movie — which, Strathan heard, was already taking a critical beating.

Strathan was never any good at taking orders. The Vyntari shards had provided the leverage he'd needed to win his independence from the wankers in the Order of Haroth.

Eliminating some of the competition on the way out the door was just icing on his freedom cake.

As for the remaining Order members, Strathan promised them he'd stay out of their business as long as they stayed out of his. He'd also still get free use of his powers which, for Strathan, was the most important part of the deal.

Camera flashes brought Strathan back from his thoughts and to the present circus surrounding him. His hand squeezed the steering wheel of his vintage Aston Martin DB4 GT Zagato.

Always one to strike against the norm, while others flocked to buy the newly minted V12 Zagato, Strathan had dug up one of the original fifty-year-old vehicles. This car wasn't one of those tired replicas, but one of the actual surviving cars from the original line of nineteen.

It took some doing, but nothing was too much for a newly independent dark sorcerer.

He couldn't resist showing it off, which is why he showed up fashionably late.

Admittedly, it would have been easier for the woman in the passenger seat to give him a blowjob if they'd been in the back of a studio-supplied limo. Strathan thought she needed a challenge.

He'd picked her up last week at a friend's pool. Fresh off the boat from the UK, she had dreams of parlaying her mid-level modeling career into acting.

He had to admit she had the ass for the casting couch. It helped that she wasn't ashamed to use it to get what she wanted. She was also pretty feckin' good between the sheets... on the counter... on the hood of a car or in the backseat.

Definitely worth keeping around for a spell.

Strathan did wish he could remember her name, though.

Whatever.

Casting a sideways glance at the woman, Strathan watched as she used the mirror on the inside of the sunshade to paint her lips with a small tube of lipstick. As he reached the end of the red carpet leading to the theater, Strathan slammed the brakes harder than necessary.

The stunt caused the girl to smear her lipstick across her overly tanned cheek.

The girl responded with a verbal curse and glare at Strathan. He shrugged. "Still getting used to the beast, babe," he quipped.

Strathan somehow managed to squelch the laughter aroused by the woman's inept attempt at a look of defiance. Far more dangerous femmes than this little girl had defied him. He had ended them with little effort and no remorse.

One femme, in particular, came to mind — Adriana Dupré.

Killing her had proved the one unadulterated joy Strathan had found in the entire Vyntari shard affair. He almost wished he hadn't killed her so he could do it all over again. In a way, Strathan owed Dupré a great deal. Her death opened the door to his emancipation.

His companion replaced her lipstick in her clutch and then withdrew a compact. Opening it, she used a makeup pad to remove the errant lipstick on the side of her face. "I can't believe you sometimes," she grumbled.

Strathan's tongue absently ran over the demon tooth in his mouth. *You shouldn't believe me*, he thought.

"Hand me a cig, babe," he said aloud.

The girl finished her makeup, put away her tools and then opened the glove compartment. She withdrew Strathan's platinum cigarette case, pulled out a cig and held it out for Strathan. He took it between his lips.

Letting one hand off the wheel, he snapped his fingers. A deep red flame ignited from his thumb. Strathan used the flame to light the cigarette.

He happened to catch the girl's eye-widening surprise. He shook the flame off his thumb as he exhaled smoke from his nostrils. "It's a kind of magic."

A mischievous grin quickly replaced the surprise in the woman's eyes. Strathan took the cigarette out of his mouth, grabbed the back of her neck and pulled her toward him, giving her a lecherous kiss.

As he opened the car door and stepped into the adoration of hundreds of fans, something nagged at Strathan's thoughts. Is this all his new life would be? Shagging girls and driving fancy cars? Where would he find the intrigue? The passion?

His thoughts went back to Dupré. She had been an invigorating adversary.

Too bad she was dead.

Lauren watched Strathan emerge from his "Wow! I have a small penis!" car. His latest flavor of the month stepped from the opposite side.

Calling Strathan an actor would be an insult to real actors. But she had to give him some credit for playing this evening's role of Hollywood star well. He paused gallantly, giving his date time to catch up before heading down the red carpet toward the cameras.

When Strathan reached her, Lauren welcomed him and started with the usual softball red carpet questions. The interview process would be quick and vapid, probably much like Strathan's date. Lauren prayed her disgust for this aspect of her job lay hidden behind her dazzling smile.

Again, to his credit, Strathan played his charm for all it was worth, his smiling Irish eyes oozing warmth, every move of his body-by-trainer a masterwork of seductive art. Lauren understood why so many women, including a studio executive or two, fell victim to his charms.

Her journalist instincts ultimately got the better of her. "Thanks for talking to us, Dwyer," she said as a false wrap to her interview. "But there's just one more thing puzzling your fans. Were you really in some unnamed rehab facility the last four months, or is there more to your breakup with Valentina Lorena than you're letting on?"

She then flashed Strathan her biggest smile. The first rule of journalism according to her professor Lane: you can ask any question, no matter how insulting or invasive, as long as you smile afterward.

Strathan ran a finger under Lauren's chin. "How can a man resist a smile like that?" he said in the Irish lilt that had seduced millions of fans. He started to say something more, but a light flashed across his eyes. The actor flinched and raised a hand to protect them.

When he recovered, Lauren saw him stare at something high above and behind her.

His charming smile dissolved into a dangerous scowl.

Lauren turned to her camera operator, Evelyn "Evie" Walker. Only a few years out of USC film school, Evie handled the gear as if she were born with a camera in her hand. She already had her camera aimed in the direction of Strathan's stare.

Lauren silently thanked the media gods for assigning her a camera op with Evie's instincts. She then turned to see what had commanded Strathan's attention.

Two spotlight beams bathed the theater's golden pagoda roof. A woman stood on the roof's curved ledge some sixty feet above the red carpet. She held what looked to be a short sword in front of her, catching the light and aiming it back toward the street.

Directly back at Strathan.

Quickly looking to the actor for his reaction, Lauren witnessed anger darkening his expression as his eyes fixed upon the woman with the sword.

Her journalist instincts kicking into overdrive, Lauren asked into her microphone, "Dwyer, do you know this woman?" She then shoved her microphone into Strathan's face. For her part, Evie had turned the camera back on Strathan, probably a tight shot. Good girl!

"Get that out of my face," Strathan demanded, his glare fixed on the woman on the theater.

Evie slid next to Lauren and gently pulled her back from Strathan. Without losing her shot, Evie whispered, "Publicity stunt. Has to be."

That could explain why Strathan was so late. Technical difficulties or something. But the menacing tone in Strathan's words had clued Lauren that she'd stumbled upon something more than an insignificant publicity stunt. "He's not that good an actor," she whispered to Evie.

A collective gasp from the crowd drew Lauren's attention back to the woman. Evie swung the camera in that direction.

The woman's sword had disappeared. Lauren assumed she had a scabbard or something on her back underneath her coat, the only place not visible to the crowd.

With her hands now free, the woman dropped from the ledge and toward the Chinese demon-head atop one of the two sixty-foot high pillars framing the theater's entrance. The woman landed on target amid the spear-like outcroppings encircling the demon head.

Leaping from this perch, she performed a mid-air somersault across the chasm between the theater's main pillars. The section of her thigh-length coat beneath her waist fanned out behind her like a small cape. Part way across, she grabbed a chain dangling from the pagoda roof.

Shifting her body, her momentum pushed the chain toward the interior area of the theater front and an intricately sculpted dragon façade.

The woman released the chain. Her momentum propelled her toward the façade. She grasped a handhold and then moved down the façade like a nimble rock climber descending a mountain.

She came to a stop atop the three sets of double doors. A final acrobatic flip brought her down at the theater end of the red carpet.

The crowd went wild with shouting and applause. Lauren suspected that, like her, none of them could believe what he or she had just witnessed, which said a great deal for a performance in front of a crowd that lived in the Land of Make-Believe.

Lauren abruptly lowered her mic and turned to address Evie. "If this were a stunt," she began, "the studio would have told us so we wouldn't be part of the show. They didn't. So let's *be* the show."

Measure Twenty-Five — Stealing the Spotlight

As Lauren approached the apparent stuntwoman, she figured the woman couldn't be much over five feet tall. She stood resolute under the scrutiny of hundreds of fans, the paparazzi's camera flashes and Evie's video camera.

Under her goth jacket, she wore black, hip-hugging pants and something that was more of a bikini top than a shirt. It revealed her toned stomach, an area of minor cleavage and her neck.

A medallion hung over the pale skin of her chest, skin nothing like the too-tanned tone of native Californians. A pair of knee-high boots completed the outfit.

You couldn't perform a stunt like hers without safety rigging, especially in this union-run town. And yet, Lauren didn't see any rigging points on the woman's costume. No, this woman was the real deal, and the journalist in Lauren had to find out who she was.

"Lauren Kahler, KTLA5," she said as she came to a stop before the newcomer. "The crowd wants to know — who are you?"

The woman ignored Lauren.

Lauren shoved the microphone into the woman's face. She wasn't far into her twenties, not much younger than Lauren's twenty-six. Her hair was pulled back in an intricate braiding pattern save two wisps of hair that fell over her face. She possessed an angelic beauty, but a haunted expression marred that beauty.

Strathan matched the girl's lack of malice with plenty of his own. Clearly agitated, he marched toward Lauren, Evie, and the mystery woman.

"I killed you!" he spat.

Lauren whipped her head around to gaze at Strathan. *He just made an admission of murder at a movie premiere!* This night was proving better than Lauren could have hoped — if she could get the story behind the admission. She charged over to Strathan, minding her heels on the carpet.

"You killed this woman?" Lauren asked. "When? And if so —"

Strathan shoved Lauren aside. At least, she thought he had. His arm had moved as if waving her away and she fell unceremoniously onto her butt just outside the red carpet. But she was too far away from Strathan for him to have touched her.

Lauren saw Evie maintaining her vigil with the camera. *Great*, she thought. *That's just what America needs to see — me falling on my ass! Cronkite never fell on his ass!* Thankfully, Evie aimed her camera at Strathan, so the illusion of Lauren's grace may be intact.

The actor stormed past Lauren and got right in front of the unknown woman. She seemed undaunted by his anger-fueled approach despite his height advantage over her. "I killed you!" he hissed as if repeating the words would make them true.

Lauren watched the girl look upward solely with her eyes and meet Strathan's gaze. She stood still and didn't seem defensive or fearful. Lauren even detected a hint of scorn as the girl said two words to Strathan:

"Did you?"

OROMIA

DECEMBER 2013

After her life had slipped away, Adriana felt nothing.

A faint memory of the Agazyan *galma* played in her mind's eye. Yet now she saw nothing of the sanctuary, heard nothing of the Agazyan people, felt nothing of the damp floor beneath her as she lay prone. Another memory played, one of her throat bruised from strangulation.

Adriana did not feel that either.

With no sensory input, she had no way to discern her location. That is if she were indeed anywhere.

In the end, Adriana realized that it didn't matter. She had failed Makeda, failed her sister, and failed herself. Her sole legacy was one of vengeance fueled by pain, leaving more pain in its wake.

Yet Adriana felt no pain now. Nor did she feel flesh. Nor bone. She felt nothing at all. All she had was the memory of a face — the last face she saw before passing into this void of nothingness.

Adriana remembered the face of the man who murdered her.

There was anger in his expression. She recognized the hatred in his eyes. It saddened her to think she had once held such hatred.

This is my true death, Adriana relented, *the death I so deserve.*

"You will not die here."

The other voice, the nearly incomprehensible growl of some beast, broke through the void. It rippled over Adriana like a wave, its source a dark recess of Adriana's mind that she feared to explore. The voice represented a sense of despair invading her emotional nothingness. She tried to fight it.

The voice would not be denied.

"You said you are not ready to die," it continued.

With every word, the voice conjured a familiar darkness. Its influence felt strong. Adriana tried to resist it.

"Rise up! Use your rage at this injustice to fuel your new life!"

Adriana knew rage.

She remembered how it had felt when it empowered her against her enemies. She also remembered the emptiness she had felt after vanquishing that enemy, the death and pain left in the wake of her actions.

This death, this nothingness, was the punishment for such thoughtless violence.

Except...

If she possessed a chance to fight back... but for what purpose? What cause?

"Revenge!" the beast-voice bellowed. *"Starting with the man Strathan! He did this to you, ending your time before you were ready!"*

The beast-voice's lure felt familiar to Adriana, comfortable. She knew it was wrong.

I deserve this, for all I have done, Adriana thought.

"Not this way! Not at his hand!" The intensity of the voice grew within Adriana's mind, pressing upon her, smothering her other thoughts.

"You will have your revenge," the voice insisted, *"and then you will continue your reign of terror!"*

The voice pushed Adriana to memories of another Reign of Terror, back in a place familiar to her, a time when she had been mortal, as she had been mere moments before.

She felt the presence of another from that time, someone she sought but could not find... a woman... no, a girl —

Adriana had opened her eyes.

The emotions stirred by the beastly voice flooded back as she felt herself rise from the nothingness she had known and flow into something other. The rush pressed her to the brink of sanity. A guttural shriek served as a release.

Sensations flooded Adriana.

The hard stone beneath her cut into her back, her limbs. The dampness in the air clung to her flesh. The stench of her death invaded her nostrils.

All other senses receded as Adriana felt a touch on her arm. Acting purely on instinct, she lashed out with her hand at whatever had touched her. Adriana knew terror as she saw the clawed fingers of her hand.

The terror grew as those same claws tore flesh, as fresh blood spilled to the stone floor.

The smell of blood transformed terror into intense desire... intense hunger. Driven by an animal's instinct, Adriana sprang from her prone position and leaped upon the source of blood.

Fangs extended from her gums, then sunk deep into the already torn flesh. Fresh blood washed upon Adriana's tongue. She drank deeply —

...until something smashed into the side of her head.

Adriana fell away from her source of nourishment, landing hard on the stone floor. In nearly the same instant, she rolled into a position from which she could launch a counterattack against her opponent.

Before that attack came, the opponent made some noise foreign to Adriana. It could have been speech, but Adriana's rage precluded rational communication. She launched herself at the new opponent, who swung something like a pole at her.

Adriana caught the pole in mid swing and then spun around in a roundhouse kick. Her heel connected with the side of her opponent's head. The attacker, a man, fell away from her. She sniffed at the air, honing in on the raw flesh and blood she desperately craved.

The source of the spilling blood was behind Adriana.

Before she could act on her desire, someone else kicked her in the back of her knee. As her leg gave out, Adriana rolled with the impact, planning to spring to a crouch. Her assailant kicked her shoulder, throwing her off balance.

Adriana ended up on her back. She prepared to spring to her feet but a foot stomped down on her chest, holding her in place.

The girl attempted her flip, but the pole came down on her knees, pinning her. A burst of white flame appeared inches from her face.

Adriana hissed as her eyes widened, horror supplanting her rage.

"*No!*" the beastly voice in her head protested. "*We will not fall again!*"

Despite the beast's impassioned words, Adriana could not combat her fear of the flame.

It suddenly (thankfully) moved aside, yet it was still close enough to remain a threat. The foot moved from Adriana's chest. The owner knelt beside Adriana, revealing herself.

She possessed a face Adriana found familiar, but could not identify. The woman moved her lips. Adriana focused on them, struggling to drown the voice of the beast and the fear welling inside.

Her efforts were rewarded. Adriana could decipher the foreign sound coming from the woman's lips.

"The demon within wants to take control!" the familiar woman demanded. "You have to fight it! You have to take control!"

Control, Adriana thought.

Control the demon.

Control the rage.

The anger.

The pain.

"*No! Use it! Destroy them!*" the beast interrupted, desperation heavy in its tone.

The flame before Adriana dissipated. The familiar woman stood, stepping away from her. Adriana felt the weight of the pole lift from her legs. She sat up, instinctively moving like a cornered animal to a position from whence she could pounce.

Adriana quickly assessed the three people who stood before her.

The familiar woman wore a brown, form-fitting jumpsuit adorned with hieroglyphs. She was unarmed, though Adriana could read the tension in the woman's muscles — a sure sign of her combat readiness. This brown-skinned woman held a regal composure.

She was definitely the leader of the three.

There was the man with the pole, which Adriana now recognized as a staff. His eyes were aglow with an indigo light akin to the flame that had threatened her. Adriana noted the man's fingers kneading the staff, not the grip of a true warrior but a man afraid of combat. Judging by his earlier actions, he wasn't against it.

A second woman completed the trio. Fair skinned and much younger than the familiar woman, she was the victim of Adriana's initial attack. This woman wore a white cloak over a white, form-fitting bodysuit. She held a hand to the torn flesh of her arm.

Blood seeped through the fabric and between her fingers, but she did not react as if in pain.

Adriana looked from the wound to the woman's eyes, hoping for a read on her combat readiness.

Surprise befell Adriana. The woman possessed no instinct for action. Instead, Adriana found compassion there. This woman, whom she had initially shown such animosity, still found it in herself to support Adriana.

Looking back to the man, Adriana found that same look of compassion in his expression. Admittedly, fear melded with that compassion. Yet he stood his ground with the women.

Finally, Adriana's gaze rested once more upon the familiar, older woman. Her expression did not mirror that of her companions. Instead, the woman's face expressed no emotion at all. She merely waited for Adriana to make the next move.

To make her choice.

"*We can destroy them!*" the demon's voice maintained. Adriana jerked her head in reaction to the force of the demon's voice in her head. She took a moment to steady herself before speaking again.

"Yes, we can destroy them," she said aloud. Adriana focused on the tiny muscles in her mouth that would retract her fangs. She forced the muscles in her fingers to do the same to her extended claws.

"But we will not," Adriana finished.

When she looked back to the three people before her, all traces of the demon within her were gone. Instead, a confused and penitent young woman slumped to her knees before them.

"Does this mean we can step down from Defcon-1?" the man asked. The compassionate woman reached behind their leader to punch him in the arm. Adriana sensed the blow was meant to scold, not to harm.

The motion and intent also came as familiar to Adriana, something she had seen before from these two, though she could not remember their identities.

"There was a girl," Adriana whispered.

The familiar woman, the leader, moved toward Adriana. "What girl?" she asked.

"I remember little of myself other than the need for violence. I do not understand what I am, these things I can do. But the girl... she was special to me, though I know not how or why... or even who she is to me."

"You are a vampire."

Adriana looked to the familiar woman as if she had just grown tentacles from her eyes. The woman made no look of jest; she stood by her words, fanciful though they were.

Thinking over her actions, what she had seen of her body, Adriana had to accept this 'vampire' state as the truth.

It would surely explain the demon voice in her head.

Thankfully, the three people gave her a moment to digest this new information. In time, Adriana spoke again.

"I hear... a voice," she said.

"When you died," the leader began, "your soul loosed from your mortal body. Under normal circumstances, you create a vampire by bonding that soul with a demon. In your case, the demon grabbed what it could of your soul upon its escape from the *ekeraa.*"

The woman allowed Adriana time to absorb the explanation.

"So," Adriana began. Her words trailed off for a moment. The familiar woman remained silent. "Are you saying my loss of memory... is a loss of my soul?"

"More of a shock to your soul," the familiar woman replied. She knelt before Adriana. The compassion Adriana saw in the woman she wounded now appeared in this woman's eyes. "I can help you find that part of you again. It won't be easy, but then, after all you've been through..."

"I wish I could remember what that was," Adriana said.

"Actually," the man said, "you may want to skip some of it. Bloody stuff, your life. But hopefully you'll remember the part where you and I went to Ibiza, and you showed me —"

The blonde woman punched the man again.

"I was gonna say 'how to use a sword!'" the man explained. "God you people have such filthy minds!"

The blonde shook her head.

Adriana almost smiled at their comedy. Instead, she looked back to the familiar woman. "And then there is the demon within," she said to the woman. "It clings to the violence within me. I fear whatever I have lost. When I find it again… what will I become?"

"That," the woman replied, "is not up to the demon, nor will it be clouded by some evil influence. It will be much more frightening."

Adriana looked expectantly at the woman.

"Whatever you become," the woman continued, "that decision is up to you."

LOS ANGELES

JUNE 2014

A month ago, Adriana was with Illyana in Orléans, France. There she encountered her sister Dominique. The trauma of the encounter forced Adriana's full memories to return.

Now she was back in the City of Angeles about to combat one of her many nemeses in front of a live, Uninitiated audience.

Much had changed in those six months since Adriana had returned from her spirit quest in the *ekeraa*. Her intent now was not to kill Strathan, as had been her method for so many centuries.

Instead, she sought to convince him to give up the Vyntari shards and be on his way.

Yes, much had changed indeed.

"Get this straight, bitch," Strathan hissed at her, not caring that the reporter and the rest of the world watched in astonishment. Spittle caught the wisps of Adriana's hair as it flapped in the breeze of a Los Angeles summer.

"I don't know how or why ya came back," Strathan continued. "The Shadowdance is fecked up that way. But know this: I've been makin' a lotta changes 'round here. I paid dearly for these changes. I like these changes."

"One thing has not changed," Adriana said calmly. "You still talk exceedingly too much."

"Big talk for somebody about to die!"

Strathan raised his hands to the height of his shoulders. Instantly, muddy red ethereal flames engulfed them.

"Again!" Strathan added.

Measure Twenty-Six — Lifting the Veil

Strathan's flame-engulfed hands came down in an overhead arc. Adriana swung her arms upward, parrying Strathan's arms at their elbows, pushing his flames away from her. She drew her arms inward and then thrust forward, putting her full weight behind a dual handed push into Strathan's chest.

The dark sorcerer stumbled backward and out of reach.

Adriana maintained her composure, standing as if the previous attack had not occurred. "I did not come to fight you, Strathan," she said, her tone modest when held against the roaring volatility of the on-looking crowd.

"With that move? Coulda fooled me," Strathan replied, his hands still alight.

Adriana looked past Strathan and to the street beyond.

Though the police barricades kept the star-struck crowd at bay for now, the potential for a fight between their brightest star and a mystery woman could provoke them. They would become much more difficult to control.

Thankfully, the uniformed police sensed this potential for anarchy and moved more officers to positions at the front of the barricades, hoping their visible presence would curtail the crowd.

Photographers bobbed and weaved between the line of police, snapping away at what inevitably would be the story of the day, at least, at the local level.

Adriana imagined the photographers' frustration when they looked at their developed photos and saw only a blurred image where she stood — one of the preternatural benefits of being a vampire.

In the aftermath, they would be unable to explain the anomaly, but every soul present would know what their eyes beheld, would know something inexplicable had occurred.

With her new attitude toward the Shadowdance, Adriana now respected the necessity of the Shadowdance's Veil, the edict by which all Initiated creatures agreed to hide the supernatural from the Uninitiated. Adriana had hoped Strathan would also respect the Veil and curtail his use of the supernatural.

That proved as foolhardy a notion as believing Strathan would peacefully relinquish the Vyntari shards.

Adriana prayed the audience would believe her confrontation with Strathan an elaborate Hollywood publicity stunt. It was the only way she saw to salvage the situation and not make her first encounter working for the Righteous an epic blunder.

The female reporter and her camerawoman remained closest to her and Strathan. They stood poised to slip beyond the Veil. They would also be the first casualties should Adriana be unable to end the conflict with Strathan quickly.

Adriana's focus returned to Strathan. He shook his hands, extinguishing the flames. He then removed his tuxedo coat and dug into the inside pocket. Strathan withdrew two palm-sized orbs, each appearing to have a cloudy substance inside. He looked at the orbs, and then to Adriana. Strathan shook his head.

"Nope," he said, sliding the orbs into his pants pocket. "I beat your ass — wait a minute. Credit where credit due. I killed your ass with my bare hands before."

Strathan draped the tuxedo jacket over an arm and then removed his diamond-studded cufflinks from his sleeves. "I aim ta do it again." He finished removing the cufflinks and then waved his arms toward the crowd. "And this time, I'll do it with a live audience!"

This last elicited a fever-pitched scream from the throngs of the Uninitiated. Strathan threw the cufflinks into the crowd.

The female reporter moved toward Strathan again. He flashed her a malicious glare. "Best stay away, missy," he warned.

"You can't expect me to back off when you're throwing around murder confessions," the reporter said. Her determination in the face of her potential death would have impressed Adriana had it not been so utterly stupid.

"He speaks in hyperbole," Adriana said.

"Hyperbole my ass," the sorcerer countered.

"Keep this between us, Strathan," Adriana warned. "And mind your… skills among the Uninitiated."

The dark sorcerer thought on this for a moment.

And then he laughed.

Strathan waved over his female companion from the car. She huffed but did as ordered.

"We don't have time —" Adriana began. Strathan extended an index finger, motioning for her to remain silent.

Strathan's date stepped to him. He turned to her and handed his jacket to her.

The girl refused to take it.

"I am not your maid," she said.

"And just who are you?" the reporter chimed in. "Do you know anything about —"

Adriana moved to the reporter so quickly it was as if she had simply manifested there. She took up a position between her and Strathan. "Let this go," she suggested.

"One and only time I agree with ya, Dupré," Strathan said. He looked back to his companion. She looked defiantly back at him. He shoved his jacket into her arms, turned her around and smacked her on her butt.

"Now stay in the car if ya know what's good for ya," he said.

The girl glared at Strathan over her shoulder but dutifully walked back to the car. In a moment of defiance, she opted to lean against the car instead of getting in. Strathan's hands curled into fists. He contemplated retaliating against the girl but must have thought better of it as he instead turned back to face Adriana.

The camerawoman had captured the entire exchange — not that appearances mattered to Strathan right now. He rolled up his sleeves, cinching them off so they'd remain up above his elbow and out of the way.

Adriana walked away from the reporter and her camerawoman. Once again standing in front of the theater's doors, she turned to address Strathan. "Is it death you want, Strathan?"

He cocked his head to the side, raising an eyebrow. "You think you're that good?"

"My wanton violence led to my death. When my life ended, what did I have to show for it?"

"Don't go getting all philosophical on me now, bitch. That shite doesn't mean a thing to ya."

"For a time, it did not. Recently, my eyes were opened to new possibilities."

"So were mine," Strathan countered as he twisted his head from side to side to stretch his neck and rolled his shoulders. "I like the freedom in those possibilities. You are not gonna take them away."

"Only you can change what you are, Strathan. If you do not…"

As the vampire's implication hung in the air, Strathan threw a few practice punches. Those hours on the heavy bag were about to pay off big. Satisfied, he frowned as he looked to Adriana. "I never did much like foreplay."

Strathan clapped his hands together. His ethereal flames ignited, again engulfing his hands. This time, he did not move toward Adriana. Instead, he thrust his right hand forward, palm toward Adriana. Flames seared the air as they projected toward the vampire.

Dodging the plume of fire proved no difficult task for Adriana, but even as she moved to the side, she grew concerned about collateral damage.

Glancing behind her, she saw the flame slam against the closed front doors of the theater. The smell of scorched paint and wood permeated the air as the door's lacquered finish turned black from the impact. Smoke billowed from the damage.

Once again, violence forced itself upon Adriana. Before her death, she would have embraced the opportunity. Now, Adriana sought to end it quickly, fearing that Strathan would not hesitate to do to human flesh what he'd done to the door if the distraction would help defeat her.

Strathan launched a second plume of flame at Adriana, this time from his left hand. She dove under the flame and toward the dark sorcerer. Without looking back, she imagined the flames burning into the wall of the theater behind her. The accompanying smell of burnt cement gave life to her imagination.

Adriana landed on her hands. Using her forward momentum, she twisted and flipped up, slamming her feet against Strathan's stomach. The dark sorcerer stumbled backward. Adriana landed on her feet with her back to him.

Strathan recovered faster than Adriana would have liked. Now that she was in range, he launched a boxer's attack against her. She ducked underneath his initial blow, then dodged two more, maneuvering so she faced her attacker.

A flaming left hook found its mark.

Adriana spun from Strathan, blood spurting from her mouth as her teeth cut into flesh. A burn quickly formed on the side of her face. Falling, her knees slammed down hard on the red carpet. Her hands thrust forward to protect her face from doing the same.

The dark sorcerer raised a foot to stomp her. She rolled to one side, the twin harnesses of her *Fukushuu* blades digging into her back. Strathan went to stomp again, but Adriana brought her foot up to catch his.

As sole met sole, Adriana pushed Strathan off balance. She spun on her back, sweeping Strathan's feet out from under him. The sorcerer fell to the ground jut as Adriana flipped up to her feet.

"I only want the shards, Strathan," Adriana insisted, her two wisps of hair crossing in front of her determined eyes. "This is not necessary."

"If yer scared o' revealing the Shadowdance, ya shoulda asked me for the shards at home, in private," Strathan countered. The conversation ended as Strathan got to his feet and went back on the offensive.

Adriana dodged or parried most of Strathan's blows, but a few key jabs broke through her defenses. Needing to bring this to an end, Adriana allowed herself the use of her preternatural speed.

Strathan threw another punch.

Adriana quickly went around it, catching his arm with one hand. She then turned the arm so that the elbow faced upwards. Adriana punched her other hand through the elbow, shattering it.

To his credit, the movie star held his scream of anguish behind gritted teeth.

Still holding the now broken arm, Adriana kicked her leg behind Strathan's legs and pushed him backward. Tripping over her leg and without an arm to soften his fall, the dark sorcerer crashed to the ground.

This time, he couldn't conceal his pain.

The flames evaporated from his hands.

The audience gasped, then cheered the fighters. Paparazzi cameras flashed.

Adriana wrapped her leg around Strathan's broken arm, applying a bit of pain-inducing pressure.

"Where are the shards?" Adriana asked. "Your answer will —"

A bullet ripped through Adriana's abdomen.

She stumbled, releasing her grip on Strathan's arm, her foot coming off his throat. Strathan shuffled a few feet away from her.

"Can always count on the cops to shoot first and ask questions never!" Strathan said.

Adriana glanced in the direction of the shot. One of the uniformed policemen stood several yards away from her, aiming his sidearm at her head. Thankfully, his companions were so busy with crowd control only this one moved forward to address her violence.

Though he merely performed his duty, Adriana could not have him interfere.

"The situation is in hand, officer," the vampire suggested while using her blood magic to heal the bullet wound.

"As soon as you get on the ground with your hands behind your head it will be!" the officer responded.

"Boring conversation anyway," Strathan interjected.

He then blasted another bolt of flame at Adriana. She dove backward in a flip, landing in a crouch.

Strathan knelt across from her, his broken arm dangling in front of him, his expression showing his difficulty in fighting back the pain.

Both stood poised like primal cats in an asphalt jungle.

"You two cut this crap out!" the policeman ordered.

The combatants ignored him. Strathan glared at Adriana. His eyes moved to the policeman.

Adriana didn't have time to shout a warning.

Strathan fired a spout of flame, this one engulfing the policeman. His screams of agony excited the already howling crowd, who must have thought this a part of the act. They did not realize that the man was burning to death before their eyes.

Adriana moved toward the policeman — but then abruptly stopped. She held her head as if getting a headache.

"Keep us away from the flames!"

The demon within Adriana showed its fear. She too realized that flames would bring them both a final death. Though she may deserve it, the policeman should not die just for doing his job.

Adriana used her preternatural speed to draw one of her blades, cut a section of the red carpet and pull the carpet loose. In the next instant, the policeman had the carpet yanked out from under him. As he fell to the ground, Adriana buried him under the section of carpet.

Ignoring the demon within and its fear of the flames, Adriana did her best to smother the very thing that could destroy her permanently. She fought her gag reflex as the putrid stench of burning flesh invading her nostrils.

The man's screams echoed in her ears.

Moments later, those screams demurred to low sobs. The flames extinguished, yet the smoldering flesh remained. The crowd now had a reason to cheer and cheer they did.

Adriana looked up.

The camerawoman stood nearby, immortalizing the moment. The reporter, her microphone at the ready, rushed toward Adriana. "Is this really a publicity stunt?" she hurriedly asked.

The reporter gagged at the smell of burnt flesh despite her best efforts to resist. "And what is this thing called the Shadowdance?" she asked. "What is Dwyer Strathan —"

Adriana swung her blade, cutting the reporter's microphone in half and rendering it useless. The reporter caught the falling piece, looking as if Adriana had just destroyed her greatest possession.

"Forget the Shadowdance," Adriana said.

When the reporter looked back at Adriana, her expression had lost its composure. The vampire swore that if the woman had a weapon, she would not have hesitated to use it against her.

While the bitch cunt vampire fumbled around with the cop, Strathan tied off his sleeve to stop his broken arm from flopping around. The pain hammered at his nerves, but he'd endure it long enough to finish her.

He kinda wondered why Dupré, once the scourge of the Shadowdance, suddenly showed compassion for an Uninitiated whelp. *Must be the shock of death*, he reasoned. *After I kill her a second time, she's gonna be Mother Feckin' Teresa.*

Looking back to Dupré, Strathan found her under the verbal assault of that reporter. Strathan had to give it to her — Lauren, he remembered. She was tenacious. And with that body, she'd make a good anchor one day. Feckin' hell, he might even give her a go.

If she lived that long.

"Is the Shadowdance a new movie? Is that what this is about?" Lauren asked Dupré despite her lack of microphone.

Adriana motioned toward the crowd. "These people know you. Use your influence to get them away from here," Saint Dupré said.

"Why?" Lauren asked. "If this is a publicity stunt, where's the danger?"

"Danger's right here, scangers!" Strathan interjected.

Dupré and Lauren looked to Strathan. Adriana moved behind Lauren. He moved in concert, joining Adriana's dance as they re-angled, Lauren their axis point.

"So ya save a copper but to hell with the reporter?" Strathan asked. "Didn't think she was doing that bad a job!"

Strathan raised his good arm. His hand erupted in flames.

"Wait!" Lauren shouted. She took a step back, bumping into Adriana. The vampire grabbed Lauren's arms, holding her against her. She stopped moving; Strathan followed suit. He lined up Adriana and, by default, Lauren.

The sorcerer lowered his hand below his eye line and took a good look at Lauren. He shook his head. "Waste of a good pair a' tits. I bet they were real, too."

Strathan raised his flaming hand and launched a torrent of fire at the women.

The vampire pulled Lauren to one side and then dove on top of her. The flames passed within inches of Adriana, singeing the back of her hair as she leaped clear of its path.

The flame shot past the women, rocketing down the red carpet and toward —

Measure Twenty-Seven — The Demon Unleashed

Thirteen months.

Thirteen months from the date of order to the actual delivery of the Aston Martin Zagato.

Strathan drove it once, for an hour, this night. The plume of fire — his fire — had struck the car, turning it into a heap of burning metal.

His jaw hung open in shock. He fell to his knees. Strathan would have cried, but that wasn't his style. He could only watch as the muddy red flames engulfed his car.

Then, strangely, the flames turned a glowing white and burned themselves out.

White flames?

To the side of the burning car, Strathan saw his little Brit chippie. She had somehow escaped the potential funeral pyre that was his Zagato.

Looking past her and across the street, the sorcerer saw the crowd behind the barricades. The explosion had driven them into a panic. They mob broke in either direction, pressing against the barricades meant to keep them off the crossing streets.

Try as the police might, the panic outweighed their restraint. Frenzied onlookers pressed through the barricades, flooding automobile traffic on Highland and Orange. The sudden chaos would at least keep the police away from Strathan's little tête-à-tête with Adriana.

As Strathan took in the scene, he felt a pinch in the hand of his unbroken arm, the hand still surrounded by Hellfire. He absently raised the hand to look at it. Blood from the wound trailed down his arm, staining his shirt sleeve.

The blade of a short sword jutted through his hand.

Strathan turned his hand to look at it from all sides as if he'd never seen the blade or his hand or this combination of the two. He allowed the flames on his hand to dissipate.

Realization hit Strathan. The blade belonged to that vampire bitch. She must have thrown it at him to stop him from burning up anything else. With his other arm broken, he couldn't even pry the blade free. He looked to the side and saw the vampire kneeling on the carpet, the reporter lying beside her.

The anger flowing through him ran hotter than his Hellfire.

"All this because you would not answer a simple question," Dupré said.

"I don't have the feckin' shards you feckin' evil bitch!" Strathan replied.

"Where are they?"

"Ask your girl Valentina!"

"I will."

The calmness in Dupré's tone annoyed Strathan. His blood painting the carpet at his feet a darker shade of red was almost as bad. The sorcerer turned his impaled hand, angling it so that the point of the blade pointed to the carpet. He slammed his hand down, dislodging the sword. He moved to grab its handle —

A booted foot slammed down on the blade, pinning it to the carpet. Strathan looked up to see Dupré standing in front of him. She used her other boot to push Strathan onto his back.

As he righted himself (a tricky task with one working arm), Adriana retrieved her blade.

The vampire licked the blood from the sword.

"Disgusting bitch!" Strathan said.

Adriana paused for a moment, seemingly savoring the taste. She then looked down at Strathan, watching him while sliding her sword back into its scabbard.

Strathan also watched, noting the Japanese script down the side of the blade. He remembered their conversation from many months ago, the night they had first met at his party. The sorcerer had asked her if the legend surrounding her blades, that they did particularly harmful damage to Daughters of Lilith, was true.

That was a piece of info he figured would come in handy later.

"I have what I came for," Adriana said. "But I have a feeling you will not let this go unanswered."

"Bet yer sweet little ass!" Strathan grunted.

"Then something must be done about you."

That nosey ass camera bitch stood a few yards away from of Strathan and Dupré. Strathan knew this because, in a movement he didn't even see, Adriana now stood next to the woman.

Another blink of Strathan's eyes and Adriana stood over him again, the camera in her hands. Strathan's closed his eyes again, planning to reorient himself when he opened them.

He didn't need sight to feel the camera slamming into the side of his head.

Blood is the life.

It carries within it the essence of the soul, the knowledge of an individual.

Adriana despised the Daughters of Lilith and all they represented. Yet the blood magic they had taught her had use. Important to her now was the power to detect the weakness of her victim by sampling their blood, effectively sampling their essence.

Having tasted Strathan's blood, Adriana allowed the wave of his essence to flood her psyche. She shuddered from the cold taint of evil but forced her way through, discerning his weakness from images in his mind. That weakness? Pride physically realized in a demon tooth in the place of a molar.

Adriana's blow with the camera had knocked this molar loose. It fell from Strathan's mouth and to the carpet. The molar didn't resemble a normal human tooth; it was closer to that of an animal.

Before Adriana could get a better look, the tooth turned a bright red. The carpet beneath it smoked as the tooth heated up. The tooth burned until white hot, its heat turning in on itself until it vaporized completely.

Only a small black mark on the red carpet remained as evidence of the tooth's existence.

Adriana looked to Strathan.

The sorcerer had curled into a fetal ball; he tucked his face into his body, hiding it from Adriana. His hair immediately thinned and grayed, clumps falling out and littering the carpet. His skin tightened, wrinkled, grew taut about his skull. Strathan's muscles withered, his body shrinking beneath his tuxedo shirt and pants.

In a hoarse voice, Strathan sputtered, "Fecking… bitch…"

Adriana heard the sirens of approaching police officers, probably firefighters too. The mob blocking traffic would delay their arrival. The policemen already on scene split their focus between keeping the too curious away from the red carpet and fighting both the escaping mob and car traffic.

The vampire knelt before the sorcerer, staring at his withering form. He slowly turned his head to face her. His skin had wrinkled, drawing tight upon his skull. His eyes were wild. Despite what was happening to him, the sorcerer smiled a nearly toothless grin.

"Yer in fer it now, bitch," he muttered.

Adriana started to inquire verbally but then noticed a gelatinous ooze trailing from Strathan's mouth. She followed the trail of ooze to the remains of the two orbs lying beside him.

Dwyer Strathan, dark sorcerer newly free of the Shadowdance, movie star who knew no moral or financial boundary, lay in the shadow of TCL's Chinese Theater as nothing more than the husk of an old man. His wounds, combined with his advanced aging, would surely mean his death. He needed an edge.

After Adriana had clocked him with the camera, Strathan huddled up into a little ball, his face hidden from the world. The broken arm non-functional, he used his pierced hand to pull the demon orbs from his pants pocket.

Lacking the hand strength to break them, he put the orbs in his mouth. Luckily, his rapidly decaying jaws had just enough strength to break them.

Dwyer Strathan would not go down like some punk bitch.

"Went through a lotta trouble fer that tooth," Strathan spoke between chuckles and gasps to get air into his atrophied lungs. "I'm gonna make this real painful for you, bitch."

The dark plasma once inside the orbs now encased Strathan's shoulder. Two fist-sized lumps of plasma emerged. They mutated, forming the heads of two small demons, both howling silently into the night.

"Denizen of Hell!" Strathan had to pause to take a shallow breath. "As I," he gasped for air, "have released you —" Again, he stopped to catch his breath. "Oh, just feckin' do your thing!"

Strathan struggled against the demon plasma as it peeled away part of his flesh in its attempt to escape his command. He turned to Adriana and smiled a nearly toothless grin, though his eyes showed the pain he endured.

"Here it comes, bitch!"

Adriana drew one of her blades from its scabbard on her back.

A gunshot.

A bullet tore through Adriana's shoulder. She jerked backward, losing her footing. As she fell onto her back, Strathan cackled like the witch in a Bugs Bunny cartoon.

The LAPD could always be counted on to shoot first and question never.

The demon heads fought in vain as the force of Strathan's will pulled their plasma forms back to him. The plasma trailed down his arm, increasing in mass, becoming a second skin to the old man's flesh. As more of the goo covered his face, he could no longer see his nemesis, Dupré.

She could no longer hear his laughter.

The demon heads finally disappeared, absorbed into the expanding plasma. It oozed over Strathan's entire body, engulfing him from foot to head. Slowly the pain of his struggle to control the demon plasma took hold.

He thought of Adriana, imagined her sitting there bleeding with (hopefully) a dozen guns trained on her. He imagined what he would do to her when he fully harnessed the demons' power. It helped blind him to the pain consuming his entire being.

Moments later, he could contain the pain no longer.

Strathan's head snapped backward. His entire plasma-covered body shook violently as the plasma on his face split open like a terrifying mouth. It released a scream worthy of great pity even for a source of such determined evil.

Reining in the pain, Strathan bellowed, "You will obey me!" in the meager voice of a dying old man, his demon-sprung mouth mutilating the words.

The plasma pulsated like a thing alive, bubbling over Strathan's body. It hardened into an armor-like form, transforming him into something... other. Something large... powerful... fearsome.

Aided by this demonic skin, Strathan rose.

The demon body armor retained the shape of a muscularly developed man. Small spikes rose from various places on the armor. Sharp talons formed three fingers and an opposable thumb on each hand. The mouth extended into a snout. Fangs not unlike the tooth Strathan had lost protruded from the snout. Three long horns grew from odd angles on the head.

His once nearly six-foot frame now towered at eight feet tall. The heat from the armor's infernal power burned through the red carpet where its hoofed feet made contact.

Two eye sockets with glowing red eyes completed the demonic transformation.

Strathan's back was to the Boulevard. He listened to the screams of horror, the running feet, the sirens, the shouted and ignored commands from the police.

They were the sounds of chaos.

Dupré knelt several yards away. She had healed the bullet wound to her shoulder. The hole through her jacket remained; a trail of blood stained her jacket front. She stared at Strathan. There was no fear in her eyes, merely concern.

Strathan would instill fear.

Before he could act, Adriana charged at him.

Strathan reached out to grab her with his taloned hands. Just as she was within his grasp, the vampire ducked down in a feet-first slide under Strathan's arms and through his trunk-like legs. Adriana vaulted to her feet behind him.

The sorcerer quickly turned and saw six police officers. Their guns drawn, they formed a half circle surrounding him and Adriana. Lauren was protesting loudly as two other cops dragged her and her camera girl away from the scene.

The civilians were clear when the police opened fire.

Adriana sprinted and made a gymnastic leap that took her over the policemen.

Two of them turned to follow her arc but wisely withheld from firing into the crowd beyond Adriana. She sprinted past the end of the red carpet and onto Hollywood Boulevard near the smoldering wreckage that was Strathan's Zagato.

The other four officers continued to fire at Strathan. Their bullets burnt into wisps of smoke as they crashed against his demon armor.

"Not getting away that easy, bitch," Strathan said in a low voice that sounded as if there were three distinct people speaking the same words in unison.

The sorcerer pulled both arms forward as if stretching his back muscles. Sections of the armor on his back broke away. Leathery wings burst from those openings along his shoulder blades, spanning ten feet in either direction. Muscles stretched from his back and around the upper edges of each wing.

The Uninitiated police backed away from the beast that Strathan had become. It was all they could do to save face by not running away.

One, two beats of his wings and Strathan was airborne. He flew up high above the red carpet area, above the crowd, out over his wrecked Aston Martin and Hollywood Boulevard. His red eyes fought the glare of the spotlights to search for his prey.

There.

Adriana raced on foot down a corner past the Dolby Theatre at the end of the block, just on the other side of the police barricade. She had a rough go of it as the crowd of once star-struck busybodies ran in all directions, smashing through barricades and ignoring police supervision as well as oncoming traffic.

Strathan flew toward Adriana, preparing a fireball in each hand.

Adriana Dupré would fall this night, even if Strathan had to burn Los Angeles to the ground.

The vampire could not contain the sorcerer's evil in proximity to this rampaging crowd. If she did not move him from this location, she risked an unacceptable level of collateral damage.

Having reached the dual spotlights at the edge of Hollywood Boulevard, Adriana broke to the left toward the Dolby Theater. She forced her way through the rampaging crowd. Law enforcement tried their best to contain the situation, but without riot police, it quickly grew beyond their control.

At the intersection of Hollywood Boulevard and Highland, Adriana leaped over what remained of the police barricade and turned left down Highland.

A policeman yelled at her as she shoved her way through more pedestrians on the sidewalk, though just as many flooded the streets, blocking oncoming traffic. Horns and profanity fought the noise of the mob and the police sirens.

Adriana had parked her BMW street cycle at a meter just down Highland. She leaped on, flipped the kill switch and dug her thumb into the starter.

The sound of metal on metal drew her attention.

The inevitable car accident had occurred near the barricade. There were no serious injuries, only frustrated and frightened pedestrians yelling at motorists.

Unfortunately, the accident would be the first of many.

As the BMW's engine roared to life, Adriana noticed people looking to the sky, pointing and shouting. She followed their gaze.

Strathan had sprouted wings as an accessory to the demonic appearance of his armor. He hovered above the intersection, a fireball in each hand.

Strathan's wings beat the air to keep him aloft; the resultant air displacement pressed down on the street, blowing loose anything not nailed down including hats, street trash, and scuttled pieces of crashed cars.

Adriana swore she could see a smile despite the armored nature of Strathan's dog-like helmet. His kind got off on this chaos; even when she was at her worst with the Daughters, at least she had kept the Uninitiated out of this violence.

Looking for an avenue of escape, Adriana almost regretted cutting her old handler Rutger loose a few months ago.

"Going somewhere Dupré?" Strathan bellowed in a voice not quite his own, something mixed with the demons he controlled, resulting in an unsettling, three-voice growl. It amazed her that she could hear him over all the other noise.

She glanced back at Strathan to see him hurl one of the fireballs in her direction. She spun the bike around and slammed the throttle, leaving a streak of burned rubber as she shot down the sidewalk heading north and away from Hollywood Boulevard.

Terrified pedestrians dove out of her way. She swerved around those awestruck and paralyzed by the events unfolding before them.

The spot of concrete where she had started melted from the heat of the first fireball. The driver of an oncoming car slammed his brakes to avoid people dashing away from the sudden burst of flame. His reward: the second fireball obliterating the hood of his car.

Adriana could not stop to witness the motorist's plight. If she wanted to prevent the same from happening again, she had to lead Strathan away from the area. She left the sidewalk, crossing into the flow of Highland's northbound traffic as death rained down around her in the form of more fireballs.

An explosion to her right forced Adriana to veer hard to the left. The move steered her into the oncoming southbound traffic. Horns assaulted her as the barely moving cars weaved and slammed into one another to avoid a collision with the wrong-way biker.

Weaving back into the northbound flow of stalled traffic, Adriana twisted the throttle again. Another fireball blasted a car close to her. She felt its heat against her cold flesh.

Adriana cursed herself for not containing Strathan back on the red carpet. Unfortunately, she had no idea about his demonic abilities.

The vampire had underestimated the dark sorcerer before, back in Africa. It had cost her her life.

Underestimating him this time would cost many innocent lives. Adriana wondered if the Knights of Vyntari made as many horrible mistakes as she had when they entered the Shadowdance.

She would have to consider that later.

Just barely swerving around a stopped car a driver had wisely abandoned, Adriana turned right onto a side street. She figured she could cut across to a less busy thoroughfare, reach the freeway and lead Strathan out of town.

Glancing behind her, Adriana saw Strathan hovering at the mouth of the street. He didn't immediately follow her.

Suddenly, a wave of intense heat from in front of her washed over Adriana. Looking forward, she realized why Strathan failed to follow.

He didn't have to.

A tear in reality opened before her. Adriana recognized it as one of Strathan's dimensional portals. Fireballs rained down all around her. She didn't have to veer around them; they weren't intended for destruction, but to herd her toward the portal. If she dared stop, one of the fireballs would surely end her.

Adriana pushed the motorcycle to its limits. Popping a wheelie as she reached the portal, she literally raced straight into Hell.

Measure Twenty-Eight — Endings

To the fleeing Uninitiated crowd in front of the TCL Chinese Theater, it appeared as if the red flames consuming Strathan's car had burned white hot, then burned themselves out.

They didn't realize that, despite the jostling Gabriella endured from the fleeing crowd, she had harnessed the fire engulfing Strathan's car with her white, ethereal flames. She then used her magic to draw the oxygen from the flames and extinguish them.

"Nice job," Freeman said from his position behind Gabriella.

"Thanks."

Both Knights wore civilian clothes and had worked their way into the crowd earlier in the day. Freeman thought it cool to hit the event as he'd never been to a Hollywood premiere. Gabriella was more concerned with watching for Adriana Dupré.

They had not talked to her in the five months since the vampire had defended Makeda before the Guardians' ruling body, the Concilium. After, Adriana left with Makeda for some spiritual journey.

A few weeks ago, an anonymous informant notified the Guardians that something major had occurred between Strathan and his Order of Haroth lodge in Los Angeles.

The informant had specifically asked for Gabriella and Freeman to head the investigation. Since the duo had a history with the dark sorcerer Strathan, the Concilium sent the two to Los Angeles.

Shamir al-Sadat, their new praetor, would accompany them to oversee the operation. There would be no more incidents like those in Berlin and Oromia.

Oops.

The trio of Knights soon learned that Adriana was the informant.

She had returned to Los Angeles from France, having regained her memories. Adriana intended to confront Strathan over the missing three Vyntari shards. She chose the movie premiere to confront Strathan under the watchful eyes of the Uninitiated.

She'd hoped their presence would curb his use of violence out of respect for the Shadowdance Veil.

The vampire shared her plan with the two Knights, who ducked out on their new praetor to watch Adriana's back.

Taking in the scene, Gabriella said, "Maybe this wasn't the best idea."

"No argument there," Freeman said while dodging passersby. "But cut Adi some slack. It's her first time doing the hero thing."

"We need to give her some lessons about —"

Freeman hit Gabriella on the arm and then pointed to something over by the theater. Gabriella looked in the direction he pointed and saw Adriana running away from the scene. Moments later, they realized why.

A demon-looking thing with wings flew up and hovered above the Boulevard. Odds were, it was Strathan showing off again.

And making things worse.

Gabriella and Freeman looked at one another. Freeman shrugged.

"Let's assume she's trying to lead him away from here," he said.

Gabriella pushed through the crowd to follow the Strathan thing. "We'd better help," she said.

Freeman grabbed her arm, stopping her. "I'll follow Adriana!" As Gabriella started to protest her partner pointed back to the red carpet. "You go help that burnt cop!"

Gabriella looked to the red carpet, saw the injured policeman and the other cops administering to him. They would be unable to dull his pain, but she could use her power to stabilize him.

Nodding to Freeman, Gabriella fought the crowd on her way to the injured cop. It was tough going, and she thought of how a salmon might feel. If she needed to talk to Freeman, they had their telepathic link to do so.

Freeman moved to a pocket of relative safety across the boulevard. Once there, he settled into his Freemanvision trance. In the astral world, he saw the people around him as a bunch of blue people only three apples high scurrying to and fro. It helped him differentiate them from his real target, Adriana.

He saw her as a video game vixen in pretty much the same costume she had on, only with sharper angles.

High above, Strathan took on a dragon's form so fierce it looked like he could kick Smaug's ass. He hurled fireballs down upon the Uninitiated blue people. If he and Adriana didn't get him out of here quickly, this Smurf village would be Azrael's unfettered playground.

For her part, Adriana made a valiant effort to lead the dragon away. Not helping her was the stalled traffic (represented by several My Little Pony-drawn carriages) backed up to a near standstill due to crowds of Smurfs running for their Smurfy lives.

Luckily, Adriana had chosen a motorcycle for transportation, allowing her to weave through the traffic.

Also lucky for her — but not for the blue folk — Strathan had shitty aim. There'd be a good deal of cleanup on this one, both physically and in the media to cover the Shadowdance. Thank the Goddess he wouldn't be involved in that!

What he would have to deal with is a scolding from Praetor al-Sadat. But how could he and Gabriella be held responsible for something an evil dragon sorcerer did?

Floating over the crowd, Freeman's astral avatar caught sight of Adriana zooming down a side street. The Strathan dragon followed her to the mouth of the street and stopped. By the time Freeman got to the same place, he saw why.

A dimensional portal had opened at the other end of the street. Lacking time to steer clear and being railroaded by a hail of fireballs, Adriana drove right in. Strathan followed her through. The portal closed up behind him.

"*Hey, partner,*" Freeman thought back to Gabriella. "*Good news for us, bad news for Adriana.*"

Adriana's motorcycle landed in a sea of bubbling lava. Its tires caught fire as the metal of the bike singed from the heat of the liquid into which it sank. She leaped to the seat of the bike, then vaulted away from it as it continued its descent. Adriana landed on the equivalent of a beach, where ash and soot took the place of sand.

Adriana turned to see the motorcycle melting in the lava. Soon its handlebars slipped beneath the surface. Looking beyond the bike, Adriana saw that the lava stretched for miles from the ashen shore. In the distance, a volcano belched lava, feeding the sea.

Behind her, the ash beach went on for a mile until it reached the remnants of a long abandoned city. Its stone structures, cracked and crooked, rose defiantly from the scorched earth.

Winged demons populated the dark, starless sky. The moans, cries, and screams of unseen damned souls assaulted Adriana's ears. An oppressive heat warmed her normally dead-cold skin. Her mind raced to the other dangers she may face here.

The demon within her probably thanked Strathan for the relocation. Secretly, she did as well. They had left the prying eyes of the Uninitiated behind. There would be no civilians in jeopardy, no need to hide what she and Strathan were.

But even if Adriana defeated Strathan here, she still faced the daunting task of finding a way back home.

Then Strathan flew through his magical portal. It sealed behind him. Adriana drew both of her *Fukushuu* blades, ready for a fight.

"We're not stayin', muzzy," the demon-enhanced Strathan bellowed with his triplicate demonic voice. "Don't want ya meltin' 'fore I tear yer limbs off."

Strathan waved his taloned hand at an area behind Adriana. That area suddenly lost its heat. Looking behind her, Adriana saw another portal. Beyond she saw a bird's eye view of what she recognized as Strathan's bedroom back in his Hollywood mansion.

Adriana turned just as one of Strathan's wings slammed into her, propelling her through the portal. She fell through the top of his four-post bed, smashing through the thick and costly mattress and box spring beneath.

She rolled out of the wreckage and set herself several yards away in the near center of the room.

Strathan flew through the portal behind her, hovering over the bed. The portal closed behind him.

The room hadn't changed since Adriana was there last December.

Set in a Victorian style and far too large for one person, the room held what remained of the four-poster bed, an antique dresser, and a full-length mirror. She also remembered that of the three sets of

French doors spread about the room, one set led to an oversized in-suite bathroom, one to a balcony and the other opened into the hallway.

The vampire steeled herself for combat. Her *Cou Re Nao Shi Xiao* martial arts style, which she'd used to unfortunately great success against the garou, would serve her well against the hulk of a monster that was Strathan in his demon armor. Combining that skill with her preternatural speed, Adriana launched into a slashing attack.

Things fared well for several volleys. Mystical steel met demon-hide armor, slashing and drawing thick, black plasma from the wounds. Plasma splattered the carpet and the limestone walls, which smoldered at the point of contact.

Thankfully, Adriana's enchanted blades withstood the plasma's heat.

Strathan howled in pain, swatting at Adriana. She proved too quick for his talons. She'd then dive under his wings and strike again. The Strathan-demon was so large, the confined space hampered his ability to turn and meet the new angles of Adriana's attacks.

The furniture in the room didn't fare as well as Adriana did. Strathan's massive wings battered the walls and vintage light fixtures. He turned the ornate dresser into a projectile. Adriana barely dodged the makeshift weapon as its drawers and their contents spilled out around her.

Then Strathan pulled a trick of his own.

A tentacle shot from Strathan's leathery hide. The new addition to Strathan's arsenal took Adriana by surprise. The tentacle slashed her shoulder. The wound threw off her balance, opening her up to a blow from Strathan.

His left wing connected full on with Adriana's torso. The force of it would have knocked the air from her lungs had she needed air for anything other than speech.

The strike propelled Adriana across the room, slamming her against the full-length mirror. It shattered, the shards stabbing into Adriana's back scabbards.

The impact rattled Adriana's blades from her hands. She landed on the floor between them, but in no position to retaliate.

Another wave of heat rolled toward Adriana. She didn't need to see what came her way. Allowing instinct to drive her, Adriana rolled to one side.

An instant later, the frame of the mirror burned to ash under the heat of yet another plume of fire.

Looking back, Adriana saw her blades just beneath the pile of burnt wood and broken glass. Before she could retrieve them, Strathan's hoofed feet landed between her and her blades. He taunted Adriana, daring her to come for her weapons.

Instead, Adriana dashed for the doors to the hallway.

Enraged, Strathan launched more tentacles after Adriana. One tripped her up as she leaped over the debris of the bed. Adriana turned the momentum in her favor, landing on her side and rolling toward the double doors of the entrance.

Luckily, the doors were open.

Strathan flapped his massive wings, launching himself into the air and smashing into the ceiling. The loser in the collision, the ceiling crumbled and broke apart, falling around him.

Adriana didn't remain to see Strathan's next move. She pressed through the double doors, slamming them shut behind her.

"That is so not gonna save ya, scrubber!" Strathan declared in his eerie voice.

He used the power of his wings to propel himself at the closed double doors. Ducking his horned head, he bashed through them, taking much of the surrounding doorframe and limestone of the wall with him. Debris rained about him.

Strathan continued across the hall outside that served as the second-floor balcony and clean through the railing.

The repeated beating of his wings kept Strathan aloft; he hovered above the wide limestone staircase. It led down to an open area that ended several hundred feet away from the mansion's entrance doors.

Strathan scanned the area.

Adriana was not there.

His red eyes narrowed as he scanned the rest of the mansion. Rooms lined both sides of the balcony that made up the mansion's second floor. All of the doors were closed, but that didn't mean Adriana hadn't used her supernatural speed to close one of them behind her.

There was also the matter of the level directly below the balcony, where Strathan could not yet see. With the mansion lights dimmed, there were plenty of shadows in which she could hide.

He could fix that.

Strathan propelled himself over the stairs and out to the center of the mansion. He threw fireballs into the area under the balcony, engulfing it in the light of his hellfire. Strathan saw everything there except what he wanted to see — Adriana's burnt corpse.

When she left the bedroom, Adriana moved just to the side of the doors. After Strathan had bashed his way out, before he stopped over the stairs, she slipped back inside.

The flames engulfing the wood of the shattered mirror had spread to the plush carpet and other pieces of antique furniture. The heat of the flames did not equal that of the fires of Hell, but Adriana still shrank before it.

The demon within her wanted out of the room. It fully understood what those flames could do to the flesh it called home. Adriana resisted its urge to run. She had an objective here — her *Fukushuu* blades.

Shielding her eyes against the brightness of the flames, Adriana looked again to the remains of the mirror. She could see the handle of one blade and the blade of the other sticking out from under the burning debris.

Holding out her hands palm up, Adriana attempted to draw the blades to her from across the room. They pulled, but could not free themselves of the detritus.

She would have to go in after them.

Adriana took a few steps into the room before the demon within asserted itself. Her body stopped. She felt her muscles pull against her will. Adriana gritted her teeth, forcing her body to defy the demon's hold.

She moved forward slowly, closer to the flame that could end both her and the demon, closer to the weapons that would help her end Strathan's evil.

It took great effort, but Adriana soon stood over the blades. She grabbed at the smoldering debris, the heat searing her flesh. Adriana pressed on, throwing the debris aside and retrieving the first blade. Its hilt burned the flesh of her hand. Ignoring the pain, she kicked the debris off the second.

A crashing sound came from her left. Adriana looked through the smoke and flames to see the dresser collapsing in on itself due to fire damage. She turned her attention back to her blades.

"Can't have that now," Strathan bellowed over the roar of the now raging firestorm.

A tentacle snared Adriana's booted ankle and yanked her foot out from under her. She slammed down hard enough to feel the limestone underneath the smoldering carpet.

Another tentacle ensnared her at the waist. Another caught her wrist as it reached for the second blade.

All three tentacles drug Adriana out of the bedroom, through the wreck of the doorway and into the main hall.

She barely managed to flip her single blade down the back of her forearm, concealing it from view.

Adriana soon found herself hanging upside down over the main staircase, some forty feet in the air. A tentacle released her leg, only to wrap itself around her throat.

Smoke from the bedroom billowed into the room, quickly rising to the high ceilings. Strathan's demonic mask of a face appeared through the smoke. His flapping wings blew the rest of it away.

"I did it wrong last time," he hissed, his voices echoing about the limestone canyon that was his mansion. "Shoulda popped yer head right off. But then, I couldn't watch ya suffer, now, could I?"

As Strathan brought down his talons, Adriana threw her blade and pierced Strathan in what would have been his palm, halting his attack. She jerked her face to the side enough to miss the projectile of thick plasma that would paint and burn the limestone below.

The damage from her blade elicited another howl from the demon.

Adriana concentrated and held out her free hand. The *Fukushuu* blade pulled from Strathan's palm and back into her hand. She slashed at the tentacle about her throat, severing it.

Three feet of the tentacle remained, trailing from its hold on her neck. More blood plasma sprayed upon the limestone floor. It bubbled and steamed, eating into the stone.

Strathan's tentacles hurled Adriana away from him. Her trajectory took her just out of reach of the second-floor railing. She'd crash to the floor below if she didn't act immediately.

Adriana threw her blade. It stuck into the railing. She then unfurled the tentacle from about her neck and wrapped it around the handle of the blade like a bullwhip.

When the tentacle drew taught, Adriana used her momentum to swing up and over the rail, landing on the second floor.

As soon as she landed, Adriana sprinted to the wreck of the bedroom door. Fireballs from Strathan smashed the walls and floor behind her.

Ignoring the smoke and flame, Adriana extended a hand palm up. Her second blade flew from the bedroom. She dodged another fireball just as the second sword landed in her hand. The handle burned into Adriana's flesh.

She ignored the pain and looked back to Strathan.

The sorcerer had slammed his two taloned hands together, rubbing the palms. Adriana took the moment to retrieve her first blade from the rail. Shaking the tentacle free, she turned her attention back to Strathan.

The demon-fueled sorcerer broke his hands apart, his wound now healed. He looked to Adriana.

"Why can't you just die?" Strathan asked.

"I have," Dupré replied. She spun her blades in her hands to throw off the demon goo and limestone. She then leaped to stand on the railing. "Now, unfortunately, it is your turn."

Adriana leaped from the second floor and toward Strathan. Predictably, his tentacles lashed out at her. She hurled first one blade then the other at him. They sailed past his tentacles. Strathan used a wing to knock one blade aside. It fell to the stairs below.

The other blade slashed Strathan's shoulder, exposing flesh beneath, before sticking into the wall behind him.

Adriana grabbed one of Strathan's tentacles and used it to pull herself closer to him.

Strathan realized his defense against the blades had left him open to Adriana's attack.

The vampire leaped to another tentacle, pulling still closer to her adversary. She ultimately landed on Strathan's back, her legs wrapped around his torso, her hands on his shoulders.

"Sexual favors aren't gettin' ya outta this one!" Strathan warned.

"But Dwyer," Dupré cooed as she ran a finger over a slash through his armor on his back. "I know you love it when girls suck on you."

The vampire extended her fangs.

Strathan cursed himself for not seeing this one coming.

As Dupré's fangs dug into the wound on his back, he wondered what the boiling plasma that was the demon blood would do to the vampire's insides — but only for a second. In the next second, he brought his talons back to bury them in Dupré's skull.

But as his talons came down, the demon armor peeled away from his hand, from his arm, melting into oozing plasma as it pulled away from his decrepit, century-old flesh beneath.

Adriana pushed away from Strathan. Where she had bitten him, one of the demon heads sprouted from his back. The other appeared from Strathan's side. As they stretched away from the dark sorcerer, they took with them portions of the leathery hide that, like the talons, reverted to its plasma form.

His concentration on his battle of wills against the demons, Strathan's wings flapped irrationally, flying him in a frenzied pattern. Adriana remained latched to him like a wee folk to a pot o' gold.

Strathan looked over his shoulder and saw his wings liquefying into plasma. He lost altitude. The two demons quickly reabsorbed the plasma, continuing their pull away from him, away from the vampire who threatened to drain them.

Dupré's eyes met Strathan's. The boiling plasma had burnt out the vampire's tongue and had done a number on her teeth. Her throat had dissolved away.

As Strathan watched, those destroyed features healed.

Adriana's lips reformed; they twisted into a wicked smile.

Without propulsion to stay aloft, gravity quickly asserted dominion over Strathan. Dupré kicked away from him, landing gracefully near the top of the stairs. The last of the demons' armor pulled away.

The dark sorcerer landed hard in the middle of the staircase with none of his demon armor to protect his frail, elderly form.

Close as he was to the point of intolerable defeat, Dwyer Strathan knew that the enchanted piece of metal he had landed on would ensure he didn't go out like a punk bitch.

Measure Twenty-Nine — Beginnings

Adriana's eyes remained closed as she focused the blood in her system on healing her wounds. When she opened her eyes, she was herself once more, albeit a paler shade.

Up above she heard the raging fire threatening to escape the bedroom. Smoke already obscured vision on most of the upper floor.

She focused instead on the two blobs of demon plasma struggling to take shape in the air in front of her. The demon within her assured her that its rogue siblings would be no threat without a host body to contain them.

True to her demon's word, the other demons' attempts to solidify failed. They fell to the ground, landing with two disheartening sloshes. The plasma pulsed for a moment, then lay still as it sizzled on the carpeted limestone of the stairs.

Adriana turned her attention to Strathan. His natural form lay prone across several steps beneath her. He retained many of the wounds her blades had created over the course of their struggle.

She concluded that his body sans the illusion of youth could not sustain itself much longer.

Strathan struggled to wave a hand at Adriana, beckoning her to come closer. Wary, the vampire descended the stairs toward the fallen man. She remembered the last time she had descended these stairs, during the party at which Strathan had introduced her to the Vyntari shard quest.

Then, as now, the sorcerer was determined to control the situation.

Strathan attempted to speak but managed only a gurgle choked by blood. Kneeling next to him, Adriana whispered, "Do not waste what precious little breath is left you."

In the past, those words always prefaced an assassination, used to send the victims of her wasteful, murderous rage to their death. Now, she meant them as a suggestion to do something right with those final moments before death.

"Your blades… enchanted for damage to Daughters," Strathan whispered.

"In a time when I foolishly thought vengeance would sustain me." Incredulous, Adriana asked, "You waste your dying words on my mistakes?"

"Just yer biggest mistake."

With the last of his strength, the dying sorcerer thrust the enchanted piece of metal he'd landed on through Adriana's atrophied heart.

The vampire felt the pain of the blow. She seized instantly, falling onto her side. Paralysis locked her body in a rigor-like state. Her blood flowed rapidly from the wound, mixing with the blood of her enemy and spilling down the stairs.

This was what happened when a *Fukushuu* blade pierced the heart of a Daughter of Lilith.

"Die... bitch," Strathan whispered.

Adriana looked to Strathan as his eyes glazed over, devoid of life. She wouldn't be far behind him.

I have set things right with my soul, she thought. *This will be a noble death.*

The demon woke first.

It felt the blade removed from Adriana's heart. It immediately wanted revenge for the wound. But it found it could not move. Through Adriana's eyes, it looked to its right hand. Limestone from the stairs had warped around it, holding it in place against the bare floor. Looking to the other hand, the demon found the same trap in place. Adriana's feet were similarly bound.

A scream of rage escaped Adriana's lips.

"Keep it down, will ya!" a male voice quipped. "Hard enough to hear with all this fire and stuff!"

The demon within Adriana raged against its bonds, but could not escape them. Adriana herself slowly came to consciousness. Testing her restraints, she felt a sense of irony that similar bonds had held her adversary in Oromia.

A bright white light sparked before them. Adriana closed her eyes to defend against it.

The demon felt fear.

"May the One Goddess grant me the power to mend this woman's wounds," a woman with an odd accent said. "Though she is far from innocent, her turn from the darkness has earned her this rite."

"*Do not let this woman's righteousness heal us!*" the demon said in Adriana's mind. "*We can heal ourselves with their blood!*"

These people mean us no harm, she thought to the demon.

A sense of relief washed over Adriana, as if the light brought with it a welcome embrace. She soon felt its power coursing through her body. Her wounds, great though they were, healed. Her demon's lust for blood was sated, and it fell silent.

"It's getting pretty old, us having to save your butt all the time," the male said.

Adriana looked up to see the familiar face of Michael Freeman. He wore civilian clothes; there was some cartoon super-hero on his shirt. Somehow it seemed more fitting than his Knight garb. Indigo-colored ethereal flames flickered behind his sunglasses.

Gabriella Doran came into view behind Freeman. Like her partner, she wore civilian clothes, ones much more fashionable and conservative than Freeman's. Her amber hair was bound in a long braid that fell to the right side of her face.

Adriana warmed to their presence, but then something occurred to her. She looked for Strathan.

He was gone.

The vampire's expression darkened.

"Where is Strathan?" she demanded.

"Funny story about that," Freeman began. "Seems his masters in Hell wanted their pound of flesh. Drug him back through a portal."

Disappointment clouded Adriana's expression, but she let it pass. Strathan had the chance to repent his ways, but chose to remain evil and harm others. At least now he was somewhere he would receive the punishment he deserves.

"Sorry about tying you down," Freeman said, bringing Adriana back to the present. "Gabriella just read 'Fifty Shades of Grey' —"

Gabriella punched Freeman's shoulder. She turned to address Adriana. "We knew you'd frenzy when the sword was drawn."

"Yeah, see, momma didn't raise a fool," Freeman said. He paused, then looked suspiciously at Adriana. "Wait a minute. Are we talking to Adriana or the demon inside her?"

"I could always stab you again," Adriana replied. "If you live, you will know which one is in control."

Freeman stared blankly at Adriana. He then palmed his forehead. "Wow! Somebody died and came back with a sense of humor!" Addressing someone out of view, he added, "Let her up, boss."

Adriana heard the limestone about her wrists and legs fracture. She watched as the limestone on her wrist deteriorated. Now able to move, she sat up. Gabriella offered her hand.

"Welcome back to the land of the unliving," she said.

"Well damn!" Freeman said while moving away from the girls and descending the stairs. "Gabriella whips out another funny! We gotta get you away from the praetor more often! You're a hootenanny! I don't know if I can take both of you ladies being all Amy Schumer!"

"Please ignore him," Gabriella said to Adriana.

In unison, both Knight and vampire said, "I usually do."

Gabriella smiled. It reminded Adriana of the warmth that had passed through and healed her. She almost allowed herself something that would just pass as a pleasant smile.

Adriana let Gabriella help her up.

Both women came away with blood on their hands. Adriana flashed Gabriella a look of apology. The Knight acknowledged the look with one of sympathy and turned to look for something to wipe away the blood. She looked down at Freeman.

He'd stopped at the bottom of the stairs to look at a gallery of movie posters hanging on the wall.

Gabriella descended the stairs. "See anything interesting, Michael?"

"Only if you're interested in posters for bad movies," he replied, eyeing the posters.

Gabriella placed her soiled hand on Freeman's shoulder, smearing the blood off her palm. He didn't notice at first, but then he felt her hand pulling away in a wiping pattern. He pushed her hand away and tried to look at his shoulder.

"What did...?" he began as he craned his neck.

Gabriella headed back up the stairs.

"Still bickering," Adriana said.

"And you're still determined to do things on your own," another female voice said.

The Knights and Adriana looked to the top of the stairs and saw Makeda Arsi there. Like the other Knights, she wore civilian clothes: dark jeans, boots, and a long-sleeved, turtleneck athletic shirt. Her hair was braided, still flowing to past her shoulders.

Adriana ascended the stairs to meet Makeda. She hadn't seen the woman in three months, ever since she left her care to travel with her vampire mother, Illyana. Makeda descended the stairs, meeting Adriana halfway.

"I contacted Michael and Gabriella," Adriana said.

"But confronted Strathan on your own, in public," Makeda countered as the two women met.

"Imagine how much more violent he would have been if the three of us had confronted him," Adriana replied.

Makeda nodded. "Point taken."

She opened her arms. Adriana accepted her embrace. "The most important thing is you seem to be yourself again," Makeda said.

"My time with Illyana did me well. No ill will toward you."

Makeda released Adriana so she could look at the shorter woman. "I fully understand the bond between mothers and daughters. I'm glad she was able to help you where I was not."

"She had a bit of unwanted help."

"A story for another day, I'm sure."

Glancing toward the bedroom, Adriana noticed the fire raging there contained behind a blue-tinted, ethereal wall. It was definitely Makeda's doing.

The vampire looked to the African woman. Before she spoke, Makeda dismissed her with a wave of her hand.

"We'll call it even," she said. "You did quite a bit for me with the Concilium. I would no longer be allowed to practice magic if not for your words on my behalf."

"My words did not keep you among the Knights, though."

"Even the mightiest of angels fell," Gabriella said. She and Freeman had ascended the stairs to join Makeda and Adriana. "I think she'll do just fine."

"Maybe she'll even get a Hell dimension to rule, huh?" Freeman added.

"Your new praetor may put you in that Hell dimension if you don't get back to him with a good excuse," Makeda said.

Both Freeman and Gabriella's disposition hinted at their discomfort at the thought of facing their praetor.

"Sorry, boss! We just wrecked part of the Walk of Fame and exposed the supernatural to hordes of Uninitiated-types. No biggie!" Freeman said. Even he wasn't buying it.

"How did you get away from al-Sadat?" Adriana asked. "When I met him in Paris many years ago, he seemed rather on top of things."

"We told him we were going for dinner in a place we knew he didn't like so he wouldn't come with us," Gabriella replied.

"Which means you owe us In-and-Out Burger. Stat!" Freeman added.

Gabriella softly nudged Freeman's shoulder. Turning from her partner, the female Knight placed her hands on the shorter vampire's shoulders. "It's good to see you on the side of the angels, Adriana. Maybe next time we try something normal like… shopping. Or maybe hit a karaoke bar and hear that nightingale voice of yours."

Adriana stared blankly at Gabriella. The Knight turned her gaze away from Adriana and began playing with her hair.

"As… odd as that all sounds," Adriana began.

Gabriella looked back at Adriana. The vampire could see the longing for acceptance in the Knight's expression. Adriana forced what almost passed as a smile.

"It would be a nice diversion," she said.

Gabriella's face brightened.

Freeman suddenly grabbed Adriana in an embrace. Surprise filled the vampire. "And I'll miss you most of all, Scarecrow!" he yelled.

Adriana broke away from Freeman and stared at him as if he were a maniac.

Gabriella placed a hand on his shoulder. "And I have to travel with this," she said. "Maybe you're on to something there with the solo act thing."

"Oh Gabriella, you know you love me!" Freeman said, puckering his lips for a kiss. Gabriella pressed her palm to his lips and pushed him away.

Gabriella headed down the stairs. Freeman looked at his arms and hands. While hugging Adriana, he had transferred the blood soaking her onto his outfit. He caught up to Gabriella, grabbed her arm and started wiping the blood on it.

"What are you —?" Gabriella asked as she tried to pull her arm away from Freeman while still managing the stairs.

"Don't like it, do ya?" Freeman taunted.

The two Knights continued their squabbling all the way to the mansion's exit.

As soon as they were gone, Adriana turned on Makeda. The vampire's expression was suddenly cold and menacing. "You owe me an explanation, Makeda Arsi."

When Makeda had scaled Mount Kanchenjunga and stole the first Vyntari shard from her mentor Chigmy, she fully realized the dark course her path could take. There were many variables: the shard could fall into the wrong hands; the players she hoped to align could make unforeseen decisions; the other Knights could uncover her gambit and put it to a premature end.

Save for the unforeseen interruption by the MKDG and Tekle's unfortunate trip to the *ekeraa*, none of these fears came to pass.

Everything had played out almost exactly as Makeda had planned, right down to this moment with Adriana. She had a reprieve when the vampire returned without her memories. Makeda tried to mold the girl further, but she wisely decided to leave with Illyana, as the woman knew far more about Adriana's past than she.

Now that Adriana's memories had returned, she'd want answers from Makeda.

The former Knight wondered if Adriana would ask the right questions.

"Strathan said he was released from the Order," the vampire began. "Presumably, that requires a word from a higher authority, one who would not show themselves without something as important as the recovery of the three Vyntari shards."

Makeda said nothing; her stoic expression gave nothing away.

"You expected me to lose the shards," Adriana said.

The two women exchanged defiant looks before the former praetor spoke again. Her stoic mask remained in place.

"Soon after we returned from Oromia, the Guardians here in Los Angeles reported a major surge in dark power. The timing coincided with the rumor, now confirmed, that Strathan had left the Order.

"The only person who could break the bond between Strathan and the Order is the demon Haroth himself... or a human proxy, the Order's only living founder."

"Malachi Thorne," Adriana spat.

She knew the man, having dealt with him back at the Sachsenhausen camp. After the events there, Thorne had disappeared. "This entire gambit was to bring him out of hiding," Adriana said.

"And, largely thanks to you, it succeeded."

Adriana frowned. She extended both her hands, her palms skyward. Her blades leaped from their positions and flew into her hands like obedient lapdogs.

"Since you lost your Knighthood and have nothing better to do," Adriana began. She emphasized her next words by pointing her blades at Makeda. "You can pursue the shards. Strathan said a vampire named Valentina had them."

As a final word on the matter, the vampire returned her blades to their scabbards. She gave Makeda one last glare and then walked down the stairs.

"Still intent to do things alone," Makeda called after her. "Even after all you've experienced these past months."

"If I work alone, on my agenda, I cannot be manipulated," Adriana replied without turning back to Makeda.

But then Adriana abruptly stopped at the bottom of the stairs.

"There is one other thing," she said without turning to Makeda. "In Berlin, you said that the Navarre and my sister still live."

The corner of Makeda's mouth turned upward into a smirk. "I did."

Adriana turned back to Makeda. "I know about my sister, having seen her a month ago. But the Navarre heirs. You said you would not disclose more until you deemed my thirst for vengeance curbed."

"I did."

Adriana looked expectantly at Makeda. The former Knight could see the snarl forming on the vampire's lips. She probably wanted to yell at her to tell what she knows.

To her credit, she held her and her demon's rage in check. Perhaps she could be taught; Makeda already knew how to control her if she couldn't be.

"In the years since your encounter with Jean-Baptiste," Makeda finally relented, "the Guardians of Faith have monitored the births of many generations of Navarre. I told them the story of the Dupré split. Cross referencing information, they found a possible Dupré in Pittsburgh."

In the blink of an eye, Adriana stood toe-to-toe with Makeda. A lesser person would have wilted before Adriana's stern gaze. Makeda stood her ground but did nothing to raise the vampire's ire further.

"I did not tell you about the split until after you told me about living Navarre," Adriana hissed.

"I know more about you than you think," Makeda said flatly.

Adriana studied Makeda's face to see if the former Knight was lying. Perhaps, Makeda thought, Adriana would cast suspicion on Illyana for telling her, just as Illyana had told Makeda things to lure her vampire daughter into this gambit.

Perhaps Adriana thought nothing of it at all. Would she even care if the information got out if she found her missing ancestors?

After a few moments, Adriana said, "Those who manipulate the lives of others in the name of the Shadowdance — either Evil or Good — shall meet justice at my blades. I will tolerate no further manipulations, Makeda Arsi. Not even from you."

Makeda remained silent. She slowly nodded. "Fair enough," she eventually said.

Adriana glared her words home, then said, "The name of this Dupré heir."

"You two should get along. He's a musician."

"His name," Adriana demanded.

"Brandon Jericho."

Adriana nodded slightly.

Done with Makeda, the vampire turned from the former praetor and walked toward the entrance doors across from the staircase.

"May you find the answers you need, Adriana Dupré," Makeda said.

Adriana turned to Makeda. The former Knight acknowledged her with a nod. Adriana slowly nodded in return.

Turning back to the entrance, Adriana continued forward. As she progressed, she used her preternatural power to cloak herself in darkness, disappearing into the shadows.

Makeda reasoned Adriana would use her contacts from her days as an assassin to locate her garou kin in Pittsburgh. More importantly, she would be in the city when the three Vyntari shards arrived, when an old nemesis would ally with new ones.

If left unchecked, their power of destruction would grow.

Makeda almost hated using Adriana in this fashion, but it was required if she would curb the evil within the Shadowdance.

###

Thanks for reading

Liked what you read?

Leave a review on Amazon.com!

THE SHADOWDANCE SAGA

CONTINUES

…with short stories revealing the missing six months of

Available for free to Initiates of the

"Shadowdance" saga

Get Initiated at Shadowdancesaga.com

Coming Winter 2016

THE SHADOWDANCE SAGA

CONTINUES…

A struggling musician in Pittsburgh, **Peyton** loses his girlfriend to seemingly random violence. She returns to him as a ghost and tells him he can get her back — if he's willing to kill a vampire's mortal liaison.

Before Peyton kills, Pittsburgh's vampires capture him. They force him to give up his ghostly accomplice —

He names vampire and former assassin Adriana Dupré.

Blindsided, Adriana rescues Peyton from the other vampires, only to learn of the arrival of Valentina, a devilish vampire masquerading as a teen pop star.

In a previous encounter with Adriana, Valentina seized the Vyntari shards. The relics imprison portions of the vengeful shadow god who created the Earth.

Now Adriana must discover why Peyton thinks she told him to murder while preventing Valentina from unleashing the shadow god.

If Valentina succeeds, she could gain the power to pervert the world into her twisted image.

Adriana and Peyton inevitably become unwitting pawns in the secret war between supernatural creatures known as the Shadowdance.

Follow the story in —

Illusion of Love

Shadowdance

Saga

Song Three

COMING IN 2017

To learn more about the "Shadowdance" Saga,

go to www.shadowdancesaga.com.

Follow the saga on Facebook and Twitter

As "Shadowdancesaga"

Sign up for the

"Shadowdance" Saga Newsletter

and

Get free eBooks and geek culture news!

About the Author

The son of a sharecropper (not really), Mark Wooden has actively pursued the dream of being a Creative since his epic kindergarten work, *Ne-Ne the Vampire Panda*. He draws inspiration from *Buffy the Vampire Slayer* and *Blade*, decades of *Batman* and *X-Men* comic books and conspiracy epics *24* and *The X-Files*. He'd be remiss if he didn't mention the influence of a certain assassin named Elektra.

Mark mines his two decades of experiences in live entertainment to instill humanity into the vampires, demons, werewolves, sorcerers and other creatures of his *Shadowdance* urban fantasy saga. The novels allow readers to confront the evil that men and monsters do from the comfort of a book.

For Her Sins is the second song in the *Shadowdance* saga. *By Virtue Fall*, the first song, is also available as an eBook and a paperback.

Look into the shadows and see horror in action.

Catch author Mark's pop culture musings on Facebook, his "Thinking Out Loud" blog and Twitter (@Shadowdancesaga).

62479872R00170

Made in the USA
Charleston, SC
16 October 2016